ENDLESS BLUE

ENDLESS BLUE

WEN SPENCER

BAEN

ENDLESS BLUE

This is a work of fiction. All the characters and events portrayed in this book are fictional, and any resemblance to real people or incidents is purely coincidental.

A Baen Books Original

Baen Publishing Enterprises
P.O. Box 1403
Riverdale, NY 10471
www.baen.com

ISBN 10: 1-4165-7385-2
ISBN 13: 978-1-4165-7385-2

Cover art by Alan Pollack

First printing, December 2007

Distributed by Simon & Schuster
1230 Avenue of the Americas
New York, NY 10020

Library of Congress Cataloging-in-Publication Data

Spencer, Wen.
  Endless blue / Wen Spencer.
      p. cm.
  ISBN-13: 978-1-4165-7385-2 (hc)
  ISBN-10: 1-4165-7385-2 (hc)
  I. Title.
  PS3619.P4665E63 2007
  813'.6—dc22
                                                    2007035651

10   9   8   7   6   5   4   3   2   1

Pages by Joy Freeman (www.pagesbyjoy.com)
Printed in the United States of America

To the House of Mews

Nancy Janda, Lara Van Winkle, and Amy Finkbinder

So much creativity in one place, it's amazing it
doesn't collapse down into a black hole.

Acknowledgements

Greg Armstong, David Brukman (of the North),
Ann Cecil, Andrew Heward, W. Randy Hoffman,
Nancy Janda, John Schmid, Linda A. Sprinkle,
and special thanks to Eraphie.

1 Out of the Blue

AT FIRST CAPTAIN MIKHAIL IVANOVICH VOLKOV COULDN'T comprehend what he was looking at in the cavernous dry dock of Plymouth Space Station. From the observation window where Mikhail stood, the thing tethered in the zero gravity looked like a rough pebble, or, considering the vastness of the dry dock, a boulder. The rock's bottom was bulbous and rough, as if it had been scooped out of bedrock, but halfway up the edges smoothed to gently curved walls. Only when he forced himself to look at the upper section by itself did he realize what the boulder truly was: a ship's warp drive imbedded in rock.

Judging by the housing protruding out of twenty meters of stone, the drive was from a very large ship, most likely a carrier. Its manifolds were buried somewhere in the stone—which didn't make sense. An impact hard enough to bury the drive that far into rock should have shattered it. The walls of the housing, however, seemed intact, although coated with a white material.

One thing was sure—the misshapen rock was why his ship, the *Svoboda*, had been requested by the United Colonies to leave the front lines and jump halfway across human space. A New Washington lieutenant, sergeant, and two Reds had escorted him through Plymouth Station security. They bristled with resentment that the U.C. required them to let a Russian like him onboard and refused to answer any of his questions. Since they were giving him the silent treatment, he was ignoring them while they all waited for the U.C. officer. Said officer was taking his time.

A tentative "Misha?" made Mikhail turn—surprised that anyone would be calling him by his childhood name.

The Minister of Defense, Andrew Heward, was immediately recognizable from his square frame and solid, heavy-jawed face. Like most people from his childhood, Heward was shorter than Mikhail remembered, coming only to Mikhail's shoulder.

The Defense Minister cocked his head and looked uncertain of Mikhail's identity, even though he was the only one in a Novaya Rus militia uniform in sight. Behind him, the Washingtonians seemed stunned that the Minister was on a first name basis with him— obviously they hadn't put much thought into Mikhail's family name.

"Minister Heward, it's been a long time."

Heward grunted slightly. "You don't look like your . . . father."

Some people avoided the labels of father and son when discussing Mikhail and his father since they were both clones of the same man, the legendary Tsar Viktor Pyotrvich Volkov. They made the mistake of thinking Ivan and Mikhail were both figureheads that the loyalist party created. They somehow discounted the fact that Tsar Ivan personally forced the Novaya Rus Empire into the United Colonies before Mikhail was born. Heward, though, had dealt with Ivan enough to know that Ivan ruled everything and everyone with an iron hand. That meant everything about Mikhail's life—including his inception—fell under Ivan's control. Biologically Ivan was Mikhail's twin brother, but in every other manner, Ivan *was* his father. So why the hesitation? Had Heward originally meant that Mikhail didn't look like Viktor? Possibly. Heward would also know that both Ivan and Mikhail disliked being compared to their famous original.

Mikhail tapped his crooked nose. "It's the nose—I broke it in the Academy—and I smile more than my father. Crows-feet. Laugh lines. Those kinds of things."

Heward eyed him. "I wouldn't have thought it would make that much difference, but I suppose it does. Ivan always looks like he has a lemon shoved up his ass. Your hair is darker too."

"He spends more time in the sun."

"Ah." Heward gave a slight grunt of understanding, adding a wave toward the black of space beyond the dry dock's great soap-bubble shield. "No, not much sun up here."

Heward dismissed the Washingtonians. Their conversation was

going to be private—or at least, that was how Heward wanted it to appear.

"You took heavy losses during your last intel run?" Heward led off with questions instead of explaining where the drive came from—more proof that it was going to be tied somehow to Mikhail's future. "How do you stand now? Are you at full strength?"

Had Heward been trying to get Mikhail to lower his guard? The truth was that while Heward had been at the palace often, Mikhail would not have called him a friend of the family.

"My ship is fully repaired," Mikhail said carefully. "My Red commander is picking up replacements for the men I lost."

Heward nodded blandly, but there was a tightening around his mouth as if the news was bad. "Anytime you take on a large number of Reds, you end up with dominance issues."

So Heward was going to want him to ship out immediately.

"I have no concerns." Mikhail put steel into his words. Most captains made the mistake of pulling replacements from multiple crèches, which resulted in all the Reds vying with each other. Mikhail deliberately tapped only one crèche at a time so the replacements already had an established dominance order. The infighting was kept to a fight between the leader of the crèche Reds and his foster brother, Turk, who was his Red commander.

Heward waited for him to add more, but Mikhail wouldn't weaken his position by trying to justify his statement.

Instead Mikhail took command of the discussion, pointing to the drive. "Where did that come from?"

"It warped into local Plymouth space seventy-eight hours ago. A crew went out to clear it and when they realized what it was, they brought it in."

Seventy-eight hours—allowing for Heward's travel time to Plymouth—meant that Heward's choice of the *Svoboda* wasn't based on convenience. There were many ships closer.

"Come on," Heward said. "I want you to see this firsthand."

As they stepped into the confines of the air lock, Heward said, "You'll have to get your nose fixed before taking over for your father. It makes you look too much like a Red."

Mikhail nodded to the last statement; that was what he liked about his skewed nose. At the time he merely just didn't want to look like Viktor or his father anymore. That it gained him respect from the battle-torn Reds was now the main reason he didn't get it fixed. Besides, he wasn't sure he wanted to inherit his father's position. Considering the mess he'd made of his life, it was also unclear if the loyalist party would allow him. That was the whole point of him being the captain of a warship: if he became a military hero his early misadventures might be overlooked.

The air lock opened to the dry dock, which was under pressure but still at zero gravity. A skimmer was waiting to take them across the vast floor, touching down and locking into place just short the rocky edge. The dry dock's floodlights cast multiple shadows of the drive on them, layering them in shades of gray.

The rock gave way to fist-sized objects, seemingly organic in nature, clustered tight together. The creatures reeked like dead fish. Under their stench was another odor, something elusively familiar, but he couldn't name it. The band of organisms was three meters wide, ending in the durasteel housing, which was coated with a rough layer of white powder. A fine grit drifted in a halo around the base. Mikhail moved closer to scoop a handful of grit out of the air. He rubbed it between his fingers.

"This is sand. This rock is coral." Mikhail recognized the underlying smell now—the briny scent of something long soaked in the saltwater. The white powder could be salt crusting the steel.

"Three different species of coral, all trademarked." Which made them Earth species adapted for terraforming purposes. "So far we've picked thirty-two lifeforms off the housing. Other than the coral, we couldn't identify any of them."

Mikhail had seen what reentry on an Earth-like planet would do to most spaceships. Gravity and wind shear tattered ships into pieces which tumbled down into the blue, at first like pebbles dropped into water, and then the pieces would start to smoke. Finally they flashed to fireballs of molten steel, becoming a firestorm . . .

Mikhail shook off the memory, focusing on the mystery at hand.

There were no scorch marks on the drive housing—which begged the question of how it got into an ocean without undergoing reentry? And where was the rest of the ship?

"What ship is it from?" Mikhail asked.

Heward took out a VID scanner, aimed it at the drive, and activated it. After punching in his security code, he held it out wordlessly to Mikhail to read its screen.

Wormhole drive, serial number WDU-290843, installed in Jupiter-class carrier UCS Fenrir.

A Jupiter-class was the largest spaceship that the United Colonies made. Years went into its construction, and it had a crew numbering in the thousands. That explained Heward's involvement. Why had Mikhail been called in? He was Novaya Rus militia, technically not part of the United Colonies force. It was only a matter of goodwill that he responded. The name *Fenrir* rang no bells, so it had been destroyed prior to him entering the military. Considering the coral growth, it might have been lost even before Mikhail was born, as the United Colonies had been fighting the nefrim years before the Novaya Rus Empire joined the effort.

"What happened to the *Fenrir*?" Mikhail asked.

"It vanished ten years ago." Heward scrolled down. "We assumed it misjumped and the evidence partly supports that. The second to last entry shows that a miscalibration took them to zero."

Mikhail frowned at the entry. A wormhole drive created a tunnel from one point in space to another. Any positive number would put them in normal space. Zero was the theorized null that the tunnel passed through—the nowhere between two points of somewhere. While the drive might think that the *Fenrir* went nowhere, it obviously went someplace. If *Fenrir* didn't simply cease to exist, standard protocol for a ship of its size was to radio High Command its new location. Even if it somehow warped into a planet's gravity well there should have been still time to launch its lifepods; there would have been a chorus of distress signals. And what of the *Fenrir*'s shuttles, which were capable of lifting off a planet and warping home? Why hadn't at least one survived to contact High Command?

A ship of the *Fenrir*'s size couldn't vanish without misjumping. Since the wormhole drive generated the warp field, it was the only piece of the spaceship that couldn't be left behind when the rest ceased to exist. The two facts directly conflicted.

"Were there signs of tampering to the engine?" Mikhail asked.

"Every test we've run indicates that those are the actual coordinates that the *Fenrir* went to."

Heward hadn't denied though that there had been tampering. In another man, Mikhail might have ignored the disparity between his question and Heward's answer.

"The coordinates are impossible." Mikhail tried to press him into answering.

Heward held up his VID scanner. "This is proof that they're not impossible, just improbable."

Mikhail scowled at the VID scanner's screen. The last entry was the coordinates for Plymouth Station. Regardless of wherever the *Fenrir* might be in truth, they'd chosen to return their engine to a recently commissioned U.C. space station deep in friendly territory—a good trick when they'd been missing for ten years. "What explanation did *Fenrir* give when it sent back its engine?"

Heward made a sound of disgust. "Everything that came back with it only makes the mystery bigger." There was a guideline set up, circling the engine. Heward hooked onto the guideline and let it arch him around the rock. "Careful on the coral, it's sharp."

As they circled the base, it was easy to see that the coral had been cut by the sudden intrusion of the warp field. The field had smoothly sheared the coral off as it shifted somewhere to nowhere to Plymouth Station. The massive steel beams of the support struts had been cut as cleanly as the rock.

On the other side of the boulder was something even more amazing: a boat. It floated in the zero gravity, anchored in place with mooring lines. It was about twenty-five meters long. Its steel wedge-shaped hull was painted deep blue, with its upper decks a crisp white. Lettering on the stern identified it as the *Swordfish*. With the exception of a heavy laser cannon turret on its bow, it seemed a simple fishing boat.

"What's that doing here?" Mikhail asked.

"It came with the engine. There was a large amount of frozen seawater and this boat. We cleared the ice before it melted and made a mess of everything."

Had the *Swordfish*'s crew been aboard when it suddenly found itself in deep space? Had they been standing on the open deck? Below where it might be airtight as well as watertight? Or had they gone through the broken windows of the bridge?

"Any crew?" Mikhail asked.

"None that survived." Heward pointed his VID scanner at the boat, entered his security code, downloaded whatever data the boat was holding, and held the VID scanner out to Mihkail.

Torpedo, serial number T-493504835472, released to UCS Swordfish.

This got odder and odder.

"It doesn't have any launch tubes for torpedoes," Mikhail pointed out.

"It's using the torpedo's fission engine as its power unit. A converter redirects the power to a crude electrical engine." Said electrical engine must be connected to the propeller now drifting several feet off the floor of the docking bay. "Look at the armory time stamp."

Mihkail frowned at the date that followed the release data. "Have you verified that?"

"Yes. The *Swordfish* picked up this torpedo from the Fort Armstrong Armory ten months ago."

The name on the boat did not bode well for the fate of the *Swordfish*. Still, Mikhail asked, "Where is this *Swordfish*?"

"The *Swordfish* was a torpedo ship. It disappeared a week after picking up this torpedo. We assumed it was destroyed by enemy fire."

"So, two ships, both lost, both in the same place."

"Yes," Heward said.

"This is obviously the work of humans." Mikhail pointed to the boat. "It follows maritime conventions started on Earth. Based on the name, I suspect the crew of the *Swordfish*."

"That's true. Come."

A second guideline ran up the side of *Fenrir*'s warp engine. It lifted them up the steep side and guided them down to a safe landing on the top of the housing. The access hatch was open. Plymouth Station had run a string of work lights into the cramped, dark interior.

Mikhail had never worked with an engine this large, but four years of warp field theory at the Academy had taught him the fundamentals. What had been attached to—and in some places replaced—the standard equipment was a collection of bizarre . . . things. He hesitated in calling them machines, although that was what they seemed to be. One looked more like cotton candy than anything mechanical.

"They were modifying the engine," Heward said. "It's not clear if the modifications were completed. We've analyzed as much as we can without removing anything. Obviously the engine still creates a warp field. What they were modifying it to do is still unclear."

Mikhail could think of two uses. "Have you considered that this may be a trap? That it might warp Plymouth Station to *Fenrir*'s location? Or destroy it?"

"We're taken out the power core and scanned for secondary power sources. We've also checked it for all known explosives."

The warp engine, the alien devices, and the *Swordfish* all seemed like pieces from different puzzles. Heward obviously wanted Mikhail's help in solving them all.

"You want me to recreate the *Fenrir*'s misjump," Mikhail said. "You want me to find her."

"I'm basically committing political suicide tapping the Tsar of Novaya Rus's only child for a mission like this. Believe me; I considered every option before settling on you."

"Why me?"

"To start with there's your ship, the *Svoboda*. As a frigate, she can enter a planet's atmosphere, fly at low attitude if needed, land and take off. As an intelligence gathering ship, the *Svoboda* has the experience and the needed equipment to move undetected while searching for the *Fenrir*. Personally—you were raised landside, which means you understand wind and weather. Also you're Novaya Rus militia. It might not be coincidence that both of these ships are from New Washington. We might be looking at sabotage."

"Over the course of ten years?"

"We've lost a lot of ships to misjumps. It's been considered unavoidable since jumps are often made by damaged ships under heavy fire. That might not be the case."

"I see."

"And then there's your Red commander."

Mikhail turned sharply to frown at Heward. "What does my brother have to do with this?"

"Brother? My God, Volkov adopted your Red?"

"No." Mikhail refused to explain more.

It still amazed Mikhail that otherwise intelligent people couldn't see that it was morally wrong to treat another as inferior just because of the circumstances of their birth. If his father was going to bring two children into the universe via bioengineering, the fact that one was genetically related and the other wasn't shouldn't have made a difference. Turk should have had every advantage that he had; God knows, his father could afford it. At least they'd been equal in Ivan's affections—which was to say, none.

"How does Turk figure into this?" Mikhail repeated.

"Perhaps it would be better to show you."

Mikhail had seen enough Reds exposed to hard vacuum to differentiate the body from a normal human. Reds were genetically adapted so they could change and adapt to extreme conditions. While a Red could survive ten times longer than an unadapted human, eventually the cold and vacuum of space would kill them.

The Red's claws, arms, and chest were covered with blood. Sometimes a Red would claw up his face and throat during the last moments of asphyxiation. There were no wounds, however, on the Red.

"Who did he kill?"

"These two." Webster uncovered two purely human males. All three wore natural cotton fabric fashioned into worn, ill-fitting, and weather-beaten clothing. There was neither rank insignia nor indication that the clothes were uniforms of any sorts.

"Who are they?"

"We can't establish an ID for either human. Moreover, the Red's serial number isn't in our system."

"Someone is cranking out unregistered Reds?"

"We need to investigate this," Heward said. "Risk everything and zero out in a jump. Find out what's out there."

We? Mikhail stifled a snort. Heward meant the *Svoboda* alone. "You're talking about a suicide run."

"We have to do this, Misha. Two of our ships in the same spot can't be a coincidence. We're looking at an organized effort. Currently all of our defenses are designed to counter the physical capabilities and limitations of the nefrim. If the nefrim are mass-producing Reds with the intent to use them against us—we'll be lost. We've lost one crèche after another, so our production is down. And I don't have to tell you about how much stronger and faster a Red is compared to a human."

"I know." Growing up with Turk, he was well aware of it. Even though Turk was nearly four years younger than he was, his foster brother had been able to win any physical competition between them shortly after learning how to run.

"Our fears are that the nefrim have acquired enough of our technology and biological samples from our Reds to start creating them. This place, wherever it is, apparently lets them overwhelm our ships and hold them for some reason. We think it might be a training grounds for their Reds. They could be teaching their Reds how to capture and disable our ships."

If that was the case, it would spell disaster for the human race.

"If this was a simple in and out, then anyone could make the jump," Heward continued. "We need someone that can think outside the box. Way outside. Take on any situation and pull out a win."

In other words, the Volkovs' reputation for pulling things out of their butts preceded him.

Mikhail ran his hand through his hair, combing his bangs back off his forehead, thinking furiously. Heward's strength was that he outmaneuvered his opposition, staging hit and run meetings. He brought things to the table that the other side didn't expect, wasn't prepared for, and then arranged deals while holding the upper hand. This meeting was classic Heward tactics. He slammed Mikhail with the huge mystery of the *Fenrir*'s drive, dropped the bomb of impending doom for the entire human race, and then commanded that Mikhail go.

The question wasn't whether Mikhail should go or not, but what Heward was trying to keep him from seeing.

Mikhail saw it then, and let out his breath. "The Novaya Rus Empire is risking a great deal—for what? Mass production of Reds requires a crèche. All of the lost crèches belonged to New Washington. If I find a crèche, I would have to bring it back or destroy it. Since production of Reds is down, it would make more sense to recover the crèche. I'm not risking everything and then handing over anything I recover to New Washington. I want anything I recover to be considered salvage, free and clear."

"Don't be stupid, Mikhail, this is a U.C. military operation. Any property recovered during all U.C. activities reverts to the original owner."

Mihkail shook his head. "No, the Novaya Rus Space Force is part of the U.C. force under the terms of the treaty. Our privately funded militia, however, operates on a volunteer basis only with the U.C. I can refuse this mission."

Yes, that was it. Heward glowered at him.

"If New Washington had a ship you thought had a chance at succeeding, you would have sent them. But you've already analyzed this and I'm the only one that meets all the criteria needed for the best success on this mission."

"I can't wave away their rights to the crèches."

"Yes, you can. There is even precedent: the *Catalina* Superliner. Declare that anything I find is free for salvage and I'll go."

Heward worked his jaw, possibly chewing down things he knew he shouldn't say. "Fine, I'll have it posted within an hour. Here's a courier packet with everything you need to know for this mission."

2 Paradise Lost

PARADISE WAS BURNING.

The *Tigertail* came in from the night side of the planet, and the continent-wide fires glowed like a red eye in the night. Daylight came as a tear-blinding crescent as they pulled into orbit and took up a geosynchronous position over the day side. Thick layers of smoke obscured most of the destruction on the planet, but the remains of spaceships were raining down in visible contrails.

Turk found it hard to count this as a human victory. He and Mikhail had visited Paradise when they were young; it had lived up to its name.

Lieutenant Grigori Belokurov lifted his hand to his ear and cocked his head, listening closely. "Commander Turk, we're finally getting a response from the planet. A minor spaceport says that they're still operational. There are sellers liquidating their prides to pay for evacuation costs, but we have to come down to get the Reds." Belokurov turned for his orders, adding, "It will be a rough ride down."

Turk growled his irritation. Going down to the planet would make them more vulnerable, but the attack probably took out much of what could climb out of the gravity well. "Fine. Tell them we'll be there shortly, and then plan a path down. Wait for my mark."

"Yes, sir."

Turk keyed open the security lock between the cockpit and the Red pit. It was good to see that his veterans were lounging easily together with no clear division into warring camps. No fresh blood, although some of the betas looked unhappy.

"Suit up," Turk said. "We need to land to pick up the replacements. We're going to treat this as a hot zone."

"But the nefrims pulled out," Rabbit protested.

Turk cuffed the yearling to shut him up. *Lightly*, because Rabbit was right. The runt of his litter, Rabbit was the cleverest Red Turk had; at his size, he had to be, else he wouldn't have survived the crèche.

"This may be a real sale," Turk explained. "Or it might be a ploy to lure down stupid bargain hunters with a spaceworthy ship."

"So we might be fighting humans?" Smoke smiled, showing off his sharp teeth.

"Yes, but only on my command," Turk said. "Anyone disobeying orders will be left behind on this hellhole. Do you hear me?"

"Yes, sir!" they roared back.

He suited up with them and checked their armor, and saw them locked into place. "Okay, Lieutenant Belokurov, take us down."

As the shuttle bucked and rocked through reentry, Turk closed his visor, shut his eyes, and blocked out the world. If he was going to be dealing with New Washingtonians, the more human he appeared, the easier his mission would be. Luckily, he was fluent in English, while a crèche-raised Red would only know Standard. The hardest part of passing as human was convincing his own soul.

"I'm human," he whispered as he forced himself to change. "I'm human. I'm human. I'm human . . ."

The spaceport's Red pits were full. Turk stalked through them, glancing into the cages, looking for replacements. In cruel irony, the Reds of Paradise had fought the nefrim off their world only to be locked up to be sold so their owners could flee. The healthiest would sell, but the sick and wounded ones would probably end up abandoned. Turk forced himself not to think of it, not to care. He couldn't take them all. He had only enough money to replace *Svoboda*'s dead if he found a good bargain, hence the reason he was here, at Paradise, instead of at a crèche getting yearlings.

What made it harder was that the Reds knew the score and

resented it, but couldn't help watching him with pleading eyes. *Take me. Save me. Get me out of here. Don't leave me trapped in here when the nefrim return.*

Damn New Washingtonians! They treated their lapdogs better than this.

"Commander," Lieutenant Belokurov's voice murmured in this ear. "Rabbit's disappeared. He was walking patrol and I lost track of him."

Turk cursed and turned to retrace his steps. Any other of his Reds he would have suspected of going AWOL voluntarily, but Rabbit was both cautious and responsible, a result of being tiny for a Red. Hell, he was small for a normal human. If he was missing, then someone had taken him. "Activate his tracking signal."

It took Turk an hour to find the yearling huddled in the corner of a large general holding cell. He was cut and bleeding.

"I'm sorry, sir." Rabbit pressed against the bars but didn't meet his eyes. "I didn't see them coming. I mean—I saw them—but—they were humans and they were moving some crates. They had their hands full. I didn't pay any attention to them . . . and then they hit me from behind."

Mostly likely the crates were empty and the work all fake to throw the young Red off guard. "How many were there?"

"Five."

"You give them hell?"

Rabbit looked up then, his eyes full of despair. He believed that Turk would leave him behind. "Yes, sir."

"Good. I'll get you out."

"You have my Red in lockup, I want him back." Turk pushed the data-stick with Rabbit's DNA registration numbers and record of ownership across the desk.

The human manning the terminal slotted the stick and grunted. "He was fighting with humans."

"He didn't pick the fight—he was jumped."

The human laughed.

"I know my Red. He keeps his nose clean and his claws in. Your people started this fight and he defended himself."

"Doesn't matter. Unrestrained Reds fighting with humans carry a mandatory fine. We keep him as collateral until you pay it."

Turk locked his jaw against his anger. "Half the Reds on this planet will be toast when the nefrim come back. What benefit would you get from keeping him?"

"If you pay the fine, that means more of us get off."

By "us," he meant humans.

"How much is the fine?" Turk reached for his credit chip.

"Fifty thousand."

"Zeny?" Turk frowned. Even with the dropping exchange rate, that seemed high.

"Standard."

"You've got to be kidding. I could buy five Reds at a crèche for that." It was half of the money he'd brought with him.

"In times like this, everything gets expensive," the man said. "We don't like having unrestrained Reds running around. They're too dangerous. The fine is to discourage people from ignoring our leash law."

In other words, it gave them an excuse to pick up Reds, and blackmail the owners to pay a jacked-up fine or sell the Red at discount to bargain hunters. Turk wondered how many of the Reds in the holding cells were shanghaied in the same manner.

"I'll pay ten thousand," Turk offered. "That's his market value."

"This isn't Novaya Rus. A fine isn't negotiable. Either pay the full amount or get out of my face."

His claws sprang out in anger. He dug them into the counter to keep from tearing said face off the man.

The *Svoboda* had taken heavy losses the last few battles. Turk needed twenty Reds to bring them back to full strength, a near impossible task except for the bargains he could get on a planet about to fall to the nefrim. He'd reassured Mikhail that dropping him on Paradise alone would let them maximize their efforts, allowing Mikhail to meet with the U.C. while Turk got their replacements. He would need every Standard he had to do so.

But he'd told Rabbit that he'd get him out.

No one would blame him if he walked away from Rabbit. The little Red made the fatal mistake of underestimating humans. Turk had warned his Reds to stay out of trouble or he'd leave them behind.

In upcoming firefights, they'd need all the able bodies they could throw into the mix. He shouldn't be wasting half his money on one undersized Red.

No one will buy a runt like Rabbit. He'd be locked in that cell when the nefrim return.

And the nefrim never left anything living in their wake.

He couldn't do that to one of his Reds.

"Fine. I'll pay." Turk keyed in the fine amount and slid his credit chip across the desk.

He took his Reds back to *Tigertail* and had them form a tighter perimeter around it. If anyone was to pick a fight with one, they'd have to take them all on—and he suspected even the scum of Paradise weren't that desperate.

"Pardon! Hey! Attention!" someone called in Standard.

Turk turned to find a tall blonde woman coming across the tarmac. She wore a flowing silk dress, cut high on one side, so that when she walked, she flashed one bare leg. She lifted her hand to catch his attention. The wind molded her dress to her and brought him her pheromone-drenched scent. He felt his groin tighten in response. A female wearing catnip perfume and looking like sex on heels meant only one thing: a cat fancier.

"Do you speak English?" she asked when she was in range.

"Yes, I do," Turk said.

"Yes, you do, very well too." She slinked up to him. "Are you the Red commander from the *Svoboda*? I've heard quite a bit about you."

He could imagine. Cat fanciers exchanged information on forums that crossed the galaxy. It wasn't the first time one of them tracked him down. He didn't have time for what someone like her wanted. "I'm busy."

"Rumor has it, that you're looking to buy Reds. I have some for sale."

"I need a pride of seasoned fighters, not house cats."

She laughed, showing off canines sharpened to fangs. "I don't have any house cats. I have a combat pride, though, and it's for sale. I'm Rebecca Waverly." She pressed her hand to his stomach, just under his chest armor. "You're Volkov's unneutered house cat, aren't you? How purrfect. You almost pass as human—it's your eyes that give you away."

She wasn't the first to say it.

He clenched his jaw to keep his tone level. She was kneading his stomach. "What are you asking for your pride?"

She gave a smoky laugh full of promise. "Oh, I know it's a buyer's market, so let me sweeten the deal."

"What do you have in mind?"

"A few hours in my shuttle," she whispered, "just the two of us, and fifty thousand for my Reds."

The price was insane for Reds, even in a market like this. He might be handing her money, but she was buying him.

She sensed his hesitation and, taking his hand, slipped it into the slit in her skirt. Staring up at him, parting her lips to breathe out a throaty groan, she guided his hand up her bare thigh to her firm buttocks. Against his will, his body reacted to her silky warmth and heady perfume. She pulled his head down and opened her mouth to him. His fingers discovered she was wearing an anal plug with a cat-tail prosthetic, which twitched realistically.

"My God, you're a kinky bitch," he growled.

"I'm not a dog, I'm a cat. A queen," she whispered into his ear, as she arched her back like a female presenting herself to a tom. "Your sticky kitty cat."

He was going to regret this. He always came away from such women feeling dirty and low. But it would make up for the money that he spent on Rabbit, and he'd promised Mikhail that he'd get the Reds they needed. Considering the number of times Mikhail had refused to sell him to cat fanciers, he owed Mikhail to put up with this.

"Fine. Let's go check out your pride. If they're acceptable, we can do the transaction and then go to your shuttle."

Her pride was in a cell block not far from where Rabbit had been held. Turk was almost disappointed to find them well fed and well exercised. One thing you had to give cat fanciers, they took care of their Reds. Their papers said they came out of Eden Crèche, which meant they'd be well trained in standard combat action. A lifetime of waiting meant most of them were napping, sleeping away the idle time. Others were doing calisthenics, burning off energy in order to nap.

They all took note of Waverly, eyed Turk intently, but only one slouched forward.

"Shouldn't you be doing something about getting us off this planet?" The Red asked Waverly. "Before the nefrims come back?"

She laughed. "Shush, Butcher. I'm working on it. I'm selling you dirt cheap with a good lay thrown in to this prime piece of meat."

The tom studied Turk closely. "You? Where's your Red commander?"

"I am Red commander."

Butcher snorted with contempt. "Humans are Red commanders, not Reds."

Meaning: *I won't obey a Red.* Turk had run into that trouble before, all with the same reason.

"You top cat?" Turk asked. While genetically varied to keep diseases from spreading unchecked through crèches, the Reds were controlled—in theory—in size both by breeding and identical diet. Still, the Reds varied in height and muscle mass. Rabbit was on the small end. Butcher was one of the tallest Reds that Turk had ever seen. Turk suspected that if you could check actual food consumption, the big Reds took the food from their smaller littermates. Over time, the differences became profound.

"Our top cat was killed," the tall Red claimed. "We haven't sorted that all out. Didn't really see the need, not if we don't get out of this trap."

That didn't ring true to Turk. Reds always seemed to put who commanded whom above all else. He wasn't sure why. Maybe it was a side effect of all the conditioning they received for following chain of command. How could you follow chain of command if all of you are interchangeable, disposal grunts? By fighting it out so there was a distinction. Or maybe the crèches were trying to inspire the Reds to excel by ranking their performances and the Reds were taking away something more, something their makers didn't intend. Someday, Turk would have to visit a crèche and see exactly how they trained the growing Reds. Someday.

"Do we have a deal?" Waverly ran her hand down Turk's front to rub his groin. There were no humans around, only the score of Reds. Butcher watched without comment, his eyes narrowing at Turk.

"I'll take them." Turk had no real choice. He'd have to deal with dominance later.

"Purrrrfect."

The title terminal was in a crowded public area. Waverly acted cool and distant as they finalized the details. The tail was well

programmed and it showed her excitement, twitching provoca-
tively under her skirt. She stayed remote the entire ride to her
shuttle.

Maybe this time it would be different, Turk thought and then
laughed at himself. Cat fanciers wanted to sleep with an animal
that could use flush toilets. They sought Turk out because crèche-
raised Reds were clueless about sex and sometimes became erratic
when molested by their owners. The last thing cat fanciers wanted
Turk to be was a normal man, a person with desires beyond a
good fucking.

"Tear my dress off me!" was the first thing she said once they
were out of prying eyes, safe in her shuttle. "Use your claws."

The material shredded away easily, revealing a supple body.
At least this wasn't going to be all misery. He paused to take off
his armor.

"Bad cat!" She slapped him hard. "Where's your fur?"

He controlled the reflex to hit her back. Besides the fact that
he'd probably break her jaw, cat fanciers didn't like bruises—they
were too hard to explain once their playing at being a cat was
done. If she called the authorities, his shuttle was far away, and
his pilot didn't have money to buy him out of trouble. He let his
stress trigger his natural tendency to fur.

"Now lick me. Make me ready."

Silently he knelt before her. She looked down at him with
smug satisfaction and then made a ridiculous attempt to purr
and meow as he lapped at her heavily perfumed skin. Of course
she wanted him to enter her from behind, mimicking what animals did. Cameras filmed them for later, projecting the feed onto
a full-sized screen which she watched intently as he moved in
and out of her. "Oh God, that's so perverted," she moaned. "So
disgusting it's sexy! I'm letting an animal fuck me! An animal
has its cock in me!"

If she wanted disgusting, maybe he should cough up a fur ball.
God, he hated cat fanciers.

3 Into the Blue

THE MISSION SEEMED DESTINED TO DRIVE MIKHAIL INSANE. NOT that it would be a very long trip at any given time according to his U.C. psych evaluations.

There was no simple way to get a boat or two in space. The *Swordfish* wouldn't fit into the *Svoboda,* and if it had anything like a longboat or dory, it had drifted into deep space before the Plymouth Station work crew showed up. Similarly wilderness survival gear was limited. The most likely reason was because Plymouth Station was in orbit around a planet still in the throes of the initial terraforming stage. Landing on it was not an option, so Plymouth stocked no planetary equipment.

Paradise, before the nefrim attack, had boats. Lieutenant Belokurov returned Mikhail's queries with news that currently the coastal towns of Paradise were too radioactive to investigate.

"Obviously the universe doesn't want you to have boats, Captain." His second-in-command Semyon Furtsev was not happy with the mission. He was maintaining a running line of sarcastic comments, punctuated by a short dry sound that was a mix of laughter and disgust. "The runabout can handle shallow water."

"Perhaps it was just as well," Mikhail said. "Most of our crew has only seen an ocean from orbit. They'd have no clue as to how to handle a boat."

Furtsev gave his scoffing laugh yet again. "The whole point of being a ship's captain is coming out a war hero, not flushing us down the galactic toilet, never to be seen again."

That was what Mikhail liked about Furtsev; he wasn't one to grovel in worship of the Volkov godhead. Nor did he grudgingly give Mikhail his proper respect. He had held his judgment, waited to see what Mikhail had been made of, and then backed him fully.

"We've gone over their data twice so far," Mikhail pointed out. "It proves that *Fenrir* has found some odd corner of the universe to fall into . . ."

"And if someone dives into the sun, we're to dive in too?"

"In this instance, yes."

Furtsev laughed again. "The loyalist party will be furious."

"It invariably is. I don't think it's ever been pleased with me, which is somewhat ironic since they're the ones that asked Ivan to create me."

"They were thinking of the madness that went on after Viktor disappeared without an heir."

"So instead they have an heir they don't want to see inherit."

"You ask a demon for his get, you get hell spawn. If the loyalists don't like it, it's their own fault."

It wasn't that Mikhail wanted to inherit either, but when his father did die, Mikhail would be a serious roadblock to anyone wanting to take power. If he managed to outlive his father—his military career might eliminate the need to worry about such things—Mikhail was going to have take over or be killed. No one would ever believe that the clone of Viktor the Great would just quietly disappear.

There was a great deal of genetic material left of Viktor, albeit now over fifty years old. He was fairly sure that the only reason his father and the loyalists didn't start the production of another clone to replace Mikhail was that there was no certainty that the next one would turn out any better. Instead everyone sat around waiting to see if Mikhail could redeem himself.

It gave his life a certain sense of being strapped to an invisible bomb. Furtsev was one of the few men that seemed able to understand Mikhail's position.

There was a scratch on the door as Turk ignored the door chime to rake his claws down the outside panel. Things must not have gone well on Paradise.

Mikhail keyed open his door. Turk leaned against the door frame, filling the doorway with tall, dark annoyance.

"No Reds?" Mikhail guessed the source of Turk's annoyance.

"I got them." Turk brushed into the room, apparently annoyed past military niceties. He was coming to Mikhail as a brother, not an officer. It meant something personally unsettling happened.

"Settle dominance?" Furtsev asked.

"No. I haven't sorted out which one is their top cat yet. The owner left dominance issues to her Red commander, but he was killed in the last raid. The Reds contend that the top cat was killed too and they haven't bothered to figure it out. More they say yes, the more I think no, and it has me worried."

"Why?" Furtsev asked.

"Because at least two would say they were top cat," Turk said.

"Someone is in control," Mikhail murmured.

"Yes," Turk said. "That he's got all them covering for him means that they're a unified group. It's going to be hard to blend them in. I'm going to keep them separated out for now."

"We're jumping in . . ." Mikhail consulted his timepiece. ". . . less than an hour."

"When we go in," Furtsev said, "the last thing we need is the Reds fighting each other."

Turk shrugged. "I'll suit them up and strap them in for a combat drop and tell them nothing else. In a combat situation, they'll hold off any infighting."

"You sure?" Mikhail asked.

"They should," Turk said. "That's the way they've been trained."

"Get us ready for the jump," Mikhail ordered Furtsev to give him a chance to talk to Turk alone. Furtsev snapped a salute and left. "You okay?"

"I'm fine," Turk growled

"You sure?" Mikhail carefully gripped him by the shoulder. Turk wouldn't intentionally hurt him, but that didn't mean he wouldn't accidentally whack Mikhail a good one if startled. "We're going in blind. We need everyone to be sharp."

Turk nodded his understanding. Mikhail hoped there would be more, some clue to what triggered Turk's mood.

Turk did, though, what Turk normally did. He took a deep breath and released it, putting his hurt and anger aside. They were polar opposites in that way. "I'm fine."

Mikhail gave Turk's shoulder a small shake. "You know that I love you?"

Turk's eyes widened. "Now you're scaring me. You've never said that before a mission before—you think we're jumping into nothing."

"If I really thought that, I wouldn't go. But . . ." Deep down he was screaming in terror. "I can't help feeling as if we're about to do a hugely stupid thing."

"We are." Turk shrugged. "When did that ever stop us?"

"I'll have you know, I've only done things I thought were intelligent . . . at the time."

Turk gave him a grin and cuffed him. "Come on, let's shake the universe and see what falls out."

War was all about acting on scanty data and assumptions. The Volkovs excelled at making the correct assumptions on the barest facts. It was how Viktor went from an indentured plaything of the idle rich to the first interstellar tsar, forging all the Russian descendant colonies into an empire. It was how Ivan made his way from puppet ruler to a tsar in his own right. Mikhail knew he had the gift, but he'd never had to act so blindly.

The *Swordfish* was a vital clue that the ships were in an Earth-like environment. One gravity. Breathable astrosphere. Bodies of water. Some land. At least partially terraformed. Compared to the hell under Plymouth Station, a viable paradise. That the *Fenrir* was on the planet and not in orbit was a clue that the coordinates would probably bring them out inside the planet's gravity well. Perhaps even at a very low altitude. If this was an Earth-like planet in regards to orbit, and the *Svoboda* came out at a dead stop, they'd be stationary while the planet moved at an orbital speed of roughly thirty kilometers per second. Hopefully they wouldn't come out in the path of the planet, else they could quickly become a bug on the planetary windshield. And any momentum that they had would speed that process up.

A quiet hush went over the crew as Mikhail walked onto the *Svoboda*'s cramped bridge. It was times like now that Mikhail felt like a conductor of an orchestra. His crew waited silently at their stations, watching for the upswing of the baton. He settled into his chair by the lift, and started the music.

"All monitors to exterior view," Mikhail said. "I want to see what we're jumping into."

Local space took form around Mikhail, cloaking him into darkness.

A light flared amber on the operations board.

"What is that?" Mikhail asked.

"We've got a fight in Alpha Red," Operations said. "They've taken out . . . the lockdown mechanism . . . and triggered damage control."

"Commander Turk is responding," Furtsev reported. "He says to go ahead with the jump."

"Keep an eye on it," Mikhail ordered. "Let's lose our velocity."

"Decreasing velocity to zero," Helm said.

"I believe we will be coming out in low planetary orbit," Mikhail said. "If we do, we need to immediately deploy the wings."

"Wings standing by," Planetary said. "VTOL engines all green."

"I want shields up as soon as we come out of jump," Mikhail said.

"Shields standing by," Defense answered.

"Velocity zero," Helm reported.

"Okay, people, let's do this," Mikhail said.

Helm counted down the jump. "Warp field generation in five, four, three, two . . ."

The field flashed over him, making the hair on his arms stand up. There was a deep hum as if the universe was picking up the tune of Mikhail's music. The vibration went down to the bone. His vision filled with the color of wine . . .

. . . and then brilliance filled the bridge. Pure, endless blue encircled Mikhail, shining off the pale faces of his crew.

"We're in orbit!" Mikhail cried as his crew sat stunned. "Deploy wings. VTOL engines ready to activate on wing lock! Shields! Status? What is our—"

Green eclipsed the front cameras.

Land? In the sky?

Mikhail glanced quickly to see if the *Svoboda*'s wings had been extended and locked. "Right VTOL engines at maximum! Hard to right! Turn! Turn!"

Turk was riding the jump out in Beta Red with his veteran Reds. He'd put the replacements in Alpha Red. Usually nothing unified a group better than engaging an enemy. Until one presented itself, though, he was going to keep the two separate.

He hated sitting in the pit in full combat gear, wondering what was happening on the bridge. He'd learned the hard way, though, that once they were in position, he had to be with his Reds to move them into action. Seconds counted.

His comline chimed and Furtsev said, "Turk, we've got an alarm in Alpha Red. The cameras showed a fight breaking out before we lost visual."

Turk swore. He'd told the replacements that they were going in hot. That should have kept them settled. "I'll take care of it."

He unstrapped and ducked out of Beta Red. Unlike his veterans, he had the replacements locked into their pit. He coded the door to only temporarily unlock, and automatically shut and seal behind him. The last thing he wanted was the replacements taking the fight into the rest of the ship.

The replacements were unstrapped and pounding on each other in a full out free-for-all. The little space was filled with grappling bodies and hoarse angry growling.

"We're going hot! Prepare for combat!" Turk bellowed, wading into them. "Get into your seats."

They were used to brawling between themselves. The crèche only taught maneuvers effective against nefrim. It was obvious as he moved through them, plucking up one after another and judo-throwing them into seats, that they'd never seen human martial arts.

He'd thrown the last one into a seat, shouting, "Strap in! We're about to jump blind!" when he felt the jump. All his senses protested being shoved through a hole in time and space. There was that jolt of heat and cold and smell and blindness and nausea all at once and then it was over. "We're in enemy territory. Prepare to . . ."

And then he saw the trap. The cover was off the air-lock control pad. Wires trailed down from the panel to the Red nearest the door. He had a moment to register that the Red was Butcher, the biggest of the replacements, the one he'd pegged as the top cat.

And then both doors of the air lock opened.

Depressurization blasted him out the door in a roaring explosion. He never had a chance to even reach for a handhold. He expected black, stars, silence, and death. Endless blue surrounded him. The roaring continued as he fell away from the *Svoboda*. They'd jumped into a planet's atmosphere! He tumbled madly for a moment. Then his training kicked in and he righted himself.

They were so deep into the envelope of oxygen that the air

was pale to almost white instead of the deep blue of the outer edge. There was a huge landmass floating in midair. Green jungle, shimmering lakes, and darting brilliant-colored birds burned into his mind. The island ended abruptly in a steep cliff, and far, far below lay an ocean. Between water and island there was nothing but sky. Both he and the *Svoboda* were falling. He was going to miss the island. But the *Svoboda* was going to hit it.

"Pull up!" he shouted into his comline. "Fire the damn VTOL engines!"

The *Svoboda*'s wings were unfolding with maddening slowness even as it careened sideways as if jerked on an invisible string. It nearly looked like they might miss.

"Come on! Come on!"

But then wings locked into place and the VTOL engines fired just as the ship rolled. The resulting vector slammed the ship into the jungle.

Turk howled in helpless dismay and continued to fall toward the water, far, far below.

4 Icarus

NORMALLY PAIGE BAILEY KEPT A CAREFUL WATCH ON VIMANAS' orbits and steered her boat, the *Rosetta*, out of the path of any oncoming floating islands. But a force-eight storm had sent them scuttling into the relative safety of Fenrir's Archipelagoes. The shoals and barrier islands acted as breakwater for the towering waves. In the seething grayness, where sometimes the sky was the next wave crashing down on them, they'd dropped anchor, huddled down, drank burn, and played poker.

Then the storm lumbered on, like a great gray beast. In its wake, the clouds tattered and then parted, revealing the vimana bearing down on them. She and her crew gathered at the railing to gape at it in surprised dismay. The vimana was still far enough off that it looked like a black pebble hung in the sky.

Their voyage had already been ill-omened. This went beyond bad luck.

"Okay." Paige finally broke the silence. "I don't know who racked up all the negative karma but I think two minutes of asking for atonement might be time well spent."

Her brother Orin laughed but backed her up like the good second in command that he was. He clapped his hands and then bent his head in prayer. The rest followed suit, although in truth her crew was more superstitious than devout. Even the teenage lovers paused in their glassy-eyed devotion of each other—although *just* for a minute—to be penitent.

27

Paige checked her own personal backlog. Nope. Nothing that rated their heinously bad luck, unless one counted wanting to drown all her crew members on various occasions. She apologized to the forces of balance anyhow. On the sea, you needed all the advantages you could get. If this was some kind of punishment, it wasn't against members of her family that were on her crew. Not that they were saints, but they had lacked opportunity to put them in such karmic debt. It was the members of the crew that weren't family that worried her. And her estranged older brother, Ethan. They'd been on their way to meet him when Fenrir's Rock went silent. Not that she could blame him for taxes, red tape, bad weather, engine troubles, electrical failure, the mass destruction of a human port, and the oncoming vimana—but it was tempting.

The two minutes' silent atonement ended and she firmly put superstition behind her.

"Okay, everyone, let's get to work. Orin, try and find out which vimana that is."

"You think it's charted?" Orin stayed at the railing, staring.

"Probably. It crosses most of the shipping lines for Fenrir's Rock."

Orin nodded and headed back to the bridge. Paige set the others to work repairing all the minor damage that the storm inflicted on them. Their situation could be even worse than it looked, but she wanted to pick the best course of action before breaking the news. The problem with having siblings as crew was they tended to debate any orders that weren't cut and dried. Once she had her crew well distracted, she joined Orin on the *Rosetta*'s dim bridge.

Orin had out all their indexes, trying to match their location with charted floating vimanas. His sun goggles were pushed up high on his head, making his sun-bleached hair stick up like sand grass.

"Almost have it," Orin said as she pushed up her own goggles to read the radar's screen.

While still a black speck visually, the vimana appeared on radar as a massive wall. From what she could tell, they were directly in the middle of the vimana's path. Fenrir's Archipelagoes had shielded them from the worst of the storm. It would offer no protection, however, when the vimana was overhead. Worse, the islets, shoals, and barrier reefs created a maze that the *Rosetta* would have to slowly pick its way through. Their safe harbor was now a trap.

In the direction of the Sargasso's spin lay Fenrir's Rock. At one time that would have been the safest place to ride out an eclipse. Before the radio gave out, though, passing boats warned that Fenrir's harbor was fouled beyond use.

Counterspin, it was only fifty miles to open ocean, and then they could head up or down the axis at full speed. They'd be fighting wind and current, more so once they hit deep water, and until they could turn to run on the axis, they only worsened their position.

She needed the speed and true size of the vimana before she could decide which direction to head.

"Orin, have you figured out which vimana it is?"

"It's—Icarus—I think." He pushed his work toward her to confirm. "This is where we are." He tapped the glass covering their chart, their position marked in grease pencil. "There are twenty vimanas on this orbit band. Only one crosses zero around this time: Icarus."

She turned the book so she could read the detailed listing. Like most vimanas, Icarus was roughly boat shaped with the tapered bow cutting the wind. It was the stern of the landmass that they needed to worry about. Icarus was sixty miles wide and a hundred miles long—one giant-sized rain collector. The overflow poured down off the back end of the vimana in a mile high waterfall. If they were hit by it, nothing on the *Rosetta* would survive.

Like most low-orbit vimanas, Icarus was traveling fast. It would be on top of them within hours. Neither Fenrir's Rock nor open water was a viable choice. The only thing they could do was make sure they weren't in path of the vimana's fall, which was the most dangerous part of the eclipse. They would still have to cope with drop nuts and other hazards, but those were survivable.

"Icarus has a center fall, so we need to get off to one side." Paige pointed at their location among the uncharted reefs. "We're going to head up the axis—towards Ya-ya."

"Ya-ya?" Orin pulled down his sun goggles to look Spinward. She knew he was looking toward Fenrir's Rock, but as always, the archipelago blocked any chance of seeing distant port. "We're not going on to Fenrir?"

He'd said it without censure in his voice, but she knew it was there. Their older brother wasn't the only family member at Fenrir when it went silent. The *Lilianna* radioed saying that they'd made harbor just hours before the explosion. They'd heard nothing since. On the *Lilianna* there had been fifteen Baileys: uncles, aunts, and cousins.

She wanted to know what happened to them. But she had the lives of her nine crew members to consider, six of which were family.

"They're saying that survivors are heading to Ya-ya," Paige said. "We'll go there, do repairs, and find out if there's any news on them. We're not going to be any help to anyone if we get ourselves killed."

Paige pulled her goggles down and studied the blinding dazzle of sunlight off water. The ocean was still choppy from the passing storm, but the sky was turning so blue that you would see distant landmasses. In the time they'd talked, Icarus had grown twice in size. She could make out the frosting of green from the thick forests growing on its crown.

"You can see it, if you look." Orin pointed at something in the water.

"See what?" Paige tore her gaze from Icarus to study their impromptu harbor, a lucky deep pool tucked among the countless barrier reefs.

"Where the fall has hit before," Orin said. "It's shifted over time. But look—it's cut grooves through coral."

She saw it then, straight wide lines moving from counterspin to spin, where Icarus's fall had drilled through rock and living coral sometime in the past. Their "harbor" was nothing more than one such cut. "We've got to get out of here."

When she tried to start up the engines, though, nothing happened.

The storm had taken out much of their electrical systems, including their radio and ship's intercom, so as Paige ran from the bridge to the engine room, she broke the news. Her little sister, Hillary, and their cousin Avery were the first people she came across, setting up to arc-weld a piece of rail that snapped.

"We're going to need to ride out the eclipse in open water." Paige hopscotched through the collection of hoses, toolboxes, and welding equipment that the two had scattered haphazardly on the deck.

"Oh joy," was all Avery said. He flipped down his visor and focused on the task at hand.

Hillary, on the other hand, gave Paige a sullen look that only a sixteen-year-old could produce. "Does this mean we're not going to Fenrir's Rock? You said that after the storm we were going to Fenrir's Rock."

Sometime in the last month—shortly after Charlene met Mitch while on shore leave at Ya-ya—Hillary left the "boys are weird" stage, bypassed "boys might be fun," and dropped immediately into "I want one for myself." All disasters were unimportant when compared to her nonexistent love life. Whatever they might find at Fenrir's Rock, Hillary was sure that they would also find boys.

"It means that we're in a state of emergency," Paige said. "When that emergency is over, we'll resume life as scheduled."

"That's what you said about the storm," Hillary said.

Paige controlled the urge to back up and smack the girl in the back of the head—she didn't have time for this self-centered pettiness. "I am not God! I can't create storms and flying masses of rock to prevent you having a social life."

"You can't keep me a prisoner on this boat."

What made sweet little kids into drama queens when puberty hit? "That I *can* do! Go tell the others about the eclipse and then come back and help Avery store all this."

Out in the Counterspin direction, the vimana had grown from a dark speck to massive black wall. It was disorienting just to look at, as her brain translated its relative size and movement into the sense that they were rushing toward it. In truth, it was bearing down on them.

"First time out in the open for an eclipse?" Kenya Jones called down to Paige from her shaded gun platform. The black woman blended into the shadows so well that she was just a voice out of the darkness. "I would have thought someone like you, born and bred here, would have been through this dozens of times."

It was hard to captain for the ex-space marine. The woman was taller, older, and in terms of book-learning, better educated. That Jones came from the universe beyond the Sargasso gave Paige a slight edge on the *Rosetta*, but barely; those that didn't learn fast on open water generally died.

"It's something we generally avoid," Paige called back. "Have you done it before?"

"Well, us newcomers do all the stupid things. It only took once to realize it's not a good idea, but it took us a while to figure out how to avoid it."

Paige had hired Jones last time they were in their home port of Georgetown Landing. While not exactly unfriendly, the woman tended to be closemouthed about herself. Paige knew little more than she was from the *Dakota*. The quip matched up to what Paige did know about the *Dakota*'s crew. Their spaceship was one of the unfortunate ones that sunk after arriving at the Sargasso, and the crew had been through a harrowing time, adrift on an open raft made of anything that would float. It was an experience that could form tight bonds between people. Or run screaming in the opposite directions, once they were safe. Obviously, it had been the latter for Kenya Jones.

"Any advice?" Paige asked.

"Pray." Kenya shrugged. "You'll see: it's all dumb luck and a hard shell that gets you through."

Paige had expected something more reassuring from Jones. "Aren't you supposed to say, 'Everything will be fine'?"

"I don't see any reason to lie to you." Jones laughed.

Paige cut through the galley to warn her younger cousin, Manny. He was up to his elbows in flour, kneading dough.

He grunted at the news. "Yell if you need me for something."

In the next room, she caught Charlene and Mitch messing around on one of the tables. "Hey! I told you: not on your duty hours! You can snog your brains out on your own time, but when you're on duty, you pull your own weight."

"Bitch," Charlene snapped.

"Yes! I'm a bitch, and that's why I'm in charge. Now get to work." Paige stopped at the door to add, "And no more screwing around where any of the rest of us have to eat!"

Paige's heart sank when she opened the hatch to the engine room and found all the various access panels open, the floor strewn with tools and grease-covered parts, and no sign of her obnao mechanic.

"Rannatan!" Paige picked her way through the tools. "Ran!"

The little alien poked up from the guts of the engine, his brown fur spotted with black grease. He worked his black triangular nose and gave a long querying whistle. "Capt'n?"

"We need to move." Paige was never sure how much Standard that Rannatan understood, so she added. "*Fisista!*"

"No, no, no, no, no." Rannatan's whiskers bristled, showing his agitation. "We no move!"

"Vimana!" She pointed in the direction of Icarus and then glided her hand sideways, mimicking the landmass coming closer.

He showed his teeth in anger and dove back into the engine. Echoing up from the metal caverns came, "No miracles! No pockets! No converter!"

She frowned trying to understand what he was saying. "What?"

"No miracles in pockets. No pockets even."

"I told you I would get you new coveralls." If they made it to a port. "What about the converter?"

He made a raspberry noise. "Converter kaput." He lapsed into muttering in his language. Spoken slow and clearly, Paige could understand a good bit of obnaoian but she only caught snatches of his rant. Apparently lightning had struck the ship during the storm, and while much of their ancient engine had been protected from such massive electrical discharges, somehow the converter had fried to a crisp.

"We don't have a spare?" Paige asked.

Rannatan's all-black eyes widened and his tiny ears twitched in obnaoian surprise. "Spare? You have spare?"

Obviously not. "I'll see what I can do."

"What's going on?" Orin asked worriedly as she banged the bridge door behind her.

"We don't have a motor. Break out the dories. We're going to have to use them to tow."

Orin cursed and went.

Paige glanced out the window to check on Icarus. Alarmingly, the sense of movement was now gone. The vimana filled up the sky to the far edges of her peripheral vision. It looked like a black cliff with roots buried deep in the water. She had to peer closely to see the slice of ocean dazzle under the floating island. Only its leading wake—air disturbance from the vimana's passage forming a white roll of water running out ahead of it—continued to report movement. The rill of whiteness swept across open water, and over sandbars and reefs, fifty miles out and closing rapidly.

Paige could barely breathe while she watched it come. Its shadow raced under the vimana, like a great sea beast. She didn't want the monstrous hunk of land to pass overhead, but they weren't going to get out of its path in time.

∞   ∞   ∞

Orin had drafted Avery into piloting the second dory. He signaled when they were ready to start towing the *Rosetta* out of harm's way.

"Take up anchor!" Paige shouted to Charlene as she took her place at the wheel.

The vimana loomed as it approached them, nearly a mile above the surface of the water, its palisade a mile of sheer rock, and then the tangle of vegetation spilling over the lip, obscuring the vimana's true height. Running slightly before the vimana, pushed by the displaced air, was the vimana's wake.

"We have to turn and take the wake straight on!" Paige shouted to Orin as the anchors ran up with a loud rattle of chain.

He nodded his understanding and the two dories started to gently pull the *Rosetta* around to meet the wave straight on, instead of sideways, which could overturn the boat.

"Brace for the wake!" Paige shouted as the dories climbed the first wave. The leading wake hit them, and the *Rosetta* canted hard to stern and then to bow, riding the wave. They climbed the smaller waves behind the first, slowly turning.

In the last minutes of full light, they came about to take a straight heading for Ya-ya and started to creep forward. Then the vimana slid overhead and instantly they were in darkness. The very air seemed heavy, pressing down on them. Sounds echoed weirdly, and the ocean growled like a beast around them.

Orin had thought to dig out their rarely used spotlights, proving why he was her second in command. The narrow beam of light played over the coral reefs ahead of them and found a break big enough for the *Rosetta*. Orin eased into the passage with Avery keeping pace on his starboard side. Gripping the steering wheel tightly, Paige focused on keeping the *Rosetta* steady as the dories towed it forward.

The pace seemed maddeningly slow. Cloaked in the darkness of full eclipse, there was no way of telling how far they'd traveled. Paige knew they had an hour before the fall could hit them, but it seemed like only minutes before she could heard the deep rumbling noise, like neverending thunder.

Kenya ducked into the bridge, seeking the harder shelter. "It's the fall."

"I know." Paige risked looking to her right, out of her starboard windows. The trailing edge was nearly to them. The fall pounded down in a column of white froth, landing in a boil that grew closer. The spray kicked up by the fall blurred the air, making it impossible to judge how close it was going to pass.

"Is it going to hit us?" Jones's voice was tense with controlled fear.

Paige studied the oncoming blur of mist and falling water. Through the smear of spray raining down, she could see the drop nuts hitting the ocean like small boulders, throwing up geysers of water where they struck. "No, it will miss us. We still have to worry about drop nuts though."

The trailing edge rushed toward them. The space between water and land overhead seemed to grow as the sky rolled back open. When the trailing edge was directly overhead, there was a deep loud bang and the ship shuddered.

"We're hit!" almost everyone still on board called.

"Find out where, you ninnies!" Paige snapped.

And then the trailing edge was beyond them. Clear sky overhead. The vimana rushing away. They made it—well—they might be sinking—but they were otherwise intact. She reached out to ring the ship's bell and found her hand was shaking.

"Please, I don't ever want to do that again," she whispered to the powers that be and rang the bell. "All clear! Orin! Avery! Bring them back in! Drop anchor!"

Dead fish littered the vimana's wake with flecks of silver. The bodies of strange freshwater fish from the vimana mixed in among the familiar saltwater ones killed by the pounding fall. For some strange reason, she felt like crying for the fish, killed by a force that they couldn't understand.

She blinked away the promise of tears and went to help Orin bring the dories back onboard. Becky showed up just as they were hoisting the first dory into place.

"The drop nut went through the deck plating in the stern," Becky reported. "It took out the freshwater tank and punched a hole in the crew's quarters. But it stopped there. It didn't breach the hull."

"Oh piss." Paige managed not to swear anything ruder in front of the eight-year-old. It meant they were out of fresh water. They were days from any human landing. And their engine was shot.

Someone had done something horrible to earn this luck.

Hopefully it wouldn't get worse.

Almost as if summoned by her thoughts, something came streaking across the sky, moving toward the Spin. Not a vimana.

It was gleaming, all angles and smooth lines. It was heading straight for them.

"It's a ship!" Paige cried in surprise and dismay.

"What?" Orin looked at her instead of upward.

"It's a spaceship!" Paige pointed at the ship as it grew larger and larger. A frigate at least. Maybe a destroyer. No. Frigate. "There's a spaceship coming . . ."

The rest of the words stuck in her throat as the spaceship roared over them and struck Icarus. A massive plume of dust, fire, and smoke bloomed at the point of impact, obscuring everything.

"Oh my God! Oh my God!" Orin cried. "It's coming down! Icarus is coming down!"

It's going to hit us, Paige thought, but then that white space in her mind with all the answers denied it. The vectors were wrong. Neither the vimana or the ship could hit them. Smoke and dust still obscured most of what was happening, but Icarus appeared to be shattering as it crashed. Large, raw boulders of the vimana rock floated upward, out of the dark roiling clouds, drifting upward. Paige closed her eyes and let the white space work. What was happening?

If the vimana shattered, then centuries of topsoil under the rainforest was being dumped into the ocean, all at once. It was rock thrown into a pool of water. Waves.

"Tsunami!" Paige shouted, opening her eyes. "Charlene, Mitch, take up the anchor. Avery, swing up around and then *get onboard*! Everyone else take cover! Anyone topside will get swept away. Go! Go!"

"We haven't lowered the anchor yet," Charlene said.

Well, for once Charlene's laziness paid off. "Then get below. Go!"

"Here it comes!" Orin called. "Twenty miles and closing!"

Paige looked Spinward again as Avery pulled the *Rosetta* around with the single dory tied to the bow. A massive wave was coming across the other wise calm ocean.

"Oh God. Avery, get onboard! Get onboard!"

He straightened them out, locked the tiller straight, and then dove overboard.

"Get him up here." Paige ran to the bridge to lash down the steering wheel. There was no guarantee that the wave wouldn't shear off the bridge. She snatched up the charts, the waveguides, the vimana indexes. What else couldn't they afford to lose?

Orin threw Avery a line and then all but hauled him up over the railing. "Paige! Paige! Get below deck!"

She had to go or they'd come after her. She knew her family too well. She could hear the wave as she hurried down into the darkness of the mess, pulling off her sun goggles to see in the dim light. Orin slammed the flood door behind her and wheeled the locking mechanism.

"Brace for impact!" Manny said, peering out one of the portholes.

Paige stumbled to a support bar and grabbed hold. Moments later, the boat dipped into the trough in front of the wall, and then the wave hit with a force that nearly jerked Paige off the bar. Something in the galley had been left unsecured and crashed with a thin metal sound. The ship shuddered as it pitched sharply to the stern, groaning as it climbed. All the portholes that should have been out of water were covered with dark green water. And then pitching downward as the boat slid over the top of the wave.

The next wave wasn't as steep and minutes later, they were back to gentle ocean. They'd made it. The question was: did they have any hope of getting safely to a port?

5 Land

"WHAT DID YOU DO? WHAT DID YOU DO?"

Mikhail opened his eyes to dark chaos. He lay in a painful sprawl in a well of darkness, a slit of light cutting through the black some two meters above him. An animal—an exotic bird or monkey or something—was screaming somewhere close at hand, its cry reminiscent of his Nyanya's accusing shouts.

But it was more than just the echoing call. The memory of his childhood nursery pressed so strongly into his waking consciousness, that he could only smell baby powder, sour milk, and the flowering lilac. He could almost feel the wool rug under him, and the slats of his bed over him, shielding him from justice.

What did you do?

"That was a long time ago." He needed the sound of his adult voice to shake himself free of the memory. "Where am I now? Am I still on my ship?"

The light flickered, as if a cloud had passed by, and the sense of being pressed down by his memories faded. Awareness of an ocean thundering close at hand, breaking against a shore, seeped in. The air was hot, damp, and heavy with the smell of salt, torn earth, bruised green foliage, and fresh blood.

He explored his small gravelike prison and discovered only one wall was earth. He was in the bridge lift, which was half filled with dirt. How did he get into the lift? He remembered the jump, the startling blue that enveloped the *Svoboda*—but then there he lost the thread of memory.

The earthen wall was the foot of a mountain wedged into the lift, preventing the door from closing. Nor was the wall just packed mud—it was a tangle of broken branches, wet leaves, and sharp edges of torn metal. Part of the bridge must have sheared open in the impact, allowing in a mountain of debris. He was lucky to be alive.

Cause and effect started to creep in. He sat closest to the lift. If he was alone in this dark womb, then the rest of his bridge crew was dead. Hard on that realization, he remembered that there had been a fight in the Red pit and then an air-lock malfunction.

Oh God, Turk.

Turk was sturdier than he was, but Mikhail knew that Turk could be hurt, could be broken. Fear condensed into a solid cold knot in his stomach. Had anyone survived? Was he all alone?

He fought the impulse to claw at the dirt. He couldn't move the mountain with his bare hands. More likely, he'd cut himself. He needed power tools and help. He fumbled until he found the service box, flipped open the access panel. The lift's diagnostic tests had been tripped, the amber display flashing "Danger. Door ajar. Air seal unable to activate." Using that dim light, he could make out the maintenance hatch overhead. He reached up, undid the latches, and popped the hatch. The lights on the emergency release handles of the lift doors above him formed a string of red pearls, gleaming softly in the shaft of darkness. After an awkward jump and scramble, he climbed through the hatch and up the inset ladder to the hangar level.

The blast doors stood open, filling the hangar with brilliance and the presence of the sea. Mikhail blinked back tears and shielded his eyes as he walked toward the door. The world beyond was pure dazzling light. Wind, hot, humid, and stinking of salt and a billion things—living and dead—blasted through the doorway, a press of white noise.

Part of his crew gathered at the open door, standing silent and numb, gazing at the ocean with bewildered stares.

Lieutenant Commander Dimitri Kutuzov noticed him and saluted out of reflex. Blood trickled down Kutuzov's cheek from a scalp wound. "Captain?"

"Are you hurt?" Mikhail asked. Kutuzov might be his new

second in command if Mikhail had lost his entire bridge crew in the crash.

"It's nothing, sir. You know how head wounds bleed like you've been laid open."

Mikhail opened an equipment locker, found welding goggles and a saws-all. "Find some more goggles, Kutuzov." They were going to need sunscreen in addition to eye protection against the glare, but that could wait until they rescued any surviving crew members off the dirt-filled bridge.

The glare filtered away, Mikhail looked out onto endless blue. It stretched out as an infinite plain of shifting water, all the blues of the universe, seething with restless energy.

"What is it?" one of the Reds asked. Its eyes had adapted already to the glare.

"It's an ocean," Ensign Sergei Inozemtsev said. "A large body of saltwater."

"Salt?" The Red wrinkled its nose.

Gripping the rail beside the hatch, Mikhail cautiously leaned out to study the water directly below. Dead fish rolled against the side of the ship with the surf. Like the fish of Volya they were mostly silver, which would act as camouflage in open water. A few were brightly colored, perhaps to hide among bright coral, or were poisonous in nature. They'd landed in surprisingly shallow water. He must have been unconscious for a while—the sand had already settled and he could see straight down to the ocean floor through crystal blue water. Multicolored coral fanned in the invisible currents. He scanned them, wondering how deadly they were, and picked out a large, dark form hiding in a crevice.

"No one goes in the water." Mikhail studied the two Reds, trying to dredge up names for them. "Coffee and Rabbit, right?" He got a nod from them. "Secure weapons. Rabbit will be with me, and Coffee will guard this door."

"What about Commander Turk?" Rabbit asked, obviously reluctant to take orders from anyone.

"Until he turns up, you're taking orders from me." Mikhail shoved away the hurt. "Keep an eye out for predators."

"Predators?" Rabbit repeated the word as if unsure of what he meant.

"Hostiles." Mikhail scanned the gathered crew. Anyone working with the Reds needed to be large enough to be respected. Mikhail picked the largest of the men in the hangar. "Inozemtsev, brief the Reds on types of predators that can be found on planets."

"Me?" Inozemtsev said with surprise.

"You were raised landside, right?" Mikhail got a nod from the big man. "I want the Reds aware that life here, even as small as a sea urchin, can kill."

"The Reds will be shooting at everything that moves," Inozemtsev murmured.

"That might not be a bad idea," Mikhail said.

"What if some of these creatures are intelligent? What if they're friendly?" Inozemtsev asked.

"Then they'd quickly learn we're not," Mikhail snapped.

Kutuzov returned with the goggles.

"Popov, Ulanova, take the goggles and come with me," Mikhail ordered. "Kutuzov, gather a team and do a sweep through the ship, starting with the lower levels. If we have flooding, we need to get everyone well above waterline—this might be low tide."

"Low tide, sir?" Kutuzov asked.

"The water might rise several meters in the next few hours."

Kutuzov's eyes widened and he threw a frightened glance at the water lapping against the ship. "Yes, sir."

"See if the infirmary is above water," Mikhail continued. Should he brace Kutuzov for his possible field promotion? No. Wait and see if anyone survived on the bridge. "If the infirmary is under water, the emergency evac in the *Tigertail* will be the backup infirmary."

"Yes—yes, sir." Kutuzov managed a salute.

Mikhail leaned out of the hangar door, caught hold of the outer hull service ladder, and scrambled up to the top of the *Svoboda*.

They were in worse trouble than he thought. True, they were in shallow water, plowing through a half kilometer of reef to bury their nose in sand, but they weren't out of the ocean. The sandbar was approximately a kilometer wide and perhaps two kilometers long. From his vantage point, he could see the whole of it. It offered no shelter, no fresh water, and no resources other than pink coral sand.

Mikhail picked his way to the bridge.

They'd plowed nose-first into the sandbar, burying them deep into the pink sand. The bridge was above the water level, but torn open, leaving behind a jagged, empty half-shell. They must have lost the bridge when they struck the floating landmass, which had been green with jungle. That was the only way to account for the black dirt and broken branches which filled the back two meters of the bridge.

In a glance he could see that he'd lost his entire bridge crew along with most of his control panels. Grief and distress solidified in his stomach with such force that he nearly vomited. He swallowed down hard on the urge and turned away from the sight.

A large bright-colored bird thrashed in the wreckage, one of its wings broken. It opened its long hooked beak and screamed, "Whatdidyoudo? Whatdidyoudo?"

Mikhail pressed his hands to his temples, trying to get control of himself. *Focus, Misha, focus.*

His bridge crew wasn't a priority anymore. He had to assess damage to the ship, deal with the wounded, and start repairs. And he should promote Kutuzov to acting second in command.

"Captain, this world is—wrong," Rabbit said.

"Wrong?"

"There's no horizon." Rabbit pointed out over the water. "And look." He swept his hand upward to a dark splotch at the eighty degree point in the sky overhead. "That's a landmass. We're inside a sphere, a very large one."

Mikhail stopped to truly look.

Floating landmasses, like the one they had hit, dotted the sky. One plowed through the clouds, roiling the white into a gray. Lightning flickered in the tight knot of polarized air, like a storm inside a bottle. That island was a wedge of stone, perspective obscuring its topside. An island farther in the distance, though, showed a crown of thick green. He would only see the top of the island if it was traveling up a curve.

Mikhail turned in a circle.

The wind had been blowing steadily from one direction, coming across the water. If this was home, he would want to call it west—with the nose of his ship pointing east—but he wasn't sure that name would apply in this place. Wind tended to follow the rotation of the planet. Was the same true in this place? Was the shell of the sphere rotating? Space stations rotated to maintain artificial gravity.

Mikhail wondered if it was an artifact or some weird accident of nature. The only difference, for him and his crew, would come if the owners of the artifact acted on their arrival.

∞   ∞   ∞

After the blasting heat of the sun, the dark of the hangar was a relief. They had both of the blast doors open, and the constant breeze scoured out the heat.

The hangar was filled with chaos as his crew had shaken off their shock and were now reacting. He found his chief engineering officer, Yevgeny Tseytlin, swearing heatedly at a heavy-duty pump with fire hoses leading down the lift shaft.

"How's the ship?" Mikhail asked.

"We had a hull breach in Alpha Red. We had to flood the deck to get the Reds out of it. The veterans were in Beta Red; they're all fine. We lost half of the replacements. Alpha Red will have to stay sealed. I'm trying to drain the rest of that deck, but there's debris clogging the intake valves on the pumps."

Alpha Red was Turk's last reported position.

"Turk?" Mikhail asked.

Sorrow filled Tseytlin's eyes and he put a hand to Mikhail's shoulder. "I'm sorry, Captain. He's not on the ship. I don't know where we lost him—but he's gone."

Mikhail had been bracing himself for that answer but it still hurt. He nodded his understanding, not trusting his voice.

"Where should I store the bodies once I get the deck drained?" Tseytlin asked.

They had a handful of morgue slots but not enough to take a quarter of the Red detachment. Normally they did all burials at space. There was no long-term storage for dead on ship. In this heat, it would only be a matter of a few hours before they would start to smell—and worse—attract predators and parasites. Burying them in the sandbar would only trap the toxin of the rotting bodies next to the ship.

"We're going have to bury the dead at sea," Mikhail said.

"At sea? You mean throw them in the water?" Tseytlin said.

"They're dead, we're not. But we will be if we don't make our survival top priority. We can't keep the dead anywhere near the ship, not in this heat. Understood?"

"Yes, sir."

"Put someone else—if you have someone else—onto this detail. I need you to make sure that the water recycling system hasn't been compromised. If it has, it's your priority above all other things."

"Water?"

"Water is like air, Tseytlin. Without it, we'll die."

"I think I've heard that before." This from a man who could tell you down to the seconds how long any amount of air could keep a human alive. Tseytlin had been raised on short-hull freighters, where none of the stops were more than a day apart. In the "world" he grew up in, even if something went wrong with the water recycling system, it would never be life threatening.

Only a few of his crew had been raised landside. Worse, none had experienced true wilderness. Never had to live off the land. Never known thirst . . .

. . . *he was so thirsty* . . .

Nyanya Nastya had left that morning. Or more accurately, she had left the night before, while Mikhail and Turk slept. The day had been full of unhappy surprises: stiff new clothes, harder classes, and a strict new housekeeper who didn't sleep in the dyetskaya *with them. Six-year-old Mikhail had managed all day to be a big boy and not cry, but late at night, thirsty and yet too scared to leave his bed, he started to cry.*

Mikhail's biggest problem was that he thought too much. He pondered things until he knew the best and worst that could happen in every situation. Only the best rarely happened, so he was usually disappointed, and he was often surprised that there were worse options available—ones he didn't know about—like discovering at the age of four that certain fast-moving objects can amputate a finger, and that while such things could be corrected, they were stunningly painful.

He suspected that there were no urody *lurking in the shadows of his bedroom suite, but one could never be sure. His crying woke three-year-old Turk, who came padding out of his cubby, rubbing sleep out of his eyes.*

"Why are you crying?" Turk asked grouchily.

He was really crying because Nyanya Nastya was gone. He knew that she left because Turk finally mastered potty training and dressing himself, but he suspected that Turk didn't know that. Mikhail had sabotaged Turk's progress to delay her leaving, at least until they started punishing Turk harshly. He wasn't sure why she had to leave. He loved her dearly. She had said that she loved him, but she lied often about things she thought would upset him. And why would his father let her leave? That was the most upsetting question of all. So many times, a possible answer to similar questions was that his father didn't love him. His father made it clear that Turk wasn't his son, but his treatment of Mikhail was not that much different. Certainly it didn't match Nyanya Nastya's shower of hugs and kisses.

Turk stood beside Mikhail's bed, waiting for Mikhail to explain why he was crying. He was stoic as well as patient and truthful; while Turk had been silent all day, he'd gone all furry.

"Do you love me, Turk?"

Turk nodded, but added, "You cry too much."

Mikhail tested the limits of Turk's love. "Get me a drink of water."

Turk never thought as much as he did. He went into the bathroom without considering what the darkness might hold. He came back, carefully carrying a cup in both hands. "Here."

Mikhail drank the water and then pulled Turk into bed with him. Turk felt like a cyber teddy, warm and soft, but better—a cyber teddy couldn't fetch water, fight urody, *or really, truly love him.*

As he drifted to sleep, feeling safe, Turk started to purr.

"Captain?" someone said close to hand, and the memory flitted away.

Mikhail pressed a hand to his forehead. For a few minutes, the memory was solid and real as the broken ship beneath his feet. He'd thought of that night before, but never with such clarity. The print on Turk's nightshirt. The blue of the cup. The taste of the water. Was he suffering from some kind of head trauma or just going mad?

Unfortunately, either was just as likely.

"Captain?" Tseytlin repeated. Mikhail recognized his voice this time. "After checking the water recycling system, what should I focus on?"

Mikhail blinked to clear the memory from his vision. It was a mark of how rattled Tseytlin was that he seemed unaware Mikhail had phased out. Mikhail had a good crew, but he just landed them in a situation that probably was beyond their ability to cope with. He had to keep himself in control. He forced himself to consider Tseytlin's question.

Watertightness was a minimal concern since the ship was compartmentalized and airtight. Even with the damage to the bridge and the breach in Alpha Red, the rest of the ship wasn't in danger of flooding even in the worst of storms. Luckily they had landed in shallow water, so it was unlikely they would sink.

"With the bridge gone, we're defenseless," Mikhail said. "We need to get the guns online."

"Is this a nefrim-controlled world?" Tseytlin asked.

Mikhail glanced out the open hangar door to the bright shimmering blue, so far innocent of anything more menacing than sharks. "That is yet to be seen. We should assume it is. Maintain covert protocol. Radio silence. Minimal energy output."

Tseytlin nodded slowly. "It will take some time, but we can modify the *Tigertail*'s weapon control to handle the *Svoboda*'s guns."

"Good."

"Captain?" Rabbit had been trailing behind him, apparently obeying the last order given to him until given new ones.

Mikhail frowned at him and realized that Rabbit was looking across the hangar. He followed the direction of the little Red's gaze. There was a tall Red that Mikhail had never seen before limping toward them, licking blood from its lips. It was one of the replacements from Paradise.

Mikhail stepped backward, wishing he had a weapon. While he trusted the Reds that had been part of the crew for several missions, these replacements were loose cannons. "What is it?"

"I'm top cat," the Red said.

So the Reds had spent the time determining who was next in command with Turk's disappearance.

"What's your name?"

"547-8210-UKU-S68."

Mikhail hardened his gaze on the Red. It was difficult to intimidate someone you knew could tear off your arm and beat you with it. After growing up with Turk, Mikhail was fully aware of how strong a Red at any age was compared to a normal human. Still, the crèche-raised had to be dealt with from a position of apparent power. "What is your name?"

The Red blinked as if surprised by the request, and hesitated, thinking it through before offering up his handle. "Butcher."

"Butcher," Mikhail repeated, digging in hooks in the Red's attention. "How much do you know about planets? Ever been out of the city on Paradise?"

"No."

"Can you swim?"

"What is swim?"

Mikhail sighed and dropped his gaze. *Oh Turk, Turk, Turk—I need you here, alive and well.* "Do you know how to do duty rosters?"

"Yes, sir. I have ten dead, three wounded, leaving me twenty-seven fit for combat. I have set up three shifts of nine Reds each and assigned commanders for each shift."

"Good." Mikhail nodded. At least the new top cat was more than a set of finely tuned muscles. "Butcher, if an unidentified boat approaches, I need the Reds to hold fire until ordered."

"You said that you wanted natives to know we're unfriendly," Butcher said. Mikhail's orders to Inozemtsev had filtered through to the Reds then. "Why the change?"

"There might be other spaceships that crashed here," Mikhail said. "If the humans survived, they might use boats to travel around on. You know what a boat is?"

Butcher put his hands together to form a prow of a boat with his fingertips. "It's a thing that floats on water."

"Just because they're humans doesn't necessarily mean that they're friendly. Consider them as *possible* hostiles." Gods, how smart was this Red? Mikhail wouldn't have had to explain himself to Turk. "But do not fire on them unless ordered. Do you understand?"

"I understand," Butcher rumbled. "Show your teeth but don't attack."

Mikhail managed not to feel for hours, keeping it all blocked out as he climbed through his darkened, half-flooded ship. Finally he couldn't hold it off any longer. He retreated to his cabin to lock his service pistol into his safe. Using a marker, he wrote "Bad Misha Bad" and drew Turk's cat face scowling at him. He felt no need to turn his pistol on himself. No. Not yet. He could feel it coming, like the sun setting on the horizon; his ability to cope was fleeing. Dark despair would set in as inevitable as night, and this time, Turk wouldn't be there to save him from himself.

He leaned against the wall and covered the cat picture with his palm. "Good God, Turk, what am I going to do?"

"You go on," Turk would say, as if it was so simple and easy. He always envied Turk that strength and had always leaned heavily on it.

He wanted to believe Turk was still alive, but the facts weighed too heavily. The air lock had opened while the *Svodoba* was still

two or three kilometers off the water. Even if Turk survived the
fall, he'd be hurt and out in open water teeming with predators.
There would be no safe place to rest or hide.

"I'll try to be strong, Turk. The last thing my people need is
me falling apart. I'll try to make you proud."

The next ship morning, they gathered under the constant noon
sun for the mass funeral. They tested one of the body bags the
shift before—made sure that it would float. It made him uneasy
to launch his people out not into space but this seething living
water. Space felt safe, its vast emptiness protected his dead from
being disturbed until God chose to gather them up. It seemed
like a betrayal, setting the dead adrift, helpless to countless forces
that would disturb them. But there was nothing that could be
done. They couldn't afford the bodies polluting the waters near
the ship.

He read his memorial speech and then the names of the dead.
Turk's name was on the list, but he couldn't bring himself to say
it aloud. One by one, they pushed off the bags, letting the current take their dead. The sky was perfect blue, the sand a delicate
pink, and the water crystalline. The black bags remained visible
for hours, slowly drifting away. Helpless.

Afterward he gathered up all the vodka in his cabin and shared
the bottles out to the crew. They needed a drunk captain no more
than they needed a dead one.

6 I Eat You

THE CURRENT BROUGHT THEM EVIDENCE OF THE ICARUS'S FALL within hours. Paige knew that Icarus had been heavily forested, but the amount that had been spilled off the vimana amazed her. The floating debris rolled toward them on the waves until the ocean was carpeted with green and brown. Drift flowers, naturally designed to ride the waves, reached them first. Then drop nuts, riding among the flowers like bald hillsides. Finally the broken bodies of dead land animals.

The chance of fouling the longboat rotors was too great. They would have to wait until the current carried the debris away. The repair to the freshwater tank was simple; filling it was an arduous process of hand-cranking the emergency desalination pump with a painstaking rate of one ounce of water per three minutes. They lacked the materials, though, to fix the hole punched through the crew's quarters. Rather than sit idle, stewing on what might lay ahead, Paige set the crew to fishing the drop nuts out of the flotsam. If she ended up having to buy a new engine, they'd need things to sell to raise money. With Jones standing guard on the gun platform, Avery and Hillary used boat hooks to herd the nuts into the cargo net to be lifted up to the deck. There Becky wrestled the large nuts out of the wet netting and rolled them into place to be dried.

"The birds I understand how they got up to the vimanas." Hillary prodded the body of a large furred animal with her boat hook. It rolled in the water, revealing that it was four-legged and hoofed. "But how did that get up there?"

"One of the many mysteries of life." Paige checked the nuts on the deck. Thanks to the baking sun of the cloudless day, the husk was already dry to the touch. "Take a break from fishing and turn these. Once they're dried, we'll move them to the cargo hold and fish more up."

Hillary made a sound of disgust. "One of the many mysteries of life. We're not savages. We still know how to build jump drives, terraform hostile planets into paradise, and alter our DNA. If we put our minds to it, we should be able to figure out anything. Can't you even guess?"

"I don't know enough to guess," Paige said.

"What is that suppose to mean? Don't know enough." Hillary shoved away the animal.

Surprisingly, it was Jones that came to Paige's defense. "How many life stages does that animal have? Kites start as nymphs and live in water. That animal there might have wings in a different stage in life."

"It could have evolved on the vimana," Avery said. "We don't know how old the vimanas are geologically speaking."

"Or devolved," Paige said. "Theoretically you could create a species that could fly up to the vimana and yet the next generation be wingless."

"Hell, it could have been catapulted up," Avery said. "It might have been the only one of its kind on Icarus."

"Catapulted?" Hillary said.

Avery nodded. "Ya-ya supposedly experimented with catapults a hundred years ago. They shot animals at passing vimanas."

"They did not!" Hillary snapped.

"Did too," Avery said.

"Hillary," Paige said as the girl opened her mouth to automatically deny the possibility. Avery had a way of mixing nearly believable lies with unbelievable truth, so you were always sure he was lying, but every time you tried calling him on something that seemed too unbelievable, he could furnish proof.

"Icarus does not pass over Yamoto-Yamaguchi," the girl said after a minute of outraged silence.

"I'm just saying that if Ya-ya tried it, then maybe someone else tried it too," Avery said.

"Why'd they stop trying?" Becky asked. "Living up there on the vimanas would be better than being down here on the water."

Rannatan whistled in a negative tone. "Stay with ship. Tech is good."

"So dismantle the ship and haul it up, piece by piece," Becky said.

"The only thing you can land on a vimana is organic material like the kites," Avery said.

"Do you think that's really true?" Jones asked from her perch. "That spaceship hit Icarus. If you can hit a vimana, maybe you can land on it."

Paige shook her head. She had tried not to think of it, but the memory of the accident had replayed again and again. There were times she wished she had a different kind of brain, one that didn't see life as puzzles that needed to be picked apart. "The ship only grazed it. Icarus was rolling even as the ship skimmed its topside." Paige mimed vimana and spaceship repulsing each other even as the ship's trajectory brought them together. "Like two polarized magnets, they repelled each other. Don't think the ship would have survived otherwise."

"Did you see what kind of ship it was?" Jones asked. "Human? Minotaur?"

"Obnaoian?" Rannatan asked hopefully. The ships from his race were few and far between and rarely survived the harsh weather long.

"It was a human ship," Paige told the little alien, and then added for the others' sake, "a Novaya Rus frigate. Probably lost its bridge when it clipped the vimana."

"We're going to go help them?" Becky asked.

"We've got enough trouble of our own." Paige told the girl what she would understand. It was more complex than that. Military new arrivals were always heavily armed and viewed everyone and everything with suspicion. When their command structure survived, they often practiced a version of "eminent domain" that was really piracy. When their command structure died in the crash, they imploded into violence. "We can't be the only humans that saw them come down. Someone not hip deep in trouble will contact them."

"Ship!" Mitch shouted from the crow's nest—the farthest point from Charlene that Paige could put him. "Ship off the port bow!"

Paige scrambled up to the bridge where Orin was already

scanning the horizon. With the debris in the water, it took her several minutes to pick out the low-riding craft.

"Good eyes, Mitch!" she called back, studying the form.

Orin made a sound of discovery, indicating he'd caught sight of it too. "That's a civ raft, isn't it?"

"I think so." Civ rafts were wide, haphazard-looking things. She could identify the nesting dome, the salvage heaps, and the holding nets.

Like all sentient lifeforms, the civ could have only reached the Sargasso after their race developed wormhole technology. Their rafts—if you scraped off all the junk and muck—bore witness that they were once skilled builders. The bare bones were of a synthetic thermoplastic polymer that floated and resisted saturation by water. And the construction across the various rafts was too uniform to suggest that they'd been lucky and raided someone else's technology. But whatever level of civilization they had when they came to the Sargasso, they lost. The civ had reverted back to complete savages.

"Is it tagged?" Orin scanned the raft. "I don't see anything."

Paige looked for symbols that humans painted onto civ rafts. "There's no ear tags on it. It's not a tribe we know."

"I think we should stay away from them. We're all but dead in the water. I don't want to end up lunch for them."

The civ saw everything as food, regardless of sentience, and they ate their prey alive. It was a nasty end, and Paige didn't want to think about the possibility that survivors of the crashed frigate might have been picked up by the civ. Statistically, it was highly unlikely. The frigate would have traveled another hundred miles or more before hitting water. The slim chance still put a shiver down her back.

On the other hand, the civ salvaged everything in their path. The definition of ownership for civ seemed to be that only when you couldn't pry something up did it actually belong to anyone. The trick in dealing with the civ, thus, was making sure you didn't get stuck to something they owned. Considering that they kept spider mites as pets, that was easier said than done.

"They might have a converter in their salvage heaps," Paige said.

"You're not thinking of trading with them? This tribe has never even seen a human before."

"All the tribes we've traded with have spoken the same language.

I can do this. Let's wait for the debris field to thin down and then I'll take the launch across."

Orin was shaking his head slowly. Paige knew that he saw the same dangers that she did and didn't like the odds.

"We need a converter," she said. "Or we'll *stay* dead in the water."

Orin glanced at their dead radio and a frown quirked the corner of his mouth as he calculated the odds of help coming to them. "I'll do it then."

"Orin . . ." She caught herself before she finished her thought. Either the Baileys' odd genetic mix or something in the Sargasso itself had given her family remarkable gifts. Each of them had their own strengths and weaknesses. Orin was her equal in reading people, and thus a capable translator. He didn't have, though, that odd mental quirk that Paige thought of as the white space, where jumps in logic took place, and answers came from seemingly nowhere. He wouldn't have her edge when faced with complications.

Unfortunately, he read what she had left unsaid and his frown deepened.

She poked him in the gut. "Suck it up. We've got too much on the line. I'm the best choice and you know it."

"I'd feel better if I couldn't kick your butt in a fair fight."

"I'll just have to fight dirty."

He scowled at her for attempting to make him laugh. She poked him in the stomach again.

"Hey, I've got the easy job," she said. "You have to deal with the crew while I'm gone."

First week out, she'd made a rule that only she and Orin were allowed on the bridge to keep all of her crew from cramming into the room. Thus all of them were outside the door when she opened it.

"We're going to trade with the civ." She forestalled them from all asking questions at once. "Charlene, we need something to trade the civ. Something that will take them time to unload from the launch. Something awkward to handle."

Charlene gave a resentful look for being ordered away first, but she went, taking Mitch with her. That boy had to grow a backbone.

Paige continued to hand out duties. "Hillary, take Becky and get everything off the launch except the motor. Even the bumpers. Avery and Manny, I want to be able to move the *Rosetta* if the current shifts and brings the raft toward us. Ran, I'll need a headset that will let me talk to Jones." She repeated the last in obnaoian, just to make sure he understood.

That left only Jones to ask questions. "I'm coming as your backup, right?"

"Yes. This is how it's going to work. Trading with the civ is like cooperative stealing. I'll go onboard their raft, find what I want, and then start the trade. At that point, they'll take everything they want—which will be everything they can carry away—and I can take anything I can carry away."

Jones nodded her understanding. "What do I need to watch out for?"

"The biggest danger is their numbers. There's anywhere from fifty to two hundred of them onboard. If things go hostile, they'll tear us to shreds."

"They can try. What weapons do they have?"

"Nothing more sophisticated than knives."

Jones frowned down at Paige with her mouth shifted slightly to the side, as if rolling something about in her mouth, trying it out before speaking aloud. Finally, the woman asked, "I take it we can't do a preemptive strike?"

"No!" Paige cried. "They're intelligent. Primitive. But intelligent."

"Yeah, I thought that would be your answer. You know, I admire your morals, but they're damn inconvenient sometimes."

"They're not supposed to be convenient," Paige grumbled. She found it a little unnerving to discover that the most heavily armed person onboard had such a homicidal attitude. "You have to fight to keep your bearings or the current will take you where it wants; the easy course is also the one that leaves you helpless."

Jones made a short disgusted noise. "Sometimes you don't have a choice."

"You always have a choice," Paige said firmly. She considered switching to someone else to back her up. No. If things went badly, Jones had the right mind-set and reactions. In the future, with more civilized races, though, Jones would be a bad choice as backup.

Luckily Charlene and Mitch returned, saving Paige from clashing farther with Jones over morality. The teenage lovers carried a large rough wooden barrel, which they eased down onto the deck cautiously.

"I think these will work well." Charlene pried the lid off the barrel. Inside were dark green glass blanks.

Paige picked one of the blanks up. They were slightly bigger than a softball, slick and difficult to hold. To a civ, with their smaller hands, the blanks would be nearly impossible to carry more than one, thus perfect for her needs. "Thanks, Charlene." Paige put the blank back into the barrel. "We have like ten barrels of these?"

"Yeah," Charlene said.

"Can you pour two barrels worth into the bottom of the launch? And be careful, they'll shatter easily."

Charlene nodded her understanding. She and Mitch heaved up the barrel and carried it toward the launch.

Jones waited until the lovers were out of earshot before asking, "What were those?"

"Glass blanks." Paige had noticed that Jones didn't like to appear ignorant among her peers. There might also be an upper limit to Jones's willingness to admit weakness to her captain. With that thought, Paige expanded her answer. "Everyone has sand enough to make glass but not the means to heat the sand until it forms glass. Minotaurs have foundries. They make these blanks in bulk. Humans reshape the glass to what they need."

"Oh, that's why you don't have glass windows in your houses."

"Why would you use glass in a window?"

"To keep out the weather." Jones's tone was as if she was explaining to a child.

Paige shook her head. "Glass would break in a storm. That's why we have shutters."

Jones breathed out a mix of disbelief and annoyance. "There are ways to make glass tough enough that it can withstand a bullet."

Paige rolled a blank around on her palm considering it. The civ weren't the only ones regressing. She hired on Jones because the woman knew how to maintain and fire the *Rosetta*'s big guns and brought with her a laser rifle. Both her knowledge and her firearm were scarce in the Sargasso. When humans set out to colonize the stars, only the colonies that received a steady supply of people and materials succeeded. While new ships were always arriving at the Sargasso, like the Russian frigate they saw earlier, they rarely expected to find themselves stranded, nor landed safely.

What would happen to them if the humans outside the Sargasso lost their war to the nefrim and ceased to arrive? The question threatened to drag her into the white zone for an answer. She shook it off; even without checking that sharply analytical part of her brain, she sensed it would be a bad thing. They needed their constant supply of people like Jones to remind them of things like bullet-strong glass.

"So why are we pouring the blanks into the bottom of the boat?" Jones asked.

"It will take the civ longer to move them and give me more time to get a converter off their raft," Paige said.

"And if you run out of time?"

"Be ready for a fight."

Because of the need to keep equipment to a bare minimum, they were quickly ready. Jones pulled out the pieces of her combat armor that survived the sinking of her spaceship. Ran had pieced together a headset for Paige that operated on the same frequency as Jones's comline. Paige made sure that she had her bowie knife tucked deep into her hip pocket. They double-checked that the launch's engine was running smoothly, and then they pushed off.

The civ raft was a kilometer long, and as they slowly approached it, it grew until it seemed like an island, complete with rolling hills. The hills, however, were the domed hives and mounds of collected flotsam. Paige had Jones troll past all four sides as she scanned the edge. True to their recent bad luck, she spotted nothing that looked like it might have a converter inside. If the infiltration scanners on Jones's combat suit worked, they could have used them to pinpoint any converter buried under the crud. Years of saltwater, however, had taken its toll on the complex electronics.

"Pull up there, where the edge is low." Paige tucked away the binoculars. "I'm going onboard. Soon as I get across, pull away again."

She moved to the bow, and the moment the two boats kissed sides, she leapt across. The surface of the raft oozed slightly where she landed. The stench of rotting matter, manure, and mold was nearly overpowering. She panted through her mouth rather than breathe through her nose and waved to Jones that she was on safe. Jones pulled the launch away, moving to a safe distance from the raft and then idled there, waiting.

Immediately, Paige was noticed. A civ scuttled up to her, its five eyes gleaming like onyx marbles, opening its long thin snout to hiss at her, exposing all its sharp teeth. She held her hands up to her mouth, cupping them so her fingers took the place of teeth, and gave the shuttering hissed greeting back. "*I eat you! I eat you!*"

"*Mine! Mine! All mine!*" It cried gesturing at piles of salvage. "*I eat you!*"

"*That mine! That mine! All mine!*" She gestured toward the launch. "*I eat you!*"

Ownership established and proper threats exchanged, she left the civ pacing the edge of the raft, eyeing her goods. While they couldn't prove that the civ were telepathic, it would certainly explain why an exchange with one would work with all of them. After the first encounter, they ignored her except an occasional, "*I eat you!*" hissed in her direction.

Civ raft ships made her skin crawl. Everything was covered by a thin layer of excrement and viscera supporting an ecosystem of fungus and plants that the civ's pet spider mites lived off of. Spider mites' eggs, little pale globes of tissue, spotted everything. She tried not to shudder too hard when the omnipresent spider mites skittered across her skin—but she did make sure that they didn't pause. The civ used the spider mites' silk to stick down their belongings.

She passed the holding nets, careful not to touch the sticky strands. They held animals from Icarus, drugged senseless by the mite venom. In smaller nets the silk was woven into fine cloth, capturing both fish and the water needed to keep it alive. No humans, though, nor anything else she recognized as sentient.

Evidence of human contact was everywhere. A life preserver. A deck chair. A set of signal flags. Some of it was nearly lost under the spider mites that worked to attach it to the raft.

"Have you found anything yet?" Jones's voice came over the headset.

"They've been in human waters for a while," Paige told her. "But everything so far has all been stuff that floats. They could have picked it up in open water after a storm. For a converter, they would have to salvage a wreck."

"Is there anything nonbuoyant?"

"Not yet." Paige clambered over a mound and found a group of civ eating something four legged and furred. While the aliens feasted on its hindquarters, the creature still panted, its eyes flicking toward her movement. Paige whimpered and scrambled backward, slipped, and fell with a cry. The spider mites skittered toward her. She leapt to her feet.

"Bailey?"

"I'm fine! I'm fine. I'm okay. I'm fine." It was taking all her control to keep from bolting from the raft. Frightened as she was, she couldn't leave without a converter. Without a converter, the next storm could be the *Rosetta*'s last.

"I don't see anything outside on the salvage heaps." Paige said. "They might have something inside one of the hives."

"You're not going inside are you?" Jones said.

Paige crouched at the entrance, staring down the low tunnel, panting out her fear.

"If the civ take you down in there, I'm not going to be able to get you out," Jones warned her.

"When are you going to learn? The correct response is, 'It's going to be fine'?"

Jones gave a dry humorless laugh. "Go in, kid, and you're on your own."

This is what it came down to. Being so fucking scared and knowing you had to go on. She was shaking as she got down on her hands and knees. One last deep breath for courage, and she crawled into the hive.

The dark tunnel connected to a dimly lit chamber. Light seeped in through what looked like paper-thin oiled skins. She didn't want to think too long on what kind of skins the civ might have used. There were four tunnels leading out of the chamber, each so low she'd have to go on her hands and knees. She couldn't imagine the civ dragging engine parts through the low corridors, but she couldn't be sure until she explored them all.

One would have never guessed that the civ actually used technology from the outside of the ship, but buried deep inside the hive, she found evidence they did retain some knowledge of technology. Machinery that she recognized, and some she didn't, sat among the organic matter, as out of place as a wrench in a pack rat's nest. Did they actually use it, or like the rodent, just liked it for the "shiny" factor? She ignored the equipment that she didn't know; it would take too long to figure out how to get them open and how they worked.

In one chamber she found a Red combat suit, its distress signal recently activated. The beacon light flared the room to red brilliance before dropping the area to utter darkness. A suit wouldn't have a converter but it would have infiltration scanners. If they still worked, she could . . .

The beacon flared red again. With a sudden deep-throated growl, something large moved in the shadows. The light gleamed red like blood on bared teeth.

Paige yelped and scuttled backward, but caught herself at the door.

"Bailey?" Jones's voice was weirdly comforting.

"They've got some fucking animal down here," Paige said.

"Not an animal." The slurred Standard came from that mouth full of teeth.

"Oh, fuck." Paige whispered and edged closer for a better look.

It was a Red male, furred over in reaction to stress, wearing shreds of a Novaya Rus uniform, pinned into place by webs, and partially senseless with venom. He growled a deep rumbling warning. Who knew what the poison was doing to his mind?

"Get me out of here," the Red snarled. "I'm not an animal. I'm human. I'm human."

"Bailey?" Jones said as the room dropped into darkness.

"They've got a Novaya Rus Red stuck to the wall," Paige whispered.

There was a minute of silence from Jones, and then, "That's not our concern. Find the converter and get out. We can't be playing heroes. We're too thin here."

It was unthinkable to leave him there, living food for the civ. But Jones was right. She was deep in the hive with Jones as her only backup. And the *Rosetta* was floating helpless without the converter.

The beacon flared to brilliance, and the Red glared at her from his prison of webbing.

"Get me the fuck out of here," he growled.

"I don't know if I can," she whispered.

"Just cut me the fuck down and give me a weapon."

Yes, it would seem that simple, but he was tacked down, which made him civ property. If she cut him down, the civ would see it as stealing, unless she did it while trading with them. A trade, however, was the length of time it took the civ to unload the boat, during which time, she could grab anything she wanted. When the boat was empty, the trade would be over. If she started the trade without having a converter in hand, she wouldn't have time to find one.

"Get me down!" the Red shouted as the beacon light turned off, as if he was afraid that she would leave in the cover of the dark.

"I can't," Paige said to let him know she hadn't left—yet.

"Then fucking kill me. I saw what they do to the things they catch. I'm not going through that."

It was a simple and elegant solution. He was so helpless she could put her knife to his throat and, with one clean cut, put him out of his misery. The beacon flared on and she looked into his dark eyes, full of intelligence and anger, and floundered in moral impasse. She wouldn't jeopardize her ship and her family for this stranger, but she couldn't just kill him.

"Just—just give me time," Paige said. "I need to find something, and then I'll come back."

"Fuck you will."

"Yes, I will. You've got to trust me."

The light died. In the dark, he gave a low, rumbling laugh, and muttered something too low in Russian for her to hear.

"I will be back," she promised even though she wasn't sure she would be able to return. "Just wait. I'll be back."

"No, don't leave me ... please." Even as helpless as he was, he clearly didn't like to beg.

"If I don't find what I'm looking for, none of us will be leaving. I have to find this first."

The light flared on. He glared at her as if he was trying to see to her core. To see if she was telling him the truth. She held his gaze, wanting him to believe in her—it would be kinder to give him hope.

"Hurry then." There was no hope in his voice.

Obviously the combat armor had been his, stripped off by the civ. It was brand new with more bells and whistles than she was used to, but close enough to the Georgetown armor that she could puzzle it out. Luckily the spider mites hadn't tacked down the chest piece, making it free game where the Red wasn't.

Judging by the way the spider mites scurried away from armor each time the distress beacon flared on, they viewed it as too dangerous to cement into place. It was intact enough for her to put it on; it was too heavy and awkward to carry otherwise. The helmet was missing, but the backup headset was still slotted into place. She took off her jury-rigged headset and snug the armor's headset into place.

"Did you find one yet?" Jones's voice over the new headset made her jump slightly.

"I'm working on it." True to her luck, the suit's commands were in Russian instead of Standard. Who expected a Red to read Russian? She stumbled through the menus, surprised to find that the system was much more customizable than any she'd worked with before. Usually there was only a small selection of preprogrammed items that the infiltration scanners recognized. Mission targets were downloaded from the command ship; thus the Reds could ignore everything but what they were supposed to find and destroy. It took a few minutes but she managed to program in the converter itself. With the scanners activated, she worked back through the hive.

Three rooms later, the eyepiece highlighted the lines of a converter installed in an excavator buried a foot under the crud. It went way past being tacked down. There was no way she could start digging without first starting a trade.

"Jones, I found one. I'm going to start the trade. You're going to have to let one of the civ on the launch."

"Fuck."

"Jones, I'm shit deep in the hive. If I start messing with the civ's stuff without a trade, they're going to tear me to shreds. The only way I'm getting this out is starting a trade—which means they have to be able to carry off what they want too."

Jones huffed but after a minute of silence said, "All right. I'm ready here."

Still, Paige wanted as much time as possible. She scrabbled at the muck until she cleared the access hatch to the excavator's engine. As she lifted the hatch, there was a rush of feet toward her. She turned and chittered at oncoming mass of civ. "Trade mine! Trade mine!"

The civs slowed, hissing at her. Did they understand her offer or were they just being cowards? Weapon of choice, other than their teeth, were clubs; the pack had sticks, pipes, and long animal bones. There was a joke about civ liking weapons that tenderized their enemies—somehow the joke suddenly didn't seem that funny.

"Trade mine!" she chattered desperately, all too aware that she was backed into a dead end and that there was a quarter mile of twisting, narrow tunnel between her and Jones's laser rifle.

"Trade mine!" the nearest one finally chattered, and they washed away, heading toward her barter goods.

"Oh thank God," she breathed, and turned back to carefully disconnect the converter. "Got it. I'm getting the Red now. How much of the stuff has the civ moved off the launch?"

"They're having a bitch of a time getting these blanks off the boat."

"That was the idea. When the boat is empty, the trade is over."

"You've got to be fucking me."

"Jones, I find you entirely too intimidating to try that."

Jones gave a surprised bark of laughter. "Better move your ass, Bailey."

Cradling the converter, she could only manage an awkward crab walk in the low tunnels. She waddled as quickly as she could back to the Red. The light reflected off the Red's cat eyes.

"You came back." The Red sounded surprised.

"I told you I would." She ignored the fact that she nearly didn't. She reluctantly put the converter down and hacked him free. Immediately she snatched the converter back up. "Come on. I can't carry you. Keep up with me, or I'll leave you here."

"I'll keep up."

Out of the hive, she had to fight through the mass of civ carrying glass blanks to the salvage heaps.

"Captain, you better be coming now. They're down to the last item."

"I'm out of the hive!"

Paige scrambled over the mounds and skittered down the last slope to the longboat. Jones was right. The civ were snatching up the last of the blanks rolling around in the launch.

"Here!" Paige handed the converter down to Jones. "Don't let go, or they'll take it back!"

"You left the Red?"

Paige turned and looked back. The Red wasn't in sight. "Shit."

If they left him, the civ would overwhelm him and pin him again.

"Get in the longboat," Jones said. "You don't have time to go back for him."

"Wait for me!" Paige scrambled back up the mound. *This is so stupid. So stupid. He's a stranger!*

Still she raced back to the hive. She found the Red in the last tunnel, the civ trying to drag him back. She kicked them away from him, chittering, "Trade mine! I eat you!"

"Come on!" She grabbed the Red by the scruff of the neck. "Come on! We're running out of time!"

She pulled the Red to his feet. With him leaning on her, she managed to get him to move faster, a controlled running stumble. They half fell down the last slope.

"Bailey!" Jones was untying the mooring lines. "Move it!"

Paige tumbled into the launch, pulling the Red in after her. "Go!"

The ex-marine picked up the last civ onboard and threw it onto the raft and shoved off. Paige sprang to the wheel and gunned the engine. The launch leapt forward and they were clear.

The Red sprawled on the bottom of the boat, heedless of the bilge water. His eyes were closed and his mouth was open, panting quickly and shallow. Now that the madness of the trade was over, and they were safe, Paige studied him. He looked first generation; he had that tall, board shouldered, heavily muscled build. His short glossy fur was crèche-bred black, which always made Paige wonder why they were called Reds. There was nothing about him that suggested he wasn't anything but crèche-raised, with all the nasty socialization that implied. What was she bringing onto her boat?

"What's your name?" When he didn't answer, she nudged him with her toe. "Hey? What's your handle?"

"Turkish Delight."

She must have misunderstood his slurred words. Crèche-raised had names like "Spot" and "Fang." Or maybe he hadn't understood her, and thought she had asked something else. He'd spoken Standard in the nest, but with a Russian heavy accent. "Turkish Delight?"

He opened his eyes to give her a look of complete disgust. His eyes were full black from being in the pit; in the glare of the full dazzle, they started to shift to a chocolate brown. He couldn't have been able to see, so the glare was meant to intimidate her.

Paige sighed. It was going to be one of *those* discussions.

Whatever his name was, it was now of minor importance. What mattered now was who could outstare who. She wished she could back down—she was exhausted, bruised, and covered with slime that was making her skin crawl—but if she did, next time would be harder. To stay in command, she had to get his name.

"What is your name?" She put an edge to her voice and prodded him with it.

His thick eyebrows and dark eyes were wonderfully expressive; they told her his thoughts even while he silently gazed at her. He was smart enough to quickly go from annoyed to a realization that they were clashing over command issues. As he pondered his options, his focus shifted from her to the endless sea beyond her. At that moment, such despair filled his face that she felt cruel to firmly push for an answer.

He wet his mouth and made the effort to speak more clearly. "My name is Turk."

"All right, Turk it is." She knew he had said Turkish Delight the first time, but she pretended to believe him. She kind of liked Turkish Delight, but maybe he found it embarrassing. What did it mean, she wondered, and how did he get stuck with it?

Turk tapped her on her foot, getting her attention. "What's your name?"

"Paige Bailey. I'm Captain Bailey. Our gunner is Kenya Jones." Paige pointed to Jones who didn't notice. The gunner's focus was wholly on the civ rift and possible pursuit. "Look, I know this is all going to be new to you, but you're only going to get one chance with me. You screw this up, and I'll throw you back into the water. And don't think I can't. Do you understand?"

"Yes." He nodded to show he completely understood.

"I don't care what you were before. You now listen to everyone on this boat. Everyone. No matter how small they are. Someone tells you to lie on your belly and show your throat, you do it. You hurt anyone, and I'll shoot you dead. You disobey anyone, and I'll put you off my boat."

"Yes, Captain." His eyes said he believed her but wasn't afraid. Nor was he hostile. He was waiting to see how well they treated him. It was a good sign that he could dig up patience when he was this battered.

"Welcome to my crew," Paige said since the *Rosetta* had just come into view. "My boat isn't much to look at, but it's home."

7 The Rosetta

TURK'S RESCUERS HAD TAKEN HIM BACK TO A BOAT OF STEEL and wood, approximately one hundred meters long. The only heavy weaponry was a laser cannon ripped out of a ground assault vehicle and mounted on the bow. Panels of solar arrays stretched out above the main deck like wings. Everywhere he looked, he could spot bits and pieces of salvaged spaceship, from the shell of a lifepod as the boat's bridge to emergency air locks now acting as deck hatches. It was a Frankenstein arc-welded together, the ugly scars of its creation visible to the naked eye.

Off the stern, a steel grate folded down to make a platform to dock up against. Crew lined the railing, waiting to make fast the launch he was on. They gazed down at him with surprised silence. While their clothes were all sun-bleached white and blues, the outfits didn't seem to be uniforms. There was no rank insignia visible. None of them seemed very old, and there were children mixed in, crying out what the adults were clearly thinking. "A Red! Paige found a Red!"

The *Rosetta* was a civilian ship. And judging on how similar they looked to each other, the crew was one extended family. No wonder Bailey had threatened to kill him on his first offense; she was putting her family at risk by taking him in.

"Hillary, Becky, go tell Manny that there will be another mouth to feed." One of the men ordered the children away from the railing. Away from danger. Away from Turk.

The children out of harm's way, the man caught the rope that Captain Bailey threw and made fast the launch.

The captain handed across the part she'd carried out of the alien nest. "Orin, get this to Ran and get the ship ready to depart. We're going to have to decom."

Orin handed up the part to another man and gave orders that scattered the crew. He waited until they were gone to say, "Is it safe to bring him onboard?"

"We'll give him a chance." Captain Bailey said. "He seems to be smart enough to realize the consequences of not behaving."

Orin eyed Turk with open doubt but said nothing more.

Uneasiness settled on Turk as he realized that he hadn't seen one Red among the crew. He'd never been completely alone among humans before. Even when he was a child, there had been the Volkov household's pride drifting at the edges of his awareness. Except for Mikhail, he'd never interacted with humans for extended periods.

"Come on." Captain Bailey held out her hand, offering to help Turk up. "We need to decontaminate."

Turk hated the fact that he needed her help to crawl out of the launch and onto the grate. Five feet and he was shaking with exhaustion. "I'm going to be the only Red?"

"More or less." She dipped a bucket into the ocean, hauled it up full, and dumped the saltwater over his head.

"*Chyort!*" He roared in Russian as the saltwater burned in a thousand tiny hurts. "Why the hell did you do that?"

"I know this hurts like sin, but if the civ mold got onboard, it could turn the whole ship toxic within a week." She doused him again. It was like having cold fire poured over him. "We're rationing our fresh water. Besides, saltwater kills the mold better. Here."

She handed him a bar of soap. Apparently trusting him to wash himself, she started to strip. She was wearing the chest piece from his combat armor. She'd turned off the emergency beacon in the alien nest, leaving him in darkness. Up to that minute, he'd thought it had been torture to hang on the wall while it blazed away, knowing if the *Svoboda* had landed safely, Mikhail would have sent a rescue team for him. In the dark, without that slim connection, he'd lost all hope. Even now, he teetered on the edge of an unfamiliar dark emotion that he didn't want to acknowledge.

"That's mine," Turk said as Captain Bailey stripped off the chest piece. It was all he had left of Mikhail.

"It was yours." Her boots, socks, and pants followed. "In this world, finder's keepers."

Had she rescued him because he was a valuable lost piece of equipment? "That includes me?"

She studied him for a minute. "Yes."

There, he was comfortably annoyed now. "What do you plan to do with me?"

"Put you to work." Captain Bailey sat down and focused on scrubbing the filth from his armor. The hem of her shirt rode up. Her underwear was modest, white, wet, and clinging, accenting her body while pretending to cover it. It was amazing how distracting three square inches of fabric could be. He had to force himself to look away, and try to remember what they were talking about. Her plans for him.

"Doing what?" he asked.

"Whatever needs to be done. Standing guard. Fishing. Scrubbing." She reached out and tapped the bar of soap in his hand. "You rub that against your skin until it foams, and then you rinse it off."

"I know." Part of the ancient imperial trappings that the Volkovs observed were scented bars of soap. Divine right via neo-Luddite cleaning methods.

"Then do it." She whistled to a male crew member, a younger brother or cousin by the look of him, and handed him the chest piece. "My cabin."

Turk forced himself not to watch them carry it away. It's not like she threw it away. Growing up under Ivan Volkov's rule, he knew the difference of something gone forever and something that might be earned back.

Captain Bailey stood eyeing him. "You need to wash. Civ mold can take down even a Red's antibodies."

He looked at the soap in his hand. Between the exhaustion and grief, he couldn't find the energy to move.

Captain Bailey sighed, crouching beside him and taking the soap. "Okay, I'll help you now, but you've got to pull your weight."

She worked the bar of soap into a lather that spilled suggestively down her bare legs. She took his hand in hers and started to wash him. She focused a nearly medical attention onto his hand, and yet, after all the practiced seduction of cat fanciers, he found it wildly alluring. "Boy, the mold has already worked into your fur. Can you shed it?"

"I can't shed on command," he snapped. Normally he could, but not now, not feeling this vulnerable. He hated being weak, dependant, ignorant, and needy. He knew that this sudden desire to fuck a complete stranger was just some emotional reaction to being lost and alone. Like starvation making plain food delicious, his complete isolation made Captain Bailey seem like the most desirable woman he ever met. The blue of her eyes wasn't truly that stunning a color. Her lips weren't that kissably full. Her smile wasn't that open and warm. Her body wasn't so fuck-me perfect. He was just imagining it.

Captain Bailey looked up to study him for a moment and then nodded. Bending her head over his hand, she scrubbed her fingers through his fur, kneading in the soap. He closed his eyes to shut out what the wet T-shirt was failing to cover.

Focus, Turk, Focus.

The captain rinsed the soap from his arm, making him hiss with pain as the salt burned into the tiny cuts she just scrubbed open. "I'm sorry." And then for the first time she moved cautiously, tentatively touching his shoulder. "I need to scrub your head."

She was aware, then, of how dangerous he could be. As she slid her hand up to his neck, he went tense, controlling the instinctive reaction to defend himself. She watched him closely as she continued to work the soap into his fur.

"Easy," she crooned. "No one's going to hurt you."

He wasn't worried about himself. He forced himself to relax. She smiled and used both hands to knead the tight muscles in his neck. It felt wonderful. As she massaged the back of skull, he slumped forward, resting his head against her shoulder. She smelt of soap and clean skin. The civilized part of him whispered that he shouldn't trust this stranger who had no reason to be good to him. The feral part of his soul, though, accepted the offered refuge.

Captain Bailey went still, holding him close, and then pulled away. He could swear she was blushing. "Get rinsed off."

He gritted his teeth through rinsing as she washed her own hair. After he dragged himself onboard, she stripped off her wet T-shirt and finished her bathing in false privacy. He lay on the wood planking and watched her bare back as foam slid down her spine. He should have stayed and offered to wash her back. Then again, it was probably better that he hadn't.

Captain Bailey supplied him with a towel to wrap around his hips, apparently for modesty only. "Lie out in the sun and dry off." She only had a towel on, wrapped under her arms, and barely covering her groin. "Stay here. I'll be right back."

Turk was on the edge of sleep when the hot sun lessened abruptly, as if something large was casting a shadow over him. He felt the movement of someone nearing him. He struggled to wake back up, growling out a warning.

"It's just me." The captain's voice came from above him.

He pried open his eyes. It alarmed him how difficult even that task was. He was still lying on the wooden deck. The sudden shadow was from a cloth awning that just had been extended over him, creating shade. Captain Bailey had changed to a swath of bright-colored fabric wrapped around her like a dress, tied so a part of her leg and hip came into view when the wind fluttered the material.

"Too much sun will make you sick." Captain Bailey locked the awning into place. "Here." She swirled a brushed steel carafe, letting him hear the liquid gurgle inside it. "I brought you lemonade."

He struggled to sit up and take the carafe. The steel tainted the lemonade, but it was cool and tart and probably the most wonderful drink he'd ever tasted. He held it in his mouth, letting it soak into the dry tissue, before swallowing it down.

"I've drunk my fill," Captain Bailey said. "You can have all of that."

He hadn't considered that they might have to share. She sat down beside him and placed a wooden box filled with slices of raw meat between them. "This is dinner."

He snarled at her, angry that she assumed he ate raw flesh like an animal.

"Sorry, it's Manny's turn to be cook and he hates to do it, so we usually end up with sashimi." She mixed a green paste with black liquid, dipped a piece of meat into it and actually ate it without signs of distaste.

"Sashimi?"

"Sushi has rice and sashimi doesn't. It's a Ya-ya dish. Hopefully you don't mind fish, because that's what we mostly eat, although normally not raw."

With shaking fingers, he picked up a piece of meat and tried it. It was surprisingly good. There were thirty pieces roughly the size of his thumb. His share, then, would be fifteen. He wolfed his half of the fish.

"You want more?" Captain Bailey licked her fingers clean after she finished her half. Did she know how erotic it was?

He felt a flash of embarrassment that he had snarled at her. "No." And because that too felt rude, he added, "Thank you."

"Good, I'm beat." She stretched out in the shade. "We took some damage in our crew quarters and we're short on bunks at the moment. We're short on everything. We can rig you a hammock someplace later, when the weather changes."

It wasn't until she closed her eyes that he realized that she meant to sleep beside him.

"You don't have a bunk?"

"We're hot bunking at the moment." She meant that the crew shared one set of bunks. "I worked through my sleep cycle."

Which meant someone was in her shared bed.

He sat in the pool of shade, watching as her breath deepened into sleep. Exhaustion dulled his thoughts and his emotions swam like fish through the murk of his fatigue. He was too tired to even identify them. Was he feeling dismay? Sorrow? Fear?

Why was Captain Bailey lying here beside him like he was her pet cat? Did she think he was harmless? Or was this a subtle invitation? If that was the case, it was too subtle for him. He looked out into the endless blue. It would be comforting to think that he wasn't completely alone in this alien world—but that would be a dangerous trap to fall into.

Paige woke when the *Rosetta*'s engine coughed and sputtered three decks below where she had slept. She lay still. Listening. Praying.

Please let it work. Please.

The engine coughed and sputtered again before settling into an uneven growl.

I'll take that.

It was only then that she realized Turk slept beside her. His chin nearly touching her shoulder. His breath warmed the bare skin of her neck. He had his arm thrown across her hips to snug her close to him. Their legs entwined. He breathed deep, fast asleep.

Not surprising considering his ordeal. He was still furred over from stress, making him velvety soft over rock hard muscles.

She sighed. It had been entirely too long since she woke up with a handsome man beside her. And Turk was dangerously good looking. When he wasn't glaring at her—which was most of the time—he had a warm, open expression with meltingly beautiful eyes. His hands were large and strong, and all his below deck equipment matched in size.

It was very tempting to cuddle up to him and let nature take its course. But she had to think of the long journey. She hadn't been able to walk away from him when he was a stranger. If she gave him her body, she'd end up giving him her heart. And after that, every decision would be that much harder to make.

She slipped out from under his arm, putting distance between her and temptation.

The ship cats, Amber and Miles, were curled up against Turk's back. They gave her evil looks as she shooed them away. Crèche training made the Red fairly safe to humans, but God knows what he'd make of cats. And Rannatan.

What the hell had she been thinking? Certainly nothing beyond getting off the civ raft alive. She thanked the gods that Turk was still asleep, giving her time to consider what to do with him next.

While in theory the *Rosetta* ran as a dictatorship with Paige as tyrant, in reality it operated much more like what it was: a family wrapped in pretensions of obedience. Orin ambushed her before she even got to the clothesline.

"Are you nuts?" he whispered. All their arguments were quiet ones so they could maintain the illusion of a united front against their younger family members. "A crèche-raised Red?"

She didn't need Orin echoing her own thoughts. "I established my dominance yesterday. I let him know he's off the boat if he doesn't obey everyone. And I *will* put him off."

"With Hillary and Becky knowing damn well that being castaway is a long, slow death?"

"Yes! If I have to." Her clothes were still damp but she jerked them off the line anyhow. She ducked behind one of the sheets drying on the next line to change. "We have to give him a chance. It's the only decent thing to do. He seems intelligent, sensible . . ."

. . . sexier than hell.

Orin heard the unvoiced part. "If you screw around with him, you're going to lose dominance."

"Do you have anything to say that I don't know already?" She stripped off the fabric she'd used as an impromptu dress.

"You're so confident in yourself that you don't think you're wrong."

Paige took a deep breath and kept in all the truthful but hurtful things she could say. Luckily he was on the other side of the sheet so he couldn't see them on her face. Telling Orin that he was reacting to a strange male in his territory wouldn't do anything but make Orin angry at her. If he was willing to be truthful with himself, he'd figure it out on his own, otherwise textbook references and photographic evidence wouldn't be enough to convince him. She pulled on her underwear and shorts, aware of the angry silence between them, but too annoyed to fill it with anything safe. She needed to say something, though, or the silence would turn cancerous.

She pulled the sheet down to shoulder height so she could meet his eyes. "No, Orin, I'm very aware that I might be doing the wrong thing. But bringing him onboard was the only decent thing to do. And giving him a chance is the only reasonable thing to do. Besides if he's sleeping with me, Charlene and Hillary will keep their hands off him."

He flinched at that truth. "That would have put Mitch's nose out of joint." Meaning Charlene sleeping with Turk.

"Yeah, Charlene being Charlene, she might have jerked both their chains just for the hell of it." Paige let go of the line and it snapped back up, giving her privacy to pull on her top.

Orin grunted agreement.

Dressed, Paige ducked under the line to his side of the sheet. "It sounds like Rannatan got the engine working. I'm going down to check on him. Plot me a course to Ya-ya, and I'll be back up to take over in a few minutes."

He nodded unhappily. It meant postponing their trip to Fenrir's Rock to make sure their family on the *Lilianna* were safe, but they'd come close to total disaster with their engine failing during an eclipse. And truth be told, they weren't out of dangerous waters yet.

She found her mechanic not in the engine room but in the galley, getting food. Manny had made minotaur gruel for breakfast.

Rannatan was eating it in his typical fashion, by eschewing a spoon and sticking his entire muzzle into the bowl.

"Rannatan, is the engine good?" Paige asked.

Rannatan looked up, licked his muzzle, and blew a wet raspberry. "Engine piece of shit."

"It's running though," Paige said.

"For now," Rannatan said.

"Will it get us to Ya-ya?" Paige asked.

A chorus of dismayed cries went up from her family.

"We'll be lucky to get to Ya-ya," Paige pointed out.

"But the *Lilianna*!" Hillary cried and was echoed.

"Might have left before anything happened," Paige said. "Might be at Ya-ya. Might be dead and gone."

Her family went abruptly silent. For a moment Paige felt bad for being so harsh. Then realized that they weren't looking at her, but over her shoulder.

Turk was in the door. He was naked except for a hand towel, hanging on his lean hips like a loincloth. He'd relaxed enough that he'd shed his defensive fur, revealing a body of chiseled muscle. All that was left was a thatch of black hair, his thick eyebrows and long eyelashes, and an arrow of chest hair pointing down to the small flap of clothing covering his privates.

Ooohh hoochee mama!

He really needed something to wear. What was left of his tattered uniform had been too impregnated with mold to salvage. Nor did they have any spare clothes that would fit him—he was broader in the shoulder than Orin, Manny, or Avery.

"Everyone, this is Turk." She broke the silence. "He's part of our crew now."

They nodded. It wasn't like there was another choice. If Turk was on the boat, he was either crew, passenger, or cargo. No one in her family would sell a Red, so he wasn't cargo, and no one expected him to pay.

Turk was staring at the obnaoian with unnerving attention.

"This is Rannatan," Paige said.

"*What* is Rannatan?" Turk asked.

"He's my mechanic."

Turk tore his gaze from the obnaoian to give her a dark look.

"He's an obnaoian, which is another intelligent race. And I need him to keep my engine working. I don't need you for anything.

You so much as breathe hard on him and I'll put you off this boat."

Turk gave a slow solemn nod. "His people control this place?"

Paige laughed. "No."

Rannatan had been staring at Turk with equal fascination. "You're a male, right?"

"Yes," Turk snapped, and then frowned. "Are you male or female?"

Rannatan whistled and chirped a moment in annoyance. "I'm male."

"Manny, he'll be working with you today." Paige assigned Turk to Manny because her cousin was the oldest male onboard after Orin and secure in his position. Also the work would be fairly simple. Washing pots and pans. "And since you have help, something more than sashimi today, please."

Manny held up his hands, warning off her annoyance. "No sashimi! I promise."

Paige noticed that Charlene had been staring at Turk. Luckily Mitch was a little slow on the uptake and hadn't noticed yet. Paige smacked her younger sister in the back of the head. They really needed to find Turk something to wear.

Working in the kitchen was a learning experience for Turk. Food was something that arrived cooked on a plate, and dishes were something that were either recycled or taken away by servants. The *Rosetta*'s crew ate off steep-sided, metal plates that could also be considered shallow bowls. The morning breakfast of cooked grain had the consistency of glue. The plates had to be submersed in hot, soapy water and scoured clean. Manny worked on the other side of the tiny galley kitchen, doing mysterious things with plants in preparation to make them into food. Like most of the crew, Manny was blonde haired, blue eyed, and lean. He talked to Turk in a friendly open tone about how to cook. Turk found it oddly comforting.

"These are potatoes." Manny held up a lumpy brown oval that didn't look anything like the potatoes Turk had eaten in the past. "We keep them in the back of the pantry, out of the light. Got to keep an eye on them though. They'll grow appendages and walk out of the galley if you don't watch them closely."

"Appendages?"

Manny laughed. "I'm kidding. You cut off these dark spots and throw them into the compost bucket. We compost everything we don't eat and keep a small container garden going. That's where I got these." He held up red tomatoes. "Which don't store, so we got to use them as soon as they ripen. They're important because they ward off scurvy."

"They're high in vitamin C?"

Manny looked up from his cutting board. "Wow, I'm impressed. Exactly right. What's handy to eat is fish, fish, and more fish. But humans can't stay healthy with just that, so we have to add fruits and vegetables to the mix. We're making a fish stew for lunch."

If Manny was willing to talk, Turk might as well learn more than how to cook. "You are Captain Bailey's . . . brother?"

"Nah, we're cousins. So is Avery. That means our fathers were brothers. We're a big family. Grandpa Bailey raised twenty boys."

"Twenty?"

Manny laughed at his reaction. "Twenty. Our dads are the youngest three; most of our other cousins are older. We all grew up playing with each other like packs of puppies. In some ways, we're close as brothers and sisters. It was a good way to grow up."

It would explain why they all had the same blonde hair and blue eyes, with the one exception of the gunner. "Jones is . . . ?"

"Kenya's a newcomer and Becky's adopted; her brother married one of our cousins. Her folks were killed in a storm. The adults went down with the ship; only the kids made it off alive. Everyone that had space took in a kid. We got Becky."

Now they had Turk. Only Becky was human and Turk was not; although Manny did seem completely at ease with him. Most likely the man had never seen a Red fight. Turk would have to be careful not to use his full speed and strength in front of the Baileys. And the more he knew about them, the better he could spot trouble coming.

"If you're all family, why is Captain Bailey in command?" Turk asked. "Because she's the oldest?"

"No, the *Rosetta* is her boat because she's the one that went to Ya-ya, worked her butt off, and earned the money to buy it. She's a very, very good translator. She could have stayed in Ya-ya and gotten very rich; but that did nothing for the rest of us, so she bought the *Rosetta* and fetched us as crew."

Manny examined Turk's efforts with the dishes and nodded.

"Good work. Here, run a little water into this pan and use it to scrub these potatoes." He held up another plant and identified it as garlic. "This has very strong flavor; you only need a small amount to make the food taste good. This recipe calls for four cloves."

"You're expecting me to cook this by myself sometime?"

"That's the plan. The more people that cook, the fewer times I'm stuck with it."

"Ah, Captain Bailey said you hated to cook."

"I don't hate it. I just don't like cooking the same things over and over again, but it's not like we have much of an option. There's only so many ways you can put fish and potatoes together."

Manny held up an impressively large knife. "Here's the trick of getting the skin off garlic. You simply lay the knife flat against the clove and press. Voila!" The cloves burst open, giving off a pungent smell. "Paige's a good captain. She knows the risks and the odds of success, and she does what is best in the long run. I suppose we do kind of stick to our ages as to who gets to tell who what."

"What about Jones?" The other outsider.

"She kind of does her own thing. When we're in shallow water, like now, she keeps an eye out for anything trying to crawl onboard. There's things that see boats as serving platters. She's pulling long hours. Once we get into deeper water, she'll probably sleep for a couple of days."

"You're spread too thin. You should have several watches, short enough that your personnel stay sharp."

Manny nodded. "We were going to take on more crew at Fenrir's Rock. A few more cousins."

"Why the change in plans?"

"Onions." Manny's expression was bleak as he held up a fist-sized sphere. "Recipe calls for four, thinly sliced." He chopped the onion in half. "Our engine has been dying for some time now. We don't have the money to replace it. My cousin Ethan—Paige's older brother—he radioed us when we were in Georgetown. He had found an unclaimed wreck, something that's never been salvaged because it's in minotaur waters. We were going to meet Ethan and some of our cousins who have a boat called the *Lilianna* at Fenrir's Rock, and go together to stake claim on the salvage. The plan was that the *Rosetta* would have stayed in minotaur waters, protecting our claim, while the *Lilianna* took what we salvaged to

Ya-ya. Even splitting the take with the *Lilianna*, we would have made a fortune."

Fenrir's Rock. As the rock belonging to the spaceship *Fenrir*? "And we're not going to Fenrir's Rock because . . . ?"

"It's not there anymore. Something blew it out of the water."

Like the engine returning to Plymouth Station. "Oh." And seeing Manny's sober look he guessed the rest. "Your cousins were there."

Manny nodded grimly. "Onions always make you cry." He swiped the back of his arm across his eyes. "The thing is the engine is crapping out. If we don't make Ya-ya, we'll be dead in the water again."

Manny demonstrated "sautéing" the onions and garlic in a pot he called a "Dutch oven." "After this we add in the tomatoes, potatoes, cloves, bay leaves, parsley, tarragon, marjoram, pepper, and water."

"It's fish stew without fish?"

"We'll add the fish about ten minutes before we serve it," Manny said. "So you have three hours to catch our lunch."

"Me?"

"Yup. Go find Paige and tell her you need to catch a couple of whiteys."

They were moving, that much was good. Paige didn't like the sound that the engine was making. It had run rough before, but now it had a rattle as if it was slowly shaking itself apart. They had no choice but to get to a port, even if it meant destroying the engine. Orin had plotted them a course; it was dangerously long.

She had the charts spread out in front of the boat's wheel, studying her options, when the door creaked open and Turk stepped into the room. Manny hadn't found him anything to wear yet. He was still naked except for the loincloth.

"Only Orin and I are allowed on the bridge," she told him.

"We need fish for the stew." Turk eyed the charts with interest. "Where exactly are we?"

"Here." She tapped the chart at their location.

He gave her a long, silent dark look. She wondered if he was top cat of his ship's pride. He had that legendary "control with a look." She wondered too if he realized what he was doing. "I mean the world. What is it? Did someone make it?"

As if she knew the answer to that. She supposed he needed

some information, though, if he was going to be useful. "No one seems sure of where we are or what this place is. Everyone has a different name and a different idea. So far as I can tell, none are better than others. The obnaoian believe we've been shrunk down to the size of atoms and we're inside an air bubble floating through a sea."

He shook his head. "I don't think they're right."

"Hmm, I'm not fond of the theory myself—air bubbles have a way of popping."

"What do you believe it is?"

"Personally I like the pocket universe theory."

"Which is . . ."

The joy of boiling physics down for someone who had only been taught to point a gun and shoot. She made sure that the water in front of them was clear, and secured the wheel so she had both hands free. "Say your ship is here." She marked a point on a scrap piece of paper. "And your captain wanted to go here." She marked a second point. "These points are hundreds of light-years apart and to go straight from one to the other would take a lifetime. What a warp drive does is this." She folded the paper so the dots connected. Then taking a pencil, she pushed it through the paper. "The warp field creates a hole that the ship goes through, instantly going from point A to point B."

"Yes." He nodded.

"The ships here, their warp engines created a warp field, punching a hole going from point A to . . . who knows. The thing is, they fell into the hole, they left point A, but they didn't get to their intended point B." She took the pencil out, and holding the paper, shook it. "If you fall off the paper—miss your universe completely—where do you go?"

"Here?"

"So it seems." She took control of the boat again. "This isn't a planet. This place—it's like an egg—and we're standing on the inside of the shell."

Belatedly she wondered if he'd ever seen a real egg. But he nodded. Did he really understand? She thought for a minute how to distill what she learned at Ya-ya down to something a crèche-raised Red could grasp. "If someone in your universe wanted to make a place like this, they would start by smashing a planet flat to build the shell. One planet would only make a little, tiny section of this place. All the planets of one solar system wouldn't be enough. If you took . . . countless . . . solar systems, you start to get enough matter."

"It's that large?"

"It's huge. The minotaur have mines that extend hundreds of feet deep. The oceans are miles deep. I can't believe any intelligent race made this place. Only God makes things like this."

"Not even intelligent races that might seem godlike?"

"I've met those and they don't lay claim to it. Besides, if someone could make it, don't you think they'd also lock the door so every monkey with two thumbs didn't wander in?"

"Maybe they like monkeys."

She was startled into laughing. The faintest of smiles flashed across his face and was gone back to the dark watchful gaze.

"So we're here?" He reached out to tap the correct position on the chart.

"Yeah. 23.29 by −12.93."

"What do those numbers mean?"

"Ya-ya is the oldest of the human landings. Oldest surviving. They chose to represent themselves as zero-zero on an x-y grid. The numbers are miles from Ya-ya on that grid. The first number is longitude. Do you know what longitude is?"

"I know."

She was pleasantly surprised. "It means we're 2,329 miles in the direction of the Spin. If we were Counterspin from Ya-ya, that number would be negative."

"Spin?"

"Newcomers talk about how most planets have a north-south pole which you can set compasses to. We don't have that in the Sargasso. Apparently you need a solid core of heavy metal spinning to create a magnetic field. What we have is the direction of the Spin. The water, the wind, and the vimanas all flow in the direction of the Spin, due to what we think is centrifugal force."

She tapped the axis marker on the map. "CS on the left for Counterspin is denoted as negative numbers, S on the right is Spin. Tells you which way is up on the map. The second number is up and down the y axis."

"Why not use latitude and longitude from the equator like you would on a planet?"

"Because people haven't agreed on where the equator is. Every ship coming in has a different universal reference that doesn't match anyone else's. Landings have fought over everything from map coordinates to time of day to what year it should be. Ya-ya's system has become the agreed standard just out of default since they're the oldest and probably the most successful of the landings."

"Where's Fenrir's Rock?"

"Let's look at a different chart." She swapped to one of larger scale. "Here's Ya-ya, smack dab in the middle. We're 23.29 by −12.93. It puts us here. These islands you can see around us, they're all part of Fenrir's Archipelago. That means an area of sea with many islands. This is Fenrir's Rock over here."

"It seems close."

"It is. But there's nothing there now. Even if we limp our way there, we won't be able to repair our engine. Also these waterways are very treacherous with sandbars and reefs. We can't just sail straight to Fenrir's Rock, we'd have to wind through a maze to find safe passageways."

"Manny said you're from Georgetown." Turk was scanning the map.

"Up here, nearly off the map. It's a long haul."

"What about this one? Mary's Landing." He tapped the Mary's flats.

"No, no, we won't go there."

"It's closer than Ya-ya."

"Mary's a dangerous place for us. We won't go there."

"Why?"

She didn't tell him the real reasons, so she stuck to ones he'd at least understand. "It's a political thing. Nothing like open warfare, but we're not friendly. One doesn't show weakness to the enemy."

He nodded.

She considered her options on who should teach him how to fish. She wasn't fond of fishing; on a bad day, it could be mind-numbingly boring. Orin and Avery were sleeping. Becky was too little to hold her own even though she knew all there was to know about fishing. Mitch? No! Orin was having issues with Mitch because Mitch somehow always managed to create issues. And if Paige loved her sanity, she'd better keep Charlene as far from Turk as possible. That left Hillary. A teenage girl looking to expand her sexual possibilities. A nearly naked, half-feral man.

Paige sighed. "Someone should just shoot me and get it over with."

"Pardon?"

"Charlene!" Paige shouted. A moment later her sister appeared. "Take the wheel. Follow the course that Orin's plotted out. I'm going to be teaching Turk how to fish."

Turk hated fishing. It was boring. It involved taking rotting animal flesh, impaling it onto a sharp hook of metal attached to a line, and throwing it overboard. And then waiting. And waiting. With washing dishes, and cooking, at least there was something to occupy his mind. They'd reached open water and the islands were dwindling to nothing in the distance. Without anything but water to look at, nothing to do but sit, he found himself at the unfamiliar edge of dark emotions. His instincts were screaming for him to run from those feelings, fill up his world with something else until they were drowned out. He was anchored, though, to one spot of the boat's deck, fishing pole in hand.

"How long do we have to do this?" he asked Paige, who sat beside him under an awning fixed over the stern of the boat. He had expected her to leave, but apparently there would be some difficult parts once the fish actually took the bait.

"Until we catch something or go hungry," Paige said. "Getting tired?"

He was, but he didn't want to admit it. It was like she said: you didn't show your weakness to your enemies. Until he was sure that the crew had nothing more than slave labor in mind for him, he had to remember that. "Why don't you catch the fish ahead of time?"

"Usually we do, but the freezer unit was one of the things hit by lightning a few days back. Fresh fish becomes inedible a few hours after it dies."

"Can't you keep them alive?"

"Normally we do, but the holding tank was hit by the drop nut. We've either had very bad luck or very good luck, depending on how you want to look at it."

"How could either of those be good luck?"

"No one was killed by the lightning, and we only lost the freezer, the ship's intercom and the radio. And the drop nut didn't sink us."

He supposed that looked at that way, they had had good luck. He supposed that he was fortunate to survive his fall and be rescued by Paige. But he'd lost his whole universe. Mikhail. The *Svoboda*. His Reds. The life he and Mikhail would have built if the nefrim didn't wipe everything out. Was his life worthwhile if it was reduced to being trapped on a boat as a slave and forced to fish?

They fell silent. Turk fought to keep his eyes open and stay awake, and yet not dwell on the things he'd lost.

"Can I ask you something?" Paige broke the silence.

"What?"

"What kind of name is Turkish Delight?" When he didn't answer, Paige guessed. "Does it have something to do with sex?"

"No!" He supposed it wouldn't hurt to tell her some things about himself. "I wasn't raised in a crèche. I was picked off a standard production line by a powerful man to be . . ." Be what? He was never sure why Ivan bought him. "Be raised with his son. He left it to my foster brother to name me. Nyanya had been reading Misha a fairy tale about a boy who was kidnapped by an evil witch. She lured him away from all that was good with his favorite candy—Turkish Delight."

"Because you were what Misha wanted most?"

"Actually, he wanted a puppy." Mikhail stated that whenever they fought as young children. He stopped saying it when Ivan offered to sell Turk and get a puppy.

"How old were you when they pulled you out of the crèche? A month old? A year?"

"Why?"

"I was just wondering how much of the viral behavior you picked up."

"Viral behavior?"

"When the crèches first developed adapted humans, they were looking at them as colonists for planets with extreme habitats. The idea was that once Reds landed on a planet, they would have to adapt not only physically but behaviorally to survive. So the first Reds were exposed to a range of animal behaviors on top of typical human behavior, so they would have a large pool of successful cultures to model on."

Turk was familiar with all crèche behavior programs. "There's nothing like that in the military production lines."

"Yes, but the experimental colonial Reds were still maturing in the crèches when they switched over. They had interactions with the military Reds. The animal behavior became viral in nature, passed on to all the following generations."

"It's a disease? Like a retrovirus?"

"No, no." She sighed out and thought for minute. "Let's play a word game. I'll start it." She looked around them, and then nudged the bait can with her foot. "Look at all that tasty bait. I one it." Paige glanced up at him. "Now you say, 'I two it.'"

Had she gone mad? "I two it?"

She nodded and pointed to herself. "I three it." She pointed to him and mouthed the word "four."

He guessed at what she wanted him to say. "I four it."

Paige pointed at herself again. "I five it." And then pointed at him to take his turn. Behind them, Hilliary came out with a basket and started to take down the sheets hanging on the clothesline.

"I don't see the point of this," Turk said.

"Just say it. 'I six it.'"

He frowned at her.

"I six it!" Hillary called from the clotheslines.

"I seven it," Paige said.

Both females gazed at him expectantly.

"I . . . eight it?" Turk said.

"You ate it? Oh gross!" Hillary laughed.

It took him a moment to understand the play on words. Paige laughed at his face.

"That game would not work in Russian," he said.

"No, I don't think it would," Paige said. "The point is that no adult ever taught me that. My older brother taught it to me. Our older cousins had taught it to him. And I didn't teach Hillary. I taught it to Orin, who taught it to Charlene, who taught Hillary."

He understood what she was trying to explain. "So the game passes like a virus."

"Yes. Just like with my family and this game, you've been infected with the inexplicable cat behavior of a crèche-raised Red. It's something you learned. It's a part of you that you can get rid of; all you have to do is decide to ignore it."

The *Rosetta* tilted suddenly, leaning hard to the port. There was the flash and whine of a laser cannon. Something large bellowed in pain.

Paige went tense beside him but didn't move to investigate. "Jones?"

"I'm getting it!" Jones called back. There was a flash of a second and third shot. There was a loud splash and the boat righted. "Got it! Sorry. Thought we were clear of the shallows."

Turk was much more awake than he'd been a few moments earlier. Also much more aware that they were just eleven souls on a small boat, out in the middle of endless water, with a failing engine and the nearest friendly port over three thousand kilometers away.

Something that looked like a cross between a killer whale and octopus floated past, its massive jaws still working even though it was clearly dead.

"Could we eat that?" he asked.

"Nah, it's poisonous. It was someone's bio-weapon that got loose. Roams free now."

"Oh." And then to show he was listening: "I one it."

8 On Razor's Edge

REPAIRING HIS SHIP BECAME A RAZOR'S EDGE THAT MIKHAIL had to walk. The damage was emotionally overwhelming; yet he had to deal with it all, every little detail. He couldn't afford to spare himself the ordeal. Their time was limited; if a new disaster caught them unprepared, it was unlikely they'd survive. He forced himself to dispassionately check each system, assign repair priorities, and then, to keep himself sane, firmly put it out of his mind.

The lower decks were the worst. The omnipresent damp scent of the ocean and muted rumble of the surf were constant reminders that Alpha Red where Turk died was still filled with water. That water waited for the smallest of cracks to flood the rest of his ship. He found it increasingly claustrophobic, and finally had to escape to the outer hull.

Outside, with his back to the ruined bridge, he let the beauty of the world distract him. Mikhail's father liked to remind him of Peter the Great's fascination with the navy, but it never occurred to Mikhail that it would mean a genetic love of open water. It seemed ironic that this death trap was so beautiful.

From his vantage point on the top ridge of the hull, he could see for countless kilometers in all directions. Their sandbar island might be an oblong swath of dazzling sand, but the coral base from which it grew was a rough mushroom-shape, full of crevasses and fissures. The water over the coral was cyan, and beyond its edge, the color deepened with the water to a sapphire. In all directions, he could see that other coral bases were growing toward the surface. A few had broken through to sandbars. None would provide safe shelter during a storm.

And a storm was brewing, off to his right, forming a gray menacing wall. Just looking at it made him uneasy. Judging by the direction of the wind and tide, the storm would move toward them. They had days, maybe even a week—distance being impossible to judge—but they were firmly stuck in its path.

Another thing he had to put out of his mind for sanity's sake.

He'd lost most of his radar crew members along with the bridge. It took him a moment to recall who fell next in the chain of command. "Moldavsky," he spoke into his com. A moment later he got a reply.

"Ensign Moldavsky here."

"Bring whatever mobile observation equipment you can lay your hands on and meet me on top of the warp engine housing."

There was a pause as Moldavsky was probably confounded by Mikhail's orders, and then, "Yes, sir."

Bracing himself against the stiff wind, Mikhail walked along the flange. He checked the condition of his ship while keeping an eye on the storm front. The rivets dotting the flange in a neat orderly row looked sound. They would have to check, though, for stress cracks at the molecular level. There had been no reentry burn, at least, with no heat discoloration anywhere, not even the safety signage, which routinely needed to be replaced.

Normally the ladder on the warp drive housing was stowed to reduce wind drag on reentry. The release on the access panel worked, but the manual hand crank refused to budge. He struggled with it for a minute and then turned to the Red that had been trailing behind him. It was the littlest of the Reds, and one of Turk's favorites, Rabbit. Despite his relatively small size, Mikhail knew the tom was much stronger than himself.

"Give this a try, Rabbit."

Rabbit looked startled at being addressed directly but saluted. "Yes, sir!"

The tom shouldered his weapon and bent to the task. The wind tugged at their clothing, trying to pull them from their narrow perch on the ridge. Here the hull slimmed and they were one misstep from a steep fall. Mikhail glanced down at the boil of white water where the surf roiled against the edge of the ship.

One step, and he would be free of all the pain riding in his chest in a cold, hard lump.

He felt a moment of déjà vu, the ship's ridge taking him back to the last time he stood on a cliff edge with unbearable pain urging him to step off. There was a flicker, like something had passed overhead. Something large loomed over him, close at hand.

He started to look upward . . . and fell into a memory . . .

Mikhail gazed over the edge of the cliff. True it was a sheer drop, but trees and tall grasses softened the foot of the cliff. Water would have been best, so he'd drown if the fall didn't kill him. He didn't want to just cripple himself. He moved down the edge of the cliff, considering ground far below. Too soft. Too soft . . .

Mikhail struggled to push the memory aside; to dwell on that moment seemed dangerous. It was the last time his life had fallen to pieces. He'd been crushed when he failed his final psych test at the U.C. Naval Academy. The military had become a refuge, a place to be wholly himself and no one else. Ironically, being seen for his own strengths and weaknesses had caused his downfall; his fragile mental state was something that the review boards wouldn't overlook, not even for Viktor the Great's clone. That day his life seemed over . . .

He found a section with rocks. He stood a moment, wondering if he should actually bother to hike the miles to where the cliff would overlook the river. This seemed sure enough. If he wasn't killed instantly, he should be hurt enough to die before anyone would find him; a little messy and painful but totally fatal.

It was like being trapped in a nightmare. The recall drowned him in details: the green smell of the freshly cut grain fields behind him, the distant growl of the threshing machines, and the gray of the rocks below. But he wasn't asleep—and that terrified him. His fear couldn't stop the memory from replaying . . .

This should do it, his younger self thought while his older self prayed that he was standing still, not moving, on his dangerous perch.

His younger self stepped out into the void—and was jerked backward, slammed to the ground, and pinned against the sharp stubble of cut grain by Turk.

"Why?" Turk snarled into his face. "Why?"

"*I just want the hurting to stop.*" Mikhail tried pushing Turk off him. His little brother was intractable as Mikhail's future. Muscles like iron bands shifted under black fur and Mikhail couldn't even struggle.

"*So what if they won't give you a posting?*" Turk growled. "*You graduated. That was the plan. Four years at the Academy and you redeem us. You can do anything you want now!*"

"*I wanted a posting! I wanted to be something other than a pale imitation of a man that vanished forty years ago. I don't want to be a puppet to father's ambitions.*"

"*You're not Viktor, and you know you aren't. And you're not a puppet. A puppet wouldn't be as stupid as this! You're Mikhail.*"

Mikhail was tired of fighting reality. "*I can't be anything but Viktor. I'll make all his mistakes including making another clone to wallow in the same pain.*"

"*What's so bad about being Viktor?*" Turk shouted. "*He was a powerful man that everyone respected and loved and obeyed. What is so bad about that?*"

Mikhail struggled to explain it to Turk but gave up. It was like trying to describe the difference between air and carbon dioxide to a rock. Turk couldn't understand why he was suffocating. "*I just want the pain to stop.*"

"*Shut up!*" Turk lifted him up slightly only to slam him back down. "*Shut up!*"

Turk's outburst destroyed the last of Mikhail's control and despair overtook him in a blinding flood of tears. He lost sense of everything but the burn of salt in his eyes and the massive growing ache that was trying to burst out of his chest and throat. Slowly, though, he became aware that Turk still had him pinned and had his face pressed hard against Mikhail's shoulder. Tremors shook Turk. It took several minutes before Mikhail realized that Turk was crying. Turk never cried.

While Mikhail couldn't find strength to comfort himself, it came easily to comfort Turk.

"*Hey. Hey.*" Mikhail rubbed Turk on the back like he would when they were little. "*It's okay. I signed all the papers to free you and I set up a bank account for you. Father can't contest any of it. It's a lot of money. You'll be able to—*"

"*Stop it!*" Turk cried into his shoulder. "*I don't want to you to die! You're the only one that ever gave a damn about me. What am I supposed to do if you leave me alone?*"

"*Anything you want! You wouldn't have to be Volkov's pet Red anymore. You hate being my Red.*"

"*You idiot!*" Without lifting his head, Turk raised his fist and punched Mihkail in the chest. "*I don't hate it. We're a team. The two of us against the universe, and the universe will lose.*"

Mikhail shook his head against the false bravado. "*You have to hate it. No one looks at you and sees you. They see every crèche-raised Red that they've met before. Sooner or later, you're going to hate me for keeping you locked in place. If I wasn't here, you could be anything . . .*"

"*Shut up! Why do you have to think so much? Nothing stands if you poke at it and poke at it and poke at it. Sometimes you just got to trust something and leave it alone.*"

"Captain!" someone cried close at hand, and finally the memory released him. He was lying on the high ridge of the ship. Rabbit had him pinned in place to keep him from falling; the same inescapable but nonbruising hold as Turk had had him on the cliff side.

Oh God, Turk! Mikhail's grief welled up as he realized that Turk would never be at his side again, calling him idiot and making him face the world head on.

But then Rabbit growled. Even in the little Red, the sound was a deep menacing rumble not to be ignored. Mikhail pushed away his grief and focused on Rabbit. The tom's hackles were up and lips drawn back into a snarl, but Rabbit wasn't looking at Mikhail, but slightly above and behind him.

"What is it?" Mikhail followed his gaze but saw nothing but the waver of heat.

"Something moved," the Red growled, scanning the area while still covering Mikhail with his own body. "But I didn't see . . . anything."

Mikhail remembered the sense of something looming over him earlier, just before he slipped into the memory and how it seemed like he was held under, forced against his will to relive that moment. *I'm not crazy; Rabbit sensed something too.*

Sensed what though? There seemed to be nothing around them now but sea and sky. Mikhail had only had a fleeting impression of something large and the shift of shadows and light. Rabbit should have heard/saw/reacted before him; Reds' senses were more finely honed. And how could anything trigger a five-year-old memory to play out in such detail? He suspected, if he'd tried earlier to recall that day, he wouldn't have remembered the fresh-cut grain fields. The harvesting had been so inconsequential to his painful loss.

And when he'd relived the night that Nyanya Nastya left, he'd remembered everything. If he tried now to think back to when he was six, he could only dredge up wisps. They'd colored the nursery shortly afterward; he knew even then it was to discourage him from clinging to her memory. The walls had been faint cream yellow the night Nyanya Nastya left. He wasn't sure what they became—what they stayed up to the day he moved to another part of the palace—what they might still remain.

But it didn't make sense that if something could make him remember an event, why it would ignore all secrets of war and state to pry out some ancient memory of childhood loss.

It would be more reasonable to assume that there was no such thing. He was just going crazy and taking poor Rabbit with him. The Red had such limited experience; could Rabbit have misinterpreted Mikhail's erratic behavior as something attacking?

Turk had told him that nothing stands if you poke at it and poke at it and poke at it. Was he driving himself insane by worrying that every oddity might be proof of his insanity? Mikhail realized that he was still poking and sighed.

"Stand down," he told Rabbit.

The Red looked skeptical. His hackles were still up and his body was tense. "I don't want anything to hurt you."

It surprised Mikhail that the yearling was so protective. "Whatever it was, it's gone. Let me up."

Reluctantly Rabbit moved off him. "Commander Turk would want me to keep you safe." He gave Mikhail an uncertain look and then added, "Captain, Butcher is not to be trusted. He killed Commander Turk."

The accusation hit Mikhail like a hard punch to the stomach. For a moment he could only stare at Rabbit in horror, and then he found his voice. "What?"

"When we were leaving Paradise, Butcher said he would be top cat. We told him that no one could beat Commander Turk. Butcher said that nothing would stop him from being top cat. After we crashed, he said, 'I took care of him.'"

Mikhail had been so busy that it hadn't occurred to him that Turk's death was anything but an accident. What had happened in Alpha Red? As anger set in, he cautioned himself that Butcher might just be claiming responsibility for something he hadn't done to intimidate the rest of the Reds. "I'll look into it."

With childlike concern in his voice, Rabbit said, "You won't tell him that I told you?"

"There's no need for him to know. I can't act on hearsay."

"What's hearsay?"

"It's a legal term to mean I didn't hear Butcher say it myself. To punish Butcher I'll need proof." He needed proof only for himself. The legal system didn't provide that nicety of protection for Reds; any Red *suspected* of a crime could be punished as the commanding officer saw fit. Turk wouldn't have wanted Mikhail executing one of their Reds on the strength of one rumor.

Rabbit nodded, trusting Mikhail. At that moment, the little Red reminded Mikhail of Turk at sixteen. The same intelligent look in their eyes, calm trust in Mikhail, and the willingness to patiently wait for him to act. Maybe they were from the same genetic lot. Somehow it felt oddly reassuring; Turk wasn't completely gone.

A clang of metal on metal reported that Ensign Moldavsky had arrived on the rooftop of the engine housing.

Mikhail patted Rabbit on the shoulder. "I'll take care of it. Just keep your head down and don't draw any fire on yourself."

Rabbit nodded again.

The rooftop was a hot griddle. It reminded Mikhail that sun poisoning was a real danger in this place. He issued orders for shelter to be set up for Ensign Moldavsky as she carefully shifted an equipment case from her shoulder to the rooftop. He also ordered a Red to be sent up to keep watch with the ensign, just in case he wasn't insane and something really was lurking nearby, unseen.

"Gravity is a bitch." Ensign Ilona Moldavsky muttered as she climbed up through the access hatch. The young officer was yet another crew member raised on freight haulers where gravity was optional. Her tall, willowy frame indicated that she experienced gravity in doses only medically required to keep her healthy. Moldavsky stretched, as if trying to escape the unfamiliar forces by sheer willpower. "At least it's not doing any of that weather shit."

"For now." He did not point out the distant gray storm front far across the water.

"So what will I be looking for? Nefrim ships?" Moldavsky opened the case and took out an antique gun sight from her personal collection. Pulled from an orbital gun platform used in the colonial wars, the gun sight had a range that far exceeded any handheld optical device. With the bridge gone and the *Tigertail* still wedged in the hangar, it was their best option for studying distant terrain.

Mikhail nodded. "Nefrim ships. Human ships. Islands. Large menacing animals. Freak weather patterns. Basically anything that might be of interest out there. Even very large waves coming in our direction."

She paused to eye him, squinting against the bright sunlight. "But what do we want to find?"

"Foremost, we need an island with a safe harbor," Mikhail said. "Then our mission is to find the *UCS Fenrir* and ascertain if it's in enemy hands. Do a spiral search outward. Find out what's sitting in our laps before you scan farther out."

Moldavsky nodded as she pulled her makeshift sunglasses into place and settled behind her gun sight. "Will do."

The only good news Mikhail had received since leaving normal space was that his warp engine was intact and theoretically capable of creating a warp field; theoretically because normally one didn't activate a warp field within a gravity well. The few that tried created a mess of themselves and the planet. The size and shape of the warp field generated by a ship's engine was carefully calibrated to the ship's maximum mass while in the vacuum of space. An atmosphere surrounding a spaceship added mass occupying the envelope of the field, and as a result, changed the size and shape of it. In essence, air would shrink the field until it no longer encompassed all of the ship.

The denser the atmosphere, the greater the mass added to the ship. A spaceship without a payload, just skimming the edge of planet's atmosphere where it was thinning to nothing, could risk a jump with little consequences. A spaceship within a mile of the planet's surface would leave sections of the ship—often vital sections along with crew members—behind to rain down onto the planet. In addition, there was a powerful implosion as the warp field punched a hole into the sky.

All in all, activating their drive while in midair would be considered a bad thing, to be done only in emergency and with a great deal of thought, calculation, and prayer. Doing it half buried in several acres of wet sand would be instant death. And Plymouth Station would have another mystery engine on its hands.

We should attach a record of our findings to our drive when we jump, Mikhail thought, *just in case.*

Mikhail wanted to go down into the Red pit, and find out for himself what Butcher had or had not done. The compartment, however, was still flooded and a low priority on the repair list. He resisted the urge to move it up the list. He'd already allocated their resources, a monster part of it dedicated to digging them out of the sand. Unless they made great strides in that project, the investigation of the Red pit would have to wait.

Mikhail went down to the beach to check on his chief of engineering, Yevgeny Tseytlin. They only had one small excavator, secured at the last moment from Paradise. He knew it had been running for hours, but there was little evidence of progress.

"This—this—this—" And not able to express more, Tseytlin turned and stomped a wide circle around Mihkail before returning. "We get a hole dug. The water goes up, and when it goes away, the hole is gone. Back to where we were. We're not digging fast enough."

Lieutenant Alexander Ufimtsev jogged up. "We're ready."

Tseytlin nodded and shouted. "Clear the beach! Clear the beach!"

"Ready with what?" Mikhail asked as they herded him toward the ramp.

"We're going to see if we can use a concussion grenade to move the sand," Tseytlin explained.

"A grenade next to the ship?" Mikhail asked.

"Armor plating should protect the ship," Tseytlin assured him. "But we're doing a test first, just to see the volume of sand moved. See if it's worth the risk."

"The grenade is buried in the sand over there." Ufimtsev pointed out a mound of sand that his footprints led to and back from. "It's wired with a remote trigger."

Said remote was handed to Tseytlin, who shouted, "Firing test shot!" and pressed the trigger.

The spot erupted upward in a column of sand which pelted down like heavy rain. A surprisingly small crater was created. Tseytlin swore and flung the remote toward the hole. Ufimtsev trotted toward the hole, saying, "I did just drop the grenade in and bury it. Maybe if I angle it."

"I can blast through duralloy bulkhead without breaching the hull. I can rig a load that will take out a nefrim torpedo ship. But I can't deal with sand. It's like blowing holes in water."

"What if we used one of the torpedoes?" Ufimstsev said.

"No!" Mikhail and Tseytlin said together.

Mikhail considered his ship. "Do the VTOL engines work?"

"We won't know until we dig them out."

"Can we dig out the intakes and fire up the VTOL engines and use them to fly the ship out of the sand?"

Tseytlin winced but slowly nodded. "We'd run a big risk that we'll just burn them out or rip the wings off the *Svoboda*. I would only recommend it as an emergency maneuver."

The entire mission was now an emergency maneuver. They still had the ability to signal for help using their shuttle, the *Tigertail*. He wanted to hold off on that until they knew more about where they were. Also he suspected that if signals could leave this abnormality, the crew of the *Fenrir* would have sent a message instead of their engine. The *Svoboda* had a full complement of lifepods, but they had no jump capability. The *Tigertail* had a small warp engine, but by the nature of the shuttle's design, it would be deadly to try. Sections of the *Svoboda* would remain airtight even if a misshaped warp field sheared off other parts of the ship; the *Tigertail* had only two areas: the cockpit and the Red pit. Both would be compromised, killing everyone within them instantly.

Still, they could use the *Tigertail* to scout nearby islands and possibly pull the *Svoboda* off the sandbar.

"What condition is the *Tigertail* in?" Mikhail asked.

"It only suffered damage to its restraining clamps. I can't get them to release. We could just break them, but I'd rather not. The way we're going through repair supplies, I'm not sure we'll have what we need to rebuild the clamps."

It was heartening that Tseytlin assumed that they were taking off again, requiring the *Tigertail* to be secured. There was the small matter, though, of how they were going to get to that point. Obviously Tseytlin was overwhelmed by their situation; he was applying brute force without thinking.

"Tseytlin, I want Ufimtsev to take over supervising here. Go back to engineering and run modeling programs. I want us making the best use of our resources."

His chief engineer looked slightly insulted, but he'd get over it.

"Also tap the Reds," Mikhail said. "It should be fairly simple to fabricate hand shovels for them. All the off-duty Reds digging should be able to make a fairly big hole."

9 Graveyard of Ships

SHELTER HAD BEEN RIGGED FOR ENSIGN MOLDAVSKY; CARGO tarps rustled overhead, casting a square of shadow on her. The equipment around Moldavsky had grown. The Red was also in place, one of the replacements. Mikhail was going to have to get to know all their names. Over the pounding of the surf, he could hear Inozemtsev struggling with his role as the new Red commander, shouting instructions to the off-duty Reds on how to use the newly forged hand shovels.

"I was only up here for a little while when I realized how difficult it was going to be to find anything," Moldavsky said. "It's like finding an enemy ship against a star field. Eyeballing it was going to be least practical method. In space, we'd use IFF."

IFF stood for Identification Friend or Foe. All human ships, including lifepods, were equipped with transponders that, when queried, would transmit a code unique to their craft. "You sent out queries?"

"No. That just got me thinking of using passive means of finding the ships. I'm looking for EM." EM was electrical magnetic waves, which were a side product of power units. "It means I can find ships but without sending out queries, I can't identify them."

Ships. "You found more than one?"

"I've picked up twenty-six so far."

"Twenty-six?"

"So far. I've only done ten degrees of scanning. Some of them are quite small, lifepod size. Only a handful are on the scale of a military class ship. In theory we should be able to see anything out there but there are islands and weather in the way."

Twenty-six. The number rocked Mikhail. He could only nod to Moldavsky while the ensign fiddled with her gun sight, discussing line of sight *inside* a sphere. On planets, where everything sat on the outside of the sphere, the curve of the world meant anything over the horizon was out of sight. Inside, however, there was nothing to obscure objects except of course weather and islands, both of the fixed and mobile variety.

Moldavsky checked the focus on her antique gun sight and stepped away to make room for Mikhail. "This is the only ship I've been able to visually confirm."

Far across the pane of water, the spaceship stood like a sudden mountain. Mikhail checked the range-finder; the wreck was nearly twenty thousand kilometers away. Mikhail's homeworld was only a fraction over forty thousand kilometers in circumference. If this was on his home planet, the ship would not only be over the horizon but on the other side of the world.

The muzzle of a rail gun cannon jutting out of the bow marked the ship as a carrier class. Mikhail was stunned that something that should never know a planet's gravity had survived landing in this ocean. The carrier, though, had been built to take a pounding from enemy weapons. The bracing to support and absorb the gun's recoil also protected the cannon's protruding muzzle from the planetlike gravity.

It wasn't the *Fenrir* though, because the engine housing was intact. Its power unit was still providing energy as a light blazed at the top of the housing like a great lighthouse. Just beyond the ship's stern, he could see that there was land with trees. The carrier had crashed onto a larger island than the *Svoboda*'s little sandbar.

Overall, though, the spaceship looked like an unfinished jigsaw puzzle. Pieces were missing—lost or taken. Had the carrier been damaged in its crash landing or had it been stripped afterward? Mikhail considered what was intact and what was gone. What remained was enough to keep the weapons operational and the ship structurally sound. Everything else had been stripped. The carrier hadn't broken into pieces from the crash; it was being disassembled. Had the salvage teams been human or nefrim?

"Have you spotted any signs of life?" Mikhail asked.

"Here." Moldavsky took charge of the gun sight, increased the magnification, and shifted it slightly. "I'm thinking that the ship is protecting a harbor between itself and the island beyond."

Moldavsky stepped back from the gun sight. Mikhail peered through to see what the woman found. Nearly hidden by the bulk of the ship was a low stone dock lined with houses painted in bright colors. The buildings seemed reassuringly human, festive even. A seagoing boat glided into view, dwarfed by the massive spaceship looming over the harbor. Mikhail switched the finder to the craft and zoomed in. Nets and buoys marked it as a fishing boat. He found the bridge and focused on the figure at the wheel. It appeared human.

The carrier's crew survived and perhaps even thrived. But if it wasn't the *Fenrir*, which ship was it?

"It seems as if the ship crashed and the crew just settled around it. No signs of nefrims at that location at all."

Mikhail grunted in answer. The town might be evidence that there were no nefrim overlords supervising the world. Or there might not be a need to gather up new arrivals as the world itself would batter down the interlopers. Smash them out of the sky. Drown in the water. Pound them against the surf.

Moldavsky reclaimed her spot behind the gun sight. "I'm starting to think that all these ships just misjumped to this place. This is the nowhere you go to when you don't go anywhere."

"Are there closer targets?"

"One is within eight hundred kilometers but I can't see the ship. There's an island in the way." Moldavsky bent to change her target.

In relative terms, eight hundred kilometers was nearly on their doorstep. Considering their condition, it could be a dangerous place for anyone to be. The IFF was an ancient system of distinguishing between allied and enemy *human* ships.

"This is the closest signal but I can't see any signs of a ship." Moldavsky moved back, giving him room.

The island was a huge rough-shaped rock, like someone had dropped a boulder out of the sky. Considering Mikhail's experience, it might have been. Even viewed from a distance, the island towered in the water, a massive wall of sheer gray cliffs. It could effectively screen any ship from view, but it should also block the EM emissions coming from said ship. He increased the magnification and scanned the foot of the island, looking for signs of human life.

He found one section, a jumble of rocks, bits of color, and blackness that suggested caves into the cliff side. Only after studying it for several minutes could he make sense of what he was looking at. There had been something built into the side of the island; only the occasional straight lines remained to denote where square rooms once stood. The rooms or buildings had been blasted into shapeless piles of rock, now half buried by landslides from the cliff above.

When a warp engine jumped out inside a gravity well, there was a violent implosion in its wake. If *Fenrir*'s engine had been near the village that the ship's surviving crew had built next to the crash site, the village would have been leveled when the engine warped out. And it made sense that *Fenrir* would be their nearest neighbors. They'd replicated *Fenrir*'s jump. The deviation from their landing site was a combination of different momentum, mass, and the collision with the floating island.

"I think you've found *Fenrir*." Mikhail searched for signs of someone surviving the engine's departure.

"I did?" Moldavsky leaned down, pressing close as if she wanted another chance to study the wreckage. He wasn't done looking. "I didn't see anything that looked like a ship. I looked the *Fenrir* up; it was a Jupiter-classed carrier. Those things are like small moons."

A moon swallowed up and eaten whole with the exception of its engine.

It was easy to judge where the engine had sat prior to the blast; the resulting crater was obvious now that he knew what he was looking at. Unless the ship came down in pieces, the rest of it had to lie within a kilometer radius of the epicenter. The island and surrounding coral reefs eliminated most of that radius, leaving only one possible orientation of the ship's hull. But there was nothing visible—only water.

"It sank," Mikhail said. "Everything but the engine sank."

"It—it's like a hundred meters tall!"

"The water must be deeper." Mikhail moved back then, letting Moldavsky see as he considered their find.

Mikhail was sure that this had to be the remnants of the *Fenrir*. But this only raised more questions. If the engine was operable, why had the survivors settled on this bleak island? If it was just to repair the engine and warp back to Plymouth Station, why hadn't they taken the effort to send back information on this place? It could be that the survivors far outnumbered the available room on the engine, and those left behind would be left with nothing. A mutiny could have taken place but where had the unidentified Reds come from? And what did the modifications made to the engine indicate?

They were questions that could only be answered by investigating the wreckage and interrogating any survivors. If the nefrim were involved, that could be a dangerous course of action.

"We need to know everything about that island. Feed images to the tactical computer and get a full rendering of it."

"Yes, sir. What about the other carrier? Should I query its IFF?"

"No. Maintain radio silence. Do the carrier when you're done with the island and see if tactical can match its profile to known lost carriers. Make sure pre–United Colonies ships are included; that ship has been there for a while."

Moldavsky nodded and then glanced beyond Mikhail at the Red who'd been standing guard. "Sir," she whispered. "Can you get me a different Red up here? One of our veterans? This one is . . . I'd rather not be alone with it."

"What's wrong?" he asked quietly.

She blushed and looked away. "It's—it's being . . . lewd."

There was a word he'd never heard attached to a Red before. "What's he doing?"

The blush deepened to a brilliant shade of red. "It's spending an inordinate amount of time looking at . . . my privates. It told me that it knew how to use its mouth. And it said that we could use wire to tie it up since we don't have restraints. I—I think its last owner slutted around with her pride."

Mikhail remembered how furious Turk had been when he returned from Paradise. Had Turk been maneuvered into using himself as part of the payment for the replacements? Turk hated cat fanciers because he knew that they saw him as nothing more than a perverted sex toy. A crèche-raised Red wouldn't bring that mind-set to the encounter. To a normal tom, sex would be a much sought-after treat. Had the woman slept with *all* of her pride? "I'll swap him out."

10 Fenrir's Rock

MOLDAVSKY'S SURVEILLANCE DURING THE HOURS THAT IT TOOK them to dig the *Svoboda* out of the sandbar showed no human activity on the island except the lone energy signature. Mikhail decided to treat it as a hot zone and that they would go in expecting trouble. By then, Tseytlin had the *Tigertail* set up to act as the *Svoboda*'s bridge.

Mikhail took the *Svoboda* in low and fast, approaching in a wide curve so the island itself screened them from view until the last moment. And then with the left wingtip nearly brushing the gray rock face of the sheer cliffs, they circled the island until the engine crater came into view. They landed in the large flat field of rubble that was once a small town and was now only a jumble of rocks. Ocean and beaches might be strange things to his crew, but bombed city rubble was familiar ground. The gunners gave the all clear signal. The hatch of both Red pits opened. Cautiously, the Reds moved out to secure the area. In the *Tigertail*'s command center, Mikhail watched the feeds from the Reds' combat suits. Three dozen eyes scanned the wreckage and fed him data.

Any doubts Mikhail had about this being *Fenrir*'s crash site vanished as the Reds explored. *Fenrir* had been named after a wolf in Norse mythology. The survivors of the crew had embraced the image. It was painted onto the prows of boats. It was stenciled onto flags. It was painted onto the gray cliff walls.

Fenrir's crew had lived off the bounty of the sea. Fishing gear was strewn everywhere. Shattered boats. Broken fish cages. Stray net floats. The military command had given way to New Washington democracy; the buildings had been homes, storefronts, and judging by one broken sign, a restaurant. When bored, the inhabitants were prone to colorful graffiti; most were joyous proclamations of existence. There had been children whose toys remained left behind. Obviously this had been a thriving town with hundreds of inhabitants, all leveled in the blink of an eye.

A third of the monitors in front of Mikhail were off, a constant reminder of the Reds that they'd lost. Mikhail avoided looking at Turk's for an hour, telling himself, "Don't go picking at open wounds. You don't need that hurt right now." Finally he couldn't resist the urge any longer and reached out and flipped it on. Turk's suit was still transmitting but the vital monitors showed no signs of life. The screen remained black; the camera must have broken.

He stared at it. The blackness of the monitor leeched into him, filling him with nothingness until he was drowning in it.

"Sectors one through five clear," Butcher reported over his comline.

Anger was better. Anger at least gave him sharp focus. Mikhail snapped Turk's monitor off and found Butcher's among the unlabeled monitors. The handles of their veteran Reds had been added to their screens; the replacements were just numbers at the moment. At Mikhail's level, top cat was usually an invisible rank, not shown by any of the displayed data. Watching the monitors, though, it had been obvious that the other Reds were centered on Butcher. They moved when he moved, took cover when he took cover, looked first to him for orders.

Butcher had the obeisance and respect that came with top cat. Mikhail hated him for it. The hate pulled him out of the darkness, but he had to hold it in tight control, lest it too became all consuming.

Tseytlin was down in Alpha Red, trying to piece together what happened. Once it had been drained and repaired, they had to use it since Beta Red had been overcrowded. With all the Reds out on the mission, this was the first time they could closely study the Red pit. Soon Mikhail would know if Turk died in a simple accident or if Butcher killed him like he claimed. But if Butcher was guilty, could Mikhail afford to execute him? The Reds were a cohesive fighting unit; putting Butcher down would trigger a dominance battle. In this strange place, they could ill afford the Reds battling each other.

The attention light flashed on Rabbit's monitor. Rabbit's feed glowed shades of green; the night vision on the camera had kicked on. Where had Rabbit found so much black in this night-less world?

"Where are you, Rabbit?" Mikhail asked the little Red.

"Captain, I've found a tunnel. Lots of tunnels actually. It seems like a good place for an ambush, sir."

Obviously, Rabbit was afraid that Butcher wouldn't recognize it as such. Turk had always valued Rabbit's intelligence, but probably not his crèche-raised replacement. Mikhail prioritized Rabbit's line with the mapping computer, letting the program try to make sense out of the confusion of greens.

Since the Reds had stayed focused around Butcher, the software had already built a detailed model of the city immediately around the ship. Rabbit had strayed off into uncharted territory. His course was a series of disjointed turns in white space.

"All sectors clear. Awaiting orders," Butcher reported. He'd done exactly what he'd been ordered to do, where Turk would have grasped what was actually needed to be done. Functioning perfectly didn't mean he was adequate to the job. Rabbit's intuition made him a better replacement, but he'd never be able to gain the Reds' respect.

"Rabbit, return to the ship," Mikhail ordered.

"Captain?" Rabbit's doubt was clear his voice.

"Return to the ship to escort me into those tunnels," Mikhail explained.

"Yes, sir!"

Turk had a spare command suit on the *Tigertail*. Mikhail took it out of its locker and pulled it on. It smelled of Turk, and for a moment, it was all not true; Turk was there, a solid quiet presence, firmly in command of the Reds. Mikhail couldn't bear putting on the helmet.

Stop picking at the wounds, Mikhail told himself and strapped on his service pistol. He checked to make sure it was loaded with tranq rounds; he didn't want to kill any survivors that they found, no matter how hostile they might be. But just in case he got into a more serious firefight, he took a clip of regular ammo.

∞   ∞   ∞

The blast doors from a fighter bay had been set into the cliff. It stood open. It had no live power running to it, but there were indications that it was in working order and could be sealed to keep out waves. Beyond, the floor of a large natural cave had been leveled with cement to make a wide hallway.

With Butcher taking point, Mikhail moved cautiously down the corridor. They went several hundred meters, passing smaller hallways and staircases branching off into darkness. At each, Butcher followed standard procedure and signaled a pair of Reds to stand watch on the opening.

Deep in the core of the island was a large cavernous harbor. Shafts of sunlight came through skylights cut into the ceiling. The soft lap of water on stone spoke of an invisible current moving the dark, still water. They'd come in at an angle to a canal leading toward the outer harbor; the landslide would have blocked the canal. A stone dock lined the edge of the harbor. High on the sheer walls were steel girders, strung with block and tackle.

"What are those for?" Rabbit asked as Mikhail played a light over the ropes and pulleys.

"I think they would haul boats up out of the water," Mikhail said. "It would double how many boats they could fit into here. See, there's one."

Mikhail spotlighted a boat far above the water, hanging on ropes. It was a twin to the *Swordfish* at Plymouth Station. The stern read *Kingfisher*. He checked it with the suit's infiltration scanners and found it had the same type of torpedo power unit as the *Swordfish* had. The hull was damaged near in the bow, perhaps the reason it was strung up here instead of out in the outer harbor at the time of the implosion.

The outside buildings had been just a small part of *Fenrir*'s colony. Inside there had been a warren of rooms adapted from the natural cave system. There hadn't been a few hundred living here, as he supposed earlier, but thousands.

Mikhail stood gazing at the grotto. This was why the survivors clung to this island. In this protected harbor, they could weather the worst of storms. But with the grotto harbor blocked, the outer harbor was much too vulnerable to large waves. Any fishing boats that survived the implosion would be destroyed in the next storm. Had the *Fenrir*'s people fled the island or had something else had happened to them?

The Reds stirred around him, growing bored.

"Do a maze search starting from this room," Mikhail told Butcher. "Look for evidence of fighting. Laser burns. Shrapnel damage."

Butcher nodded his understanding and turned to the Reds.

The wall along the dock was whitewashed and then painted with messages. Some were carefully detailed like "Crew of the *Passport* went to Georgetown Landing on the *Ben Franklin*." Others were much more cryptic, requiring some knowledge of the people who left the messages: "John Q., Went to Mom's, H." The most poignant was "Everyone dead but me. Don't know where I'm going, Dennis Finway." Hundreds of messages, in dozens of paint colors, done neat and sloppy, big and small, bending and twisting not to overlap, lest their message be confused with the others.

Nor were all in Standard; there was at least one of every language that made it into space. Japanese. Chinese. Arabic. German. Russian. He'd need to feed the images into a translator to understand what all but the last said. Eerily, the Russian stated, "*Svoboda* is no more. Everyone but I am dead. I go on. Mikhail Ivanovich." *Svoboda* was a popular name for a ship, as Mikhail and Ivan were for men. Still it felt like he stumbled across a message from himself.

Only a few offered up the cause of the destruction. "Explosion in harbor," stated one. "Engine exploded," read another.

The destinations interested Mikhail the most. The survivors hadn't all fled to the same place, but scattered, suggesting a multitude of human havens in this world. What's more, the sanctuaries seemed to be all ship names. He recognized the *Constitution*, *Requin*, *Whyalla*, and *Buffel*; they were United Colonies ships lost in infamous battles. While he didn't know the others, their names resonated as ships. The only ones that didn't were "Ya-ya" and "Mary." If each name represented the crash site of a ship with its crew setting up an outpost of human civilization, then there were dozens of "lost" ships listed on the wall.

What confounded him was the time frame. The *Svoboda* arrived only a few days after *Fenrir*'s engine appeared at Plymouth Station; Moldavsky should have picked up a fleet of small boats moving purposely away from this island. And *Fenrir* had been lost for only ten years. That seemed far too short a time for the survivors to pull themselves out of the ocean, build fishing boats, and carve out these caves. Even if they had accomplished so much in such a short time, it didn't account for places where the stone was worn smooth by casual wear. Or the ring of coral that had grown on *Fenrir*'s engine.

Time seemed to run differently in this place.

Fenrir might have vanished out of normal space ten years ago, but its people seemed to have lived here for decades. The engine might have appeared at Plymouth Station less than a week ago, a few hundred hours, but more time than that had gone by in this bubble world.

Time was affected by gravity. At the event horizon of a black hole, time shuddered to a stop. But run fast? How could there seem to be normal gravity here and yet time was accelerated?

Mikhail heard the splash of water and the slap of wet on stone behind him as he searched his com for the ship names he didn't recognize. The sound filtered slowly through his consciousness. First as an awareness that the two noises, connected, meant something had left the water and landed on the dock. Secondly that Butcher had neglected to leave any Reds with him. He was alone on the dock.

A second wet slap echoed through the cavern, sounding closer.

Correction. *Had* been alone.

He spun around.

There were two fish lying on the dock, half a meter long each, twitching in puddles. Their mouths worked, desperately trying to find something to breathe. The harbor churned with silvery bodies, darting through the shafts of sunlight in a frantic pace. Mikhail stared at the fish, both in the water and the dock. *Why in the world would fish jump to their death?*

The school of fish in the harbor suddenly veered away from one shadowed area to race toward the dock. Individuals leapt, here and there, as if trying to flee the water itself. No; they were fleeing a shadow moving through the water behind them. There was something in the water; most likely a predator of some sort. A very large predator. The shadow widened as it arrowed toward him, as if something black was surfacing out of the depths even as it grew closer. The creature was black with spots of white, long and lean, and huge. It ignored the fish leaping out of its way, seemingly intent on him. Or something in the water right in front of Mikhail.

There was a lip built into the edge of the dock. Someone was tucked under the ledge, just the tips of their fingers showing where they were holding on.

"Get out of the water." Mikhail pulled his service pistol and changed the clip. He doubted his tranq ammo would work on anything as large as the incoming sea monster.

The person in the water peeked over the stone edging, dark eyes peering through a wet mane of black hair. The black on black of a Red.

"Something is in the water. It's coming straight at you. Get out of the water." Mikhail took aim at the creature. It was nearly at the dock. Hoping that the creature followed Earth physiology and kept its brain between its eyes, he took careful aim at the center of its head. The muzzle flashed brilliant in the grotto's shadows, the shot echoing through the cavern.

"Oh shit!" The Red came scrambling out of the water. She was unmistakably female—wearing almost no clothing to hide that fact—and furred. A female Red.

Reds were always male. Always.

Mikhail was so stunned and amazed, he stopped tracking the creature. It was a fish in the water, after all, and the impossibly female Red was on the dock, beside him, but fleeing quickly. "Wait! I won't hurt you! I just want to—"

The creature heaved out of the water and slammed into him. Massive jaws with an impossible number of jagged teeth clamped down on his side. The combat suit flashed warning as its projectile dampers resisted the sudden onslaught. Then the creature whipped its head to the side, in a move that probably was supposed to rip a hunk of flesh free, and Mikhail went tumbling across the dock. He slammed against the cave wall and lay there stunned.

I really should have put the helmet on.

The fish was heading toward him but he couldn't get any of his limbs to obey him.

Then the woman was there, jerking him up with the ease of a Red. She was surprisingly short for a Red, and lean, but apparently just as strong. Her eyes were as dark as a Red's. She had their glossy black hair, only hers was curly and long, a wild mane instead of the crew-cut that all his pride sported. She wore strips of cloth pretending to be clothes; one tight black band crossed her full breasts, and another barely covered her groin. She had a knife strapped to her thigh, and the hilt of a swordlike blade showing over her shoulder. Other than an annoyed look and black fur, she had nothing else on.

There was a metal catwalk overhead that Mikhail hadn't noticed before. It had been hidden by the deep shadows of the grotto. He was made forcibly aware of the catwalk as she flung him up onto it. His suit complained again that it had saved him from grievous harm. The woman landed next to where he lay.

"Idiot," she growled. "How close does death have to get before you recognize it?"

The creature splashed heavily across the dock to stand under them. Its huge mouth opened, a sudden cave ringed by thousands of jagged teeth. Its breath blasted over him, an explosive hot exhale of carrion.

Mikhail gazed down through the metal grate flooring at the huge open jaws just inches away. "Apparently very close."

"I could have let that thing kill you," she said. "But in this world, the only thing you can control is yourself. I don't want to be a mindless monster that concerns itself with only feeding its belly. Fix that firmly in your mind. To be is to be and no storm can change your course."

Mikhail refrained from pointing out that he'd saved her first; because she was right, she could have left him laying there half stunned.

"Oh shit, it's still coming." She jerked him to his feet again. "Come on, come on. It can climb."

"It's a fish."

She slammed him to the wall and pinned him there. "Why do you think you know anything? This isn't your universe! It's a rogue bio-weapon. It's fast. It's smart. It's nearly impossible to kill. And it can climb!"

The catwalk clanged and rattled as the creature hooked a tentacle onto the railing and started to haul itself up.

"Point taken," Mikhail said.

The woman released Mikhail. The catwalk had ended before another set of blast doors from a fighter bay. This one, though, was sealed shut.

"Oh give me a break!" The woman growled and threw open the access panel to the manual crank. "I don't know why I deserve all this bad luck. We're so dead."

The creature was coming at an alarming speed, although Mikhail suspected that due to its size, any speed would be alarming. Amazingly, he'd kept hold of his pistol. Unfortunately, he'd only brought one clip with him. He had only a dozen bullets to kill the monster, and then he was out of ammo. He took careful aim for its right eye and fired. The bullet ricocheted off the eye as if striking steel.

"That's only going to piss it off," the woman growled as she struggled with the crank. "As will those peashooter rifles your Reds are carrying. You need something big—like a cannon."

Judging by its speed and his experience with such machinery, they weren't going to get the door open before it was on top of them. He glanced around, trying to form a plan. He realized that the catwalk let people access boats suspended from the trusses overhead.

There was another catwalk beside the *Kingfisher*, not connected to the one they were, but only a short jump away.

"Follow me." Mikhail holstered his pistol. "We're moving to the next catwalk."

She burst into curses but still let him pull her to the railing. "That doesn't go anywhere! That door is without power too!"

"I have a plan!" He scrambled up onto the railing and leapt across.

"It better be a good plan!" She landed lightly beside him. "It can jump this easy."

"I'm hoping it can."

"What?" She nearly squeaked the word in startled amazement.

Mikhail scrambled onto the *Kingfisher*. Just escaping the beast would leave his crew endangered when they came looking for him. He had to kill it. On Plymouth Station Mikhail had spent hours climbing over the *Swordfish*, looking for any overlooked clues as to where it might have come from. Luckily the *Kingfisher* was very much a twin for the *Swordfish*.

He kicked on the engine and then set it at a high idle. As he dashed for the engine hatch, the creature leaped the gap, flinging itself across with surprising grace and ease. The catwalk shook violently as it landed.

In a cabinet beside the engine hatch, there was a heavy duty power cable with alligator clamps on one end and a crude old-fashioned pronged plug on the other.

"Here!" Mikhail called to the woman as he threw open the engine hatch. "Help me! Plug this in."

"What?" She scrambled to his side and snatched up the plug. "Now?"

"No. Wait for my mark."

Attaching the clamps to the railing required getting close to the creature. His suit would protect him from both the monster and electricity. Theoretically. With clamps in hand, he ran to the railing, aware that the creature was rushing toward him.

They reached the railing at the same time, reaching for each other with outstretched limbs. The bio-weapon was faster. Its climbing tentacle whipped around Mikhail, crushing tight, and jerked him toward its mouth full of teeth. Mikhail clamped the right lead to the tentacle holding him, but his left hand was trapped to his side.

"Plug it in!" he shouted.

"Are you insane?" the female Red shouted back.

"Plug it in!" He wriggled his left hand so the metal end of the lead pressed against the tentacle.

Apparently she obeyed him. The creature jerked wildly as the power surged through it. His suit screamed warnings that its ability to protect him was failing. The smell of cooked fish filled his senses.

And suddenly he was on the floor of the ship and the creature was a still mass draped over the railing. The sudden silence was amazing.

"Are you okay?" The woman pressed a hand to his neck, feeling for a pulse. Her hand was soft with fur.

"I'm fine," Mikhail croaked and sat up.

"That took a lot of guts." She looked at him with surprised awe. "You know, I could have done the clamps and you plugged it in."

He wheezed out a laugh. "I had the suit to protect me."

"Yeah. I see you don't need to be told to watch your course."

"Captain!" Someone shouted in the distance, and came running through the darkness at a speed only a Red could produce.

"Captain!" Mikhail recognized Rabbit's voice. He sounded in a near panic as he turned in place, looking for Mikhail.

"Up here!" Mikhail called down.

Rabbit looked up, spotted the catwalk, and leaped up onto it. A moment later Rabbit was at Mikhail's side, worry on his face. "Captain, are you hurt?"

"No." Mihkail put a hand on the yearling's shoulder to calm him. Annoyingly the hand wanted to shake. Mikhail controlled it and cleared his throat to make sure his voice stayed firm. "I'm fine."

The woman was gone, silent as a shadow retreating before the light.

11 Yamoto-Yamaguchi

PAIGE BOTH LOVED AND HATED YAMOTO-YAMAGUCHI.

The gods had smiled on the ancient spaceships. Both had landed nearly intact and within miles of each other. The colony ship *Yamaguchi* had the manufacturing facilities to make and repair practically anything. The battleship *Yamoto* supplied military power to protect a sprawling wealthy settlement. They had the means to make a beautiful city; thus Ya-ya was an opulent flower resting between the two great ships.

Coming to the landing when she was a child was like having her eyes forced open. For the first time she realized how the other landings were built with a plethora of salvaged material poorly redesigned and haphazardly placed. They suddenly seemed as ugly as a broken hand-me-down toy that someone else had the joy of owning when it was new. She loved the landing's beauty, and hated how grimy the rest of the world seemed compared to it.

As usual, she felt torn as they finally made the busy harbor.

The *Rosetta*'s engine had stuttered and stalled for the last five hundred miles. It was a huge relief to settle into a boat slip and tie off, safe. *Safety* was a relative word though. They had to deal with treacherous economics now instead of the dangers of open water. Everything came at a price in Ya-ya, from the pilot that came out to guide them in, to the tugboat that was eventually needed to get them to the docks, plus a daily fee on the boat slip

113

itself. She couldn't force her crew to exist without money, so she would have to pay their wages. They needed food staples such as coffee, flour, and sugar. The fridge, ship's intercom, and their radio were all fried. And both Turk and Rannatan were still naked.

She set aside wages, sent Manny out with money to cover the staples, electronics, and clothes, and considered what was left. Two thousand yen. Not a sum to be sneezed at, but a new engine would run three to four times that amount. Without a new engine, the *Rosetta* was merely a floating house. And the longer they sat idle in harbor, the more they would have to pay.

Orin came onto the bridge with two cups of coffee, which meant Manny was back from his shopping. "Manny says there's no news on Ethan or the *Lilianna*. If they survived, they didn't come here."

"Once we get a radio in, we can call Georgetown—see if anyone went back home."

Orin nodded to the wisdom of this. "How are we doing moneywise?"

"We're not broke." Paige handed him his coin string. "There's all the cargo we were going to sell at Fenrir's Rock. And the drop nuts we picked up." That might scrape in another thousand. "We're going to have to take some local jobs, though, before we can afford another engine."

They went over the duty schedule. While Ya-ya was safe from storms and dangerous sea creatures, it was thick with thieves. They would have to make sure that at least two adults were onboard and awake at all times. Taking jobs to raise money would stretch them thin.

Paige was just finishing up with Orin on the dock when Turk caught up to her. As always he drifted up close to her but stopped short of touching her. There were times she wished he would just take his distracting presence away. There were other times she wished he'd press his body full against her. Her awareness of him was so acute that even when they were inches apart, his nearness felt like a touch.

At least he was no longer naked. Manny had gotten him a blue cotton shirt, white linen pants, and leather sandals.

"Did you get new clothes too?" His gaze went down over her slowly.

She had changed into her best kimono, a brilliant red *furisode* with peonies. She had gotten it secondhand, as new it would have cost a hundred times the price. "No, this is old. And it's annoying to wear." She held out her arm and loosed her sleeve to show off the fact that the sleeves trailed the whole way to the ground. "I only break it out when I'm going to be spending a long time on land."

"It makes you even more beautiful."

Damn, the man could go through all her defenses and make her blush. Other people would have said, "You're beautiful in it," as if implying that beauty lay only in the garment.

"Thank you." She distracted herself in gathering up the sleeve again. "Here, this is yours."

She handed him the coin string she had tucked into her sleeve. His was the last she had to give out before leaving.

"What are these?"

"They're yen. It's the coins that they use as money here. You do know how money works?"

He frowned at the money so intently that it was easy to see he was puzzled by something. There were times he was so easy to read, while other times he continued to mystify her.

"They have how much they are printed on them. See, here's a *one* on one yen. A *five* on five yen. And these are fifty yen. Five yen can get you lunch or a taxi ride. Fifty yen will get you some boots if you want, or a good knife."

"Why are you giving this to me?" he asked.

"That's your pay. Twenty yen a day for every day you've been on the *Rosetta*, minus out the cost of the clothes we've given you."

"You're giving me a salary?"

The total look of bewilderment on Turk's face made her laugh, covering her mouth with her hand. Five minutes in a kimono and she was slipping into old habits. "Yes. For the work you've been doing. Fishing. Cooking. Cleaning. Keeping watch. It's not as much as I would have liked but we're tight on money right now."

"Why are you paying me?"

"Because you're part of my crew—for as long as you want to be." The last few days had been a torture of temptation; she resisted because she didn't want to be heartbroken if he left when they reached Ya-ya. It had been fairly obvious that he loathed fishing, and it would be a while before he could cook a meal himself. "If you don't want to stay with us," she forced herself to add, "you could look for a job here in Ya-ya; newcomer Reds are well thought of as guards. If you sign onto another ship, stay away from those out of Mary's Landing."

Turk jingled the coins, scanning the city as if with new eyes. He was considering going.

The other annoying thing about the kimono was that it made her take little steps, as if the clothing was designed to force women to be demure. She started down the dock toward where the *Rosetta*'s launch was tied off, going as fast as the tight hem allowed.

And yet another thing was it made men pay attention to her. Of course, that was the whole point of the kimono. The length of sleeves and style of the garment denoted the age and marital status. Hers was a loud and clear advertisement that she was a woman over twenty years old and available for marriage. The men working along the dock all paused in their work to watch her move past them.

It also seemed to work like a magnet on Turk, as he drifted alongside of her. "Where are we going?"

"We? We are going nowhere. I've got errands to run."

"You can barely move in that. You're asking for trouble."

"I can take care of myself."

He gave her one of his long dark looks. "I can wander around lost by myself, or you can let me come with you and show me the city."

Damn the man. He made entirely too much sense.

This was the much talked about Ya-ya? There had been something vaguely surreal about sailing toward the great spaceships stranded in the ocean, rising like cliffs out of the water. Turk had expected that once in the city, with the buildings closed in around him that the sense of the unreal would fade. It would be like any other spaceport he'd been in. However, everything about the town was so alien to what he knew that it felt like he slipped into a dream. Unlike spaceports, there were no skyscrapers to balance the massive spaceships. The city was of stone buildings, none over three stories tall. The spaceships loomed like mountains, shrouded in a morning fog. Boats slid in and out of the fog, horns blaring, a cacophony of tones and timbres. Obviously established before the United Colonies adoption of Standard, all the signage was in ancient Japanese. And the animals ... There were never animals at spaceports. Ya-ya had a nightmarish zoo of strange creatures roaming free or sitting in cages, adding their calls to the noise of the ships.

And the most dreamlike thing of all: Captain Bailey in a silk kimono sitting beside him. He had thought that maybe his desperate situation had made her seem more alluring than she truly was. But watching the men of the city react to her, he knew it hadn't been his imagination. Captain Bailey was as stunningly beautiful as she appeared in his eyes.

The coins she'd given him had holes punched through their middles and they were strung on a piece of leather. He fingered the strand like a rosary.

She'd paid him.

He'd thought that Captain Bailey had claimed him as her family's property when she rescued him off the civ raft. All the kindness and patience the crew had shown, he'd discounted as simply taking care of their belonging. As a final blow, Bailey had told him that he was free to leave if he wanted. He nearly bolted, like a zoo animal who sees only a chance to escape from a cage. Running just to run would be stupid. Where the hell would he go?

When Mikhail freed him when Turk turned eighteen, Turk had had years to consider what he wanted to do with his life. Like Bailey, Mikhail had pointed out alternatives to staying with him. To Turk, though, there had never been any other sane decision except to stay with Mikhail. It went beyond the affection and respect that they had for each other. Much as Ivan would never admit it, Turk was Ivan's son. As with Mikhail, Turk's every waking moment as they grew up had been dedicated to understanding politics and the art of commanding others. As a lone Red, the best Turk could have hoped for would have been the Red commander of a modestly wealthy man. With Mikhail, he would be part of ruling an entire empire.

If the *Svoboda* had landed safely, nothing would have kept Turk from searching for Mikhail. But all odds and indications were that the *Svoboda* had sunk after hitting the floating island. There was a slim chance Mikhail could have survived that disaster, but Mikhail had a tendency to self-destruct when life slipped out of his control. A helpless Mikhail tore himself apart with self-recrimination. Since Mikhail maintained a stonewall façade of strength, it'd be unlikely that anyone but Turk would notice him falling into suicidal despair . . .

Turk stopped himself. *Mikhail is dead. The question is what do I do now?*

He glanced at Captain Bailey sitting beside him. She'd been good to him, as had all her family. Even when he thought they'd enslaved him, he'd begrudgingly grown fond of them. With the Baileys, he'd lucked into a safe haven. But life on that boat—the hours endlessly focused on the act of barely surviving. Did he want to resign himself to that?

Then again, did he want to throw himself into the complete unknown and trust he would land as safely a second time? He didn't like to think of himself as a coward, but after his brush with the civ, that idea scared him. Besides, giving himself time to learn the world before making a choice would be wise.

They turned a corner and the canal widened in front of a busy stone plaza. Actual land rose beyond the plaza in the form of a tree-covered island. The dock was crowded with small boats. Captain Bailey found a space between two boats and guided them up to the dock. She lifted her chin to indicate the ropes coiled at the bow. "Get the rope and tie us off."

The crew of the *Rosetta* had been drilling Turk on tying knots until he was sure he could tie them in his sleep—which was probably the point.

Bailey waited until Turk tied the boat off before cautiously picking her way to the bow. The kimono was lovely but obviously impractical. She was going to have a difficult time stepping up and out of the boat. He reached out and swept her up. She laughed, wrapping her arms around his neck to hold on tightly. "I told you it was a pain to wear."

"Why wear it?"

She glanced into his eyes, lips close enough to kiss. Something like desire filled her face, but then she blushed and dropped her gaze. "Because I was coming here; a kimono is proper dress. Because I like to wear pretty things now and then."

He put her down, reluctantly. It had felt good to hold her; she had been surprisingly light, warm, and soft. As his hands slid over her bottom, he could tell that she wasn't wearing her normal modest underwear. He tried not to think about what she may or may not be wearing under the kimono. There was something good and pure in the way that she blushed; he didn't want to sully that.

He focused instead on the other people. The women all wore colorful kimonos. The cut of the men's clothing varied, from something that looked like a male version of the kimono to his own new clothes. He and Bailey, though, seemed to be the only non-Asians in the plaza.

There were booths lining the edge of the plaza. Some were selling food. Others had umbrellas and fans. On the far side, the island rose, forming a gentle hump, crowned with flowering trees. While the hill wasn't steep, people only climbed it using a set of stone steps with red wooden arches standing over them.

"What is this place?" Turk asked.

"This is Ise Jingū." She took his hand and pulled him toward one of the booths. The vendor was cooking pieces of meat on a thin wooden skewer. Paige held up four fingers, received four skewers, and paid with a five yen coin. "Ise Jingū means shrine island. It's a holy place."

"And this is holy food?" he asked.

She smiled. "No. It's chicken!" She handed him two of the skewers. "For once, no fish!"

He had to admit that the change was delicious. As they ate, she led him to another booth, this one selling roast corn. "We're going to eat our way across the plaza?"

"What? You don't like this plan?"

"Just surprised by it."

"I translated here for ten years." She held up the corn she just bought. "I got addicted to some of the food. We can't grow corn on the *Rosetta*."

"Manny says you're very good at translating."

"I'm the best." She smiled up at him. "I really loved doing it. It pays well. And it's safe work. No fighting storms. No treacherous waters. No man-eating fish." She took a bite of her corn and moaned at the taste. Did she know how erotic it sounded? "And you eat nice."

"Why did you quit?"

The smile fled her face. She concentrated on nibbling the kernels off the corncob without making a mess of her kimono. Only after she finished, and licked her fingers clean, did she answer. "My parents died when our boat ran aground on a reef off of

Omaha Landing. Ethan and I were here in Ya-ya translating. Orin and the others were left stranded and orphans at Omaha. I'd been saving my money to buy a house here in Ya-ya. I decided to buy the *Rosetta* instead."

"Why not buy the house and bring your family here? It seems safer than putting them all on a boat."

"I . . . I thought about it. There were too many reasons why getting a boat outweighed moving them here. Orin and Avery love the sea. Avery can't translate, and Orin doesn't like it. Nor does Charlene; as you might have noticed, she doesn't like to do hard work."

Turk laughed. "I would have thought translating was easier than working on the boat."

"Mentally, translating is a wonderful challenge. You're an invisible negotiator between two unreasonable parties. Each side says rude comments about the other, makes impossible demands, and you have to make it seem as if everyone is being polite and reasonable. And translating between two groups of humans is actually the hardest. Humans, more than any species, seem to have this 'I must come out on top in this deal' mind-set. You have to manage the deal so both groups think they're walking away with more than the other party."

"The other species don't think like that?" Turk said.

"Not in the same way."

Fish-shaped cakes filled with sweet bean puree were next.

Following her was like applying a male intelligence test to the crowd. Every man noticed her. The smart ones looked first to see if she was alone and accurately determined that they couldn't take Turk in a fight. The less intelligent would try to intercept her, and only notice Turk as he blocked their path. Only one idiot was stupid enough to try to go around Turk, but luckily he understood the warning in the low growl that Turk gave.

Thankfully the crowd thinned as they climbed the steps. Bailey had a hand pressed to her mouth. It was only when she glanced at him that he realized that laughter danced in her eyes.

"I can take care of myself," she murmured, "but thank you. That was the easiest I've ever gotten through a crowd."

He refrained from pointing out that was exactly why he came with her. She took his hand again even though there was no reason to; they were nearly alone when they reached the top of the stairs.

A lush garden stretched out before them, with pea-gravel paths meandering away in several directions. She guided him down the path, the gravel crunching underfoot.

Only when they were completely alone did she quietly confess, "The only thing I didn't like about translating was that so many men assumed that since they'd paid for my services, they'd paid for all of me."

He didn't ask for details. Certainly he'd spent enough years with people assuming that just because he existed, they could gratify their sexual whims with him. When he realized that ten years of translating meant she'd started younger than Hillary was now, he growled low with anger.

She leaned against him, touching her forehead to his shoulder. "You don't need to growl so. Nothing worse happened than a few conversations with human octopi."

"Octopi?"

"It's the plural of octopus."

"Oh." He understood now. He'd had a few conversations like that when he was very young. "Not octopuses?"

"No. Octopi."

"What are we doing here then?"

"I need to make money before making the *Rosetta* seaworthy again. I'm nearly broke."

"How are we going to raise money here?"

Mysteriously, his question drew a radiant smile from her.

"What?" he asked, and glanced behind him to see if there was something amusing behind him.

She ducked her head, shaking it. "Nothing."

"Tell me."

"You said 'we.' It made me happy." She continued to study the path before them. "I'm hoping that you'll stay with us."

That jolted emotions through him, much akin to a sugar rush on a roller coaster. In the past, women either ignored him, or viewed him as a perverted sex toy. He had no experience in anything else. Was this something else? Was she indicating that there could be something between them? He became acutely aware that she still held his hand. With the Baileys being his only known refuge, could he risk misinterpreting her?

"So, how are we going to raise money?" he carefully skirted around the issue.

"We're going to visit my teacher, Ceri. Most people that need translating come to her."

After what she'd told him, he was surprised. "You're going to translate?"

Bailey nodded. "It will be better than fishing."

"Anything would be better than fishing."

They'd turned a corner and stopped in front of a small wooden house. On a knee-high porch, an old woman in an elegant silk kimono sat drinking tea.

"Sensi." Bailey greeted the woman, bowing low with respect.

Turk stared speechless. Bailey was striking, from her honey gold curls to her vivid blue eyes. The roughness from work and weather, however, made her real and touchable.

Ceri was beyond beautiful; she was perfection only slightly touched by time. Her long thick hair was glossy silver, gathered into a loose braid with silk ribbon wove through it. Her skin was so pure white that it was ethereal. Her eyes were a deep shade of lavender that outside this world he would have suspected to be contact lens or artificially dyed. With her kimono artfully arranged around her, the woman seemed like an expensive doll.

The woman gazed into his eyes. It was a look of want and the promise of sexual release of such intensity that he felt his body respond even as he growled warning.

"Please don't play with him, Sensei," Captain Bailey murmured.

"Indulge an old woman." Ceri obviously had taken voice lessons; her tone was as perfect as her looks. "You have come begging."

Captain Bailey stiffened, breathing in sharply.

Ceri glanced at Bailey, frowned slightly, and looked away. "Yes, you would, foolish, foolish child."

Turk felt like he'd missed a full section of the conversation. What would Bailey do?

"You're almost as bad as your brother," Ceri said. "Entirely too much pride in your family."

"Compared to?" Bailey asked.

Ceri laughed. "That's your father's blood speaking there. Ready to fight."

"Ceri, I did not come here to fight with you. I put in ten years of doing anything you asked of me. I earned the right to leave without recriminations."

Ceri gazed into her teacup for several minutes of silence before murmuring, "Oust, love."

Only then did Turk realize that the woman wasn't alone. An old man stood in the shadows of the porch. His stance said bodyguard. Turk nodded to him; one warrior to another. The man returned the nod.

"Please fetch me my book," Ceri said to her bodyguard.

Oust went into the house and returned with a book stuffed with scraps of paper.

"It's Ethan that I'm angry with." Ceri untied the ribbon that held shut the book and leafed through the pages. "Every spare moment he had, he focused on the seraphim. Trying to build a lexicon for creatures with no commonality with us."

"No profit."

Ceri gave a slight motion, conceding that Bailey was closer to her objection to Ethan's obsession. "You at least had good cause to go. He disrupted everyone's life with his wild goose chase."

"Have you heard anything from Fenrir's Rock?"

Ceri shook her head. "Nothing of your family. From what I could tell, there was nothing but chaos afterwards. A hurricane was closing on Fenrir's Rock, the inner harbor is inaccessible, and the outer harbor has been destroyed. Everyone scurried away to safer harbors before the storm hit."

Bailey nodded.

"This is the list of those confirmed dead." Ceri took out a paper and held it out to Bailey.

Bailey ran her finger down the list of names, her face registering degrees of hurt. She blinked away any chance of crying, but her nose started to run. "Shit," she murmured, pressing the back of the hand to her nose, and then looked up and saw Turk watching her. "There's a lot of people from Fenrir and Georgetown that I know one way or another. The Becker twins lived about five houses down—they are—they were my age. Janni Thompson—she—she dated Orin—" She gave a slight laugh. "—but she was a complete bitch, and I was happy when she dumped him. And—and—"

Bailey stared at the floor, her shoulders squaring to a stubborn set. There were times she reminded Turk of Mikhail. Misha would get the same "I'm not going to tell how bad I hurt" look. He'd keep it all inside until it had the force of a black hole, and then he'd collapse. It was frightening to think that Bailey might share the same self-destructive tendencies. Pushing never worked with Mikhail, so Turk wrapped his arms around her, laying his cheek on her forehead, and waited. After a minute, she poked him in the ribs, like she knew what he was doing, but then hugged him. Taking comfort in his presence.

"As it stands, I can use you." Ceri took back the list and replaced it in her book. "A goodly number of Fenrir's people came here, and I'm shorthanded."

Bailey nodded, and then for Turk's sake, explained. "The people of Ya-ya usually only know a smattering of Standard, and the Fenrir people don't speak any Japanese."

Bailey sighed, and Ceri tsked her. Again Turk felt like he missed something. It was like they shortcut through the conversation, taking detours that bypassed him completely.

"You have a bodyguard now." Ceri gave an elegant wave of her hand to take in Turk. "You will not have the same problems as before."

Turk understood then what had gone unsaid. The Fenrir's Rock people were the ones most likely to expect more from Bailey than just translating. They would want sex too. And Ceri was right; Turk would make sure that wasn't a problem.

Bailey laughed. "In that case, I'll have a different problem."

"There is that," Ceri said. "I'll send word to you when I have something for you."

Captain Bailey was quiet as they walked back through the crowded plaza. Only after they cast off did she break the silence. "I'm sorry. Ceri assumed you were staying."

"I don't see how I could find my ship," he started to explain his reasoning for staying. "I don't know where it went down. It probably sank. I have no way of searching for it . . ."

"Why would you want to find your ship?"

He wondered how he could explain it to her. "What if a hole opened up and dropped you onto Volya's northern steppe?"

"Where?"

"Exactly, you're not sure where you are. As far as you can see, it's grass and nothing else. Some seemingly kind but eccentric people find you. Luckily you can speak their language but they don't speak Standard or English. They say you can stay with them as long as you want, but you need to get used to eating borscht and help take care of their horses."

"Borscht?"

"Borscht. No fish. The sea is too far away."

Captain Bailey shook her head, obviously unable to grasp the idea of no ocean. "What exactly is . . . horses?"

"They're very large animals that you ride, but they're very skittish and spend an extraordinary amount of their time trying to get you off their back."

"You've ridden on a horse?"

"Misha's family put a good deal of importance on the trappings of old royalty." After revolting against his original owner, Viktor had cloaked himself in the mysticism of divine right. God had chosen the Tsars of Russia; Viktor maintained that God had brought forth their bloodline to once again act as God's will in flesh. Viktor reinforced that line of thinking by copying much of the ancient imperial lifestyle. "You can't imagine how unsettling it is to lose everything from your world. From your language to the color of the sky—gone."

"I know how Reds are treated on military ships. You might be better off than most, but why go back to a place where you're a slave?"

"I was raised in the house of a powerful man. One thing I learned well: no one is free. Even the rich and powerful still have masters. I've seen men who rule cities of several million people grovel."

Bailey shook her head. "I don't have a master."

"You have a cruel and heartless master: this ocean. It doesn't care if you live or die."

"It's not the same."

"It's completely the same. You picked facing the ocean on your little ship instead of staying here at Ya-ya as a translator. You made the ocean your master."

"At least I'm not a slave."

"I'm not a slave. Misha gave me the same choice you did; I chose to stay with him."

12 Eraphie

WHEN MIKHAIL WAS YOUNG, ONE OF THE HOUSECATS HAD HER kittens under the crawl space of an outbuilding. By the time the kittens were found, they were several weeks old and feral. Mikhail and Turk used food to lure them into live traps and then spent days holding the kittens, forcing them to be tame beasts.

Mikhail doubted his female Red would trust him if he caught her in some kind of trap. Nor that prolonged physical contact would tame her; it would be much like trying to gentle a Bengal tiger merely by holding it.

But he could leave out offerings to lure her out. He tried to put himself in her mind-set. She was alone on an island where a military ship just landed. That she was hiding from them indicated she was frightened of them. What kind of things would make her trust them? Things she needed. Food. Clothing. Blankets.

Could she read? Crèches used Standard so that Reds could be used on any United Colonies ship without a language barrier. While pictographs were heavily used with Reds, they were also taught the rudiments of reading. What the female had spoken, though, had been true English. Without the usual Red training, it was possible that she hadn't been taught to read. Regardless of her ability, she might interpret his assumption that she could read as proof that he saw her as a human being. He dug up a spare reader and downloaded all of his books which were in English.

He took the precaution to have Tseytlin bug the reader so they could track the woman's movements.

Mikhail carried his offerings to where he last saw her. "Hello? I realize that you're stranded here. I brought you some things you might need." It felt awkward, talking to the dark. She probably wasn't even listening, but he couldn't pass up any opportunity to communicate. "We don't mean you any harm. We just arrived at this place and we could actually use a native-born guide."

He carefully positioned the bundle where it could be easily seen and made sure it appeared purposely left. The offering would be moot if she thought someone just mislaid it. "My name is Mikhail Ivanovich Volkov and my ship is the *Svoboda*. And in case I forgot in all the excitement, thank you for saving my life earlier."

He added a note, hoping that she really could read. There were no pictographs for Mikhail Ivanovich Volkov and thank you.

He backed away from the bundle and waited a few minutes. With the kittens, he and Turk would have to leave the area before they would venture out from the crawl space. Apparently at least that much held true.

"I can't take this, Mikhail."

Mikhail still felt claustrophobic in the sea-scented confines of the *Svoboda*. He'd found shelter at the edge of the rubble in a building still standing. He wasn't sure what the *Fenrir* people had done in the bare structure, but the sides of the building folded back until it stood completely open. He'd settled at the center of the bare concrete floor. Butcher set up guards all around him so that he saw a Red every time he looked up.

Thus he was stunned when he looked up and found the female Red crouched down in front of him, close enough to touch. Somehow she had slipped past all the guards. No wonder his Reds hadn't spotted her on the island earlier; she could come and go like a ninja. Her appearance startled him so much that he said, "*Izvinitye*," and had to repeat himself in English. "Pardon?'

"I can't take this!" She repeated and pushed the reader at him. "It's too expensive."

"No, no, it's practically disposal." He waved off her attempt to hand it to him. None of his guards had noticed her arrival. The ocean and wind, he realized, was generating white noise that was screening their conversation.

"Maybe in your universe it's disposal but not here!" She gave the reader a small shake. "This is worth a month's wages. Maybe two. I can't take it."

"You saved my life."

"That was for me, not you. I knew if I just watched you die, that would eat at me, make me someone I don't want to be. I need to respect myself, and I can only do that by being a person that I can respect."

He didn't want to take the reader back, especially if she considered it very valuable. Ruthless as it might seem, he needed her in debt. "Let's consider it a month's wages then. I need help. You could use the work. I'm guessing that there's a lack of job openings here at the moment."

Her eyes widened at his quip, and then narrowed slightly. "I don't want to be part of your pride."

"No, no, you'd be my native guide. There's so much we don't know about this place, and that not knowing could get us killed. As I've already demonstrated."

She weighed the reader in her hand considering if it balanced out to a fair trade. "I can't translate. You need a Blue to do that, not a Red."

A Blue? To translate? Maybe she didn't mean the females genetically engineered to be beautiful sex toys for the wealthy. Or maybe translate was their term for sex. "See, I didn't know that. And I have not a clue where to find a Blue."

"And I won't fight, not unless something comes at me personally. I'm not a meat shield."

"No fighting."

"And I won't be free to just anyone that wants some piston action."

It took him a moment to understand her. "No! No sex."

She glared at him for several minutes. Then she swept a look over the desolate ocean and the rubble. "Okay, Mikhail, I'll think about it."

He'd insist on "Captain" later, when she was a little less feral. "Thank you." To keep her from disappearing, he asked, "What's your name?"

"Eraphie." She put out her hand for a handshake that was strong and firm. "Eraphie Bailey of—" And she paused as sorrow filled her face. "Currently of nowhere."

"Currently? Until recently of . . . ?"

"Of the *Lilianna,*" she whispered. "But it's—it's gone. I'm the only survivor."

"What happened here?"

"I don't know." Eraphie started to stand.

He reached and caught her hand. "Please tell me what you do know."

Eraphie eyed him suspiciously for several minutes and then blew her breath out in a loud sigh. "It just happened so fast." She crouched down to be eye level with him again. "One minute everything was same-old, same-old and then the next . . . everyone was dead. There was almost no warning. There was this noise, a deep hum, you felt it all the way down into your bones. I had no idea what it was or where it was coming from but it felt wrong. It felt like it was something you run from, but I didn't know which way was away from it. I was just standing there, scared shitless. There were some people—newcomers—that recognized it as a warp field setting up. They started to run down harbor, away from the engine that was out on a peninsula by itself, shouting at people to get away. One of them went past me. I didn't even understand what he was screaming, but it was like he cut me loose, and I was gone, running flat out, without a clue where I was going or why. Then the sound changed and I looked back and the sky had gone all purple, and then . . . I just remember a loud boom and being picked up and flying and the air was full of dirt and stone and people. I came to later, lying on a pile of rubble."

She pointed at the edge of the destruction, which was probably why she was still alive.

Much as Mikhail wanted to know what happened to the colony, he'd seen all the end results. He wanted to hear about the things he didn't know. "So, you were born here? You've never jumped?"

Again the suspicious look, as if looking for hidden weapons. "Yes. I was born at Georgetown Landing. My grandfather came here on the *Georgetown.* My mother is out of Zephyr Landing."

Georgetown was one of the ships he was researching. He'd pulled its name off the wall as a destination of the survivors. It matched up with the ship they had spotted, sitting in the ocean, thousands of kilometers away.

"If *Fenrir*'s engine worked all this time, why hadn't anyone used it before now to warp back?"

She shook her head. "The engine didn't warp, it just imploded."

He opened his mouth to correct her, but caught himself. Why was she so sure? "It didn't warp?"

"No. Engines don't create a true warp field here. Power up your warp engine. See for yourself. It doesn't work."

Her calm assurance terrified him. What if she was right? What if he'd stranded his crew in this godforsaken place?

"Warp engines are designed to operate in normal space," she explained. "They open a wormhole from point A to point B in normal space. We're at point C."

"But . . ." He was going to argue that the physics should stay the same. His eye was caught though by one of the huge floating landmasses drifting in the sky. Water plumed down from it in a waterfall, defying everything he knew about gravity. And if time was running differently here, then basic laws of physics could have different constants.

Certainly it would make sense that Eraphie was right. It went against all odds that none of the ships arriving had ever returned with information on this watery graveyard. Something was keeping them all trapped. Someone, though, had made a scientific breakthrough and sent back the *Fenrir* engine.

"Was someone working on the engine when it imploded?" he asked.

She shrugged. "I don't know. We're not from Fenrir's Rock. We arrived right before the engine leveled the town."

"We?"

Pain filled her face before she looked away. "My family owns . . . owned a salvage ship. We pulled into port just hours before. We weren't even going to stay more than a few days; the salvage was in minotaur waters. My dad and mom and brothers and sisters . . ." She sobbed and pressed her palms to her eyes and sat hunched in silence.

It was like watching someone drown and being afraid to go in to save them, lest they pull you under with them. Mikhail watched her fight with her grief, wanting to comfort her but unsure if he could survive the resonant pain.

"It sneaks up on you." She was still balled against her pain. "You think you're all done with it and put it behind you and then suddenly this big black hole opens up in front of you."

"I know." It was all he could offer her without risking himself.

He distanced himself more by thinking back over what she had told him. "There were other survivors?" She nodded mutely. "Are there any others still here?"

"No." She uncurled and sighed, scrubbing tears from her cheek. "We were supposed to meet cousins here. They were coming from Georgetown Landing. We'd been at Ya-ya, selling scrap, so we had a shorter haul. After—after the blast, I wasn't thinking clearly. I just wanted to be with family so I decided to wait for them. I tried to give them a holler, but a radio was too dear to come by. They're late. They should have been here days ago. I'm starting to think they heard the news and gave us up as dead."

"Captain!" His guards had finally noticed Eraphie's presence. Trigger and Smoke had their rifles leveled at her.

"Hold your fire!" Mikhail got to his feet to make himself a more commanding figure. "Stand down."

Eraphie made another attempt to hand him the reader.

"Keep it while you decide." Mikhail needed her and so far the reader was his only successful bait.

For a moment she looked like she might fling it at him, but she controlled the impulse. With the muscles along her jaw tightening in defiance, she shoved the reader into her pocket. "I'll think about it."

She stalked off. People called Reds cats all the time, but this was the first time Mikhail had seen one walk with all the fluid grace of a lioness.

The United Colonies had claimed to be panicked by finding unregistered Reds among the wreckage that showed up at Plymouth Station. The Reds' speed, strength, durability and ease of reproduction would make them a dangerous weapon in the hands of the enemy. At Plymouth Station, it seemed a valid fear. Having talked with Eraphie Bailey, Mikhail had to question everything from the moment he met Minister of Defense Heward.

Eraphie's claim of being born to a mother made elegant sense. Male Reds weren't sterile and, while extensively adapted, they were human enough to breed with a woman. Turk's life was proof that there were even women that would welcome sexual activity with a Red. And checking through the reports, the "unregistered" Reds were simply just not numbered.

Any Red created on a production line would be numbered. Everything from taxes to inventory control to body identification on the battlefield required a number encoded into the Red's cells. That part of the automated system was tamperproof, starting a data trail for the United Colonies to track every Red ever initiated. It would be risky for the nefrim to tamper with the system just to remove the numbers.

The Reds that the United Colonies found with the engine were born in this world. Had Heward known? Perhaps.

All in all, Mikhail had a mountain of information to shift through and no real answers.

Mikhail opened the files that the United Colonies had supplied him. They had seemed thorough when they left Plymouth and were assuming that the nefrim were involved in *Fenrir*'s disappearance. But the records only went back to the first recorded encounter of the nefrim, nearly fifty years ago. If the nefrim weren't responsible for the ships disappearing, there were nearly a hundred years since the development of warp drives not accounted for.

Luckily he had full data on Eraphie's hometown, the *Georgetown*. The battleship had been lost at the beginning of the war. It had been evacuating the Tau Ceti Space Station when nearly overrun and forced to jump. With the odd time dilation of this world, there was no telling how long it had actually endured.

Mikhail searched the crew list for Eraphie's grandfather, but there were no Baileys listed. Nor were there any on the *Fenrir*. It occurred to him that Bailey might have been a civilian evacuated from Tau Ceti. Heward had included the space station data, a fact that struck Mikhail as odd until he noted that Tau Ceti had contained a crèche. Lo and behold, John Orin Bailey had been a White Star Crèche employee.

Starting in the combat training area, John Bailey had been promoted up through the ranks. He had gained experience enough to be entrusted with the younger, more fragile Reds, until he worked in the decanting room itself.

If the *Georgetown* had rescued the White Star gene banks, and Bailey had survived the crash, then the *Georgetown* could still be producing Reds.

"At ease." Acting Commander Inozemtsev's barked commands to the Reds pulled Mikhail out of his research. "At ease. Widen the perimeter."

Inozemtsev wasn't alone. He had Chief Engineer Tseytlin and Commander Kutuzov with him. By their dark looks, the three were bearing him bad news. Mikhail closed up his work with his stomach sinking.

The problem of a small ship was that information rarely could be kept secret. He'd asked Tseytlin to check Alpha Red to find out what really happened to Turk. Mikhail would have liked to have a chance to review the facts by himself. Getting Tseytlin in and out of Alpha Red required coordination with his fledging Red commander, Inozemtsev. Somewhere along the line, Mikhail's second in command, Kutuzov, became involved.

"What did you find?" Mikhail asked Tseytlin after Inozemtsev had the Reds move out of ear shot.

"They killed Commander Turk," Tseytlin said. "Killed him in cold blood."

"How?" Mikhail asked even though he really didn't want to hear the details.

"They rigged both air-lock doors to open at the same time. They started a brawl to lure him in. And then they took out the monitors so we couldn't see what was happening in the pit. They expected to space him. Since the atmosphere was thin where we warped in, the results were just as deadly. It was a cold-blooded ambush, the bastards."

"They?" Mikhail glanced to see again which Reds had been guarding him. Trigger and Smoke. Both veterans. "Not just Butcher?"

"It was all of the replacements, working together," Inozemtsev said. "A handful did nothing but participate in the staged riot, but ironically, they're the ones that drowned."

Most of this ran counter to typical Red behavior. Dominance fights were always one-on-one. Reds weren't taught how to bypass security. Nor should they have known how to booby-trap the air lock.

"Have you found out anything about their previous owner?" Mikhail asked. He'd asked Inozemtsev to confirm that the woman, Rebecca Waverly, had actually slept with some number of her pride. Until they knew which of her toms she'd introduced to sex, he'd ordered that none of the replacements be left alone with female members of the crew.

"From what I can tell, she was a crime boss on Paradise," Inozemtsev said. "She seems to have taught them a lot of nasty habits. They have dice and gamble off duty."

There was no telling, then, what the replacements were capable of. Because of their strength, speed, and intelligence, the most effective control over Reds was via their behavioral training that conditioned them to obey. Waverly might have seriously compromised her Reds' training.

"Say we eliminate Butcher." Mikhail didn't want to say "put down" like the man was just a sick animal. "Can you tell which of the Reds would make top cat?"

"In a fair fight, Coffee would be top cat," Inozemtsev said. "But I doubt if it would be a fair fight. Butcher is using his status as top cat to give the replacements first choice in everything. It's probably why they cooperated in killing Commander Turk. My guess is that the replacements would make sure Tricks replaced Butcher."

Mikhail didn't recognize the name, which meant Tricks was one of the replacements.

Kutuzov glanced at the Reds on guard and then lowered his voice to say, "We're going to have to isolate the replacements one by one and quietly put them down. There's no way we'll be able to deal with them all at once."

"We could just siphon the oxygen out of Alpha Red," Tseytlin said. "It would be fitting; that's what they planned for Commander Turk."

Cold revulsion washed through Mikhail at the idea of ordering a mass execution. Somehow the fact that it would be done quietly and secretly made it seem even worse. Mikhail lifted his hand and waved them off. "We can't afford to put down a third of our Reds."

"They killed your brother!" Tseytlin said.

"I know. I know. But the safety of this ship has to be my focus. Not vengeance for my brother. We have no idea what we will face in the following days. So far we've encountered a bio-weapon and a female Red who is most certainly not off any human ship. If there are more weapons, or if the Reds of this place are hostile, we're going to need all of our Reds. Even the replacements."

13 Red Gold

THE REDS HAD FOUND AN OBSERVATION DECK ON THE HIGHEST point of the island. From its height, the remains of the great spaceship *Fenrir* were visible under several hundred feet of crystal clear water. The island sat on the edge of a land shelf; beyond it the floor of the ocean dropped away dramatically. Only *Fenrir's* warp engine had landed on the shelf, and then sheared off as the rest of the ship sank in the deep water. The crew had platforms floating over the wreck where, apparently, they had still been salvaging parts of the ship. The gun batteries were gone. The antenna array too; but that was sitting behind him on the observation deck. The rail gun was in place, but the crew compartments were skeletal.

So ends the search for Fenrir, Mikhail thought as he gazed down at the object of his mission. What should he do next? Attempt to go back to Plymouth Station and report his findings? Not that he had any firm conclusions on what he found: a mystery place, seemingly outside normal space, not a world but something else, something that didn't obey the same rules of physics. Was that information worth Turk's life? It didn't feel like it.

So far, though, he'd found no signs of the nefrim. The *Fenrir's* crew seemed focused on a life of fishing and surviving the weather, not fighting aliens. Nor was there any indication of powerful overlords bringing human ships to this place. The ships seemed randomly placed and the humans roamed freely. The unregistered Reds were most likely born to survivors of various ships.

Nor did it seem likely he *could* get back to Plymouth Station. Moldavsky continued to find spaceships wrecked into the ocean and a goodly number still had their warp drive intact. Statistically, it was impossible that not one ship managed to send something back to normal space—unless the laws of physics were different here. Then Eraphie Bailey's claim that a standard warp engine couldn't create a true warp field in this place seemed extremely reasonable.

Whoever had sent back *Fenrir*'s engine had made modifications to it. Those changes obviously adapted the engine to the physics of this place. He'd gone over the scans of the modifications with Tseytlin, but his chief engineer couldn't even begin to guess what the odd equipment attached to the engine had done. Nor, without understanding the fundamental nature of this place, could Tseytlin start to make modifications of his own.

Their best hope for getting home was finding whoever made the changes to *Fenrir*'s engine. Between the messages written out by the survivors, Eraphie's account of the implosion, and what they've found searching the island, Mikhail believed that a group of outsiders had done the work.

Fenrir's original engine crew was all dead and buried in a small cemetery that escaped destruction. While the *Svoboba* found evidence that the island kept up maintenance on the warp engine's power unit—which they were using as their primary electrical source, there was no indication that they were working with the field generators. The island's inhabitants had been caught unaware, and afterward been unsure what had happened. And Eraphie's story indicated that it wasn't unusual for ships from different ports to arrive and do business, substantiated by the fact that the survivors fled to various ports. Nor was there any sign of scientific research into establishing a modified warp field, or clues where the experimental equipment had been created.

Then there were the two humans killed by the Red. A fight had broken out just before the warp field was activated. Obviously, someone found out what was going on and tried to stop it.

All of which told Mikhail that someone had arrived with the parts already manufactured, installed them, and activated the warp field without permission from the people of *Fenrir*. It didn't tell him, however, who. Nor did it tell him which side the mauled humans and the Red dead of vacuum had been on. Had the Red attacked the outsiders, or defended them from the men he killed?

And most importantly, it didn't tell him if any of the outsiders survived. Assuming that Eraphie Bailey wasn't lying through her teeth and she had nothing to do with modifying the engine, if the outsiders were still alive, they'd fled the island.

"Sir! We're getting company!" Moldavsky pulled Mikhail out of his contemplations. "There's a boat heading this way."

The sea vessel heading toward them was ugly and misshapen. Bits and pieces from spaceships had been cobbled together into what could generously be called a boat. The bulk of the hull was a large troop lander with a bow welded onto its blunt nose to cut through the waves.

What worried him most about the boat was what looked to be gun turrets. He highlighted sections of the boat. "Are those weapons?"

"They appear to be." Moldavsky ran them through pattern matching software. "Yes they are, sir. They're out of New Washington Spitfire fighters."

Humans then. Specifically most likely New Washington. Mikhail didn't like the idea of not knowing any more about them. Opening lines of communication, though, would require giving away information on themselves, something he'd avoided up to this point. Until they were sure that there were no unfriendlies of alien or human origin, he would like to keep it that way.

Mikhail glanced at the antenna array beside them. "This is operational, isn't it?"

"Yes. I think they left it as a navigational beacon. It's got a solar array powering it."

Like a lighthouse. Lights are on, but no one home—except a visitor from outside the world.

"See if you can tap the *Fenrir*'s transponder and query that boat. It looks like a troop lander; it might still have its transponder working." Using the *Fenrir*'s transponder would at least disguise who was at the island.

"Yes, sir." Moldavsky worked for a few minutes in silence before saying, "Captain, the troop lander is the *Red Gold*. It's off the *Dakota*."

The *Dakota* he knew; he'd asked for placement on the ship when he graduated from the Academy. Odd, that fate seemed determined to strand him in this place. Ironically, when the *Dakota* vanished shortly after his father bought him the *Svoboda* to command, he felt it was a validation that he was going the right direction with his life. He scanned the *Dakota* records, reacquainting himself with the ship. Like the *Fenrir*, it had been a massive ship with a crew of thousands of men, women, and Reds. Obviously, the United Colonies data on the spaceship had very little relevancy to the incoming boat.

"Ensign Moldavsky, keep an eye on the boat." Mikhail needed to talk to Eraphie, who might know current information on the *Red Gold*.

He used the bug they put in Eraphie's reader to locate her. She was in one of the top level rooms. She'd answered his knock with "Door's open." Mikhail tentatively opened the door, feeling like he was invading her private space. It was a small storage room lit by a skylight. Judging by the bedding and collection of foodstuff, she was living there.

Eraphie was curled on a nest of the blankets he'd given her. Reading. She'd shed off her defensive fur. At ease like this, she looked young and vulnerable. Perhaps even too young to realize how sexy she looked, lounging in the makeshift bed.

"This Mark Twain," Eraphie said without looking up. "He doesn't seem to know how to spell and he uses lots of words I'd never heard of but he's fun to read. I like his hero, Huck Finn."

Mikhail leaned against the door frame since there were no chairs, and joining her on the blankets seemed too forward. "Mark Twain wrote in a time before humans ever left Earth. It was a long time ago. Words have changed."

"People haven't. Before they had Reds, they had these—" She paused to check the word. "—niggers."

"Unfortunately, yes." Mikhail decided that it was most likely that the dead Red in *Fenrir*'s engine had been attacking not defending the people modifying the engine. He was tempted to show her a picture of the male Red, but until he knew where she stood, he wasn't sure if he should tell her anything about their mission.

Until then, there was the incoming boat.

"I need your help as native guide," he told her.

"Okay." She turned off her reader and rolled onto her back, putting the reader on her stomach. "What do you need to know?"

"Anything you can tell me about a boat called the *Red Gold*."

"The *Red Gold*? It's coming here?" Eraphie sat up, no longer at ease.

"Yes."

Eraphie bit her lip.

"What do you know about it?" Mikhail asked.

"It's a salvage ship."

"Your cousin's?"

Eraphie shook her head. "No, no, the *Red Gold* aren't Georgies. They're what's left of the *Dakota*."

He nodded. He knew that. Then stopped himself and actually analyzed what she said. "All that is left?"

"Pretty much. They landed in the open. Water isn't like air. It gets . . . heavier the deeper you get. You understand?"

Mikhail nodded. It actually was exactly like air, but he didn't see the point of detouring the conversation.

"When a spaceship lands in open water, it's too heavy to float. As it submerges, it's slowly crushed, and air seals start to rupture. Most ships don't realize their danger. Air is replaced with water, and the ship gets heavier, and it sinks deeper. Eventually all the compartments are breeched. Only some of the *Dakota*'s crew managed to get off. Then they were adrift for a long time."

Total crew of *Dakota* numbered over eight thousand. He doubted if the *Red Gold* had a crew of more than a hundred. It was a staggering loss of life. At least the commander didn't have the guilt of purposely bringing his crew to this place. The *Dakota* had been under heavy fire when it warped.

Thoughts were playing across Eraphie's face. Something about the *Red Gold*'s arrival had her upset.

"What's wrong?" Mikhail asked.

"Well, I knew salvage ships were going to show up sooner or later. I was hoping someone from Georgetown Landing would arrive. I'm not sure if I trust Hardin."

"Who?"

"John Hardin. He's the captain of the *Red Gold*." When Mikhail frowned at the name, trying to place the man among the *Dakota*'s command, Eraphie added, "He was the highest officer left alive, but I think he was only a lieutenant."

Mikhail nodded to keep her talking. He'd check the records later. "Why don't you trust him?"

She gave him a dark look. "No reason."

"I need to know if I can trust this man. He's a U.C. officer."

"He *was*." Eraphie stressed the past tense. "There's no such thing as the United Colonies here. Things have happened to him, horrible things. Don't think of him as the same man."

"Okay," he said and then cautiously pressed for an answer to his original question. "What did he do that makes you not trust him?"

She considered him for a minute with her dark eyes. "I don't like repeating things I don't know for sure are true. There are rumors. I don't know if I believe any of them, but they make me . . . cautious."

"What kind of rumors?"

She was silent for another minute before sighing. "He doesn't have any Reds. The *Dakota* was an assault ship. It had a pride of nearly three thousand. There are all sorts of stories about how he . . . lost . . . them."

Yes, it would make sense that she wouldn't trust a man who failed to protect his Reds. Who might have considered the Reds as acceptable losses, or even worthless to save.

"But like I said. I don't have any way of knowing which stories are true, so I'd rather not say."

Mikhail nodded. "Anything else I should know?"

"He won't risk coming into the harbor," Eraphie said. "That's too dangerous. He'll come around and tie up to the salvage docks and come in on a launch."

Mikhail returned back to the observation deck to do a search on John Hardin. As Eraphie said, John Hardin had only been a lieutenant on the *Dakota*. Mikhail frowned at the photo attached to Hardin's service file. The name and the face seemed familiar. Mikhail scanned Hardin's history; there were only a few places where he would cross paths with an officer from New Washington. Hardin spent a childhood in Capital slums. Worlds apart, and by more than just spatial distance. They had crossed paths, however, when Mikhail was eighteen and forced to attend the United Colonies Military Academy. Hardin had been one of the ambitious, overachieving upperclassmen that the instructors wanted Mikhail to emulate.

The ambition clearly continued onboard the *Dakota*. In the year between his graduation and the *Dakota* being lost, Hardin became highly decorated. But the man had a temper, and with every honor, there was a black mark. Despite the pressures of war to fill command positions, Hardin was still only a lieutenant.

"Sir," Moldavsky said. "The *Red Gold* has launched a small boat."

Mikhail looked up. As Eraphie predicted, the *Red Gold* had tied up to the floating salvage docks tethered over the wreck of the *Fenrir*. The boat looked like a water bug skating above the great sunken spaceship. A launch had left the *Red Gold* and was heading to the island.

"We're getting company!" Mikhail broadcast via his com. "Station rules apply—no shooting unless shot at. No inciting a fight, or I will punish the person who starts the fight. Secure the ship. Assume we've got thieves coming. Keep me posted on our guests."

There was an air-lock door set into the top of the stairs with a high lintel to keep out torrential rain. Beyond it was a ladder down into a well lit by a skylight. The metal was hot as he slid down to the landing below.

. . . and dropped down into a memory.

. . . they were still covered with blood. Mikhail had blood on his shirt and holding fast to his anger, because if he lost it, fear would crowd in. Eight-year-old Turk was furred over, wide-eyed with fear, with blood on his mouth. They were both scared for the same reason: Reds that attacked humans were put down . . .

Mikhail struggled to push the memory aside. He didn't have time for this. But it was like being trapped in a nightmare, the recall drowning him with details: the coppery smell of blood mixing with scent of leather and smoke of his father's personal study, the distant roar of the visiting dignitaries enjoying full rein of the palace, the monitor scrolling updates on the crisis he created—no—not him or Turk—but everyone else . . .

"If security had been doing its job right, this would have never happened." Mikhail clung to the hope he could shift the blame off of Turk. "He belongs to me! No one has any right to do anything to Turk without asking me first. Security should have stopped the Ambassador."

"Security had their hands full." His father ground out his cigar. "And there are more polite ways of denying someone their perversions than bashing their brains in with a hockey stick. But you know that."

Yes he did, but Turk had already bitten the Ambassador. If Mikhail hadn't attacked the diplomat and done serious damage—harm that couldn't be ignored—then Turk alone would have been blamed. The problem of being clones of the same man, he and his father thought too much alike. His father clearly saw through Mikhail's attempts to divert attention to himself. It was the same cycle of each knowing how the other thought which boiled all Mikhail's childhood down to a battle of wills. This time, though, Turk's life hung in the balance.

"I will not allow Turk to be punished. If he's harmed in any way, I'll refuse to cooperate with your succession plans." The danger of playing that card was his father could simply make another clone. Ivan was young and had time enough to raise another replacement. One that would probably be more stable.

"Yes, I know." Ivan acknowledged the truth of what Mikhail said and, perhaps, what wasn't said. "The question is how to salvage what you've left us with."

This was the start of his military career, Mikhail realized. He tended to think of his reluctant first days at the Academy as the start, but that bloody night had been the true start. But why dwell on it now?

"Mikhail?" Eraphie said close at hand, and finally the memory faded, leaving him free to see the inner harbor. Sunlight streamed down from the skylights overhead. Steam lifted where the hot sun hit the cold water, wafting into the sunlight to turn it into shafts of misty gold. Something moved through the light and darkness, catching his eye. Was it a bio-weapon like the one that attacked him earlier?

As he stared, he made out a sinuous form gliding toward him. Less than a shadow, it was merely a suggestion of a body, a distortion of light. As Mikhail watched, the creature slid closer, blurring the stones under it.

Close up, it was harder to see. Some trick of his brain eliminated the distortion when it filled his visual field. And *big* was one of the few definite things he could tell about the creature. He took a couple steps back, trying to bring it back into focus.

It took five steps so that he could once again see the outline of the distortion and get some sense of the creature's presence. He got the impression of a snake rearing up, its massive wedge-shaped head looking down at him.

"Do you see—" He started to ask Eraphie if she could see the creature too.

But the creature suddenly moved, flowing over him, through him . . .

. . . *Mikhail could hear Nanny Ingrid's soft breathing from her bed as he crept to his old crib. Since his baby brother arrived the week before, Nanny Ingrid had been napping in the afternoon. She would be asleep for a long, long time. Now was his chance to play with his new brother . . .*

"No! Not that!" Mikhail flailed out blindly. His vision snapped clear as his hand passed through the creature and hit the stone. He welcomed the pain. He wouldn't be pressed and drowned in that memory.

"It's not me!" he said out loud to fill the vacuum in his mind left by the implosion of the recall. "It's making me remember."

The creature was deliberately dragging him through his past. Nothing would have made him think of that day in such clarity; he'd locked it away for years until the U.C. psych evaluations shook it loose. And he'd buried it again, determined not to think of it. He'd been three years old. He—he—he . . .

"I won't!" To dwell on it would only taint his whole life. What had happened that day. What he had lost. What he had gained.

The creature had forced him to remember. It had slipped into his mind somehow and started a cascade of thoughts. How though? And why? Was it deliberately probing for some specific memory or was it making his neurons fire randomly? When the creature had touched him—seemed to touch him—he hadn't felt anything. No movement of air. No sense of pressure. No change in heat. Like it was a ghost made of his own memories.

"Are you okay?" Eraphie whispered from behind him.

"Can you see it?" he asked, pointing at the phantom.

"The seraphim?"

"Whatever the fuck it is!" His voice rasped and his hand was shaking.

"It's a seraphim," Eraphie whispered.

The mist swirled out in the harbor and Mikhail realized that a second creature had glided up to a piece of lumber floating in the water. The creature reared up, and this time he could see that it had forelegs resting on the flotsam. The wood didn't shift under it, as if the creature had no volume or mass.

He could detect no sound or movement between the one in the water and the one on the dock. The second, however, released the flotsam and swam away, and a moment later the first glided down into the water, following.

"What exactly are seraphim?" Mikhail asked.

"Seraphim are the first rank of angels which encircled the throne of God, existing off the love emanated by Him."

"Angels?"

"Yes, they're angels." Eraphie said it with complete conviction of someone who completely believed what she was saying. "Seraphim are described as vaguely snakelike, and you can see for yourself that these seraphim look like big snaky things."

"They could be some kind of aliens. Or even . . ." Mikhail struggled to come up with something that they could be. ". . . a bio-weapon."

"Bio-weapons try to kill you. Seraphim protect people. They saved me. They moved me out of the blast range. They save people all the time by moving them out of danger."

So while they couldn't be felt, they could interact with people more than just making neurons fire. "You didn't mention this before."

"Because you hadn't seen the seraphim. Newcomers don't believe in angels until they've seen them."

The seraphim had spent entirely too much time threatening Mikhail's sanity for him to think of them as angels. "Just because they save people, doesn't make them divine."

"The hak say that they're holy beings."

"Who the hell are the hak?"

"The hak are gods."

Mikhail comline chimed. "Captain, the launch from the *Red Gold* has landed. What should we do?"

"I'll be out to meet them." Whatever the seraphim were—and any ties they had to his painful memories—had to wait. He had to meet with Hardin.

"Can you do me a favor, Mikhail?" Eraphie trailed behind him.

"What is it?"

"Can you ask Captain Hardin to check with Ya-ya and see if my cousin's ship, the *Rosetta*, is in port?"

Mikhail really needed to get Eraphie to call him captain if she was going to be part of his crew. "If things go well, I will."

∞   ∞   ∞

The salvage dock had survived fairly intact. A row of buildings, now rubble, protected it from the implosion. It followed the
island's *L*-shaped harbor. The longer leg against the town had a
high wide awning to provide shade for workers. Mikhail wanted
a strong façade when the crew of the *Red Gold* arrived, so he
had all his Reds at ready in the dock. Hopefully Hardin would
assume that the *Svoboda* was maintaining a standard three work
shifts and that Mikhail had three times the Reds than was at hand.
Not that Mikhail expected an attack. He did, however, want to
appear too strong for the thought to cross anyone's mind.

The *Red Gold*'s launch was a sleek speedboat, obviously con-
structed on this world and not cobbled together from spaceships
that crashed into it. It was encouraging to see that somewhere
manufacturing was taking place and not everything was jury-
rigged salvage.

Hardin had four armed human guards. No Reds, just as Eraphie claimed. The launch hove up beside the dock. Hardin didn't
wait for his guards to clear the area. Instead he stepped off the
launch before the others could even disembark. The *Dakota* had
only been lost for four years, but Hardin looked older than his
last fleet picture by about twenty years. Time had ridden the man
hard—his skin turned leather by sun, his hair gray. But it was
definitely Hardin—his solid chin, thin lips, and long nose. As
he moved into the deep shadow of the walkway, he took off his
mirrored sunglasses. His steel gray gaze swept over the *Svoboda*
perched in the rubble and the Reds standing guard.

When Mikhail moved forward, though, Hardin focused on him.
He cocked his head to one side as he studied Mikhail. "Volkov?"
Hardin tapped his nose in the spot where Mikhail's had healed
crooked. "You look so damn young, Volkov, I thought maybe
they cloned Viktor again. I remember you breaking your nose,
though, and not letting them fix it."

Mikhal had been thinking that he and Hardin were virtually
strangers to each other. He'd forgotten that being Viktor's clone
gave him celebrity status even at the Academy. Hardin might
know him in great detail despite the fact that they never directly
interacted. "No, there's been no new clone."

"I would say something about Novaya Rus weeping over its
lost prodigal son, but I guess they'll just make another once they

realize you're not coming back. God forbid they let someone new take command."

Odd, how having someone else voice his opinion made Mikhail's hackles rise. "Unfortunately, we Volkovs are just too damn good at it."

"Good is the enemy of great." Hardin smiled as if trying to take the sting out of his words. His eyes stayed hard and bitter. "But that's not ours to worry about now—seeing that we're stuck here. Welcome to my paradise."

"Paradise?"

Hardin laughed at the skepticism in Mikhail's voice. "Yes, paradise. Look around you." Hardin swept his hand out to take in the endless blue water and the sky. "The Japanese call this the Cradle of Life; where God tested creation before he made the universe. Perfect air for humans. Water easily made drinkable. A sea teaming with life. Open your eyes and see the bounty! A hundred planets worth of living space all at ideal human conditions. Best of all—no nefrim. This is the salvation of man."

"Put that way, it would seem a paradise. I'd argue that the obvious problems with landing safely outweighs its benefits."

A frown flitted across Hardin's face, but he forced himself to laugh. "Yes, a few kinks to be worked out." He looked past Mikhail to study the *Svoboda*. "Christ on a donkey, Mikhail, but God does love the Volkovs, doesn't he?"

"Pardon?"

"You hit land. Do you know how rare that is? *Fenrir* here is considered a good landing, despite the fact they didn't hit land so much as sink beside it. Half their human crew dead. A mutiny within the first week killed what they had in the way of officers. But still, a safe harbor and supplies enough to make a go at it."

"All gone now."

"Yes. Shame about that." Hardin pulled his gaze away from the *Svoboda* to sweep over the rubble. "They'll be back. You err toward overly cautious here. Without fishing boats, this rock doesn't produce enough food to feed more than a dozen people. You protect the boats first, then organize supply chains to feed workers. A hard thing to do when everyone scattered to friendly ports up and down the axis."

Friendly ports? Then there were unfriendly ones too.

"Any come to the *Dakota*?"

Hardin frowned at him. "No."

"Why not?"

"That's a long sad story."

"If you hadn't noticed, I'm not going anyplace anywhere soon."

"True, true." Hardin sighed. "The *Dakota* is gone." He made a fist and then flung open his fingers, like a star going nova. "Poof. There one minute, gone the next."

Mikhail waited, giving Hardin silence to fill.

"We'd been under heavy fire off the shoulder of New Haven, providing cover for the evacuation of civilians. When the order came through to jump out, and the warp field powered up, we actually cheered because we thought we'd survived."

Hardin glanced to Mikhail. "You've been through it. That blinding blue where there should have been black. A few seconds to think you're in shallow orbit around a planet. Desperate maneuvers to pull out of a gravity well—and all you've done is make matters worse. Then you're in the water and sinking with a ship full of people who have no clue how to swim.

"Your damn Volkov luck put you down on land. We landed in deep water." Hardin moved out into the blazing sunlight. "You would never know how by looking at it, but water is dark as space when it gets deep."

Harden fell silent. The sea birds cried overhead like lost souls. After several minutes of the wind whirling fine rubble about their feet in dust devils, Mikhail asked, "You had to abandon ship?"

"We had no choice. The pressure started to crush the ship. You could hear the metal groaning. We deployed everything we could launch off of the *Dakota*. Troop landers. Fighters. Escape pods."

"How many were you able to save?"

"Less than a thousand."

Thinking of Eraphie, Mikhail asked, "None of your Reds?"

Hardin stepped close and spoke lowly. "We were adrift for a long time. Sacrifices had to be made."

Meaning he had killed all the Reds that had survived the crash.

Hardin saw the realization in his eyes. "Don't you judge me," he whispered. "You landed pretty but you used up all your luck. You don't even know how badly you're screwed."

"Trust me, I'm aware that my situation is tenuous, but that does not mean I'm helpless."

Hardin glanced at the Reds. "Yes, I can see. But a warship is stocked with only a hundred days of rations. Once it's gone, you don't have the tools to catch enough to feed your Reds. Or the knowledge. All that muscle bulk needs twice the food as a normal man, and they start to waste fast."

"Did you just sacrifice Reds, or did you have to move up to humans too?"

Hardin scowled darkly at him. "No. We were spotted by Tonijn Landing. They're a small subsistence landing. Once we were able to cobble together the *Red Gold*, we went nomadic. We move around the Sargasso without a home landing."

"The Sargasso?"

"One of this place's many names. The Sargasso Sea on Earth was known as a graveyard of ships. It seemed fitting to name this place after it."

"What do you think this place really is?" Mikhail asked. "Was it made? Or is it natural?"

"Well—it's not the afterlife. I don't believe in the afterlife. We live and then we die. All we get is the time between that first breath and last to chisel our name into stone."

"And billions of humans over thousands of years who believed in heaven have been wrong?"

"Heaven is a placebo for the poor and helpless. It deludes them into thinking that their existence has meaning that will last. That their lifelong struggle leads to something more than a puff of dust. When I was a child, you had to take your ID chip with you to the bread lines. It had your genealogy records; you used it to justify your existence to get your share of food. It had my parents, and grandparents, and so forth back ten generations. Hundreds of people reduced down to some ones and zeroes on a data chip and nothing else. Their own flesh and blood knew nothing about them beyond that. If it wasn't for a hundred pounds of meat on two feet, it would be as if they never existed."

"But there was you."

"Ha!" Hardin spread his hands to take in the world around them. "And I'm there to stand testament? Hell, no, I'm stuck in this obscure corner of nowhere. In the mysticism of immortality, the ancient Egyptians stumbled across the truth. Tutankhamun. Nefertiti. Ramses. Seti. We know their names a millennia after their language stopped being spoken. That's immortality."

"Biblical heaven implies a time longer than millennia."

"Well, I'll settle for a few hundred years."

They had wandered off the subject. Mikhail pushed to get it back on track. "Is there any proof that an alien race created this place?"

"None that humans have found. If another race knows, it hasn't told us."

It stunned Mikhail that Hardin could speak so casually of alien races. The nefrim had been humanity's first encounter with another race.

"Exactly how many alien races are there?" Mikhail asked.

Hardin actually had to count on his fingers. "There's the hak, the minotaurs, the civ, the obnao, the kites—although I'm not sure if they're intelligent per se—the barbies, the kelpie, the nixies. Ten. Maybe eleven. That we know of."

Hardin hadn't named the nefrim as one of the other races.

"No nefrims?" Mikhail asked.

"Their ships are here. No one has ever seen a live nefrim though; there's something that kills them here."

"And how many human ships?"

"How many arrived here?" Hardin shrugged. "Countless have vanished without a trace. There are a hundred human landings. The largest and oldest is Ya-ya: the *Yamoto* battle ship and the colony ship *Yamaguchi*."

"What's the total human population then?"

"Less than a million. Because *Yamaguchi* was a colony ship, Ya-ya has the means to support scientific research and a college, but most landings are hand-to-mouth."

"And you consider this paradise?"

"Ya-ya is proof that humans can prosper here given the right equipment and a large enough population pool."

"And luck at landing."

"If I could get out and gain access to the right equipment, incoming ships could have safe flight paths and a selection of landing sites." Hardin said it as if it was something he'd put a great deal of thought into. Was his arrival at *Fenrir* after the engine warped out no more coincidental than Mikhail's?

"Have you figured out how to get out?" Mikhail asked.

Hardin gave a weak laugh and shook his head. "No."

"Someone here at *Fenrir* figured it out." Mikhail waved a hand at the rubble around them.

"This isn't proof that it went back home. It could have just gone to another universe we don't know about. Or reduced down to a black hole which collapsed." Hardin paused and cocked his head. "But you should know. You jumped out of normal space after the implosion. Did it show up?"

To hesitate in answering would be the same as admitting the truth. Denying it would limit what he could ask Hardin without tipping his hand. So Mikhail nodded. "It came out of warp near Plymouth Station. No survivors. No explanation as to where it had been. No clue as to what happened to the rest of the ship and why only the engine appeared. Minister of Defense sent me to investigate."

Hardin's eyes widened in surprise. "So Command doesn't know about this pocket universe?"

"It knows that *Fenrir* is in an ocean someplace." Mikhail didn't elaborate on what else Command knew and feared.

Hardin looked out at the dazzle of sunlight on water where *Fenrir* lay.

"Do you know who was working on the engine?" Mikhail pressed for answers. "How they modified it so it could function in this place?"

"No."

It was a quick, firm denial. It could be the truth if Hardin had little to do with *Fenrir*'s people. Or he could be lying.

14 Blue Blood

THE STORM WAS NEARLY ON THEM. THE HEART OF THE STORM, according to Moldavsky, was still two hundred kilometers off, but already the winds were blasting over Fenrir's Rock. It was clearly visible to the naked eye, a black wall sliding toward them over the darkening ocean.

"You're making it challenging to come and go," Eraphie said when she appeared at his side while they were setting up perimeter security monitors around the *Svoboda*. Once again his personal guards had yet to notice her standing beside him, well within striking distance.

"Yes." Mikhail decided that he was partially at fault too. The clothes he'd given her could be easily mistaken for standard issue uniform at a distance. "Entirely too many things are coming and going unseen. Like you."

"Pft, Reds are easy to get past. Stay downwind, move silently, keep to shadows, and whoosh." She made a sliding motion with her hands. "You are super ninja."

"Super ninja?"

"Super ninja!" She repeated only this time with a thick Japanese accent in a deep bass voice and made several karate moves, complete with quiet little *ya*'s as she chopped the air. While it was only mock fighting, her moves were clean in form, indicating that she'd been trained to fight. "It's a game we played as kids. Super ninja. Hide and seek. Marco Polo. Blind man's bluff."

153

"And you always won?"

She laughed, relaxing out the fighting stance. "No, no, Reds are good, but Blues are scary."

It was the second time she mentioned Blues in a way that didn't fit what he knew—but he was by no means an expert in them. Viktor had outlawed the production of Blues in Novaya Rus shortly after he came into power. He foresaw Reds were going to form the bulk of the military force against the nefrim and were thus a necessary evil. Blues, though, were created only to fill the sexual desires of their owner. Other colonies still produced Blues, and many of the envoys that visited the palace certainly owned one or more. Knowing Novaya Rus's stance on them, the envoys always left their Blues behind. The pictures he'd seen of the women were always stunningly beautiful, as perfect in form, dress, and makeup as china dolls. Mikhail couldn't imagine any of them roughhousing with Reds and coming away the winner.

"What exactly is a Blue?" Mikhail asked.

His feral ninja kitten pressed her lips thin obviously weighing what was safe to tell him. "Ya know, when they first made Reds, they were trying to create humans to colonize the first planets that they found. Back then, they thought it would be easier to fiddle with humans instead of trying to fix an entire world."

Mikhail nodded. That was before the development of warp drives that could quickly move the human race to an uninhabitable planet and a host of terraforming tools to make said planet a paradise. The production of Reds probably would have been phased out if not for the nefrim wars.

"Well, Reds were made to be adaptable," Eraphie said. "Not just them, but their kids."

The ramifications were starting to dawn on Mikhail. Reds were never allowed to breed before. Here in this world, not only had they reproduced, with the time dilation, they'd been given generations to adapt.

"And Blues are . . . ?"

"When you cross a Red with a Blue, you get a lot more than a pretty kitty. Blues have something going on up here." She tapped her temple. "And the Red brings it out, makes it kick ass. Reds might be stronger, faster, but Blues can outthink them. Fighting a Blue is like fighting your shadow."

"Where did the Blues come from? They're not on military ships."

"Here and there. Some of the bigger civilian ship landings have a shit load of Blues. And *Georgetown* rescued a crèche off of Tau Ceti; it produced both Blues and Reds."

Mikhail hadn't thought to check if White Star Crèche had a second production line. No doubt that it did; Blues were lucrative. Sex sold well. But why had the *Georgetown* survivors decanted both and bred them together?

He had no chance to ask as his guards came alert as Hardin approached from the direction of the salvage yards.

Eraphie looked like she wanted to bolt. It was gratifying to see that she was feral for everyone, and that she'd come to trust Mikhail to some extent. "Did you ask him to . . . ?"

"Yes," Mikhail nodded in reassurance. He'd forwarded her request just before Hardin returned to the *Red Gold*. He'd also set Moldavsky on eavesdropping duty; unfortunately no one on the *Svoboda* spoke Japanese, so the result of the conversation was still unknown. He wondered if Hardin might have deliberately avoided Standard. Not knowing protocol for Ya-ya, it was difficult to tell.

Eraphie wavered, but chose to stay, hedging a little closer to him.

Mikhail saluted Hardin, who returned the salute. "Eraphie was just asking about her cousin's boat."

Hardin studied Eraphie, looking down over her slowly from head to toe. After a minute, he asked, "Eraphie Bailey?"

"That's me." She held out her hand, demanding a handshake and the respect that went with it.

Hardin shook her hand. "You a Red or a Blue?"

"Red." Eraphie raised her chin up slightly as she said it.

Hardin nodded. Nothing in his face changed, but Mikhail had the distinct impression that his interest in Eraphie waned. "Ya-ya port authority says that the *Rosetta* was towed into their harbor a short while ago. The *Rosetta* had engine problems and lost their radio too. They didn't have any more information but hazarded to guess that the *Rosetta*'s going to be in dry dock for a while. Apparently Ceri put out word that your cousins will be working under her."

Eraphie visibly relaxed. "Oh good. They're safe."

"I was actually here looking for one of your other cousins. Ethan?"

"Ethan?" Eraphie said in surprise. "Why?"

"He was finding me ships to salvage. He sent word he'd heard of something new," Hardin said.

Eraphie shook her head slowly. "He'd found our family a ship that he thought might be a seraphim ship, but he didn't say anything about a second ship. You'll have to talk to him—if you catch up with him."

Mikhail looked at her in surprise. The way she had spoken earlier, he was sure that all of her family had died.

"He survived?" Hardin beat Mikhail to the question.

"God loves idiots," Eraphie snarled. "Yes. He went to Mary's Landing."

"You didn't go with him?" Mikhail asked. Mary's Landing was one of the sites he hadn't been able to gather any information on except that it existed.

"No!" Eraphie cried. "I'd rather be dead than to go to Mary's."

"That idiot," Hardin said. "He knew I was coming. Why did he go there?"

"Because he's an idiot," Eraphie said. "You said so yourself. I don't know what he thinks he's doing; you can't outthink bigotry. I wouldn't have thought anyone in my family would ever willingly go to Mary's Landing."

"What's so horrible about Mary's?" Mikhail asked.

Eraphie combed her mane back from her eyes. "Georgetown says that anyone born and raised here has the same rights as any other human, even if they're fully adapted. *Mary* was an old luxury cruise liner; it had three Blues for every first-class passenger. They've been using their Blues like they were a crèche gene bank. They breed the Blues and sell out the children."

Mikhail swore softly. It was bad enough to use the Blues as sex toys. To make them pregnant and then steal away the babies was pure evil.

"Most people that buy a Mary's Blue marry them," Hardin murmured as if that made things better.

"Not all," Eraphie growled. "*Mary* also collected a file of genetic markers of every adapted on every ship in the Sargasso. Both Blue and Red. If someone goes into debt, *Mary* checks their DNA, and enslaves them if they have any of the markers. *Mary* claims that a debt to them overrides the rights given to a person by their own landing."

"They enslave people who were raised as free?" Mikhail asked.

Eraphie nodded empathically. "Oh, yeah! What's more, *Mary* makes up debts just so they can hold someone. No one from Georgetown will do business with them."

Hardin saw the look on Mikhail's face and said, "Oh, it's not that virtuous. Georgetown lost eighty percent of its crew the first year. They started up production on the crèche just to keep from dying off completely. They're into their third generation; there's almost no one without one grandparent who was adapted."

Mikhail was appalled that third generation could still be considered adapted. "Mary's extends ownership into grandchildren?"

"Once a Blue, always a Blue." Eraphie said it like she was quoting something. "Ethan was fucked in the head to go there. And I told him that before he left."

"You'll have to be careful, Volkov," Hardin said. "I heard a rumor once that Viktor had a good deal of patented genetic material, in addition to that reclaimed Tsar bloodline. If that's true, Mary's Landing might even lay claim to you."

While Hardin's tone was of mild concern, his eyes held laughter at Mikhail's expense.

"I'll keep that in mind," Mikhail said coldly.

Hardin seemed to realize he'd tipped his hand and the laughter faded out of his eyes. "Did Ethan have anyone with him?"

Eraphie shrugged. "There was a minotaur by the name of Caan and an adorable little obnaoian by the name of Mahoruru tagging along with him. Neither one spoke any Standard or English. I think they were with Ethan because he was the only person that could communicate with them. The shame about Caan was that a minotaur ship showed up after everyone had left."

"So, minotaurs are friendly?" Mikhail asked.

"Usually," Hardin said in a tone that suggested that the aliens could be dangerous.

"If you pick a fight with a minotaur, you're too stupid to live," Eraphie clarified.

"Did you talk to them?" Hardin asked.

"I'm not a Blue." Eraphie seemed to think this was answer enough. Hardin nodded as if it was.

"Did they head back to Midway?" Hardin asked.

"No. They seemed to head toward Mary's. Maybe Caan got hold of them and they were going to pick him up."

Hardin nodded slowly then looked away, studying the sea. "I

was shipping out soon. A storm is coming in. There's a small safe harbor a few hundred miles out."

"Not much protection here, no," Eraphie agreed.

"After that, I'm going to Ya-ya," Hardin said. "You're welcome to come with me."

Eraphie's eyes widened slightly.

"The *Svoboda* will be leaving for Ya-ya too," Mikhail countered. He didn't want Hardin taking away his native guide. Nor did Mikhail completely trust Hardin. He hadn't decided his next course of action, but his instinct said that if Ya-ya had dry docks and shipyards, then it was a better place for the *Svoboda* than this desolate island.

"I—I think that I'm staying with Mikhail." Eraphie said.

"*Mikhail*?" Hardin loaded his name with sexual innuendo.

Eraphie blushed and looked away. "It's nothing like that."

My God, this man is manipulative. Hardin's insinuation was nothing more than trying to get Eraphie to come with him to prove she wasn't sexually involved with Mikhail.

"I consider her part of my crew." Mikhail warned Hardin with a look to stop what he was doing. Was the man attempting to steal Eraphie away just because Mikhail desperately needed her help? Did Hardin resent him that much?

Hardin acknowledged Mikhail's rebuke with slight smile. "If you change your mind, Bailey, just send out a signal and I'll have a launch pick you up."

Hardin saluted and strolled off.

Eraphie was still blushing.

"You're going to have to call me captain," Mikhail said gently as he could.

She nodded. "Mik— Captain, what did Hardin mean about the patented genetic material?"

It was something Mikhail normally wouldn't talk about but she'd been open about being a Red. It seemed only fair to admit to his own genetic makeup. "There was a Russian crèche that invested in DNA mining, before it became illegal. Actually, they were why it became illegal. They started with actors and actresses, mostly as part of their Blue line. But then they branched out and tried to recreate famous political figures. Viktor Volkov was made from DNA from Peter the Great. The DNA was fragmentary, so they spliced it with what they had on hand. It's not exactly clear what all went into making Viktor."

It was the main reason they made Mikhail instead of letting Ivan have a normal born son. It was fully expected that most of the genius of Viktor would be recessive.

"What does that have to do with you?" Eraphie asked.

"I'm Viktor's clone."

"You are?"

Mikhail nodded.

"Wow," she breathed. "Yeah. I guess. It's the nose. With that broken like that, you don't look like him. But then, he killed himself before I was born; I've only seen photos of him."

Mikhail had been nodding along with her comments and felt like he'd just stepped off the end of a dock. "He killed himself?"

"Yeah. It was a huge surprise. Everyone thought he was dealing well with his wife dying, but one day . . . he shot himself."

"Tsar Viktor Pyotrvich Volkov?"

"Well . . . he wasn't a tsar here. He was a fisherman."

Mikhail opened his mouth to protest and then shut it again. Viktor had vanished with the *Queen Mary IV*. The cruise liner had been the largest one ever built, back in the day when individually owned jump drives were unheard of, even for the rich and powerful. During a summit meeting, terrorists caused the warp field to activate and the ship was lost. Lost . . . to this place. The *Queen Mary* had landed safely and Viktor survived? Wait. Mary's Landing. "*Queen Mary IV*'s Landing?"

Eraphie shook her head. "No, he left Mary's Landing and came to Georgetown Landing. We went through bad times right after we landed, and things looked bleak. Mary's Landing knew we had a crèche onboard and was going to take it by force. Viktor found out and took what was left of his security team and came to Georgetown to keep the crèche out of the hands of Mary's Landing. He planned to blow it up, but he met Marion, that was his wife, and she talked him out of it. She was yearling Blue."

"Viktor married a Blue . . . and had children?"

"Four girls . . ."

Good God, does that make me a father?

". . . and . . . um . . . twenty-two grandkids, and I'm not sure of great-grandkids. That number changes every few months."

Great-grandfather? Mikhail stared at her slack mouth for several minutes before he could find his voice again. "He killed himself?"

"My aunt said he was always a little touched. None of his kids were all that surprised. Upset, yes. Surprised, no."

He'd always believed that Viktor had been made perfect. That Ivan continued that perfection. That he was the only one flawed. Were all his suicidal tendencies part of the original package then? Did that mean Ivan hid a dark streak? "What about his children? Are they . . . are they as crazy as he was?"

Eraphie bit her lip as if the truth was bad. "Well," she finally admitted. "They're all half-Blues. And Blues are angsty by nature. It seems to come from having their empathic nature ramped up so high for the sex stuff. His grandkids, though, are all rock solid."

Children. Grandchildren. Great-grandchildren. All his life he'd been able to count blood relations with one finger. The only people he could claim as grandparents were dead for hundreds of years.

"You really are going to Ya-ya, right?" Eraphie asked.

Mikhail blinked at the change in conversation, still slightly dazed at the idea of an extended family. "We've searched the island. There's nothing more we can learn here."

"We should leave soon, then, before the storm hits. It's going to be a granddaddy."

Like me.

"We can take off at the last moment and just fly above the storm," Mikhail said.

"Ugh!" Eraphie made a face.

It would help if his native guide was a little more informative. "What?"

"If that's the plan, I'm going with Hardin."

"Flying above the storm is a bad idea?"

"Very bad."

It occurred to him that if flying was a safe option, then they would have spotted at least one plane. The total lack of aircraft should have told them that flying wasn't safe. They weren't prepared, though, for a speedy takeoff; they had people and equipment scattered all over the island.

"We have a lot of work to do if we're going to take off soon," Mikhail said. "Go get anything you want to take with you."

She flashed him a smile and took off like a gazelle.

He had Ensign Moldavsky gather weather patterns before pulling all her equipment down off the observation deck. Eavesdropping on Hardin had given them Ya-ya's position and radio frequencies the settlement used and an idea of standard protocol for reaching authorities. Ya-ya lay to the northwest several thousand kilometers. If they went straight north, before heading west, they could outrun the storm.

"All crew onboard," Lieutenant Ulanova reported.

"Is Eraphie Bailey onboard?" Mikhail had left instructions that she would be allowed to board.

"Yes, sir," Lieutenant Ulanova said.

He almost left it at that. But then he wondered where on the ship Eraphie might be. In the rush, he'd forgotten to leave orders on what part of the *Svoboda* she could have access to. With the bridge out, once Eraphie was on the ship, there wasn't any way to track her movements. "Who escorted her onboard?"

"I did," Inozemtsev said as Ulanova read off his name.

Mikhail turned to his Red commander. "Where did you put Eraphie Bailey?"

"In Red pit, sir," Inozemtsev said.

"What? Why?"

Inozemtsev looked as confused as Mikhail felt. "She's a Red, sir."

"You bigoted idiot!" Mikhail snapped before catching himself. He was fraying at the edges if he was losing control of his temper. "No, she wasn't to be put in with the rest of the pride."

He started for the Red pits with Inozemtsev trailing behind him. Hopefully Eraphie wouldn't take offense for the temporary placement. He would need to find a place for her and make her position clear with the crew. He should have thought of this beforehand. The enlisted were hot bunking, and convincing them to share their bed with "one of them" might be difficult. There were officer cabins empty, their owners dead in the crash. Putting her into one of them could cause resentment, but if he shuffled the people he'd made acting officers into those cabins, it might come off as a sign that their position was permanent. As in the *Svoboda* was stuck in this place. Which was the lesser of evils?

The word *evil* made him think of the replacements' previous owner.

She had sex with her Reds while they were restrained.

"Oh fuck!" Mikhail spun and caught hold of Inozemtsev's shoulder. "You put Bailey in with the veterans didn't you?"

"No. That was full. I put her with the replacements."

"You fucking idiot!" Mikhail snapped and took off running for the Red pits. Oh, God, let the stupid things not decide that proper behavior with a Red was tying it up and forcing it to have sex. Bailey might be a Red and trained in combat, but she was locked in with a dozen males, all taller and more muscled than she was. Butcher had used his pride to kill Turk. Butcher organizing a gang rape was all too possible.

Mikhail dropped down to the last deck to the Red pits. Eraphie's screams were audible even through the thick steel. Swearing, Mikhail punched in his override.

They had torn her clothes off and used strips of cloth to tie her arms behind her back. Butcher was trying to enter her, but even tied and pinned on her stomach, Eraphie was fighting.

"Stand down!" Mikhail shouted. "Stop it now!"

"Get him off me!" Eraphie screamed. "I told you! I wouldn't be part of a pride and no sex!"

"Butcher, stand down now!" Mikhail shouted. He knew better than trying to grapple with a Red.

"I'm top cat and she's a Red," Butcher snarled. "Humans have no say on dominance fights. She's going to do what I tell her to do if I have to beat it into her."

Mikhail pulled his side arm, placed it at Butcher's head, and pulled the trigger. The gun kicked in his hand, the explosion deafening in the enclosed space. Blood and bits of brain splattered the wall and rained down on Eraphie. Butcher slumped down on top on of Eraphie. Whimpering, she squirmed out from under Butcher's body and rolled onto the floor. There she scrambled back into the corner.

"What did you do?" Eraphie echoed the cry of his childhood. "Are you insane?"

Possibly. At least she didn't call him a monster, even if that was what she probably was thinking.

Mikhail turned and all the Reds backed away from him. "Listen very closely. First off, I am the captain, and you will obey all my orders. There is no part of this ship that is not mine to command.

"Secondly, we will be encountering other female Reds. Regardless of what your last owner said or did, what Butcher was attempting will not be tolerated. You will not treat females—part of this crew or civilian—human or adapted—in this manner.

"Lastly, I know what Butcher did to Commander Turk. I know he made the air locks open after we jumped. I know he killed Commander Turk, and caused the flooding that drowned the Reds in this compartment. Any Red that harms another member of the crew—and that includes the Reds—or attempts to force himself onto a female, will be punished."

He stood panting, gun aimed very carefully at the floor. They could tear him apart before he could get another shot off. The only reason he was in control was years of deep conditioning. And it seemed to be holding. He keyed open the door.

"Eraphie, get out. Go," he said as calmly as he could. Her reader was on the floor among the tattered remains of the clothing he'd given her. He snatched it up without taking his eyes off the Reds, then stepped out of the pit and locked the door behind him.

He'd killed one of his own crew. He stared down at the sidearm in his hand. He'd put it to an unarmed man's head, one of his own, and pulled the trigger. Tiny drops of blood splattered his hand past his wrist. He was nearly overwhelmed with the need to wash the blood off. Out, out, damned spot.

Eraphie was braced against the wall, as far away as she could get from him in the short hallway, glaring at him through her long hair.

He put his sidearm into its holster before even trying to approach her. "I'm sorry." He held out his hands to show he wasn't armed. "I'm sorry. I—I made a mistake. I forgot to make sure that you were taken care of in the right way. I'm very sorry. Are you hurt?"

She shook her head.

"Let me untie you." He held out his hand and then realized it was covered with Butcher's blood.

She flinched but shifted slightly so he could reach her makeshift restraints. He tucked her reader under his arm as he worked at the knots. She trembled as he untied her.

"I'll get you some new clothes," he promised in what he hoped was a soothing voice. *I killed one of my crew.* He held out her reader once she was free. "Here, you dropped this."

The statement was so normal sounding compared to the circumstances that it seemed a ridiculous thing to say.

She was slow to take it back, but she did.

∞   ∞   ∞

Mikhail put Eraphie in Furtsev's cabin for the time being. He gave Lieutenant Ulanova orders to find another set of clothes for Eraphie and make sure she knew how to operate the toilet and shower. Eraphie temporarily settled, Mikhail went to deal with cleaning the mess he made in Alpha Red. Sometime later, Lieutenant Ulanova caught up with him with a stack of clothes under under her arm.

"Sir." Lieutenant Ulanova held up the clothes as evidence. "I've been looking for Eraphie Bailey to do what you ordered. I can't find her."

"I put her in Furtsev's cabin for now. I need to find a place for her." Mikhail stressed that the situation wasn't permanent.

"I looked there. I also checked the other empty cabins, the galley, the sick bay, and the Red pits. I don't think she's on the ship."

After the attempted gang rape and Mikhail shooting Butcher, he wouldn't be surprised if she had left. Nobody should have been able to get off the ship unnoticed, but she'd shown herself quite practiced at coming and going.

Mikhail put a call through to engineering. "Tseytlin, can you check the tracking device we put in that reader? Is the reader still on the ship?" If it was, it still might not mean anything because Eraphie might have left it behind.

After a minute, Tseytlin said, "No, sir, it's not the ship. Not on the island either, sir. It's about a hundred kilometers out."

Mikhail turned to Moldavsky. "Did the *Red Gold* leave?"

"Yes, sir, it pulled out a few hours ago."

He'd scared Eraphie badly enough that she ran to the man she didn't trust.

"You want me to . . . ?" Tseytlin didn't finish; he obviously couldn't think of what a proper response would be.

Mikhail sighed. "No. Thank you, Tseytlin, that's all."

Inozemtsev had "I've done something wrong" written all over his face. He studied the floor instead of looking Mikhail in the eye.

"What is it, Ensign?" Mikhail asked, aware that the last time he spoke with the man, he'd called him a "fucking idiot." Hopefully the man wasn't going to live up to that title.

"Sir, I've triple-checked. There's Reds missing."

"Missing? How many?"

"Over half of them."

"Half!" Mikhail headed for the Red pit, aware that once again Inozemtsev trailed behind him. *Fucking idiot* had been dead on. How did you lose that many Reds? "How long have they been gone?"

"I'm not sure, sir. I haven't checked on them since after we removed the Red you killed."

"Did you do a head count then?"

"Yes, twenty-nine Reds. Twenty in Beta and nine in Alpha."

"All the ones in Alpha are gone?"

"Yes. All the replacements. And ten of our veterans are missing from Beta Red."

The replacements he could see fleeing for some reasons, but the two groups weren't getting along, and the top cat was dead.

"Where did the remaining veterans say the missing Reds have gone?"

"I didn't think to ask them."

Fucking bigoted idiot!

They reached the bottom deck and he keyed open the Alpha Red. It still smelled of blood. There were no Reds inside. He had locked the door after they took Butcher's body out—hadn't he? He turned and opened the other pit.

Beta pit was nearly empty with the remaining Reds huddled together, looking scared.

"Where did they go?" Mikhail asked.

They shook their heads.

"Just one moment they were here," Smoke said. "And then they'd be gone."

"Something took them," Coffee said. "But we didn't see what it was."

"We couldn't see it," Rabbit clarified. "It was that thing we couldn't see on the hull."

Seraphim took his Reds? Eraphie had said that angels "rescued" people. Had they seen the Reds as in danger and needing rescued? She'd implied that people were only shifted short distances by the seraphim when they were "saved."

"Gear up, we're going to see if we can find them."

They couldn't find the Reds anywhere on the island. It had started to rain in sheets of gray. Waves were growing taller, crashing over the breakwater. Mikhail stared out over the seething ocean, feeling sick. None of his Reds could swim.

"Let's go back to the ship," Mikhail said.

"Captain?" Rabbit whispered. "Do we really have to go back to the pit? It might come back."

Mikhail patted the yearling on the shoulder. "We're leaving here. There's nothing here on this island for us."

15 Promises to Keep

TURK WOKE WITH CAPTAIN BAILEY RUBBING HER TOES AGAINST his stomach.

He and Captain Bailey had pulled duty on the *Rosetta* while the rest of the crew had shore leave. They'd spent the day gutting the crew cabins which had been damaged by a drop nut. Afterward, they created a temporary common sleeping area on the top deck, complete with privacy barriers. Too tired to cook, they'd splurged on dinner off a passing boat, a mobile restaurant, billowing out fragment smoke and calling out its wares in singsong Japanese. Roast duck. Corn on the cob. Hot fruit pastries. And something that had a kick like vodka that she called Burn. Tired and full, they'd sprawled out in the new sleeping area to rest.

Turk opened his eyes and gazed up Captain Bailey's bare legs. She lay on her back studying a reader. Almost as if she didn't realize what she was doing, she flexed her foot and caressed her toes across his abdomen.

He leaned up and rasped his tongue across her instep.

"Hey," she laughed.

Smiling, he followed her foot as she tried to move away from his mouth. He ran his tongue up the back of her calf to the hollow behind her knee. She tasted clean, warm, and oh so female.

"Hey!" Her laugh deepened to a throaty groan. She reached down without looking and caught him by his collar. "Stop that."

167

She gave a slight tug to pull him away from her knee. He crawled up her, the smooth skin of her inner thighs caressing his sides as he did. Her shirt rode up, showing off the sensual dip of her belly button at the center of her flat stomach and the swell of her breasts. He wanted to lick the beads of sweat from her skin.

She had tilted her reader, though, to eye him. "What are you doing?" she asked as if it wasn't obvious.

So he continued upward until she was totally under him. In this position, she felt smaller than before. Was this really the same woman that had dragged him out of the civ hive? Even the kinkiest of cat fanciers would be afraid of being under him, helpless, but she continued to gaze up at him as if she trusted him completely.

He found that he didn't want to betray that trust. "I think I'm trying to seduce you."

"Just think? You don't know if that's what you're doing?"

His groin kissed into her softness, and her eyes dilated with anticipation.

"I know what I am trying to do, but I don't know if I'm succeeding. Seduction usually requires a positive response to work."

She lowered her book completely to study him. "Usually."

Her eyes may have been wantonly soft, but her voice was carefully neutral. Not what one would call "positive."

"Believe it or not, I'm not totally sure of what I'm doing. I usually have to beat women off with a stick."

She laughed. "Oh, I believe it." She let go of his collar and slid her hand up to rest on his cheek. "You probably just need to look at a woman and she melts."

"Are you mocking me?"

"No. I'm making an observation." She turned her attention back to her reader. "You have beautiful eyes."

He wasn't sure what to do next. She hadn't pushed him off her, or told him to stop, but she was paying more attention to her reader than to him. "What are you reading?"

"I had Manny buy some children's books."

So he was less interesting to her than children's books? He shifted off her body. Why had he started this? As he wondered, Paige stretched out her foot and wriggled her toes against his thigh. Oh yes, he acted in response to her touch.

She didn't move her foot, and the tips of her toes remained a hairsbreadth from his leg. It made him aware that a moment before, they had been casually intimate, like old lovers. The loss of that closeness ached inside, and slowly turned to anger. Was she just playing with him?

"Why are you reading those books?" he growled lowly.

"They're in Russian. I thought if you ended up stuck with us, you should have someone that could speak your language."

The low burn of anger vanished. Some strange emotion he couldn't identity but suspected was love flooded through him. He leaned forward and kissed her. She made a small, startled noise that ended with low moan. The sound of it made him move over her, bringing their bodies back together.

Several minutes later, she tried to push him away, murmuring, "I shouldn't be doing this."

He resisted, nuzzling into her neck, delighting that her breath shook when he touched her. "You want it."

"Yes, I want it." She gasped as he slid down to lick the sweat from her stomach. "But you haven't said you're staying."

He kissed down her body, pulling loose the drawstring on her pants and nudging the band down so he could bury his nose into the three inches of white fabric that had tempted him so on that first day. The heady smell of her excitement flooded his senses. He wanted her under him, in proper missionary style, watching her face as he pushed himself into her, but he restrained himself. It would come to that. It would be better to savor the experience.

"I can't do a one-night stand." She whispered, but lifted her hips so he could slide off her pants. He nuzzled her soft mound, and then, hooking the fabric of her underwear with his thumb, he slid them aside.

"Turk," she murmured his name but he couldn't tell if it was in faint protest or desire.

"I'm staying," he promised.

When he put his mouth on her sex, her breath caught and came out a soft moan. "Oh, yes," she hissed. "That's so good." And after that, she only whimpered softly in delight.

When Paige released, it wasn't with the cat fancier's rake of his shoulders, inflicting pain even as they took pleasure. Her hands stayed gentle on the back of his head, pressing him into her. He couldn't restrain himself anymore. He surged up her body. Paige reached for him, drawing him eagerly into her and then locked her arms and legs around him. He was too close to make it last as long as he wanted. He was keenly aware of her slight body under him. He gazed into her eyes, watching the echoes of her pleasure play across her face.

Afterward, he lay nestled into her, still conjoined to her. Her eyes dreamy with drink and sex, her breath deepening toward sleep. When her eyes finally closed, he felt sorrow seeping in. He didn't want to lose this closeness, this first taste of mutual pleasure. He was afraid that when she woke up, she'd remember he wasn't a man. Or worse, she was simply a tamer variety of cat fancier.

16 Parting Is Such Sweet Sorrow

FOG SHROUDED YAMOTO-YAMAGUCHI IN THICK GRAY, REMINDING Mikhail of early dawn, as the harbor tugboats maneuvered the *Svoboda* through the waterways of the sprawling settlement. Visibility was only a few hundred feet. The two great spaceships were suggestions of mountains within the clouds, all detail lost to the mist. The sea had been rough out beyond the massive seawall behind them, and they'd hovered, waiting to be guided into the harbor. Here, though, the water lay nearly still with a faint sheen, looking like mercury between the high dock walls. Boats of every shape and size moved around them, ignoring their passage to the point that they nearly collided. The largest number were bargelike crafts, riding so low they seemed as if they were about to sink at any moment. As if to support this impression, a constant stream of bilgewater poured out of a pipe on their sides. The rest, though, were as small and rough as a rowed gondola to needlelike powerboats to large freighters. Massive cranes made from steel girders lined the shores, like great insects, loading and unloading the ships.

Gray and grungy as the harbor and boats appeared, Mikhail found it all comforting after the desolate ruin of Fenrir's Rock and the endless sea. This was life. These people were thriving in this place. The *Svoboda* wasn't alone in this strange place.

The tugboat slowed, churning up water to check the *Svoboda*'s forward momentum. Keeping its nose to the *Svoboda*'s side, the tugboat swung around and slowly nudged the spaceship up against the dock. The tugboat's crew had set up lines to tie the *Svoboda* off at pilings and now moved as a team to secure the *Svoboda* into place.

Kutuzov was ashore first and was met by a wizened old man the size of a child.

"*Konichiwa!*" the man called and bowed to Kutuzov.

"We don't speak Japanese," Kutuzov was saying in Standard as Mikhail joined them on the dock. "Does anyone speak Standard?"

The old man displayed his thumb and forefinger close together and then squinted through it. "Rittle Standard." He had to say it twice before they understood that he was saying, "Little Standard."

"We stay here." Kutuzov pointed at the dock space. That was greeted with a blank look. "Here. Ship. Here."

The old man rubbed his together. "A hundred yen."

Kutuzov waved off the price. "Fifty yen."

"*Iie! Iie!*" the old man yelped. Mikhail thought he was upset until he added, "Ninety yen!"

The two haggled for a few minutes, hampered by the fact that the old man only knew a handful of words. While Mikhail wondered where Kutuzov planned to get the yen, he was nevertheless impressed that his second in command was doing as well as he was. Once they agreed on price, Kutuzov produced a toy hoverjet with remote. A toy meant for his son. Kutuzov showed off how the hoverjet worked to the old man's great interest. With a little difficulty, Kutuzov managed to convey that he wanted to sell it, not trade it directly for docking fee. The reason became quickly clear, as he set an initial price at two hundred yen. They haggled over the price of it, finally settling on a hundred sixty yen for the toy, seventy-five of which would go toward the docking fee. The old man hobbled away with his hard-won toy.

"Good job," Mikhail said after the negotiation was done, relieved he didn't have to do it himself. Since shooting Butcher and his Reds being taken, he'd felt fragile, as if the next blow would break him. "You didn't have to use a personal item though."

Kutuzov shrugged, jingling his hard-earned coins in his hand. "I'll buy another when we get home. Now what, Captain?"

His crew's trust in him was intimidating. "We find someone that can speak Standard and Japanese fluently. Can you see if the old man can point us in a direction where we might find someone?"

"Yes, Captain." Kutuzov laughed and jogged after the old man, saying, "Once more into the breach my friends!"

Mikhail smiled and turned his focus back on the city around him. Eraphie had implied that this was the hub of manufacturing and ship repair. They should be able to get the *Svoboda* repaired here, although it might mean gutting the *Tigertail* for parts. That step would only make sense, though, if the people that adapted *Fenrir*'s engine survived the implosion. Otherwise their resources would be best spent finding a place in this world.

The mist shifted and he realized that something was moving toward him. He only had a moment to recognize the seraphim before it wrapped around him . . .

. . . *Mikhail could hear Nyanya Ingrid's soft breathing from her bed as he crept to his old crib. Since his baby brother arrived the week before, Nanny had been napping in the afternoon. She would be asleep for a long, long time. Now was his chance to play with his new brother. His father had told him that baby Viktor was his little brother, made so Mikhail wouldn't have to grow up alone, like his father had. And baby Viktor was a clone, just like him, so they'd grow up exactly the same, which meant baby Viktor wouldn't get bored playing chess like Nyanya Ingrid did. Yet no matter how many times he asked, Nyanya Ingrid wouldn't let him even hold his baby brother. He had long ago figured out how to turn off all the safety alarms on his old crib and escape out. This time he would just escape in. He tapped in Nyanya Ingrid's code to turn off the alarm, pushed his chessboard and chess pieces through the bars, along with a bag of yum-yum beans . . .*

Mikhail recoiled in horror. No. Not this memory. But he couldn't drag himself free.

. . . *Mikhail wasn't sure why his father thought Viktor would be fun for him. Viktor seemed to do nothing more than squirm on his back, waving his hands and feet. It was interesting how tiny his fingers and toes were, but he ignored all the chess pieces that Mikhail tried giving him. Perhaps he'd like yum-yum beans. Mikhail carefully shared the candy out. One for him. One for baby Viktor. He couldn't get Viktor to pick the candy up, so he put the candy into Viktor's toothless mouth. Viktor made gurgling noises and waved his tiny hands and kicked his little feet. Mikhail took a second for*

himself and put another into Viktor's mouth. Mikhail was chewing
on his third piece of candy when he realized something was wrong.
Viktor had gone dark blue in his face and his hands and feet were
no longer moving. Mikhail stared in horror at the limp baby. He'd
broken his little brother somehow . . .

No. No. No.

It'd been his own crying that woke Nyanya. She came running
in and jerked Mikhail out of the crib.

"What did you do, you evil little monster?" She dumped him
onto the floor, snatched up Viktor, and started to scream. It was
a primal wail of terror and distress. Terrified by her screams, he
fled her. Under his bed was safety, his big-boy bed shielding him
from justice.

He was a monster. They always kill monsters.

"What did you do?" Nyanya wailed again. "You've killed him,
you monster!"

The door flung open and his father's voice demanded, "What's
wrong?"

"Misha killed the baby!" And she held out the proof: his brother's
limp body.

"Oh, no, no." His father cried in a tone so hurt and broken that
it tore Mikhail's heart. His father took his brother from Nyanya, his
body bowing as if receiving a massive weight instead of the slight
body. "Oh please, God, no . . ."

"Stop it!" Mikhail shouted. "Stop!"

"Captain?" Rabbit's voice finally broke the hold that the alien
creature had on Mikhail's mind. But the damage was done. Mikhail
felt like a hole had been torn through him. He grieved now as
if his infant brother was freshly dead. That he'd been three years
old at the time was no solace. He understood all the ramifications
so much more clearly now. Viktor's existence had been erased to
protect Mikhail. The official statement about Viktor's birth had
been delayed to coincide with the Empire's anniversary, so no
notice of death needed to be made. No funeral was held. No
official gravesite. Even now Mikhail did not know what they did
with the tiny body. Gone as if he never lived, and Mikhail was
responsible. He'd utterly destroyed his baby brother.

Irony was that Viktor's death triggered Turk's adoption—the
one good thing in all of his life. Ivan had stood firm on the idea
that Mikhail should have a brother but would not approve the

creation of another Volkov clone. Bad enough to murder Viktor and let his death go unpunished. Unacknowledged. It would have been far, far worse to pretend that another person could utterly replace him. But a Red? A Red would have been easy to dispose of. A Red could have been replaced. But Mikhail had been oh so careful with his little brother from then on.

Careful until he brought him to this world of death on a mission he'd known was suicide.

"Captain, is something wrong?" Rabbit asked.

Mikhail shook his head and struggled to appear solid and unshakable. "Everything is fine." But it wasn't. Mikhail had stranded his crew in this watery graveyard of spaceships. Turk was dead. He'd utterly destroyed both his little brothers. And some alien creature was forcing him to remember it in exacting detail. What was next? Eraphie's rape? Butcher's death? Eraphie had said that the aliens were angels. Was this some divine justice to punish him for all his misdeeds?

He couldn't take that. His crew was safe here in Yamoto-Yamaguchi. Safe as he could ever make them. They didn't need him protecting them anymore. God knows, if the seraphim succeeded in driving him insane, his crew would probably be better off without him.

Turk had no warning of the attack. He'd spent hours working with Paige and Orin learning carpentry as they rebuilt the ruined crew quarters. He was tired, thirsty, sore, and looking forward to what the *Rosetta*'s crew called a shower.

Turk wasn't expecting the ambush at all. One minute he was alone on the top deck, tasting his first attempt at lemonade, and the next he was looking at Hillary wearing a skintight yellow dress that covered far too little. She spun in a circle in front of him, ending with her back to him, showing off the fact that the hem of the dress barely covered her panties. "Well?" She looked over her shoulder at him. "I have to go buy supplies. What do you think? Is this good?"

"No!" he snapped once he got done choking on his lemonade.

"What's wrong with it?" She turned around to face him. "Is the color wrong for me?"

It was a perfect color for her. It was young and flirty and far too little of it. True, the women on Paradise wore much less, but they were in private enclaves with high security to protect them from the dregs of society. Here at Ya-ya, they were shoulder to shoulder with the seedier crowd. Paige had moved the *Rosetta* to a cheaper berth, and their neighbors showed it.

"Go change," he growled at the teenager.

"Why?"

"Because it gives men the wrong idea."

"No, I think that's exactly the idea I want them to get."

"This is not the place for something like that. Go change."

She shook a finger at him. "You are not the boss of me."

Luckily Paige was Hillary's boss, and appeared behind Hillary.

"Look at what Hillary's wearing." Turk wished he didn't sound like a five-year-old.

"I know." Paige held out a hand, forestalling him from saying more. "I know. I know."

"You're going let her leave like that?" he asked.

"I can take care of myself," Hillary said as Paige said, "She can take care of herself."

Obviously they were both naïve and delusional. He had no choice; it was clear what he had to do. "I'm going with her."

Paige laughed and kissed him. For a moment, with her soft and warm in his arms, he almost changed his mind. With the Baileys, though, there always seemed an unspoken element to any interaction. Paige hadn't told him not to go and the kiss may have even been a reward for accompanying Hillary.

"It's going to be hard for me to pick up boys if you're along," Hillary complained as they worked through the maze of anchored and moving boats in Ya-ya's busy harbor.

He laughed but didn't add that was the point of him accompanying her. "A man likes to hunt, not be hunted."

"Oh, is that why Paige and you took so long, *Oni-chan*?"

It still amazed him that none of the *Rosetta*'s crew seemed upset that Paige was sleeping with a Red. He wondered if Paige threatened them with bodily harm to keep them all complacent. While they neither flaunted nor hid their relationship, he wasn't comfortable in talking about it. Discussing it meant defining it and he didn't want his nose pushed into any ugly truths.

"What does *oni-chan* mean?" he asked instead.

"Big brother." Hillary gave him an impish grin. Did she know how unsettled she was making him? "Do you want to know what the word for 'little sister' is?"

"No." That was a dangerous game to play. "I'm not your big brother."

"You will be if you marry Paige." She gave him another grin and sang, "*Oni-chan.*"

Either Hillary had forgotten that he was a Red or she was even more naïve than he thought. Reds didn't get married. And how did Paige think her little sister could go off alone? Or was Paige just as naïve as her sister? That had to be it; else Paige would never let Hillary off the ship wearing such a skimpy outfit.

"I can take care of myself, *Oni-chan,*" Hillary said. "I don't need a big, sweaty brother glowering over my shoulder, chasing everyone away with his evil looks and manly smell."

He gave her a dark look in an attempt to quiet her. "I'm missing what you think passes as a shower to come with you."

"You don't like our shower?"

"No." The *Rosetta* lacked abundant fresh water, the means to heat it beyond tepid, and anything you could call "pressure." Showering was like being repeatedly spit on.

"We could go to the bathhouse!" She veered the boat wildly to head off in a new direction.

"Bathhouse?" The idea of a good shower was appealing, but somehow he didn't think this was a good idea.

"Ya-ya has public bathing facilities."

"Really?" There had to be a catch. "What are they like?"

"You pay a fee to get in and can stay as long as you want."

"Why would you want to stay?"

"It feels good to soak in a hot tub. Relax. Talk." She smirked at him. "Wash each other's backs."

"They're . . ." He didn't know the word in English. "How you say it? Both sexes?"

"Co-ed. Yes!"

"*Nyet!*" Good God, Paige would shoot him!

Hillary laughed at his discomfort.

Turk turned his back to her, looked across the harbor and forgot how to breathe.

The *Svoboda* sat tied off at a dock. The *Svoboda* hadn't sunk.

He stared dumbfounded at it until he realized that Hillary was going to go past the ship without stopping.

He bolted up. "Stop!"

"Turk!" Hillary cried as the boat rocked wildly under him.

"That's my ship!" He scrambled to the back of the boat and took control of the rudder.

Hillary followed his gaze and went wide-eyed.

The bridge had been sheared off by its collision with the floating island. Mikhail would have been on the bridge. Had Mikhail survived?

There were Reds on guard. The nearest was Rabbit, who recognized him with a stunned look. "Commander Turk? You're alive?"

"Yes, I am." Turk scrambled up onto the dock beside the little tom.

The yearling surprised him by hugging him. "I'm so glad! I'm so glad!"

"What about Captain Volkov?"

"He'll be glad too!" Rabbit misunderstood the question. "I've been worried about him. I know you would want me to keep him safe, so I've been watching him. It's like he's growing smaller and smaller, growing inward. When he went off shift, he said goodbye to me. Like he was leaving."

Oh, that idiot. Of course, Mikhail would have fought to stay together until his crew was safe. Coming to Ya-ya, with all the obvious signs of civilization, would have been "safety." It would release Mikhail from his sense of responsibility. Turk nearly bolted to the *Svoboda* but then realized that he'd be leaving Hillary alone. In that dress.

"Rabbit. This is Hillary. Go with her. Keep her safe. Hillary, this is Rabbit. You can trust him. He's a good man."

His responsibilities to the *Rosetta* covered, he hurried to the *Svoboda* to save Mikhail from himself.

Mikhail turned the gun in his hand, feeling the cool metal warm with his touch. Guns were always so messy and uncertain. There was a slim chance he could survive—well—at least back home, on a safe and sane world he might. The noise would bring people, and medical crews would be summoned, and parts of him might be salvaged—enough most likely for a clone to be made. He laughed tiredly. Perhaps it was just as well he was someplace where that was impossible—he would hate to think of leaving a helpless part of him behind, forced to go through his hell, this time alone. There would be no Turk.

So, was it to be the gun or something less dramatic? The door chimed. He reached over and snapped on the Do Not Disturb sign.

There was a slow scratch at the door, a Red running its claws down the panel the same way Turk used to when he locked Turk out of his room.

Mikhail hit the door pad. "What?"

"Misha, let me in."

Interesting. He never had audio hallucinations without being a great deal more medicated. He went cautiously to the door and keyed it open.

Turk filled the doorway, smelling of the sea.

Mikhail blinked at him, fighting the sense of relief that wanted to flood through him. Turk couldn't be here. Mikhail must have taken some drugs without remembering it. This had to be some kind of mental trick, the part of his brain that didn't want to die. The hallucination gave an exasperated sigh, took the gun away from Mikhail, and pushed into the cabin to close the door behind him.

"Turk?" Mikhail gripped his brother's shoulder to reassure himself that he wasn't imagining him. He felt the solid muscle and hard bone.

Turk stunned him by pulling him into a hug that threatened to break bones. "Oh, you stupid little brat," Turk growled into his shoulder. "When am I going to be able to go off and not have to worry about you imploding?"

One sentence, and the floodgates on everything Mikhail had been fighting with, from the darkest pain to giddy relief, burst. Tears like fire washed into his eyes, and he clung to Turk, sobbing.

"Misha. Misha, please stop crying." Turk rubbed his chin along Mikhail's, an old habit of seeking reassurance. "We're both safe and sound. I'm tired. And dirty. And . . . I haven't had a decent shower for weeks."

Mikhail scrubbed at the burning tears. "I should have known that you're too tough for a couple-kilometer drop to kill you. You can use my shower. But talk to me."

"Misha."

"I was counting bullets, Turk. I need to hear your voice."

"Fine, fine, fine," Turk groaned and put the pistol back into Mikhail's safe and locked it shut again. He gazed at the cartoon of himself that Mikhail had drawn over the safe. "Oh, Misha . . . I'll leave the door open."

Mikhail sat with his eyes closed, listening to the comforting deep rumble of Turk's voice as he briefly recounted how he fell from the *Svoboda* and was captured by aliens. Apparently one of the first things that the aliens did was strip him of his combat suit, thus the reason it was broadcasting no life signs. Thankfully, he'd been rescued by Eraphie's cousins who had been trying to get to Fenrir's Rock, but needed to turn back because of engine trouble. It was ironic that Hardin had told Mikhail days ago that the *Rosetta* had reached Ya-ya safely. All this time, there were links between them; Mikhail could have found Turk if he'd pursued the right information.

"I found out some information concerning *Fenrir*," Turk said. "But I thought you were gone. I didn't see the point of finishing the mission."

The dryer snapped on, and Turk used its roar as an excuse to fall quiet.

"We found its crash site." Mikhail broke the silence.

"Fenrir's Rock?" Turk turned off the dryer and came out of the bathroom in Mikhail's bathrobe.

"Yes." Mikhail told him about the crash, using the EM waves to find *Fenrir*, and investigating the ruins. "It's just a gut feeling, but I'm sure that the work had been done by outsiders."

"Your gut is rarely wrong." Turk paced the room. Where Mikhail liked to keep still while he was thinking—lest his body distract him from an important thought—Turk thought through motion. "We've been repairing the *Rosetta* and looking for new engines for it. It takes us down to the salvage yards. They spray-paint a complex numbering system onto the parts as they're salvaged off wrecks. The marks on *Fenrir*'s engine were from the salvage yards here in Ya-ya."

"Whoever bought the salvaged parts are probably also the people that used them to modify *Fenrir*'s engine."

"Most likely," Turk said.

"I don't suppose that the people running the salvage yard speak Standard."

"I don't know. Paige only talked to them in Japanese."

"Do you think she'll act as a translator for us?"

Turk nodded. "Financially, though, the Baileys are in a tight spot. I want to help them. They've been nothing but good to me. They have treated me like I'm family."

"Certainly." Mikhail sighed. Turk had been avoiding asking about the ship, probably trying not to dwell on the things that had depressed Mikhail. "Turk, I—I lost most of our Reds."

Turk studied him for a minute, before tentatively asking, "How many?"

"I have a dozen left. All veterans." Mikhail named them. "I don't know what happened. The last night on Fenrir's Rock, something just . . . took them right out of the Red pits. We searched for hours. Didn't find any trace of them."

"What did surveillance show?"

"Cameras have them there one minute, gone the next. And I shot Butcher."

"What?"

"He was raping Eraphie Bailey. He wouldn't stop. So, I put my gun to his head and pulled the trigger. I killed them. I killed them all. Furtsev. The bridge crew."

Turk leaned forward and gripped his shoulder and gave him a little shake. "Stop it. We're a warship, and this is an important mission, and we all went in with our eyes open."

Mikhail scoffed at the importance of the mission. "A graveyard of ships?"

"Mikhail, this place holds so many mysteries. So many possibilities. Alien races that humans are already living in peace with. Alien technology. Alien weapons."

It was so Turk-like to make it seem so simple and clear.

Paige was starting to think that Ceri was more than a little annoyed with her. It had been days since she spoke with Ceri and there had been no word from her teacher. Paige had started repairs, confident that work would be forthcoming. So far, she'd laid out two-thirds of their cash for materials such as a new radio, ship's intercom, refrigerator, and wood to rebuild the crew quarters. If Ceri didn't give her work, they'd be out of money soon.

It filled her with relief to see Oust finally pull up to the dock and tie off.

"*Konichiwa!*" Paige called to him and then swore at herself.

The Japanese greeting had become habit in just a few days. She knew that Oust preferred English. "Hi, Oust!"

Oust waved back. He strolled down the dock, eyeing the boat with faint disbelief. "I still can't believe you gave up everything to go off in this ugly bucket."

"Hey! Don't trash my boat!"

He gave her a steady look. "It's ugly, Paige, and you loved translating."

Oust was mostly Red, but he had enough Blue in him to know the truth when he saw it. She just hated to hear it.

"I love my family more," she told him.

He acknowledged that this was true with a nod of his head.

"I hope you're coming about a job." She forced the subject off herself. "We need the money."

"Yes, I am. Boats coming into harbor are reporting seeing minotaurs on the Outer Banks."

The Outer Banks was a long narrow strip of islands not much more than sand dunes along the coast of Ya-ya. While sheltered from the brunt of storms by the landing, the islands were still too exposed for anyone to live on.

"Minotaurs?" Paige said. "What are they doing on the Outer Banks?"

"That's what the city council wants to know. They're hiring you to go out and talk to the minotaurs. Find out what they want. Settle it in Ya-ya's best interest."

Whatever the reason was, the humans wanted to get the best out of the deal.

"How much is my cut?" Paige knew that Ceri would be taking a percentage of her pay. It was the price of business.

"Five hundred to go out to the islands, find the minotaurs, and find out what they want. There'll be a bonus hundred yen if you can get them to peacefully go away if they have no plans for trading."

In other words, Ya-ya's city council was slightly afraid that the minotaurs planned to lay claim to land that the humans weren't using. As herbivores, the minotaurs lived off land that they terraformed. They were masters of claiming landmass out of the ocean; much of minotaur mainland was in fact ocean floor sectioned off with dikes, drained, and farmed.

"If minotaurs want to trade?" Paige ignored the fact that she had no clue how she would get out to the Outer Banks. Taking the *Rosetta* out would require more money than it was worth in tugboat and pilot fees. The islands were too far, though, to take one of the launches.

"Ya-ya will pay an hourly rate on top of the initial fee for you to negotiate a trade—if they want what the minotaurs are offering."

It could amount to a good deal of money. If Paige didn't know that Ceri refused to leave the city, she might have thought that Ceri was being nice to her.

"Okay, I'll do it. Come on up. Might as well sit and have some lemonade while I sign the contracts."

She used the delay of making the lemonade to consider the deal. If she signed the contracts, she'd be committed to figuring out how to get to the Outer Banks. No matter how she did it, it was going to cost money. If it wasn't for the possibility of a trade after the initial contact, she would turn it down immediately. Odds were in her favor, though, that the minotaurs weren't trying to claim the land. It went against everything she knew about the aliens.

She served the lemonade. Orin made small talk with Oust while she read over the contracts. It was all standard clauses and penalties. Most Ya-ya business was transacted without such lengthy contracts. Only translators had such contracts. There was something about having no idea what was truly being said made people paranoid.

"Do you have a pen?" she asked Oust when she finished.

Orin gave her a look that clearly said, "but how are we getting out to the Outer Banks?"

"All my crew is out at the moment." She accepted Oust's writing set. As she mixed up ink for the brush pen, she said for Orin's sake, "I'll need to wait for them to get back before hiring a boat. I can't leave the *Rosetta* unattended."

"Speed is of the essence," Oust said. "The city council is afraid that hostilities might flare up if the minotaurs are left to roam unchecked."

Yes, humans tend to kill what made them afraid.

"We'll leave in an hour," Paige promised. She might have to send Orin out to track down some of her crew.

She dipped the brush into the ink and signed her name. They were committed now.

Once the ink was dry, Oust carefully tucked the contract away.

"It might be wise if you leave your man behind." He meant Turk. "He's not going to deal well with the minotaurs."

She blushed. Did the entire landing know she was sleeping with Turk? "He's going to have to learn."

"I can take Ceri being with other men much easier than I can deal with her trading with minotaurs," Oust said.

Oust was a male Red; he'd understand Turk's mind-set better than her. "I'll keep that in mind."

Orin waited until Oust was gone before saying, "I don't like this."

"Even if we don't get the hour rate for the trade, we'll still be ahead. This is a job that Ceri doesn't want. If we do it, she'll owe us a favor. Right now, we need her in our debt."

"The city council knows more about the minotaurs on the Outer Banks than we do. If there was any hint that a trade might be possible, they'd be sending a council member with us. Something could have pissed the minotaurs off and it's a war party."

"If the minotaurs were pissed off, why would they sail a hundred thousand miles and then stop ten miles out of the landing? I've signed the contracts. We're committed."

Orin glanced behind her and an odd bleakness filled his face. "Paige," he said quietly and lifted his chin to indicate something on the dock.

She turned and felt her insides go cold. Turk was walking toward the *Rosetta*. He was in a clean, crisp dark blue uniform. Behind him was a clean, crisp runabout with Reds in combat suits.

Somehow, against all odds, Turk had found his ship and clearly gone running back to his brother.

"Fuck," Paige breathed. Turk stopped at the edge of the dock. She went to the railing and looked down at him. Either he didn't care about her as much as she thought, or the idiot hadn't thought it all out yet.

"You found your brother." Paige supposed he couldn't be faulted, really. If she'd lost Orin, and found him again . . .

Turk nodded. "He's here with our ship."

Our ship. Paige nodded. She heard all the undertones. It didn't say why he'd come back with obvious intentions. "So . . . ?"

"We need your help."

She remembered then how he'd left the boat. Was this subtle blackmail with her little sister hostage? "Where's Hillary?"

He frowned and glanced to where the launch was normally

docked. "I—I guess she's still shopping. I assigned one of my Reds to protect her. A yearling named Rabbit."

Oh good God, her teenage sister out with a teenage boy? And Turk thought he was protecting Hillary? Men! She pressed her palm to her forehead to ward off a sudden headache. Carve out her heart and set up a major family crisis. At least it wasn't as bad as it could be.

"We have our own problems we have to deal with," she said.

"I know. We can pay you and you can use the money to solve your problems."

"Pay us with what?"

"Anything we don't need to survive."

"Anything?" *You?*

He nodded, clearly deaf to her unspoken question. "Within reason."

Gods must hate her. There were so many reasons to say yes, and only the ache in her heart to say no. "Fine. We'll help you. But not right now." At least she had the means to escape him now. "Ceri lined up a job. I need to find a way to get out to the Outer Banks immediately to talk to minotaurs."

"Minotaurs?" Turk echoed. "As in aliens called minotaur? Are they dangerous?"

Paige shook her head. "They're big, and pushy and loud, but harmless."

"Fairly harmless," Orin grumbled.

Turk pounced on the word. "Fairly?"

Paige glared at her brother. Didn't he realize that he was making it difficult to get rid of Turk? Or was he hoping that Turk could lend them military backup? Didn't he realize how dangerous that might get? "Fairly."

"If you could call something that big and that heavily armed harmless." Orin ignored her glare.

"Are they ever hostile?" Turk asked.

"We have an alliance with them," Paige said.

"Which means we make nice by lying through our teeth about our basic nature," Orin said.

"Orin," Paige growled. "Go find someone to watch the *Rosetta* while we're gone."

"You're not taking the *Rosetta*?" Turk asked.

My God, it's like swimming in a sea urchin patch! "No."

Turk watched Orin go and then trailed behind her as she gathered gear. "You're angry at me."

"Yes. I'm angry at you."

"Why?"

"Why? Why? Because you're leaving me! No. You've already left! You ran back to him and you even didn't stop to think about how hurt I might be. You walk back here and don't even say you're sorry, or good-bye, just that you need my help for him!"

"I didn't think . . ."

"Obviously!"

He pressed up against her, pinning her to the wall. "Finding Misha doesn't change that I love you."

Now he says it. She'd been patiently waiting for him to say aloud the words that his body whispered to her. She clenched her fists to keep from hitting him. The stupid idiot.

Paige fought to keep her voice level. The words clear. "I'm only in Ya-ya until the *Rosetta* is fixed—and then we leave."

It finally dawned on him. For a moment he stared at her, stricken. She fought the urge to comfort him even while some small dark part of her soul was glad that he was feeling some of the same pain.

He took a deep breath, stepped away from her and smoothed down his uniform. "I see." When he looked up, he'd closed off all evidence of his pain except for grief that lingered in his eyes.

It only served to make her want to hit him more. She wanted him out of her sight before she did something that she'd regret.

"Go back to your brother and tell him that we'll help him when we get back." *We* was a safe pronoun, much less dangerous than *I* at this moment. She was sure the word would stick in her throat if she tried to say it. Could someone choke to death on polite discourse?

"How are you getting there?" Turk asked, his voice flat.

"I don't know yet."

"How many minotaur are there?"

"I don't know!"

"What do they want?"

"I don't know! I don't know! I don't know!" She fled to the bridge to look at charts. "Nobody knows. That's why they hired me!"

Annoyingly he followed. "You don't have to do this. We'll be paying you enough money that you can back out of it."

"I signed a contract. I'm obligated to fulfill it. If I back out of it, it's less likely I can get another translating job. Don't you newcomers understand that relationships stretch across lifetimes? Is it because your universe is so big, that you can break your word and fly away and never see that person ever again?"

The word "never" seemed to strike them both like a blow. She stared at the chart but the words all blurred from the tears starting to burn in her eyes. She squeezed her eyes shut, trying not to cry. She didn't want to cry in front of him; it would only make things worse.

"Let me help you," Turk said quietly. "We have a small troop lander. We can fly you out. It won't cost you any money."

She didn't want to say yes, but it would be stupid to say no. They were running too close to being broke and losing everything for her to spurn his offer.

17 The Time Has Come to Talk of Many Things

MIKHAIL FOUND HIMSELF WONDERING EXACTLY HOW CAPTAIN Bailey was related to Eraphie. Captain Bailey turned out to be a beautiful young woman with blonde curls and deep blue eyes. She didn't look like she had any Red in her. Mikhail would have thought that the Red's dark coloring would have been the dominant genes, but she could have been third or fourth generation with possibly strong Nordic bloodlines mixed in. Or maybe their Bailey fathers were human brothers and only Eraphie was half-Red.

Mikhail would ask, but Captain Bailey was obviously not thrilled at the idea of helping them. Turk left in a good mood, but came back brooding like a thunderstorm. As they explained to Mikhail about the minotaurs—and not about why they were fighting—the two alternated between giving each other hurt looks and pointedly ignoring the other. Mikhail saw no reason to add fuel to the fire when they so desperately needed Captain Bailey's help.

Normally Mikhail would have let Turk go solo on a mission that could escalate into violence. He felt, though, that he should act as a buffer between Turk and Captain Bailey.

"It would be best if I just go out alone." Despite what Captain Bailey said, she sat down beside Turk in the Tigertail's cockpit.

"The *Tigertail* is too valuable to risk." Mikhail tried to stay impersonal.

Still studying the ceiling, Turk growled, "I'm not going to let you go alone."

"I can take care of myself," she said without looking at Turk and then appealed to Mikhail. "I don't think he should go."

"I'm Red commander, I go with my Reds," Turk stated.

And Mikhail wouldn't want it any other way.

Captain Bailey frowned at Mikhail as if he had said it aloud. "Fine. Then I need to lay down some rules and you have to obey them. Translating across species is like defusing bombs; I can't have someone running amok or it will all blow up."

"I understand." Mikhail acknowledged that she wanted rules but didn't agree to them. He would need to hear them first.

Something in the way she studied him reminded him of his father. Perhaps it was just the blue of her eyes. "Minotaurs are a patriarchal society. A social unit will be a bull, a harem of females, and children. Interactions between social units are through the bulls only. It means that I have to pretend that I'm a bull."

Turk gave a bark of laughter. "Your true form is revealed."

"Hush you." She poked him in the ribs. "I'm the only one that gets to talk."

"Since we don't know how to talk to them, I doubt that will be a problem," Mikhail said.

"You have to stand back and not interfere." Captain Bailey poked Turk to underscore her point. She was building to something.

"Why would he?" Mikhail asked.

"The conversation can get physical," Bailey said. "The minotaurs can be very . . . brutish. Whatever happens, unless I go down and don't get back up again, you stay out of it."

Turk hunched in his seat, stared at the floor, and growled lowly.

"You can't protect me." Bailey poked him once more.

Without looking, Turk caught her hand and pressed it his cheek.

"You can't," she said again, but leaned her head against his shoulder.

They were lovers! Mikhail realized that the trouble lay not in her helping them but in Turk leaving the *Rosetta*. Except for childhood crushes that ended badly, Turk had never taken a lover. Women that expressed interest in Turk had always been either maneuvering to get into Mikhail's bed—and be the empire's first

Tsarina—or cat fanciers wanting to wallow in perversions. In one little act, Bailey was showing Turk more humane tenderness than any woman had ever done. Leaving Bailey was going to hurt Turk deeply—and his little brother was just realizing it.

"Sir, we're over the islands," Lieutenant Belokurov said.

Spread out north and south was a dotted line of islands, only about a kilometer wide, but thirty or forty kilometers long. There was no sign of aliens.

"They would have put up some kind of shelter from the sun," Bailey said. "It's blending with the sand."

"The minotaurs would have gotten there somehow. Scan for a boat," Mikhail ordered.

"Found something." Lieutenant Belokurov brought up an image. A small garish-colored catamaran sat stranded on a reef, a dozen meters from shore. One of the twin hulls had a hole punched into it.

"Yes, that has to be them," Bailey said. "That's a minotaur craft."

"Looks human to me," Turk said.

"A human wouldn't have picked those colors to go together." She pointed out the lime green, orange, and pink.

Mikhail had to agree with her there. "Put us down as close as you can on the island."

"If they're shipwrecked, at least that explains what they're doing out here," Turk said.

Captain Bailey shook her head. "Not completely. The minotaur mainland is a hundred thousand miles away. There's no way they could have made it here in a boat that small. There has to be another minotaur boat close by—probably a much bigger one."

The minotaurs had abandoned their small boat. There were tracks in the sand that ran in all directions.

"I think they went this way." Captain Bailey pointed out that most of the tracks went north. "Please, stay here with *Tigertail.*"

"I'm coming with you," Turk said in a tone that meant he couldn't be swayed from his decision.

Captain Bailey must have recognized the tone too. She sighed and nodded. They went off together. Just before they disappeared over the sand dune, she reached out and twined her fingers around Turk's.

Why hadn't Turk told him that about Captain Bailey? Turk was in love; that much was clear. And she seemed genuinely fond of him—if not something much deeper. Could it be that Turk was blind to it all? Or was he refusing to see the truth? It was possible that Turk didn't think any woman would love him because he was a Red.

Mikhail loved his brother dearly, but there were times he wanted to smack some sense into him. Turk had to see himself as human before the rest of the universe would.

If it hadn't been for her fur, Mikhail wouldn't have guessed that Eraphie Bailey was a Red. Talking to her, she seemed wholly human. She didn't have the pervasive catlike behaviors that all Reds—Turk included—displayed. Was it because she wasn't a full-blooded Red, or was it because she wasn't raised in a crèche and subject to their training methods? If the cat thing was learned behavior, then when did Turk pick it up? He had spent only three months in a crèche. Had they laid some subtle pattern down on him then? Or had he picked it up later, when he interacted with their father's house pride? Was it something Mikhail could have prevented, if he had stopped and thought about how much damage it was going to do in the future? The thought stained him with guilt.

Luckily Lieutenant Belokurov distracted him from the sense of being dirty. "Captain, we have visitors."

About two kilometers down the beach, five beings were enacting a pantomime of excited discovery. The distant figures were too oddly proportioned to be human, though, with large heads and blocky feet. The beings came running toward Mikhail at an impressive speed. Something about their gait reminded Mikhail of a herd of horses. For a moment, Mikhail thought they were going to run him over. At the last moment, they came to an abrupt stop just out of reach.

They stood, panting only slightly from their two kilometer run. They were tall with a reddish hide and the heavy square heads of horses. Their oversized ears, however, pointed downward like a cow's, and the male had a small set of black horns, about ten centimeters in length. Captain Bailey's legendary minotaur. While they had hooves for feet, their hands were long-fingered. They were mammals—the females wore bright-colored cloth tied like makeshift bikinis over rounded breasts. The females also had black manes braided into beaded rows. The male had a sarong that covered his sex and a line of stubble to show that his mane had been shorn short.

They carried spears with metal tips with such ease it seemed as if they'd forgotten they held the weapons. Almost two meters tall, the minotaurs looked down at Mikhail.

The minotaurs gazed at Mikhail, all talking rapid fire among themselves. Their language was deep and breathy with no word breaks that Mikhail could make out. Their eyes were wide set in their square heads, the large, dark pupil taking up the entire eye. Despite their very alien nature, Mikhail got the impression of wide-eyed surprise.

Mikhail was at a loss what to do next. Alien contact normally meant nefrims, and that was always kill or be killed. Communicating would be good—but without Captain Bailey—how?

"Hello? Greetings?" His speaking drew the minotaurs' attention. The male fell silent, but the females chattered on, giving the male nudges and pointing at Mikhail with their spears.

Coffee snapped his rifle up to his shoulder.

"Hold your fire!" Mikhail cried.

"So I'm to wait until they stab you with those spears?" Coffee asked.

"Yes," Mikhail said. "Stand down!"

"Suit yourself." Coffee lowered his rifle.

The minotaur apparently didn't recognize the rifle as a weapon because none of them reacted. Or maybe they were too focused on their argument to notice.

The male finally spoke. Throwing back his shoulder, he bellowed, "*Haalahorthraraharo.*"

There was no helpful hand waving or pointing involved. Mikhail couldn't tell if this was a ritual greeting or if the male was giving his name or telling them to bug off their beach.

Mikhail tapped his chest. "Volkov. I am Volkov."

The minotaurs looked at him and then scanned the beach. After a few more nudges from the females, the male blew out its breath and bellowed again—slower this time, so that Mikhail could catch the word breaks. "*Haala horth ra ra haro.*"

Had it just repeated itself?

"I am Volkov. Welcome."

This brought the minotaurs to complete silence.

While they stood gazing at one another, the sea birds wheeled overhead, giving their shrill cry.

So now what? Apparently that was what the minotaurs were

asking too—as they put their heads close together and conferred. They seemed to expect him to know what they wanted. Captain Bailey indicated that humans traded with minotaurs often. Perhaps a visual would help.

Mikhail crouched down in the sand and smoothed out a writing area. He drew out a rough sketch of the stars and stripes symbol that the New Washingtonians loved to paint on everything. If the minotaur had contact with the Georgetown Landing, they would recognize it.

He looked up to find that he'd lost his audience. The minotaurs were heading for the *Tigertail*. One of the females was out ahead of the rest, running backward to point out the troop lander to the others.

"Captain?" Coffee had his rifle back on his shoulder.

"Let them near it." Mikhail hoped it wouldn't be a mistake. While the minotaurs were tall and sturdily built, he was sure that the Reds could kill them before they could do any serious harm with their primitive spears. "Call Commander Turk." Mikhail trotted after the minotaurs. "Tell him to bring Captain Bailey here. Quickly."

Paige ran toward where they left the *Tigertail*, her heart in her throat. She could trust her family to stay calm in the face of a minotaur invasion, but newcomers? It'd been a mistake to bring them. Minotaur bulls were huge. She wasn't sure what frame of mind these minotaurs might be in, especially since Ya-ya hadn't been able to establish communication with them earlier.

Turk was keeping pace with her, talking with his Reds on his comline.

"Tell them to stay calm," Paige said.

"I have," Turk said.

They came over the last sand dune. The minotaurs were gathered in a knot beside the *Tigertail*, obviously arguing about something. Simply taking the *Tigertail*? As far as she knew, theft wasn't in the minotaur's mind-set, but then, you can only steal from "people." And humans might not classify as people. As she jogged toward them, she noticed that something seemed odd about the minotaurs, but she couldn't put her finger on it. The group consisted of one bull with a harem of four females. A fairly standard group. They had fishing spears but no heavier weapons, which was unusual.

Then it struck her. They were too small to be adults. This was a group of children.

She stumbled to a stop in her surprise.

"What is it?" Turk stopped with her.

She motioned him to wait, thinking. The nearest minotaur settlement was Midway, nearly a hundred thousand miles away. There was no way children could have come all the way by themselves. There had to be adults somewhere close by. Very protective adults; every time she had done a trade with the minotaurs in the past, the children were herded out of town. *Oh holy hell, this could get messy.* Maybe talking to them wasn't wise. Maybe waiting for adults to arrive would be better.

But the minotaur children had noticed her arrival and were now galloping toward her.

"What's wrong?" Turk growled.

"It's fine. Just wait." She waved him back and then stood her ground as the children charged up and stopped.

"Try it! Try it!" The smallest female minotaur cried.

"It's not going to work." A mid-sized female snorted and tossed up her head, a gesture of contempt. "They don't have a mouth."

"One of these two might be a mouth, although this one is tiny." The tallest female peered down at Paige. Was size any indication of their ages, thus this would be the oldest of the group? The female was slightly taller than the bull, which would mean she was definitely older than the male since minotaur bulls were normally much bigger than females.

"Talk to them!" the other two females said.

The females all prodded the bull.

The little bull swallowed hard and then bellowed. "I demand to talk to your mouth."

At least he had the traditional phrase down. That was encouraging. How old were the kids? Preadolescent? Adolescents? She knew that at some stage young adults moved on to form herds of their own. Was this such a group? Or was it a sibling group, too young to be out on their own?

"I am the mouth," Paige said. "I speak for this herd."

"It's a mouth!" The children cried and bounded around with excitement. It was stunning to see how high excited minotaurs could leap. For a few minutes they sprang about her. Strange how she never considered minotaurs as hyper before. She glanced at Turk; he was tense but was patiently waiting.

The tallest—and possibly oldest—female regained her composure first. "Ask it for a trade!"

"Ask it for food!" The smallest continued to bound around.

"They eat animals." The middle one settled down. "And we don't have anything to trade it."

"Ask it for medicine for Zo," one female cried.

"Ask it to fix the communicator," the other female said.

"Hush." The oldest stomped her foot in the sand. "They're civil not real."

At least that was what Paige thought the female said. Paige had never heard the words used in that way before and wasn't sure what the phrase meant.

"We can use my armband." The little bull was already removing its finely crafted gold armband.

The females all reacted as this was a stunning announcement.

"But Toeno!" the littlest cried. "That's your stake money!"

"I got us lost." The bull held out the armband to Paige. "I offer this up for trade."

"You got to tell him what you want first!" The mid-sized female snatched the armband out of the bull's hand and held it tight to her chest. "It's the only thing we have. We have to get the most we can for it."

This triggered a squabble as they argued what was needed and what the humans might actually have. The phrase "civil not real" was used again, making her wonder. Trading was usually fairly regimented, but Paige could see that the kids were out of their element. She decided to hint that the wounded child was the most pressing of their needs.

"What is wrong with Zo?" Paige asked.

They went wide-eyed and silent.

"Is Zo hurt?" she pressed. Whatever gender Zo might turn out to be. Paige was guessing female. "We might have medicine for Zo."

After several minutes of the minotaurs eyeing her and each other, the littlest finally blurted out. "Zo broke her leg." She pointed back toward the direction that their hoofprints came from. The littlest was probably also the youngest. Little, of course, being comparative to the other minotaur. The female was still taller than Paige.

"Hush," the tallest said. "Toeno talks to strangers."

And they all turned expectantly to the bull who backed up a step under the collective stare.

"Z-z-z-zo broke her leg," Toeno kept backing up. "She seems very sick."

"The trade!" The middle female stomped her foot.

"We're establishing what goods my people can offer in exchange," Paige soothed. "Why don't you show me where Zo is?"

The children led her down the beach several kilometers to a small tent shelter tucked between two sand dunes. In the tent was a female clearly in the same age range as the rest. Her right leg was broken. The bone had pierced through her hide. Paige flinched at the damage. Worst, the female didn't stir as they crowded around the tent's entrance.

"Has she been like this since you came ashore?" Paige said.

They made the little noise that meant yes.

"Have you given her any water?" Paige said.

They glanced at each other and the bull was elected to ask, "Should we?"

"Yes," Paige said.

They looked at each other again, and this time the oldest said, "We didn't know."

God, they had to be just babies. Either that, or the minotaurs were lousy at teaching their children how to survive. She might not able to provide "medicine" to the children, but she could lend basic care.

"How long have you been lost?" Paige said.

She couldn't imagine beings as young as these obviously were had come from Midway. They must have come off a minotaur ship. The question, how far way was it?

The little bull stated a time that equated to several weeks. "Our herd was going to the human settlement of Mary's Holt." He meant Mary's Landing; a holt was an alliance of herds, sometimes but not always living close to each other. It was the close as the minotaurs got to the concept of "settlement." Apparently bulls were so territorial they couldn't stand living near a nonallied bull. "On the way, we stopped at an island in the human waters to do some maintenance on a navigation beacon there." He pointed toward the Fenrir Archipelagos, which lay between Midway, Ya-ya, and Mary's Landing. "There was no beach where our ship anchored. Hoto said we could take the catamaran out to a nearby sandbar to run on firm land."

She knew Hoto. He was the bull that controlled Midway. She had never seen Midway's children as humans were never allowed near them. She made the noise that meant that she understood and that Toeno should continue with their story.

"We—I got bored of that." Toeno couldn't blame the females since their society expected males to lead. "So we sailed to another sandbar . . . which could be even called an island because it had three trees. Mia could see—I could see that there were pai fruit at the next island which had more trees, so we—I sailed to it."

Paige felt bad for the little bull. The other children had been as much to blame if not more so but Toeno alone would shoulder the responsibility for the disaster that followed. She knew what it was like to suddenly have to act as head of the family. There were times that her siblings ignored all common sense only to later claim Paige should have headed them off. Charlene was the worst offender; Paige often wondered if her sister would one day blame Paige for letting Charlene marry Mitch. Or how much blame would be placed on her if something happened between Hillary and Rabbit?

"You got lost?" Paige guessed at what happened to the children as they weaved their way from island to island. Close to the water, unable to see any great distance, and movement changing the appearance of any nearby landmarks, it would be very easy to lose track of which way their main ship lay.

The bull bleated out a yes. "I thought I would be in less trouble if we just found our own way home, and then a storm caught us."

It must have been the recent force-five storm that swept up the axis. Its rotation must have carried them Counterspin hundreds of miles for them to end up at Ya-ya's outer banks. They'd done well to stay afloat if they'd been caught out in that storm.

It meant, though, that their parents weren't close at hand. She wasn't even sure how to get a message to the minotaur ship. While people liked to call their relationship with the minotaurs an alliance, it was more often peacefully ignoring one another except to occasionally trade goods. Communication was always handled face to face. She'd have to radio to all human ships with translators onboard to pass on a message.

Until then, she would have to take care of the children. To get their full cooperation in their own rescue, she needed to make a trade. The question was, what should she ask for in return? She didn't want to take the armband if it represented a much needed resource for the little bull. It would be bad juju to take advantage of lost children.

"How about you trade me the catamaran?" Paige figured that the catamaran would be lost soon anyhow. "Surely you have no more need of it. I can take it back to the human city and fix it."

The children considered the offer.

"Toeno can keep his armband?" the middle female asked.

"Yes," Paige said.

They conferred via glances.

"Yes," Toeno said. "We will make that trade."

Captain Bailey stomped up the *Tigertail*'s gangplank and stopped in front of Mikhail. The minotaurs trailed behind her, like a herd of calves suddenly convinced that they were ducklings to her mother duck. Turk brought up the rear of the strange parade, looking as mystified as Mikhail felt.

"What did you find out?" Mikhail wondered why she'd brought them back to the *Tigertail*.

She bellowed out a curse. "This is all screwed to hell."

"How exactly is it screwed?"

"What we have here are six lost children, one of which will die if we don't do something quickly." Said children towered over the petite Bailey. "Their boat is scrap. Their communication device is broken, and they don't know how to fix it."

And the *Rosetta*'s engine needed to be replaced.

"I feel like we're creating a parade of the blind leading the blind," Mikhail said.

"I told them that I would help them. And I will, even if you won't." She leveled at him a gaze that reminded him of his father when he laid down the law. It said, "You will be sorry if you think I'm kidding."

"I will help them," Mikhail said. "But I'm going to need you to show me how."

She studied him and then nodded. "We need to move them

to Ya-ya, along with their boat. The communicator is built into
their boat and I'm not sure we can remove it—and the boat could
wash away and sink with any large wave."

"Done," Mikhail said.

"And the wounded calf needs to be given some basic care."

"Done."

"I will have to get my mechanic and see if between me, him, and
your engineer, we can fix their communicator and call their family."

"Done.

She relaxed slightly then, and gave him a slight smile. "Thank you."

The invasion of the *Svoboda* became a storm of activity in the
hangar as the minotaur children and their catamaran were unloaded
from the *Tigertail*. The crew of the *Rosetta* joined Mikhail's crew,
helping to translate and assist with the repairs on the minotaur
communication device. Captain Bailey was at the eye of the storm.
One moment she was bellowing out the breathy minotaur phrases.
The next she was whistling and chirping at her mechanic, who
reminded Mikhail of an otter. Mikhail noticed that she changed
how she held her body and moved as much as her language. For
the minotaurs she stood up straight, stomped a lot, and tossed
her head, mimicking the children's gestures. For the mechanic,
she'd duck down, wrinkle her nose, and occasionally wriggle her
butt as if she had a tail.

Maybe she was playing at being a human just as well as she
did at being other species.

Mikhail's medic, Lidija Amurova, looked at Mikhail as if he was
mad and complained that she hadn't had so much as a hamster
for a pet as a child. Captain Bailey, though, guided Amurova
through simple first aid for the minotaur child as Bailey coaxed
water into the wounded alien.

"Normally I'd do a glucose drip for someone in this condition
but I don't know what it would do to them," Amurova said. "If
they have something to feed it . . . her, I'd recommend it."

"Toeno!" Captain Bailey called to the bull. "*Hoofynaveyenyadoo?*"

The bull bolted off and returned with two paper-wrapped squares.

"This is what little food they have left," Captain Bailey explained.
"I have some more on the *Rosetta*. Considering Zo's fragile condition,
I think the female should only get something the minotaur them-
selves prepared."

Mikhail and his medic eyed the squares.

"What are they?" Mikhail asked.

"They take baked grain and soak it in honey, form these bricks, and then wrap them in waxed paper." Captain Bailey unwrapped one of the bricks. "Humans can't chew them; we don't have the jaw strength. We can eat them boiled down to a thick gruel."

Amurova tapped on the hard grain. "But this is solid. Only liquids boil."

Mikhail locked his jaw to keep from sighing. Again and again, his space-raised crew was in over their heads. "You put it in water and bring the water to a boil until it becomes a pastelike consistency."

"I can get Manny to make the gruel." Captain Bailey shook her head. "Your crew is going to need to do some serious adapting to survive, Misha."

Only Turk called him Misha. She said it with the same gruff affection.

"Thank you for helping us," Mikhail said.

"All things considered, it's the right thing to do." She studied him intently for a moment. "I need to ask you something. Volkov—as in Viktor Volkov? Because you look like him."

"I'm his clone."

Her eyes widened slightly. "Clone? Oh. I didn't realize they cloned him. I thought maybe you were from a bastard child that took his name." She thought a moment, growing troubled. "Turk—he's not really your brother—genetically—right?"

"I consider him my brother." Mikhail kept his face neutral. He'd faced this bigotry over and over outside the Sargasso, but he was surprised that would make a difference to her of all people.

"He's off the standard production lines." She pressed. "Not from some cocktail of Red and Volkov DNA?"

"What difference does it make?" Mikhail asked coldly.

"Viktor Volkov was my grandfather."

"Oh." Mikhail couldn't force any other words out.

"My aunt said that he was always a little touched," Eraphie had told him. Mikhail hadn't realized Eraphie meant that her aunt was Viktor's daughter reporting on her father's condition. That Eraphie's cousin was Viktor's granddaughter. Mikhail's genetic granddaughter.

And if Turk was a mix of Viktor's DNA and standard Red— making him more a true "brother" instead of a straight clone identical twin like Mikhail—she'd been sleeping with her genetic great-uncle.

"Oh." Mikhail wet his mouth and managed, "Turk isn't genetically my brother."

"Good."

"Does Turk know about . . ."

Captain Bailey shook her head. "We're careful about inbreeding here. With any native-born man, I would have compared family trees before the nookie. I didn't think I had to worry with Turk."

Within a crèche, each lot of Reds were identical. To keep disease from sweeping through the crèche, each lot was slightly different, along the lines of children of the same parents. Luckily, because of patent protections, however, every crèche produced Reds that were genetically different from other crèches'. If any of Bailey's parents were Reds, then the fact that they were White Star Crèche and not from the same crèche as Turk would keep them from being genetically father/daughter or uncle/niece.

Which Captain Bailey most likely considered.

If Turk was genetically Mikhail's brother, then she would have had a mess on her hands.

"I checked once," Mikhail said. "I was hoping that our link was less tenuous since my father always encouraged me to think of Turk as my little brother. But Ivan literally just walked out on the production floor and picked at random one out of thousands. Took Turk out of the crib, leaving an identical brother to either side, and carried him home."

She looked slightly alarmed. "I hope you've never told Turk that."

"No. No. I wouldn't hurt him that way."

It had been a long, hard day. Paige had lost track of time, easy to do on the *Svoboda* since there was no ship's bell marking time. She was starting to suspect that she'd been awake for more than twenty-four hours. She'd made the mistake of sitting down to discuss plans on what to do with the minotaur children, selling excess equipment off of the *Svoboda* for yen, repairs to the *Rosetta* as payment, and . . . Turk was shaking her awake.

"We'll need to move the *Rosetta* closer." She rubbed her face. She wasn't looking forward to threading her way across the harbor to her boat. How did she get here again? Did she have a launch to get back on?

"You can stay here tonight," Turk murmured into her hair. He was a comfortable wall of warm to snuggle into.

"I'm angry with you," she said to remind herself more than him.

"I'll keep my hands to myself," he promised. Apparently that didn't cover his mouth as he kissed the nape of her neck. It felt annoyingly good; it would be easy to melt back into his arms.

She reminded herself that she was going to be leaving with the *Rosetta* once the *Svoboda* was on its feet, that Turk probably wouldn't leave his brother—that he never mentioned his brother was Viktor's clone! Good gods, he nearly lured her into incest! She whined her annoyance.

"The crew quarters on the *Rosetta* are all torn apart," Turk reminded her. "You'll have to sleep out on the deck, and it's raining."

Damn him for being right. Now that she listened for it, she could hear the drumming of a hard rain.

"You can use my cabin. Take a hot shower."

Double damn the man. She knew what he was doing. He was trying to seduce her into leaving the *Rosetta*. She'd seen this dance played out too many times not to recognize it. The problem of only having family on a boat was that the only way to fall in love was to meet someone not on the boat. Then the struggle started; who stayed where they were and who had to leave. Charlene and Mitch had just gone through it a few months ago. With them, though, there wasn't much choice. Mitch's family couldn't take another person on and the *Rosetta* was shorthanded. Still Charlene had to woo Mitch into marriage by showing off all that the *Rosetta* had to offer.

The *Rosetta* was Paige's boat. She'd worked long and hard for it. She wasn't going to leave it and strand herself with a pack of newcomers who all needed a nursemaid.

There was a rumble of thunder that made it through the *Svoboda*'s thick hull. She'd have to wait for the storm to pass or go out in the pouring rain . . .

"Fine, fine, I'll stay," she grumbled.

He hovered close as they walked down the halls to his cabin, but tensed every time someone brushed past them. It made her wonder about his position on the ship. Mikhail treated him with warm affection. The other members of the crew seemed to respect him. Turk, though, didn't seem at fully at ease. Or was it her? When they were alone or with Mikhail, he pressed close to her. When there were other people around, though, he'd drift away, creating distance.

Was he ashamed of her somehow? Had he found out what she truly was? No. That wasn't it. It was more like he was trying to protect her by keeping his distance. She was starting to think that in terms of relationships, Turk went with his heart and rarely thought things through. How could she stay on the *Svoboda* if he thought he could only protect her by keeping his distance? It made her head ache just to think about it.

His cabin was twice as large as hers on the *Rosetta*. He showed her how to work the shower and kept his promise of keeping his hands to himself.

The shower was a mistake. She could kill for such a shower. Leave her ship? That one she'd have to think about—when she wasn't so tired.

Turk had always taken pride in his decisiveness. Lying in bed beside Paige as she slept, he realized that making decisions fast and clean was easy when you had no real choices. For the first time, he had a real choice, and he couldn't decide.

He knew how much he would be asking Paige to give up: everything he thought he'd lost himself. Part of him didn't even want to think about subjecting her to that. And what did he have to offer? The future he'd always envisioned required him to stay on the *Svoboda*, fighting alongside Mikhail, until Mikhail proved himself a war hero and moved into politics. It could take years. Any other future was a huge step down, from being a major power in the empire to struggling to stay above common house cat.

The lower his level, the worse people would view Paige. One thing to be lover to the Tsar's trusted advisor. Quite another to be lover to a poor man's house cat. And the basic truth was that they were just shades of the same perversion; she'd always be "that cat fancier."

But he loved her. He didn't want to lose her. And he was afraid that the sea would simply swallow her up. She wasn't safe on the *Rosetta*, no matter how much she might love it and her family.

He wanted her to go back with him to his universe.

He didn't want her to give up her universe for him.

He had no place in his universe for her.

He loathed the thought of staying in her universe, trapped on that tiny boat, helpless and bored stupid.

Life had been easier when he had no choices.

∞   ∞   ∞

The bed was heavenly. It reminded Paige of drifting in a quiet pool without the wet. Perhaps it was like sleeping on a cloud. Turk had kept his promises and only slept, spooned against her back. When she woke up, he was already gone.

She took another shower. It was a dangerously decadent shower.

Turk had left out a clean shirt for her: a seductively soft short-sleeve pullover in a beautiful shade of blue. It matched her eyes. Damn, the man was good. Well, two could play this game. She'd have to work on countermeasures. The problem being that she wasn't sure what the *Rosetta* could offer—other than herself—that might appeal to him.

It felt a little underhanded to toss his cabin for clues . . . actually it was extremely underhanded. Oh well. All's fair in love and war. It was also fascinating to see how a new spaceship worked, as opposed to one that had been sunken in saltwater for countless years. The drawers were so flush to the wall that they were nearly invisible. They opened with a light touch and were lit from inside. How ironic that while Turk had spent so many days naked on the *Rosetta*, he had two weeks worth of socks and underwear folded neatly up and waiting his return on the *Svoboda*.

In the second drawer down was a photo frame. She turned it on. It had photographs of Turk and Mikhail. Meeting them as adults, she thought of them as roughly the same age, but the photos made it clear that Mikhail was three or four years older. Their solidarity showed even in the earliest pictures; they leaned close together and looked at the camera with cautious eyes. They were allies against whoever was taking their picture. She didn't notice that they weren't smiling until she came upon later photos, showing them as young men, and obviously entrusted with a camera of their own. The enemy behind the lens was gone, and they grinned for the pictures, showing warmth and affection for each other.

The third to the last picture was of a man Paige thought was Mikhail until she cycled to the next photo. It was the same man posed with Mikhail. They'd cloned Viktor more than once! This then was Mikhail and Turk's "father." The older clone and Mikhail were dressed formally in Imperial regalia. Tsar and future Tsar. No sign of Turk in this official portrait of power; but then, he was just a randomly selected Red. The last photo was candid; the camera caught the "family" in motion. It looked as if it was taken the same day as the official portrait. The Tsar was talking to the boys. Little Turk, who may have been only five or six in the photo, leaned against their father, looking up at him with full adoration. The Tsar's focus was on Mikhail, a hand on the boy's shoulder and a stern look directed at his heir. Mikhail, though, was holding Turk's hand, almost absently, as he was being lectured to.

"Poor Turk, did you ever get your father's attention?" Even alone, though, she couldn't say aloud, "Does he even think of you as his son?" That was too pitiful to say.

The frame cycled back to the first photo. She set it aside. Turk seemed to get along with her family well enough, but she doubted that they could compete with Mikhail and the Tsar.

On the floor, beside the trash chute, she found a data-stick which could be slotted into some device. She checked the photo frame and discovered the stick fit into it. She slipped in the stick and turned the frame back on.

In a small opulent bedroom, Turk was tearing the clothes from a beautiful woman. What the hell was this? Paige gasped as the woman slapped Turk hard.

"Bad cat!" the woman said like she was scolding a dog. "Where's your fur?"

While clearly furious and able to break the little bitch's neck easily, Turk furred over and let the woman force him down onto his knees to service her with his mouth, like he was a street-corner whore. Paige tried to jerk the stick back out, and triggered some fast-forward function. The speed compressed the following sex into unbearable abuse and humiliation. Turk couldn't have enjoyed this—could he? His rage seemed to shimmer just below the surface and there were moments she was sure he would snap and lash out. Wincing, Paige tried to free the data-stick and stop the flow of images, but the data-stick wouldn't come out while it was playing. With some fumbling, Paige got it off fast-forward. The sex, though, had all been played out. All that was left was the woman rubbing salt in Turk's wounds. The woman reached down the camera saying, "Let me give you a stick of what I'm going to post to the forums so that everyone can see what a magnificent animal you are."

God, what a bitch. Who was she? Why had Turk let her abuse him? He didn't seem to enjoy it—or had he?

18 Of Shoes and Ships and Sealing Wax

AS ALWAYS, TURK'S OPTIMISM PROVED TO BE VIRAL ON MIKHAIL. It was slow to start, but after hours of incubation, Mikhail was fully infected. Of course having Turk back alive and well, a translator in hand, docked at a bustling city, and peaceful aliens to study helped too.

The mistake would be letting optimism dictate his actions. He had to plan for various outcomes. He dearly hoped that they would be able to repair the *Svoboda* and return to their own universe. The worst case scenario wasn't being stuck in Sargasso. It was actually second best. As Hardin had pointed out, it was close to paradise. Unfortunately, preparing for it ran completely counter to the best case. Instead of funneling all their resources into repairing the ship, they would focus on creating a permanent life here in the Sargasso.

The worst case was that they found the people that modified *Fenrir*'s engine. Made the needed changes. And the warp field distortion because of added mass of the atmosphere was so great that they scattered parts of the ship and crew across two universes. In that case, once again, Plymouth Station would end up with an engine and a mystery.

The worst case threatened to overwhelm him with the bleakness he'd newly escaped. He kept it at bay by laying plans. Eliminating mass prior to the jump, shutting all blast doors, having the crew suit up and located at the heart of the field would protect his people. Documenting what they found would prevent a second mystery.

Mikhail believed in the adage that a picture was worth a thousand words. He clipped on a recorder headset and set about recording. If and when the time came to go back to their own universe, he'd make sure there was a record of their time here in the Sargasso on the engine.

He started by climbing to the top of *Svoboda* and slowly panning over the harbor. "This is the crash site of the *Yamoto* and the *Yamaguchi*. It's home to hundreds of thousands of humans, many of who were born here in this place they call the Sargasso. We've been here—" He paused to check his com. "—nearly twenty days. So far there have been no signs of nefrims and the only aliens we have encountered seem to be friendly."

He spent several minutes using the eyepiece to zoom in on the great marooned spaceships. Once again the morning was foggy and he had to use filters to pierce the gloom and get clear shots. As he finished, Captain Bailey scrambled up the side of the ship to join him.

"Good morning, Grandpa." She grinned at him. "What are you doing?"

"Covering all my options." He erased her greeting and turned off the recorder. He wanted to strictly control what got back to the United Colonies. "And trying to decide what to do next. Are there Novaya Rus Landings?"

"Russian ships don't land well," Captain Bailey said. "Where the ship was headed when it comes here seems to rule where it lands. We think that's why the *Yamoto* and the *Yamaguchi* are together and most of the New Washington ships are on the Washington Archipelagos. The area that Novaya Rus ships come down in isn't over shallows."

"They all sink?"

She nodded. "During the Colonial Wars, Novaya Rus was for the most part, nonaggressive. Then Novaya Rus stayed out of the beginning of the Nefrim War . . ."

"Ah, yes." Mikhail saw where this was going. Since the Novaya Rus hadn't jumped ships in large numbers into Japanese or New Washington space, few would have landed near Ya-ya or Georgetown.

"I've heard that there are a few small landings, far down the negative beyond Mary's Landing, but they don't have the where-withal to come this far up the axis."

The distance involved and the relative smallness of the Novaya Rus landings made them high risk. It would be better to settle in a larger landing. Both Ya-ya and Georgetown seemed good candidates. Ya-ya was the largest, most prosperous landing and they were already there. The language barrier, however, was enormous. Standard borrowed heavily from English and used the same alphabet. All of his crew had taken years of Standard and were at least marginal at speaking it.

"Would Georgetown take us in if we wanted to settle there?" Mikhail asked.

"Probably," she said slowly. "If it wasn't you, no. But people knew and trusted Grandpa. And our family has a lot of pull there."

By "our family" did she mean the Baileys or the Volkov descendents—or was there little difference between the two?

Speaking of family and language barriers, they'd made their way to the minotaur encampment set up in the *Svoboda*'s hangar. "How are the children?"

"Growing restless," Captain Bailey said. "I sent a message over to the *Rosetta* for Hillary and Becky to come over and babysit. They can keep the calves distracted by teaching them our games and learning theirs."

Mikhail had only vague memories of how unmanageable bored children could be. And these children were over six feet tall. "Thank you."

"I also sent a report to my mentor, Ceri. The city council was going to pay an hourly wage for negotiations. I'm hoping that they'll be willing to cough up something for babysitting, but I doubt that will happen. There's no profit in it for them."

Mikhail supposed that it was a true sign of how acclimated the humans of the Sargasso were to their circumstance: a host of aliens generated only a minor squabble over who would "babysit." Tseytlin had reported that they were still trying to understand how the communicator was supposed to work. It might be days before they could send a message out directly to the minotaur parents. In the meantime, they could gather information on the aliens.

"Are there other aliens in Ya-ya?"

"There are the hak," Captain Bailey said. "They're at Ise Jingū.

There might be some seraphim floating around. Other than that, most species tend to steer clear of others."

Mikhail heart jumped at the mention of the seraphim. He hated that just the thought of being dragged through his memories again frightened him. "What do you know about the seraphim?"

"Not much. You're asking the wrong Bailey. My brother Ethan . . ." She shook her head as if she was at a loss for words.

Mikhail wondered if this was the same Ethan that Eraphie called an idiot for going to Mary's Landing. "Ethan what?"

"I don't understand my brother. I mean, I do, but I don't. Ethan can't be happy with life," she reluctantly added. "Sometimes I think it's merely because he's a self-centered prick, and it kills him that the world doesn't revolve around him. Being able to interact with the seraphim set him apart, so he obsessed over them."

"He can talk with them?"

She fell silent, thinking. She had the rare trait of actually considering the question before answering. People often held the belief that they understood a question upon hearing it, and the first thought that came to mind was the correct one. It was rare that someone actually turned a question in their mind, seeking the truth instead of giving an easy reply.

"I don't think so." She squared herself to him and looked him in the eye. "You and I right now are talking. I am communicating information to you, and while you might be perceiving something slightly different than what I'm intending, there are points of commonality."

It was his turn to ponder. "If there were no meeting of your intentions and my perceptions, then we're not talking?"

"Exactly. One of the most difficult things about translating is your own perceptions get in the way of what the other person is trying to communicate. A simple example. Pretend we're meeting for the first time. I'm Captain Paige Bailey." She put out her hand for a handshake.

He shook her hand, wondering what the catch was. "Captain Mikhail Ivanovich Volkov."

She held tight to his hand instead of letting go and ending the handshake. "Your perception was that I put out my hand for you to shake it. You believed that since I gave you my name, that to be polite, you had to give me yours. Since I used my rank, you used yours. But what if I held out my hand, wanting you to hand me your sidearm? Or if I wanted you to slap my palm with yours?" Her point made, she let go of his hand. "Because of commonality, though, you understood me correctly."

"Ethan is misperceiving the seraphim?"

She sighed. "Let's just say, I strongly doubt that he's putting his preconceptions aside long enough to correctly translate whatever they're trying to communicate to him."

Was that what they were doing to him? Trying to communicate? Much as he hated to admit to the mental rape the seraphim were committing, he'd have to tell Captain Bailey something to get her advice.

"The seraphim keep crawling into my mind," he told her. "They're triggering memories to replay. The worst of my memories. It's—it's been driving me *bezumny*—crazy. I need to know what these things are. What they want? How do I stop them? Why are they doing it? Are they trying to talk to me?"

She frowned. "What are they doing?" Her gaze unfocused, as if she was looking inside for answers that couldn't be found outside. The frown smoothed away as her face went lax. She was still for over a minute, before she murmured, "They're trying to communicate something to you." She blinked and returned to herself.

"*When you cross a Red with a Blue*," Eraphie had said. "*You get a lot more than a pretty kitty. Blues have something going on up here.*"

"What is it they're trying to say?" Mikhail asked.

Captain Bailey opened her mouth but said nothing for a moment while she searched for words. "I—I don't think I could even guess. I know what you're talking about; I've had them do that to me. But only once. I'd gotten angry at Ethan and we were fighting and one came into the room we were in. And it made me remember being put down for a nap out in our shanty. There were cracks in the floor, and you could see down into the water below. For a moment it was like I was back there, staring through the cracks, just on the verge of sleep, watching the minnows dart in and out of the shadows.

"And I think . . ." She paused as if she was worried about telling him the wrong thing. "I think what it was trying to tell me, was to be at peace. To rest easy. To wallow in the feeling of being safe with my family. But it might not have been that at all."

"That memory meant safety to you. So it depends on what my memories mean to me?"

"Maybe. For all I know the seraphim was relating to being disconnected from the minnows as they darted through the water. How can you know what the minnows are thinking when they're so far below you, running from shadows?"

It took him a moment to realize she was referring to the seraphim seeing humans as minnows. Which he supposed was just as possible a translation of the moment as the first version.

"I see." Mikhail didn't want to divulge details of what the seraphim forced him to remember. She was hinting that even if she knew the details, it wouldn't necessarily help. While he might be able to somehow bare his soul enough for her to come to understand what the events meant to him, there was no telling if the seraphim were viewing them in the same light.

"It really depends on what the seraphim really are," Captain Bailey said. "If they're angels, then one could suppose that they know the human soul. If they're aliens . . ."

"Why assume that they're angels?"

"I've noticed that newcomers are often atheist. Hell, the word *atheist* doesn't do justice to the way you think. It's like the question of 'is there a god' is something you've never even considered. Maybe because out there, humans have taken control of what could be considered the prerogatives of God. If you want a child, you don't pray to God for the miracle of birth, you design the child you want and give it life. You don't pray for good health, you eradicate illness from your body. It's not that I think this is necessarily bad. There is a level of maturity that comes only when you realize that you are responsible for your actions."

He wasn't sure where she was going but nodded in encouragement.

"That's not how we are here in the Sargasso. We believe in divine intervention. Sad to say, but probably because we're so helpless all the time. But once you open that door to belief, it's hard to close it. A lot of people think the hak are gods, or at least *kami*, which are spiritual beings along the same lines of a god. English really doesn't have the words to explain them and Standard tends to be devoid of religious ideology."

"And the hak say that seraphim are angels."

"So the legend goes. But I doubt it is completely correct. Generally speaking, translators only use Buddhist concepts when dealing with the hak."

"And 'angel' isn't a Buddhist concept?"

"Technically, no." Captain Bailey shook her head. "It's possible that the hak used a Buddhist concept and it later got translated into English as *angel*."

"What do you think they are?"

She sighed. "I don't know. I've heard so many stories about them saving people. They perform miracles by foreseeing disaster and moving people out of harm's way. I just don't believe that these creatures are supernatural beings of good. I do think that somehow they can see beyond what we can sense. But I hold the unpopular belief that they have their own agenda and they're helping us only for selfish reasons."

"You don't trust them?"

"I have found that every species, with maybe the exception of the hak, has a common trait: they act in their own self-interests first," Captain Bailey said. "Usually I can figure out what the other being is getting out of any one action. You give me cargo because you want me to keep helping you. I understand that, so I trust you—to a degree. Because I can also guess where you might turn and bite me in the hand and I can guard against it. You know I can guess it, and that I'm guarding against it, so it's unlikely you would try it. Trust is a game of checks and balances."

On a certain level, he agreed completely with her. He would like, however, to think that the trust between him and Turk wasn't a game. That their trust was unquestionable and unbreakable. But if it was unbreakable, he wouldn't have to worry about damaging it. He had always been careful of protecting Turk for fear of losing his trust and affection. Was it that way with all families? Or was it just because he was Turk's brother only in his own mind?

He shied away from probing his own inner scars and considered the seraphim. "As far as I've been able to determine, I'm the only one that they've attempted to communicate with. Why focus on me? Why try to talk to humans at all? Why don't they deal with the hak? Or the minotaurs?"

"Humans are kind of unique in the Sargasso. We're the only race that will talk to anything, including our cats."

"The only ones?"

"That I know of." Captain Bailey patted her hand on the *Svoboda*. "This is the *Svoboda*. She's a good fine ship, trusty and true."

Mikhail sensed she was trying to make a point. "I don't understand the connection."

"We see everything like us until even objects become people. No other race does that. Take the minotaur. If we were minotaurs, instead of humans, this wouldn't be the *Svoboda*, it would be *Mikhail's frigate*."

"So you're saying that the minotaur don't talk to other races because they don't see them as people?"

She nodded. "With the minotaur, sometimes I think it comes from the fact that they're herbivores. Certainly, they're the most egocentric of the races. They don't share their space with anything that doesn't benefit them. They don't have pets. They don't keep plants beyond what they eat. They barely seem to be able to tolerate themselves. With humans we have that hunter/animal husbandry stuff going on that lets us empathize with other creatures. From the very beginning of our race, we had to get into the minds of other animals to survive."

It made sense that the seraphim would attempt to communicate with the one species willing to listen. It still begged the question: why focus on Mikhail? Could it be because Viktor had done something that caught the seraphim's attention and now that he was dead, Mikhail was heir yet again to Viktor's legacy? Or could it be because he was perhaps the captain of the only human ship that came here on purpose? Or was it simply because he was already slightly insane? Who knows, pushing him over the edge might bring joy and delight to aliens far and wide.

"Is there anyone who is an expert on the seraphim?" Mikhail asked.

Captain Bailey shook her head. "Not exactly. We can ask the hak, see if the legend is true. We could also see if Ethan had friends here in Ya-ya that shared his interest. Ceri seemed to indicate that he had some success in communicating with them."

Mikhail nodded. "I would also like to go to the salvage yards."

Captain Bailey misunderstood the reason for his request. "Georgetown Landing has a shipyard. It would be easier to create a boat out of the *Svoboda* in Georgetown than do it here and try to sail there with an inexperienced crew."

"Turk thinks . . ." Mikhail paused. What exactly had Turk told her about their mission? He'd assumed that Turk would have told her once he thought that the *Svoboda* had sunk. But Turk could have considered their mission so moot that he didn't see the point of explaining it. There was no way, though, that they could investigate the modification of the engine without her understanding what they were trying to find.

"Turk thinks what?" Captain Bailey said.

"We didn't come here by accident." Miksail decided on an edited version of their mission. "We were sent here to find the *Fenrir*. Its engine returned to Plymouth Station with no indication what happened to the rest of the ship."

At first she was merely startled by the information, but as connections were made, she frowned. The frown worked deeper and deeper. "You think you can warp out of the Sargasso?"

Mikhail nodded. "If the people that made the modifications weren't killed. The parts that were used to modify the engines had markings from Yamoto-Yamaguchi's salvage yards."

She stared at him mutely for several minutes before saying, "I—I don't know if I should help you with that."

"Why not?"

"Georgetown Landing is a small independent colony. If the United Colonies gained access to the Sargasso, they're not going to see us as that. They'll see us as lost New Washington property. We go through this every time another New Washington ship lands in the Sargasso. They get on the radio, announce that Captain So-and-So is calling for our commanding officer, and when they discover all our original crew is dead, they think they own the place."

Yes, he could see that happening. He thought frantically of how he could sway her; while there might be other translators to be had, Bailey could be dangerous opposition.

Luckily, though, he could offer what no other person could. "Novaya Rus will recognize Georgetown as an independent colony."

She considered it a moment before shaking her head. "No, United Colonies wouldn't allow it."

"I knew that there might be—" He edited out the word *crèche* and inserted, "—important items here in the Sargasso. Ships, certainly, if the *Fenrir* was here. I wasn't sure what I'd find, but I didn't want to risk everything and then hand over whatever I found to the United Colonies. I negotiated that Novaya Rus has salvage rights for anything I discover."

"You did?"

"I am the clone of Viktor Volkov and someday the Tsar of the Novaya Rus Empire." Whether he wanted to be or not.

She bit her lip, her face filled with uncertainty.

Mikhail pressed on, hoping to win her over. "If the people who modified *Fenrir*'s engine are still alive, it might not matter what you and I agree on. They know that the engine warped out. They had something close to success. There's no reason why they wouldn't try again."

Captain Bailey's eyes went wide. "You're right! They might try again. The Sargasso is littered with parts. They might even try to do it here in Ya-ya." She looked out at the bustling harbor and city spread beyond.

Mikhail gave her a minute to consider all the awful implications. Let her realize that by doing nothing, she could be allowing the people that leveled Fenrir's Rock to destroy another landing. "What happened at *Fenrir* might have been an accident, or it might have been a total disregard for human life. I want to find out. I need your help."

She nodded, and kept nodding, as if agreeing to things that went unsaid. "I'll help you. I can't let that happen again. Let's take your runabout to the salvage yards."

Spoken like a true Volkov.

Captain Bailey gave them a travelogue and history lesson on Ya-ya as she navigated the runabout through Ya-ya's waterways. It seemed as if she was pointing out the best features of the city.

Turk, Mikhail noticed, took up a position beside Captain Bailey, standing with one arm braced behind her. They weren't touching, barely seemed aware of each other, and yet radiated a "we are a couple" feeling. As they wove their way through city, Turk smiled time and time again at things Bailey said. It made Mikhail realize how rarely Turk smiled. Seeing how happy his brother seemed, Mikhail began to worry about the future. If all went well, he and Turk would return to their universe. The only way Turk could live happily with Captain Bailey was if one of them would give up everything they knew.

Who would sacrifice everything for the other?

Mikhail couldn't imagine Bailey giving up the boat she had worked years to earn and leaving her tight-knit family. Besides Mikhail, what was there to keep Turk on the *Svoboda*? Like himself,

Turk was friendly with the rest of the crew, but not necessarily close. Turk's universe saw him as nonhuman, a rogue piece of property that somehow owned itself.

The more Mikhail considered it, the more likely it seemed that Turk would stay with the *Rosetta* when Mikhail found a way to return to his universe. Would knowing that Turk was happy be easier than when he thought Turk was dead? Was he strong enough to keep on going without Turk? He felt ashamed that not only had he to consider the question, but there was a tiny spark of terror deep inside him that didn't believe he was.

The canal opened up into another harbor area. Here, shrouded in the mists, was a sudden graveyard of small personal space-ships. Fighters. Shuttles. Troop landers. And something he didn't recognize.

"What is that?" Mikhail moved the headset's eyepiece into place to eliminate the effects of the fog and zoomed in on the alien ship.

Captain Bailey followed his gaze. "That's a minotaur ship lifepod. A salvage ship out of Fenrir called the *Gleipnir* found a very large minotaur ship just on the edge of the Minotaur Flats. They've been floating the lifepods in for a few months now."

"There's only one," Turk murmured.

"Human salvage sits for a while because people often buy them whole." She pointed to the troop lander. "Reshape the bow on a troop lander and they make good sturdy boats. It already has water filtration, bathroom, showers, crew quarters, and such built in. People don't like working with alien ships. The sizes are wrong. None of the subsystems are set to human standards. And they're kind of creepy; it's like at some very deep level that they strike you as wrong. So they get melted down for scrap."

When Paige had been begging for bargains and offering nothing to sell, she'd dealt with the foreman out in the salvage yard. Mikhail, however, with his newly arrived riches and need for massive and speedy repairs, was escorted to offices she'd never seen before. There they met with the salvage yard's owner, a thin Asian whose *yakuta* hung on him as if he was a clothes hanger. His thin long fingers danced over the abacus before him, flicking beads up and down the rows. He had a pair of glasses balanced on his face that he seemed to need only for reading as he took them off every time he paused to talk to them.

"Yes, yes, I recognize these." The manager waved his glasses toward the far end of the salvage yard. "There was an odd motley crew that would come and climb around all the new arrival stuff. They pick out what they want and Hardin would pay for it. They favored the exotic."

The glasses went back on.

Exotic meant "alien technology." "What were they doing with it?"

The glasses came back off. "Who knows. Exotic is usually melted down since so few people can make heads or tails of the stuff."

Paige turned back to Mikhail, who had been trying to follow the conversation of rapid Japanese without success. "He knows the people that bought the items. Says Hardin paid for it."

"John Hardin of the *Red Gold*?" Mikhail asked.

The manger spoke enough to Standard to recognize that. "Yes, John Hardin." The rest was in Japanese. "He paid for everything they took. A hundred thousand . . . two hundred thousand yen of salvage. Very good customers."

"How much?" Paige said. The amount was staggering

"Hardin made over a dozen payments," the manager said. "All ten thousand yen or more. He'd pay every time he was in port, and this motley crew would come buy more parts."

"What is it?" Mikhail asked.

"Hardin paid out a shitload of money for the parts. You can make good money doing salvage, but I can't imagine Hardin being able to afford something of this scope."

"Maybe he had a credit line? Or a backer?"

Paige shook her head. The cautious moneylenders of Ya-ya wouldn't lend that much money to someone whose sole collateral was their salvage ship. Especially someone with as legendary bad luck as Hardin. "Did Hardin have a backer?"

The manager looked startled, as if he realized for the first time how odd it was. He put the tips of the earpiece into his mouth as he considered. "Yes, I believe so."

"Who was his backer?" Paige said.

"I only know that he paid for things he couldn't otherwise afford." The glasses went back on and he bent over his abacus. "He must have had a backer."

Paige thought back over the conversation. Something had slipped past her, she was sure.

"What did he say?" Mikhail murmured when she had been silent for some time.

Paige held up her hand to silence him. It was coming to her. On the surface, what the manager said seemed as if he was talking about Hardin's crew, but when considered carefully, actually implied the opposite. "This motley crew? They weren't *Red Gold* crew?"

"The three humans may have been but there were also a mino-taur, an obnaoian, and two Blues, translating."

Paige's heart jumped. "Who were the Blues?"

"Evangeline." He breathed her name like a lover, although the effect was ruined as he stumbled over the *l* in her name. "Such grace. Such beauty."

Paige knew Evangeline. She was Ceri and Oust's daughter. "Who was the other one?"

The manager thought and then slowly shook his head. "I—I never paid much attention to him."

Men! "They're here in Yamoto-Yamaguchi?"

The thin shoulders shrugged. "I haven't seen any of them for weeks."

He bent over his abacus again.

Mikhail caught her eye and lifted his eyebrows in query.

"Hardin had people that weren't his crew working here in Ya-ya," Paige told him. "From the sounds of it, they stayed here as he came and went."

"So they might still be here," Mikhail said.

"Maybe," Paige said. "But he doesn't know anything more."

"Did he say anything to give us a clue to how we can find them?" Turk said.

"Hardin was working with a woman called Evangeline," Paige said. "I really don't know her well, but I do know that she lives on Ise Jingū and works as a translator."

19 Ise Jingū

SINCE MODIFYING *FENRIR*'S ENGINE OBVIOUSLY TOOK PLACE IN Ya-ya, Mikhail decided to commit his resources to repairing the *Svoboda*. The lack of knowledge on part of Fenrir Rock's survivors suggested a secretive organization, and one unlikely to risk everything to discovery. Chances were good that Mikhail could uncover enough to recreate the success. As Captain Bailey pointed out, the Sargasso was littered with spare parts, and the *Svoboda* already had an undamaged warp drive.

Captain Bailey negotiated the purchase, exchanging parts for *Svoboda*'s spare equipment. She was less than overjoyed to carry out the deals, but Mikhail had to trust that she bargained in good faith. It was unnerving to know that his success ran counter to his translator's happiness. Captain Bailey, though, seemed to embody the same moral compass that Eraphie had; to do the right thing because it held true to the type of person you wanted to be. It would have been nice to think that Viktor was the fount of this ideology; but more likely, it was from the Baileys' other grandfather, John Bailey.

The following day, they went to visit Ise Jingū to see Captain Bailey's mentor and the aliens called the hak. It was to be just Mikhail and the Red, Rabbit, going with Captain Bailey. Turk added himself, and Mikhail couldn't deny him. Then, as they were untying the ropes to cast off, Captain Bailey's teenage sister, Hillary, slipped into the boat with them. Hillary was wearing a simple kimono, unlike the ornate one that Captain Bailey was in.

"Where do you think you're going?" Captain Bailey asked.

Hillary pressed a hand to her chest. "I'm your placeholder! Or do you really want to be stuck sitting and waiting for the hak to talk?"

Captain Bailey gave her sister a dark look, glanced to Turk sitting beside Rabbit and then sighed. "Fine. Fine."

"*Oni-chan*, slide over!" Hillary tucked herself between the two Reds.

They moved into the foggy harbor, the horns of passing ships bellowing like great beasts. A flock of birds went overhead, flickers of white to vanish into the haze.

"Why is it so foggy here all the time?" Mikhail asked.

"Who knows. Nature of the beast." Captain Bailey concentrated on maneuvering around a slow barge. "The water around Ya-ya is much cooler. It might because there is a pocket of extremely deep water just outside the city. Some people think there might be crack in the shell under Ya-ya and water making contact with the outer void is freezing solid, sealing the crack, but also transmitting the cold up to the surface. Other people think the hak are cooling the water in order to make the fog."

"Could the hak be the creators of the Sargasso?" Mikhail said.

Captain Bailey shrugged. "They say they aren't, and lying would go against everything they seem to believe. Personally I think the hak are here because of the weather conditions, not that they're causing them."

"Who was here first, humans or the hak?"

"The hak. *Yamaguchi* landed first and found them. Being Shinto, they decided that the hak were *kami* and that Ise Jingū was sacred ground. Not sure what would have happened if the *Yamoto* landed first."

Both ships loomed like mountains in the fog. It occurred to Mikhail that there wasn't a third, alien ship.

"Where is the hak's ship?" Mikhail said.

Captain Bailey shrugged. "We're not even sure they use spaceships."

"You haven't asked them?" Mikhail said.

She gave him a look of pure disgust. "This isn't like a conversation between a Russian and a Georgie, where you can pull out dictionaries and look up meaning of words if the discussion strays into unknown waters."

"I understand," Mikhail said. "But it seems to me that the first thing you try to determine about another species is—"

"If they're going to try to eat you in your sleep," Captain Bailey said. "Trust me. That's the first thing."

"I'll take your word," Mikhail said.

"Here, take the wheel," Captain Bailey said.

Mikhail leapt to the wheel as she stepped away from it. She scooped up a bucket, leaned over the edge, and filled it with the harbor's slightly greasy-looking water.

"Here." Captain Bailey thumped the full bucket down beside him and pointed at it. "If I say *dodecah* what does it mean?"

"Water?" he guessed. He wondered which language the word was from.

"No, *dodecah* means 'bucket.'" She filled her cupped hands with water and held it out to him. "*Jaxin?*"

He skipped the obvious, which would be again, water. "Wet?"

"No, I'm offering you a drink," she said.

"I'm starting to see why understanding the hak might be difficult."

Evangeline hadn't been at the shrine. Paige scratched out a message on the shrine's chalkboard and then led the others off in search of the hak. The pea gravel crunched underfoot. The smell of incense hung in the air, mixed with the fragrance of the cherry blossoms. As usual, a sense of peace smothered the place, so that even Hillary's energy seemed muted.

She went to the places that hak liked to meditate in and considered each of the aliens. Whereas it was usually possible to identify one minotaur from another, it was nearly impossible to tell the hak apart. The human priests had discreetly marked the hak's shells so that they could be identified. *Fifty-nine* and *Nineteen* were by the koi pond. She could still see the faint line of their tails in the dirt leading up to meditation points, meaning they had recently been awake. There was no use to talking to either of them. *Eight* was beside the knee of the Buddha in the main sanctuary. As she watched, an elderly woman clapped her hands and made a seaweed-wrapped rice cracker offering to *Eight* and whispered a prayer. There were four other crackers on the floor in front of the alien, so *Eight* had only settled in hours ago.

Fifteen had a translator's placeholder sitting in front of the alien, waiting for the sleeper to awake. Paige kept moving.

There was a hak under the cherry tree, covered with a thick layer of pink petals. She brushed them off the shell to undercover the hexagram. It was *Thirty-six.*

Paige knelt in front of the mediating alien and genuflected. Mikhail settled beside her, looking mystified.

Turk remained standing. "Is the boulder the alien, or is there something else that I can't see—like the seraphim?"

"Hak are turtles," Paige said.

Turk eyed the hak as if trying to judge how to kill it. "Very large turtles. Are they dangerous?"

"We'll be lucky if it even moves." She patted the ground to the left of her. "Sit."

"I'd rather stand," he grumbled.

"Turk," Mikhail said in a tone that was half pleading, half warning.

"I told you this would be tedious," Paige said. "They've proven to be more willing to talk to someone who is sitting than standing."

Turk chose to sit to her right and slightly back, perhaps so he could easily reach either her or Mikhail. She tried not to let it seem more than it was.

"What are turtles?" Rabbit whispered to Hillary.

"Here, I'll show you some little turtles." Hillary led the boy away. Paige suspected that Hillary's plan all along was to get Rabbit off alone.

They sat in quiet as the cherry blossoms drifted down. Both men were surprisingly patient and went unmoving for a long time. Paige tried to ignore them and focus on meditating; reaching that clear state of mind that seemed to help establishing contact with the hak. The stillness though only gave her time to think of all that was troubling her. The fact that Turk might not stay with her. That Ethan might have been the male translator working with Evangeline. That her little sister might be heartbroken when Rabbit left. That she might be putting her family into harm's way. It was almost a relief when Mikhail broke the silence.

"What's the symbol mean?"

"It's a hexagram," she said. "The priests marked the hak to be able to tell them apart."

"It's some kind of Japanese hexadecimal system?" Mikhail said.

"It's an ancient Chinese symbol system. The six lines are actually two sets of trigrams, or three lines, of solid and broken lines. The broken lines, the ones with spaces in the middle, represents yin, and the solid line represents yang."

"Two to the third power; eight possible trigrams," Mikhail murmured. "Two to the sixth power; sixty-four possible hexagrams."

"Yes," Paige said. "And each hexagram has a very complex meaning. They use them sometimes for divination."

"How many hak have they numbered like this?" Turk said.

"Sixty-four," Paige said.

"Because they ran out of symbols?" Turk said.

"No," Paige said. "That just happened to be the number of hak that come and go here."

"That's . . . odd. Exactly sixty-four?" Mikhail said.

"Yes," Paige said.

"Which one is this one?" Turk pointed to the hak before them.

"*Thirty-six,*" Paige said. "Darkening of the Light. The inner trigram is *li*, radiance or fire. The outer trigram is *kun*, field or earth."

"If you were doing a divination, what would this hexagram tell you?" Mikhail said.

Paige wondered why Mikhail would want to know. "Darkening of the light. He lowers his wings. He finds difficulties and does not eat for three days."

"He who?" Turk asked.

"Truthfully, I was never really clear on that part," Paige said.

"Anything else?" Mikhail asked.

"Stay on track, but beware of difficulties," she said. "The correct path is not always the easiest or most popular. Explore disorder to conquer it. However do not deal too harshly with disorder which has been the standard for a long time. Change must be gradual. He enters the left belly of darkness. He sees the true nature and understands that which is obtainable and that which must be avoided."

Turk grumbled something too low for her to hear, then asked, "We just sit here until . . ."

"Until it comes out of its shell," Paige finished his sentence.

So they waited as the cherry blossoms drifted down.

Hillary and Rabbit returned with food they'd purchased from street vendors. It was amusing, although a little sad, to see Rabbit puzzle over the new form and tastes; the boy had eaten prepackaged protein bars his entire life.

After they ate, there was nothing to do but sit and wait. Time seemed to slow down until it nearly stopped. Nearby a cicada had taken up its drone, somehow even more timeless than silence.

"This reminds me of Urashima Taro." Hillary yawned.

Paige murmured agreement. "It always makes me think of him too."

"Who is Ur—Ur—" Rabbit stumbled on the Japanese name.

"Ura-shi-ma Ta-ro." Hillary pronounced out the name slowly. "He was a young kind-hearted fisherman who saw some children tormenting a sea turtle. Taro bought the turtle and released it into the ocean. Sometime later, the turtle returned and invited Taro to visit an enchanted palace of the dragon king. He was welcomed there, given wonderful things to eat and drink, and fell in love with the beautiful Oto-hime, or Princess Oto. But after three months, he grew homesick, and asked to be returned to his village. Reluctantly, Oto-hime granted his wish. She gave him a box with instructions never to open the box. So Taro left the wonderful palace under the sea. Unfortunately, when he arrived at his village, he found everything had changed. He'd been gone not for three months, but for three hundred years. Everyone he knew was dead. Everything he knew was gone."

"What was in the box?" Turk asked.

"The effects of time on him," Hillary said. "He opened the box and poof, he aged three hundred years in a moment."

"Why would he open the box when she told him not to?" Rabbit asked.

"Because he was a man," Hillary said.

"What else could have he done? He'd lost everything important," Turk said.

"He could have gone back to Oto-hime," Paige said.

Turk frowned, perhaps recognizing the connection that could be drawn between Taro and himself.

"Was Taro's turtle one of the turtles in the koi pond, or one of these big turtles?" Rabbit asked.

Hillary shrugged. "It might have been a hak."

"It's an old story," Paige said. "I think it was first told on Earth. There are stories from almost every culture like it. There's the tale of Oisin, who fell in love with the fairy woman called Niamh.

She took him to a magical land to live with her, but after what seemed to be three years, he returns home only to discover three hundred years had passed there."

"It could have still been one of the hak." Hillary clung to her theory. "They say that hak jump using their chi instead of spaceships."

"That's never been proven," Paige said.

"But why do the men leave?" Rabbit asked.

No one could answer him.

Mikhail was called away, taking Rabbit with him. Hillary volunteered to ferry Mikhail back to the *Svoboda*. It left Paige alone with Turk with lots of uncomfortable silence to fill. Luckily, Oust appeared to save her. The old Red paused at the edge of the clearing and eyed the hak, looking to see if the alien was stirring.

"It's still mediating." Paige stood.

Turk started to rise. She didn't want him in tow until she was sure Ethan wasn't involved. It was unlikely that he had been; Ethan left Ya-ya some time ago. But there was a profound lack of male translators. Paige motioned that Turk should stay seated. "Stay here and play placeholder. Someone will take our spot if we all leave."

Turk settled, trusting her completely.

"You're looking for Evangeline," Oust murmured once they were out of earshot.

"Yes, I want to ask her some questions about some translating she's done."

Oust shook his head. There was sorrow in his eyes. "She's not in Ya-ya. She went off with Hardin."

"She left?"

He darkened. "That bastard treated her like she was one of his cats. Nothing. Expendable. And the worse he treated her, the more addicted she was to him."

And the hard question. "Was Ethan working with her and Hardin?"

"Yes, he was."

Even expecting it, it hurt.

"How did they get involved with a man like that?"

Oust looked away, something like shame on his face. For several minutes, he was silent, and then, wetting his mouth, he said, "I didn't realize what Ceri was doing. Not at first. I thought she was just teaching our little girl to be good. I didn't realize how quietly her mother had destroyed Ceri. How quietly Ceri was destroying our daughter."

Paige covered her mouth to keep in the gasp. Oust was talking about the traditional Blue training. She had heard how it ingrained into a woman the need to please a man. Any man. All men. That *good* little girls were sweet, and gentle, and gave to men whatever they wanted. She thanked the gods often that her family avoided passing on the training, although she wasn't sure how.

"The men here in Ya-ya, they are in awe of those that talk to the gods. But Hardin, he saw Evangeline as a Blue, and he treated her that way, and she craved it, because that's what her mother had taught her was the only way of being good."

She didn't know what to say in the face of that horrible confession. What worried her was that Evangeline's sick love somehow involved her brother. "How does this relate to Ethan?"

"Ethan had been working to establish a lexicon for the seraphim. He asked Evangeline to help him. He needed someone to be placeholder for him with the hak, but she became more involved. I think she realized that ultimately Hardin would see value in Ethan's work. As soon as they had some success, she went straight to Hardin."

Blues were very good liars. Evangeline was one of the few people in Ya-ya that could have kept Ethan from realizing that she meant to betray him.

"Why was Hardin interested in communicating with the seraphim?" Paige said.

Oust looked uncertain. "I don't know. Ethan had started building odd machines in an attempt to talk to the seraphim. Ethan rented a workshop and hired some workers. It was a strange mix of people. A couple of humans from here in Ya-ya. A few newcomers. A minotaur. An obnaoian. He had some success before he ran out of money; Hardin gave him more."

There seemed to be a weird hiccup of logic. She knew that ultimately Ethan had built something that allowed *Fenrir*'s engine to warp out of the Sargasso—but how did he go from trying to communicate with the seraphim to that? "What exactly were the seraphim telling Ethan?"

Oust shook his head. "I don't know. I do know that the first device allowed them to talk to the seraphim. Ethan thought of whatever the seraphim told him as a mandate from heaven. Hardin didn't see it that way, so Ethan started to keep parts of what he was doing hidden from Hardin. Ethan was afraid anything he told me would find its way to Evangeline. Ethan realized after he saw her with Hardin that she'd tell Hardin anything she learned."

The last part sounded like Oust was quoting Ethan, which meant Ethan was obviously still talking to Oust about something. Namely Hardin. "He told you he didn't like working with Hardin?"

Oust nodded. "He kept coming to me. Encouraging me to do something about Evangeline. He needed the money that Hardin was giving him. He was sure that if Evangeline wasn't leaking his secrets that he could control Hardin. I think he underestimated the man."

For a Blue, Ethan could be blind. "What did Evangeline tell you?"

Oust sighed and spread his hands helplessly. "Hardin told them both not to tell anyone about Ethan's project, and that included me. And then Hardin took them both away."

"Ethan didn't tell you anything?"

"He didn't want to jeopardize his source of money."

That sounded like Ethan.

Hillary and Rabbit returned while Paige was off with Oust. Turk was about to track Paige down when she returned to the hak. Oust had delivered bad news; Turk could see it on Paige's face when she rejoined them.

"I have the address of Hardin's workshop." She studied the hak for a moment. "I don't think it's going to come out soon. We might as well go and check out the workshop. Hillary can stay and be my placeholder."

The girl pouted. "How am I supposed to contact you if it starts to stir?"

Paige let out an exasperated breath. "You should have thought of that before you volunteered. I'll check back every few hours."

"Rabbit can stay with her." Turk didn't like the idea of leaving the young girl completely alone, unarmed, without a boat or any way of contacting them. Rabbit could keep her safe. "He can radio me."

Paige gave him a dark look but said, "Fine."

They left the two teenagers watching the unmoving alien and headed back to their boat.

"Evangeline is Ceri's and Oust's daughter," Paige explained. "Oust says that Evangeline went with Hardin. He's quite upset. Hardin sees Evangeline as nothing but a Blue."

Turk realized then that Ceri had been a Blue. It seemed a small betrayal that Paige hadn't told him the truth about the woman. "Why didn't you tell me Ceri wasn't human?"

Paige gave him an odd look. "She's human."

"She's a Blue," Turk said.

Paige shifted uneasily. "Blues are human."

"They're adapted. Like Reds."

"Doesn't make them less than human," Paige snapped.

Turk wasn't sure why it seemed to bother Paige. He tried edging around whatever was making her angry. "So Ceri's a Blue?"

Paige studied him a moment before nodding. "Her mother was one of *Mary*'s original cache of Blues. The woman had been 'classically trained,' which is fancy words for the brainwashing they do to Blues in crèche before selling them. They're taught that their value comes from how well they sexually please men. They're worthless if they're not visually perfect and fuck any man silly."

Turk nodded. He'd known about the training but he'd never met a Blue. Before, the knowledge had been a set of facts. Now it was distasteful.

"Ceri showed her ability young and was switched to be trained as a translator before she was eight, but not before her mother had instilled classical training into her. The reason everyone expects sex from translators is because Ceri thinks that all business dealings have to end with sex."

"Even after all these years as a translator?"

"Telling lies to a child is like pouring concrete over it. Even when it knows the truth, it can't escape that mind-set that the lies created. You tell a child that it's ugly, and it doesn't matter what it sees in the mirror, it will believe the lie for the rest of its life."

That explained how he much he hated what he was.

I should tell him, Paige thought. She hadn't told him about her family when she first rescued him, thinking that it would otherwise cause dominance issues. It was clear, though, he was deeply prejudiced against the very thing that he was. What her family was. What she was.

If she told him, though, would he look at her with disgust? Should she even want him if that was how he felt?

The *Yamoto* had been a troop carrier. Its attachment of troop landers had long been salvaged and turned into boats. The lander bays and launch tubes were rented out as warehouses. The expensive ones overlooked the bay with access to the water. Ethan had rented the cheapest: second to the last bay on the far end of the landslide row. Landside was the widest street in the city, cobbled with two-foot-square stones cut from coral beds. On one side, *Yamoto* created a duralloy cliff and the bays five stories up with cantilevered cranes to lift up material. On the other side were the tall, narrow houses with shops occupying the first floor. Unlike the stores of Georgetown, which had a normal door leading into the dim interior, the Ya-ya stores had walls that would fold back, opening up the entire store to the fresh air. The weather was fair, so the stores had extended out into the street, showcasing goods in movable display racks.

While the other warehouses had elevator platform rigged from their cranes. Ethan's workshop was only accessed by a series of wooden ladders leaned against the *Yamoto*'s hull.

"Up the outside of the ship? Why?" Turk eyed the ladders. "The fighter bays have air locks."

"The ship was being illegally gutted by the people renting the warehouses." Paige led the way up the first ladder, which was more like a very steep set of stairs up to a wide ledge in the ship's hull, which seemed to be used as footpath to another part of the ship. The stairs seemed communal, and despite their flimsy appearance were sturdy and well-made. "City council had a host of fears, from deliberate sabotage of their remaining weapon systems to the accidental damage to the ship's structural system, so they locked everyone out."

Every twenty feet there was a ladder from the first ledge up to wooden landings built into the old torpedo hatches. Each landing studding the mile long hull was shared by three fighter bays. The landings were twenty feet long but only three feet wide, allowing only one person at a time to climb up onto them and move to the next ladder.

Turk studied the landing overhead and said, "I'll go up first."

The last ladder was rickety to the point of being frightening. Turk caught hold of Paige's wrist and hauled her up into the bay when she reached the top, proving that she wasn't the only one rattled by the ladder.

"I should have just come up alone," he growled, "and lowered the crane cage."

"Hindsight is everything," she said.

"We're using the crane to get back down."

Considering she'd made the mistake of coming in a kimono, that was fine with her.

The workshop looked like a civ nest, minus the spider mites. Disassembled spaceship parts were heaped into piles. Some of the equipment came from human ships, but most were of alien origin. She could differentiate between the technologies because of the racial style. Obnaoians' machines tended to be transparent, wispy things. Theirs were the most fragile of spaceships—like so much fairy dust—that did not survive the ocean well. Minotaurs built on a massive scale and had a great love of the color red. Their machines were large and clunky as if the idea of "compact" never entered into their minds. Humans liked streamlined equipment, often with molded covers that fit the machine perfectly. Even disassembled, she could tell which parts belonged to which race. None of the human machines seemed to be related to warp engines. She couldn't tell what the alien machines had done while assembled and working. Nor could she tell—yet—what Ethan might have been making with the merger of the various machines.

Paige drifted through the mess, poking into everything, trying to glean enough information that her ability might kick back an answer on Ethan's secret projects.

Some of Ethan's crew had lived in the warehouse alongside of the equipment. With the husks of the gutted machines standing in for walls, they created several sleep alcoves. The sleeping pallets were gone but traces of their owners remained. The largest alcoves reeked of minotaur. The smallest had obnaoian mystic symbols painted on the wall. And course, there were human-sized sleeping areas.

Ethan's handwriting covered the countless scraps of paper littering every surface. Each was a shard of a Rosetta stone of whatever they were working on. In two or three languages and often accompanied with complex mathematics and diagrams, Ethan obviously had been the language hub. Some of the notes were clearly about warp engines, but there were other machines and research scattered in among them. She gathered the papers together as she found them. Mikhail might be able to use them to recreate some of Ethan's success with *Fenrir*'s engine.

There were several cleared areas, signs that Ethan or Hardin had taken things away. The basics of day to day life. Tools. And whatever they'd been building. Judging by the dust on the floor and the lack of footprints, no one had been in the warehouse since before the explosion at Fenrir's Rock.

Despite all her skills, Paige never understood Ethan. What moved him? Why he was so different from her? As they shared parents and upbringing, they should have been much alike. He seethed at the world for reasons he could never make clear, even to her. Whereas she had been able to chose a direction for her life and pursue it, Ethan always seem to flounder in aimless misery.

Obviously, the seraphim had given Ethan a direction to go. But what did the seraphim tell him? How did it lead to warp engines?

Turk was studying a map taped to the wall. More of the Rosetta shards were taped around it.

"What's that?" The intensity of his focus on it drew her to his side. It was a map of the Fenrir Archipelagos. A circle had been drawn around Fenrir's Rock. A radius line from the smallest to the largest was labeled "r=10.5 miles."

Turk touched one of the scrap pages. It was one long equation that filled the paper. "This is a warp field equation. Given a known engine size and distribution of mass, what is the radius of the resulting field? This calculates out how much area would warp with Fenrir's engine."

It was one thing to know that Ethan had created a machine that Hardin perverted into mass destruction. It was another to learn that Ethan knew perfectly well what Hardin intended to do and yet continued working with the man. It was like Turk had punched her in the stomach. She gasped out in pain and horror.

"No! I can't believe that idiot would have purposely triggered a warp field next to Fenrir's Rock. That couldn't have been the plan."

Turk eyed the map. "The radius listed here is much larger than the result of the equation. I think the map is showing the range the engine needed to be *outside* of when triggered. This was supposed to be the necessary safety zone."

Did it make it any better than Ethan had at least given thought to the danger before leveling an entire landing? That he hadn't originally planned on killing hundreds of people? Killing members of their own family?

What was Ethan trying to do? She sat down to sort through the papers she'd collected. She sensed that there were two different directions to Ethan's work. One led to the warp drive and the destruction of Fenrir's Rock. Hardin figured prominently in those plans. The other work focused on the seraphim. Ethan had built something that looked like a spiderweb using obnaoian phase shields. She scanned the workshop. There was nothing that looked close to it among the machines that were left. Near the back of the warehouse was a void in the clutter that matched the machine's footprint. Ethan still had the device then—was still listening to whatever the seraphim were telling him.

Turk's comline buzzed quietly and he tapped it. "Commander Turk here."

Commander Turk.

"Sir, this is Rabbit. Hillary . . ." The little tom started.

"Hillary-chan!" Hillary called in the background.

"Hillary-chan," Rabbit corrected himself to use the endearment. Did he even know what he was calling her? Did Turk? Probably not. "Hillary-chan says that the hak is stirring."

"We'll be right there," Turk answered without even glancing at her.

It took nearly thirty minutes to race to the island, but even then the hak took another ten minutes of shifting almost imperceptibly in its shell before emerging. By then Mikhail had rejoined them and they'd fully updated him on what they'd found at the workshop.

"I know this is slightly late to ask," Mikhail whispered, "but how do we know we're talking to the hak that can answer our questions?"

"It's considered that when you ask the universe a question, the entire universe answers." Seeing that Mikhail didn't understand, Paige rephrased. "That this is the hak that we chose is part of the universe answering."

"But you chose it." Mikhail obviously wasn't getting the zen of her answer. "Doesn't that somehow negate the universe's answer?"

"I'm part of the universe." Paige wondered if this was how the hak felt when they talked to her. It was clear to her, but Mikhail obviously was having trouble following the logic.

With a quiet rustle, its plastron lowered slightly, revealing part of its scaled legs folded back inside its shell, and its hard beak. It breathed out through the small nostrils on the top of its beak, sending the cherry petals swirling away. The blast brought Paige its smell of old leather and the scent of the air after a thunderstorm. It made her arms prickle as the fine hair on them stood up.

Mikhail came alert, excitement clear on his face. Paige motioned him back, trying to caution him with a look and hand gesture to be quiet and patient.

The hak sat for several more minutes in its half-open position, and then, slowly, emerged from its shell the rest of the way. The hak's eyes were always startling, dark with a flare of white ringing the black pupils. It slowly blinked at them. When it spoke, its voice was like static on a radio tuned to a dead station. "I am awake."

It was the ritual greeting.

"I am yet asleep." It took her months to learn how to make the clicks and pops and hiss of their language. "I wish to be awakened."

"Open your eyes and awaken."

She had had hours to consider how to pose this question and yet it still seemed daunting. One reason the priest hadn't picked names for the hak was because they didn't seem to use them. The hak had no names for humans or seraphim. "There are beings that move among us. We cannot see them clearly. We cannot touch them. We cannot hear them. We do not know what they are and we do not know how to speak to them."

Slowly, the hak's eyelids lowered to slits. For a panicked moment, she was afraid it was about to go back to meditating, which was not unheard of after someone asked a hak a difficult question.

But then it answered. "Those you speak of are bodhisattvas."

In Buddhist terms, bodhisattvas were enlightened beings who were not yet a fully awakened Buddhas. They were more like saints than angels, if one had to translate it to Christian terms.

"They are awake?"

"They are no longer in the *manusya* realm but they can be seen."

Manusya realm was a buddhist term, using the sanskrit word *manusya*, which meant human, to indicate the reality that humans lived in. It did not automatically mean that the seraphim had been human, just that they once existed in the same realm as humans. At one point in time, the hak had confirmed that the minotaur and obnaoians also were all in the "human" realm. The *tiryag-yoni* or animal realm was considered a lesser realm than the human realm, but humans could still see animals. Above the realm of humans there was the realm of the *asura* or demigod realm and the *deva* or god realm.

The hak claimed that they were Buddhas and existed in the *deva* realm. Being that hundreds of years had gone by since the island had been discovered and in all that time, the hak had never died or reproduced, eaten, drank or—for months at a time—not even moved seemed to support that claim.

"Can you talk with them?" Paige asked.

"We hear them and understand them," the hak said. "They cannot hear us. They cannot understand us."

"I can hear you."

The hak tilted its great head and eyed her closely. "Can you?"

This is what she hated about the hak. One moment she was sure where she stood in the conversation, and the next moment she was lost in a sea of philosophy.

"I hear something," she said carefully.

"You hear echoes of the truth. You see shadows of the truth. To see my true form and hear my true words, you would need to be enlightened. This world would not be an egg for you, trapping you as it protected you."

"I think that the bodhisattvas are attempting to speak to . . . me." She wasn't sure what difference it would make if she kept to the total truth, but the slight change was easier to communicate.

The great head dipped as if to nod. "As each race has their own voice and their own words, they have their own course to enlightenment. We each found our own way, swimming alone." It meant the hak. "Your people swim in a school, never as one, but rarely alone. The ones that you speak of were once one, moved as one, were becoming enlightened together as one. But then they were divided into two, and madness followed. The bodhisattvas seek to save their race which has sunk from the *manusya* realm, to the *tiryag-yoni*, to realm of the *preta*, and now dwells in the *naraka* realm."

Paige sat stunned the information, trying to grasp it. An entire race sinking into oblivion of unreason? Was this what the seraphim were talking to Ethan about? Somehow she couldn't imagine him struggling to save another species. It seemed almost too selfless of him. And what could Ethan possibly do to save an entire species? Perhaps the seraphim were beginning to realize that they'd made a bad choice, which was why they were now focusing on Mikhail. "Do they want me to save their people?"

"They are desperate for someone to hear them." The hak said. "They are seeking your people out for help. They are still new to the demigod realm; their powers are too limited to save their people. They have realized that your people listen well enough to catch echoes."

"If you can hear them, why haven't you helped them?"

"To help, one must be heard as well as listen. They stand close enough to you to hear your echoes."

She wasn't sure how well the seraphim understood the human via their echoes. And what did they expect Ethan/Mikhail to do to save their race? While it might be maddening to try to figure out what the seraphim told Ethan via the hak, currently they were the only ones available to ask. "There are some of us trying to help these bodhisattvas. Did you act as an intermediate between them and us?"

"That was a mistake. Truth can be distorted by too many voices. Our attempt to help has made things much worse."

While she wasn't sure that the hak were truly gods, there was something very frightening to have one of them admit that they made a mistake.

"Worse how?"

The hak closed its eyes and retreated ever so slightly into its shell. Paige struggled not to think "no, no, no" at it. There was no real proof that thoughts could influence the hak, but you could never be sure with them. Peaceful thoughts. Peaceful thoughts.

"A stone thrown into an ocean makes small waves that disappear quickly. A stone thrown into a puddle, disturbs the entire puddle."

Oh that did not sound good. "This place is the puddle?"

It slowly tilted its head and blinked. "This is the first of puddles from which all puddles were made. To throw a stone into this puddle is to throw a stone into all puddles."

"Maybe I shouldn't try to help them." Certainly her life would be much simpler if she just ignored all the people that needed help.

"Time is an ocean with many shores. You can let the tide take you where it will, or you swim where you desire. The one thing you cannot do is stand still."

Mikhail sat mesmerized by the hak as Captain Bailey spoke to the alien. Sleeping, it had seemed like a great rock. Awake, though, the hak was a different creature. Mikhail was filled with the profound sense that there was more than he could see, something huge and ponderous, focused onto them. He understood why the natives considered the turtles holy; he wasn't even religious and yet he felt awestruck.

He was amazed too that humans had ever learned enough of their language to carry on a conversation. Their language was like listening to a star's electromagnetic waves. The air distorted slightly, like that of an energy shield. And as Captain Bailey spoke with the alien, the cherry blossoms that had been floating down stopped in midair, and then the pea gravel started to drift upward. Captain Bailey ignored it all, focused intently on the alien. Toward the end, she too began to drift upward while still kneeling in front of the alien. Communing with it.

Then the great turtle finished speaking, blinked its eyes that looked like solar eclipses, and withdrew into its shells. Bailey was the first thing to settle onto the ground, then the pea gravel, and lastly, the cherry blossoms.

"What did it say?" Mikhail asked.

"I'm not sure." Captain Bailey was still frowning, focused inward, trying to understand what had been said to her. Mikhail waited. "According to the hak, the seraphim are the bodhisattvas of another race."

"Are what?"

"Are bodhisattvas. Those who are enlightened are Buddha. Those who delay their own final and complete enlightenment in order to save others out of enormous compassion are called bodhisattvas."

"Apparently something has happened to their race, the hak didn't say what, but it's devolving. It's moved through the realm known as the hungry ghost. It means they're sentient beings with the insatiable hunger for a particular substance. Usually it's something disgusting like dead bodies or feces. It's always bizarre. They're now in the *naraka* realm or in English, hell."

"Literally?"

Paige threw up her hands. "Who knows?" She recounted then in detail what the hak had told her.

"The seraphim wanted Ethan to help them," Mikhail summarized. "Something has gone wrong, and their situation can get worse?"

"I'm not sure how," Paige said. "But yes."

20 You Say Tomato . . .

I SAW THIS COMING, PAIGE THOUGHT WHEN HILLARY CREPT out of the forward hold. Her little sister looked well-tousled and had a half-dressed Rabbit trailing behind her.

On the way back from talking with the hak, they decided to split up again. Mikhail took the notes that she'd salvaged from Ethan's workshop back to the *Svoboda* while Paige returned to the *Rosetta*. The plan was for her to move her boat closer to his ship. Her family was translating for his crew. His Reds were standing guard over the *Rosetta* while her family was gone. It made sense to have the two vessels together to eliminate the constant coming and going. Turk, of course, came with her to oversee his Reds, and Hillary made sure that Rabbit was included. Somewhere between paying off the charges for their old berth and reaching the *Svoboda*, Hillary must have snuck Rabbit down below to make love.

Hillary glanced toward Paige to see if Paige was watching and realized she'd been caught. After a blush of embarrassment, Hillary lifted up her chin in defiance. Her look said, "He's the one I want."

Oh joy. It was Hillary's right to decide, since falling in love sometimes meant leaving your family and home behind for the rest of your life. Rabbit came with entanglements. Making arrangements was probably going to be more complicated than just deciding which boat was in a better position to take the newlyweds.

Paige had to admit that in some ways, Rabbit was a better choice than Mitch had been for Charlene. The little Red was genetically designed to be without defects, raised with expert medical care, and was proving to be quite intelligent. Mitch was a distant and not very bright cousin whose immune system had been slightly damaged by a brush with a killer virus. Mitch, though, had been freeborn on this world. Rabbit was property from another.

Turk was lounging beside her, close enough that they were actually touching lightly at the hips. Now and then, he seemed to become aware of the contact and move away, and then, as if subconsciously drawn to her, drift back. Yet another male with entanglements.

"Rabbit is a yearling?" She tentatively waded into that pool.

Turk paused to scan over the boat to find the said Red before nodding, as if her comment was a way to point out some problem. "He's been on active duty for six months."

Reds were given sixteen years to mature, so Rabbit was the same age as Hillary.

"He's your runt?" Runts were lowest rung on the dominance ladder, nicknamed that because they were also usually the smallest, like Rabbit.

"Yes, but he's my smartest. That's why I picked him."

Well, if she had to take a combat-trained Red out of the crèches, a runt who was used to taking orders from everyone would probably be best choice.

She took a deep breath and stepped deeper into the treacherous waters. "He's got a standard contract?"

Turk pulled away and turned to face her fully. "Why?"

No, he didn't like the way this conversation was going. She could table the subject and take it up with Mikhail, who probably could handle it with less emotional difficulties. Talking about it with Turk, however, might create openings to discuss their own impossible relationship.

"We want Rabbit. Mikhail said I could have anything off the *Svoboda*. We want Rabbit."

Turk shook his head, moving farther away from her. "Why Rabbit?"

"Hillary's taken a liking to him."

"Your sister is a cat fancier?"

"What's a cat fancier?"

"A sick, perverted little slut."

He meant like the woman that humiliated him on the data-stick that Paige had found in his cabin. He was comparing her virgin baby sister to that? Paige punched him. Even as she swung, she realized it was a bad, bad knee-jerk reaction. She'd been brought up that if someone slurred you, it was one thing, but no one could slur your family. She also recognized that if she only hit him lightly, things could get messy fast, so she committed to it, and hit him with everything she had.

It was kind of gratifying to know that a Bailey could still bring down a full-blooded, combat-trained Red in one hit.

"Well, I knew our relationship was impossible." She rubbed the hurt from her fist. "It just wasn't going to work out."

He wouldn't stay down for long, and when he got up, he was going to be pissed. Time for damage control. Thank God the bridge was high enough that none of his Reds saw what was happening. She wrestled his body onto his stomach, and got his arms levered behind him before he came to.

She expected him to come to fighting. He jerked once, realized that she had him pinned, and went still.

"Now you listen to me, and you listen well," she said. "I could have left you in that nest. I didn't have to help you."

"You were stuck," Turk growled.

She smacked him on the back of the head. "Wrong answer. You say 'Thank you,' and mean it."

He growled lowly.

"You do not come onto my ship and call my baby sister a slut. Not when Rabbit wouldn't be doing anything to her that you haven't already done to me. Or are you implying that I'm a sick, perverted, little slut too?"

She was tempted to hit him again. She was angry that he had pushed the issue when she tried to keep her distance. Hurt and furious that he might think her perverted for giving in to him. It was really hard not to punch him again, but she had to get control before things got totally out of hand.

Turk had stopped growling, though his breathing was rough with anger. She kept him pinned, aware that their bodies were close as they'd been when they made love.

"Do you even know what a Red is?" she asked him. "They're

humans made faster, stronger, healthier—better. You do understand the word? Better? It means superior in every fucking way that could be imagined. Reds are humans—only better."

The door to the bridge opened. Rabbit stood in the door. He reacted instantly to Paige pinning Turk down. Rabbit brought up his rifle and fired, hesitating only a moment because it was her, not the normal target he'd been trained on. It was enough for her to jerk out of the way of the bullet. She followed the momentum of her body, rolling off Turk and behind the cover of the map table.

"No! Cease fire!" Turk roared, surging up to throw wide his arms in an effort to block a second bullet. "Stand down and get out!"

"Sir?" Rabbit sounded all his sixteen years.

"Get out!"

The door slammed shut. Paige scrambled back more as Turk turned and started toward her.

"Easy." He put out his hands to show he was unarmed. "I need to see where you were hit."

"Paige?" Orin called from the other side of the wall. There was a clink of a gun being loaded.

"I'm fine! Don't do anything." She'd run out of floor space. Like it or not, she was going to have to let Turk get close to her.

"I thought he hit you." Turk's hands shook as his quick search found the burn of the bullet's path across her shoulder. "I thought he killed you."

"I'm fine." She could see that he wanted to hold her, be comforted by offering comfort.

Mikhail had been watching the *Rosetta* sail up to his ship. Everything had seemed fine as it paused to let a barge go by. At the last minute, though, a single gunshot rang out. Mikhail watched through binoculars as the focus of everyone on the boat turned toward the bridge. He scanned through the crowd and couldn't find Turk.

If Turk had been hurt, his Reds would be reacting. The Reds on the *Rosetta*, though, were alert but in stand-down position.

Minutes later Turk finally appeared, coming from the bridge. Even at this distance, Mikhail could read his distress.

What was going on? *Oh, please God, don't let it be that one of my crew hurt one of the Baileys.*

One of the *Rosetta*'s dories were lowered and Turk bullied his Reds into it. Captain Bailey came out of the bridge. She and Jones climbed down into the boat, but there was an obvious "us" and "them" going on in the cramped quarters.

Mikhail met the launch out on the dock. Turk was the first one off.

"What's going on?" he asked Turk.

"I don't care who they are," Turk growled lowly. "You're not going to give them one of my Reds."

Bailey stayed on the boat as Mikhail's pride unloaded. "If I had known you were such a two-faced bastard I'd never have slept with you."

Turk jerked around, his body stiff with anger.

"Secure your pride." Mikhail caught Turk by the shoulder before he could do anything.

Turk glared at him.

"Commander," Mikhail growled at Turk.

Turk worked his jaw, but his eyes flicked to Paige and sudden despair filled his face. He barked commands at his Reds and stalked away.

"Which Red?" Mikhail asked.

"Rabbit," Bailey said.

"Rabbit?" He could understand Turk's reluctance to part with the little Red. Mikhail liked the small tom. What he couldn't understand was why that particular Red.

"You put a sixteen-year-old boy on my boat with my sixteen-year-old sister. She might already be pregnant by him. I would like the father of my niece or nephew to be living with us, not locked in some Red pit getting the shit beat out of him because he's small."

How did I not see this coming? Once he actually considered it, Hillary's and Rabbit's courtship had been fairly obvious. He had no idea, though, how it escalated to gunfire. He sat on the edge of the dock, and indicated that she should come join him. "Let's talk this out instead of shouting at each other."

She swung up onto the dock and sat with her back to the piling.

"What does Rabbit think of this?" Mikhail asked.

"He's more than happy to sleep with my sister."

"And he wants to transfer to your ship?"

"You don't ask someone like him what he wants. He doesn't

know how to choose. Your people have never given him the chance to pick anything in his life. He doesn't pick what he wears. What he eats. Even what he's allowed to say to most of the people he interacts with."

"So you just take him away from everything he knows?"

"Yes, it sucks, but that's how it is in this world. Everyone on one boat is usually related. To find a partner, you hook up with someone from another boat. Then one of you has to leave everything you know behind."

He rubbed his temple, wondering again how this led to a shooting. "You and Turk?"

"Was a mistake." She stood up.

"Because he's a Red?"

"Because he thinks any woman that would sleep with a Red is a sick, perverted slut."

That sounded like a quote, and a possible cause for violence.

Mikhail sighed. "I don't suppose you mentioned that you're a Blue mixed with Red?"

It was always bad when someone made their face completely neutral.

"I don't care what you are," Mikhail said. "All I care about is how you treat my brother."

"How did you know?" she asked, meaning her parentage.

"Eraphie told me about her cousins. She had no way of knowing I'd ever meet you. So how exactly are you and Eraphie related?"

"My grandfather had been a crèche technician. After the Georgetown crashed, he raised twenty Reds out of the same lot as his sons. All of his sons consider themselves brothers."

"Making you and Eraphie cousins."

She nodded. "Genetics is an odd lottery system. Eraphie came out mostly Red. My brothers and sisters and I came out mostly Blue."

"And it won't bother you that your sister's children will be full Red?"

"As I told Turk, Reds are humans—only better."

Apparently she wouldn't be bothered in the least. Too bad things were not working out between her and Turk; her attitude toward Reds would probably be good for his brother. Normally he wouldn't even consider her request, even though he desperately needed the Baileys' goodwill. But all things considered, the yearling was probably better off with the Baileys. Runts lived a hard life and were usually the first to die.

"You can have Rabbit," Mikhail said. "Give me time to deal with Turk. I'm going to have to beat on him to see reason."

"Thank you."

Turk fumed the whole way down to Beta Red. He knew what was happening behind him and he was furious with both Mikhail and Paige. It was Mikhail's father, Ivan, all over again, doing what was politically good, and disregarding what was good and right for Mikhail and Turk.

It wasn't until he was tagging in his Reds that he realized that Rabbit had fallen behind. He found the little Red curled in a ball, sobbing.

"Rabbit?" He knelt down beside the Red.

The tom looked up, tears streaming down his face. He was furring over from stress. Turk realized for the first time that the tom had spent most of his time in Ya-ya shed down to bare skin. "I just realized—I'm never going to see Hillary again, am I?"

Turk sighed. "The *Rosetta* asked to buy your contract."

"Hillary said they would, but then I shot Captain Bailey. I shot a human! They'll probably want me put down."

Would they? He'd been so concerned about whether Paige had been hurt that he hadn't considered that Rabbit's actions might have changed the *Rosetta*'s demands. Well, he wasn't going to give his Red up, for either reason.

Turk pushed Rabbit's head back so that the little Red looked up into his face—to see Turk's level calm promise. "I won't let them hurt you. And Captain Volkov would never agree to it."

Mikhail might sell one of his Reds to the *Rosetta* as a sex toy to get continued help, but he wouldn't kill one of his own crew without good reason. Turk was sure of that.

Rabbit sniffed and scrubbed at his eyes. "Why—why does it hurt so much?"

Turk sighed. He'd never had this talk with one of his Reds before. There was never any need. With the exception of cat fanciers, Reds never interacted with women. "It's called love."

"No, Hillary taught me about love. Love feels all warm and soft and good. This feels like someone pushing something through my chest."

"Love is mostly about pain," Turk said. "What happened on the *Rosetta*?"

"I heard what sounded like a body falling, so I investigated and found Captain Bailey assaulting—"

"No, I mean with Hillary. When did all this start? How long have you been . . . ?" *And how the hell did I miss it? Scratch that, I know: I let myself be distracted by Paige.*

"The first day, when Hillary was shopping, I felt so stupid and clumsy. But then she started to ask me questions. What was space like? How dark was it? Do stars actually twinkle? What's it like to be weightless? Were planets really balls? And I realized that we just knew different things. She knew her home and I knew about our home."

"I meant the love part."

Rabbit looked at him in confusion. "It is part of the love part. She said she liked talking to me and I said that I liked talking to her. We went to this place in the hold, where no one goes, and we talked."

"Just talked?"

"At first." Rabbit studied him. "Am I in trouble for doing more than talking?"

"No." Turk kept all anger out of his voice. He was no longer sure who all he was angry at. Rabbit, though, was the most innocent person on the list.

"The space in the hold was really small, so we had to be close together while we talked. And I realized that I liked being close to Hillary. And she said she liked to be close to me."

God, at this rate, it was going to take half an hour until he found out if they had had intercourse. Worse, it sounded more innocent than any teenage fumbling that Turk had witnessed, meaning he insulted Paige's little sister for nothing.

"Did you make love?" And in case that wasn't clear enough, Turk added technical terms for body parts and used hand motions to make it obvious.

Rabbit gave a tiny nod. "Many times."

So Rabbit had lived up to his name while Turk wasn't paying attention.

"Commander?" Inozemtsev called down the hallway to Turk. "The captain wants you and Rabbit in his cabin immediately."

Despite being just a kitten, Rabbit was a seasoned warrior.

Heartbreak he couldn't understand, but walking into a war zone he knew how to deal with. He took a deep cleansing breath and stood, sealing away all fear and uncertainly behind icy calm. Turk envied the crèche-raised; sometimes he wished he could shut off all feeling except anger, because anger was useful.

It was the first time he ever dreaded stepping into Mikhail's cabin the same way he used to dread going into Ivan's office.

"Commander Turk and Private Rabbit here as ordered." Turk snapped a salute.

"At ease. There is something I need to show Commander Turk." Mikhail cued something up to his monitor.

Turk took a deep breath as he realized that the nearly naked woman on the screen was a Red. He wanted to ask Mikhail questions but not in front of Rabbit, who might repeat it to Hillary.

"Eraphie?" Rabbit asked.

"Yes, soon to be your cousin, Eraphie Bailey."

"Bailey?" Turk's stomach gave a sickening lurch. No, he must have misheard.

"What's a cousin?" Rabbit asked.

"It means Eraphie and Hillary's fathers came from the same Red lot," Mikhail said.

"The Baileys . . . are Reds?" Turk asked.

"What's a father?" Rabbit asked.

Mikhail studied Turk before saying, "Rabbit, report to the *Rosetta*. They've bought you. Ask them to explain *father*, since you might be one soon."

"Does being a father have anything to do with shooting Captain Bailey?"

"No. Go on. They're waiting for you."

Rabbit snapped a salute and left.

"They're Reds?" Turk asked again.

"No. They're not," Mikhail said quietly. "Reds are humans raised in the dehumanizing crèches, where they're mentally shaped into weapons and nothing else. The Baileys are all natural-born humans, raised by loving mothers and fathers with a wide extended family."

"That"—Turk pointed at Eraphie—"is a Red. How much more catlike does she have to get before you see her as a Red?"

The comline chimed as Mikhail stared at him in amazement. Mikhail slapped on the intercom. "What?"

"Sir, I need to talk to you about . . . something." Tseytlin's voice came over the com. "You really need to see this."

"I'll be there shortly." Mikhail slapped off the com. "I would have thought that you, of all people, would understand. Rabbit might have just walked out of here as a Red, but the main reason I'm letting him go is because I believe in ten or twenty years, with the Baileys beating that Red mentality out of him, he will be just as human as you are."

"I'm not human."

"Yes, you are," Mikhail cried and came to grab his shoulders. "Turk, I was brewed in a petri dish and decanted out of a bottle just like you. I know I'm human, and I know you're just as human as I am."

"When you can fur over under stress, we'll talk about being the same." Turk didn't trust himself to stay in the room. He was angry enough to hurt someone. He didn't want it to be Mikhail. Blind as he was, Mikhail still meant well. It wasn't Mikhail that he was angry with.

Paige had lied to him. He'd asked that first day if he was the only Red onboard, and she had told him yes. They were all Reds, and she had told him that he was the only one. He'd been so gratified that she didn't look at him in horror, that she treated him with compassion. All the while, she kept the truth from him. That under the skin, she was no different than he was.

Upset as Mikhail was over the fight over Rabbit and Turk's whole reaction to it, he put it aside when he saw Tseytlin. The man looked completely distraught.

"What's wrong?" Mikhail put out a hand to steady the man and was dismayed when he flinched away.

"There are nefrims on the ship," Tseytlin whispered.

"What?" Mikhail reached for the alarm but Tseytlin caught his hand.

"No, no, no, they don't know that we know that they're there. We have to get the upper hand here." Tseytlin scurried to a parts locker and started to dig out equipment. "I have to apologize to you, Captain. You told me that they were there and I thought I was thorough, but I should have trusted you and looked harder. Instead I just thought you'd gone a little loony on us. Considering your family history, I thought it best not to comment on it."

What was Tseytlin talking about? Mikhail hadn't said anything about nefrims being on the ship. And what did he mean—family history? Did he mean the infamous bloody reigns of various Tsars of ancient Russia?

"Calm down man, and tell me what's wrong," Mikhail said.

Tseytlin scurried back to Mikhail, his arms overflowing, to whisper, "Back at *Fenrir*, when you asked me to look for invisible aliens, I was worried you were going over the edge. Especially when I set up a standard perimeter security line and not a thing showed up. I was worried that you were losing it. I truly was."

You and me both, Mikhail thought. But he had Tseytlin looking for seraphim, not nefrim. "What's happened?"

"I found the bastards!" Tseytlin winced at his own loud outcry and dropped back to a whisper. "The ship is crawling with them! Invisible—or something."

"Nefrim?" Nefrim were two meters tall with half a dozen limbs. The seraphim were—as far as he could determine—snakelike. "Are you sure?"

Tseytlin nodded vigorously as he piled the equipment into a cart. "The notes you gave me earlier—most of them I can't understand—had details on the results of sensors used to detect 'ethereal' beings." Tseytlin indicated quotes around the word with his fingers. "I had to look that word up. But it made me realize that our standard security system was inadequate for this place and—and—I had the *Rosetta* people get me sensors for testing a myriad of things. Not the standard motion and heat—just—just— everything. I threw together a small grid in the hangar, just as a test run, and fed them all through pattern-recognition software to a rendering engine."

"Okay." Mikhail tried for a soothing and calm answer. "The seraphim become visible then?"

"Seraphim hell!" Tseytlin pointed to a bank of monitors. "Look!"

Each sensor reported in a different color of light. As each sensor was mapped out, it was just a mass of disorganized colors playing through the vast space. It overlaid the slight distort in the air that Mikhail recognized as a seraphim moving through the hangar. He scanned the monitors, looking for the composite image, expecting to find the snakelike form of the seraphim. But the composite was the familiar multilimbed body of a nefrim.

"But that's not what I—" Mikhail stopped. He couldn't truly

"see" anything any of the times he "saw" the seraphim. He had only gotten impressions. The seraphim were already messing with his mind; perhaps they were influencing what he saw too. "Are they using some kind of camouflage gear?"

Tseytlin shook his head. "They're passing through walls, equipment and people. It's like they're not really there, but they are."

"Ghosts," Mikhail murmured.

"Kind of. Out of phase with us somehow. Most of the crew doesn't seem to perceive them. Only a handful of Reds react to them but don't seem to be able to track them."

Hardin had said there were no nefrim in the Sargasso. He might have been lying, but more likely mistaken. If this was the nowhere that you went when you misjumped—and the only such nowhere—the universal constant for failing to safely arrive back to normal space—then it would also be where lost nefrim ships went.

21 War Room

TURK WAS STILL GLOWERING WHEN MIKHAIL CALLED A MEETING of his officers. Mikhail didn't know how to make things better for Turk, so he ignored him, hoping that giving Turk time and space to work it out would help.

"Our mission was to find the *Fenrir* and the other missing human ships." Mikhail had set up the recorder to include their briefing with the engine if they ever reached that point. "We were to determine if they were in enemy hands. At first there seemed to be no nefrim activity here, but now we've found that the seraphim are nefrim with abilities we've never seen before."

"Nefrim ghosts," Turk grumbled from where he was holding up the wall.

Hak had claimed that the seraphim were enlightened beings but the rest of their race was descending into hell. Certainly the description matched the nefrim's habit of reducing planets to rubble, uninhabitable even by them. Mikhail wasn't sure he wanted to drag his crew through the metaphysical. He decided to stick with the concrete facts.

"What's more, the humans here consider the seraphim as holy beings. Ethan Bailey, most likely, believes that angels are speaking to him, giving him commands."

"Can we trust the crew of the *Rosetta* if that's the case?" Kutuzov glanced to Turk for the answer.

Turk darkened. Mikhail expected him to say no after his fight with Captain Bailey. But Turk looked away, and gave an unbiased accounting. "There was no reason for them to lie to me about Ethan's activities; we all thought that the *Svoboda* had sunk. Their radio was broken, so they couldn't have known the truth. They had been out of contact with Ethan from when Paige—Captain Bailey bought the *Rosetta* and left Ya-ya, nearly two years ago. They thought he was here in Ya-ya translating. He contacted them when they were in Georgetown Landing and asked for them to meet him and their cousin's boat, the *Lilianna*, at Fenrir's Rock to do salvage on a ship in minotaur waters."

"What Eraphie Bailey told us confirms most of that," Mikhail said for Turk's sake. "Ethan was working independent of his family and called them in without giving them all the details of what he was working on—and that led to the deaths of *Lilianna*'s crew."

"Ethan Bailey was working with the nefrim though?" Kutuzov said.

"Yes," Mikhail said. "But we don't know what the nefrim's agenda is."

"Kill. Destroy. Leave things in ruin," Turk growled.

"That fits the description of Fenrir's Rock," Kutozov said.

"There seem to be simpler ways of destroying a landing," Mikhail said.

"Every landing will probably have an engine," Tseytlin pointed out. "And if the humans think they're escaping this place, they'll be more than willing to do the work for 'the angels.' It's an insidious trap if you ask me."

Mikhail shook his head. "It feels too subtle for nefrim."

If it wasn't for the visual evidence, he wouldn't believe that they were dealing with nefrims at all. What the hak told them *felt* like the truth: the race had been cleanly divided into the ethereal, benign seraphim and the corporeal, malevolent nefrim. "Captain Bailey felt as if the notes she collected from her brother's workshop showed two agendas."

"I'm not making much headway in understanding these notes." Tseytlin was leafing through the papers. The engineering chief rubbed at his temple as if the paper was giving him a headache. "I've studied what United Colonies High Command gave us on *Fenrir*'s engine and I—I don't think I can re-create this work, not without years of work, the help of the *Rosetta*'s mechanic and one of the Baileys translating. A minotaur who knows what the hell it's doing would be helpful too. The ones we have know nothing."

Which was what Mikhail was afraid Tseytlin would say. Said minotaurs thundered overhead. The newest game introduced to them was kick ball.

"Why do we have these minotaurs onboard?" Lidija Amurova interrupted. She'd been the crew member assigned to "ride herd" on the minotaur children, as Captain Bailey put it. "Surely someone in the city knows more than I do about how to treat them."

"I want to gather as much information as possible on these aliens," Mikhail said. "The human ships seem to be grouped together based on what star system they were trying to jump into when they were lost. In the Sargasso, the minotaur landings are close enough to trade with. It's possible that in our universe, we could make contact with the minotaurs."

"We have enough trouble with the nefrim," Ensign Inozemtsev muttered. Mikhail had included him in spite of his demotion from Red commander to Turk's second in command. Despite his fight with Captain Bailey, Turk might decide to stay with the *Rosetta* when the *Svoboda* chased after Hardin.

"The minotaurs might be our ally against the nefrim," Mikhail pointed out. "For all we know, they might even be fighting with the nefrim on another front."

They thought about it and nodded as the implications soaked in.

Mikhail steered them away from the minotaurs and back to Ethan Bailey's notes. "The question is: is there evidence that we're looking at two divergent agendas?"

Tseytlin blew out his breath and started to leaf slowly through the papers, laying them out in piles. After a minute, he nodded slightly. "I think there are three actually, or to be more specific, there's the original start point, and then the two branches. The start point is this pile." He placed a hand onto it. "It has nothing to do with warp engines. They're obviously building an experimental device, using scientific methods, and keeping close track of their attempts and failures. It's from this work that I got the idea for the sensors. They seem to be attempting to interact with the invisible nefrims but the focus was on audio, not visual."

"Nefrim talking, that would be a first," Inozemtsev said.

It would. Humans had never detected communication between

the nefrim ships or had even been able to establish that the nefrim used language. If the seraphim were nefrims, and Ethan Bailey had learned their language, that in itself would be important information.

"This pile." Tseytlin tapped the second stack of papers. "They're all warp engine information. There are huge jumps in logic missing. Like all their no-brainers have been left out. I'm guessing that every . . . being . . . that worked on this part was on familiar grounds. There was no need to grapple with translations on paper.

"That leaves these." Tseytlin motioned to the smallest pile. "They're so cryptic, it's like they're nearly written in code."

Mikhail shifted the pile to in front of Ensign Moldavsky. "I believe you're the expert on cryptology."

Moldavsky winced but nodded. She started to leaf through the papers.

"This supports what we've been told," Mikhail said. "Ethan was working on communicating with the seraphim. Project number one. He has a breakthrough and Hardin gets involved . . ." Mikhail paused to consider the facts. "Hardin gets involved because Ethan's next project for the seraphim is developing a working warp drive."

Turk grunted. "If Hardin doesn't know that the seraphim are nefrims then he's only seeing Ethan's work as a way back home."

Mikhail nodded. "But it worries me that Hardin lied to me when I told him what our mission was and asked him what he knew about *Fenrir*'s engine."

"He paid for everything," Turk growled lowly and started to pace. "He had to know what was going on."

"Exactly," Mikhail said.

"Why would he lie?" Tseytlin asked. "We have a spaceship with minor damage and intact warp engines. You'd have to be blind not to know how rare that is here."

"Because we're Russians," Inozemtsev said.

If it had been Mikhail in Hardin's place, he would have joined forces with an old classmate. Was Inozemtsev right? Had Hardin lied because the *Svoboda* wasn't a United Colonies ship? No. Mikhail had stated that their orders originated from the U.C. High Command. Inozemtsev stirred restlessly, reminding Mikhail that his crew was waiting on him.

"Hardin's motivation will have to remain unknown." Mikhail

made a note to go back and consider it. "We have to consider him 'hostile,' but I don't think he's working with the seraphim. If he and Ethan Bailey were both working with the seraphim, Ethan wouldn't be encrypting his work. Since Ethan is the one that started the work with the express purpose of communicating with them, let's assume he's the nefrim collaborator.

"Hardin funded the work." Mikhail returned to the chain of events. "But he wasn't there when the *Lilianna* arrived with Eraphie onboard."

"Assuming she didn't lie to you," Turk growled.

Mikhail couldn't see any benefit for Eraphie to hide a connection to Hardin, but Turk was right, he had to stay skeptical of everyone and everything, least he blind himself. He had to make some assumption, though, to follow threads of thought. "If what the Baileys are telling us is true, Ethan needed two ships to do salvage on a seraphim ship. He arranged for the people he trusted most, his family, to meet him at Fenrir's Rock instead of working with Hardin. I don't think it's coincidence that the *Lilianna* arrived while Hardin was elsewhere. If things had gone the way Ethan wanted, his family would have been on their way long before Hardin returned."

"Do you suppose the navigation system on the nefrim ship is intact?" Tseytlin suddenly asked.

They all stared at Tseytlin dumbfounded. In fifty years of war, they'd never been able to capture a nefrim ship with its navigation system intact. Unlike human ships, the nefrim engines didn't record jumps. They had never been able to tell where the nefrims were jumping from. The coordinates of the nefrim home worlds were still unknown.

"They couldn't have the self-destruct alarmed while jumping," Tseytlin said. "We've ascertained that weakness in their self-destruct mechanism. If they jumped in here like we did, no enemies in sight, there's no reason to arm it, and then—bang—they could have bought it just like us."

"Oh Christ, if it is . . ." Kutozov gasped out what they were all thinking.

"Motherlode!" Inozemtsev murmured.

"I think finding the nefrim ship just moved to the top of our priorities," Mikhail said.

"I think, sir, that these might be map coordinates and dates."

Moldavsky pointed to symbols on the encrypted notes. "These symbols here are minotaur numbers." When Mikhail looked surprised that she knew, she added, "Becky was teaching the minotaur children hopscotch in the hangar. They marked the grid in chalk and used minotaur numbers. They use hexadecimal instead of base ten. So this set of symbols are two numbers separated by a nonnumber character. They could represent longitude and latitude. And here, in the corner, someone has translated this other set of symbols into a human date YYST."

One of the first things that was explained to them once the *Rosetta* crew started working with them was "Yamoto-Yamaguchi Standard Time." All spaceships kept Earth Greenwich time. But with the odd time dilation, each newly arrived ship soon discovered that their clocks and calendars didn't match any other version in the Sargasso. Apparently the closest the human landings had ever come to war was over time standardization. In the end, they settled on adopting Ya-ya's clock and calendar. The *Svoboda* was still trying to determine what the dilation would mean in regards to their return.

"Eraphie said that the seraphim ship was in minotaur waters," Mikhail said. "This might be a listing of wrecks that the minotaurs know about. One of them might be the ship we want."

Moldavsky made a sound of disgust as she flipped the paper over. "There's dozens."

Mikhail nodded. He nearly asked Turk to check to see if Ethan had given the *Rosetta* the location of the salvage, but then just made a note to ask himself. What would be ideal was tracking down Ethan and trying to pry the truth out of him. Eraphie said he went to Mary's Landing. Mikhail paused, considering. "If Ethan had a workshop here in Ya-ya, and both the *Rosetta* and *Red Gold* are on their way to Fenrir's Rock, why would Ethan go to Mary's Landing?"

"It doesn't make sense," Turk agreed. "The Baileys hate Mary's Landing. When we were out in the middle of nowhere with a failing engine, Paige refused to even consider going there, even though Mary's Landing was closer."

"Eraphie couldn't believe Ethan decided to go," Mikhail said. Eraphie had said that Mary's Landing made up debts to enslave anyone with adapted genes. Hardin claimed that almost everyone out of Georgetown fell into that category. As a newcomer, though, Hardin had nothing to fear from Mary's Landing. "I wonder if

Ethan had a choice. Hardin was fronting a lot of money for the project. What if Mary's Landing was Hardin's silent partner? Hardin kept it secret because the Baileys wouldn't work with Mary's Landing. Everything went smoothly and the project was nearly at a successful end."

Turk understood where he was going with the logic. "Mary's people go to check on the engine and a fight breaks out as Ethan realizes who is paying for the work. Somehow during the fight, the engine gets activated and warps out ahead of schedule."

"Yes. Wait. No." Mikhail frowned. Something wasn't meshing. "It . . . It couldn't have been Ethan that started the fight. He was outside the blast zone."

"That blows a very good theory," Tseytlin complained.

"Maybe." Mikhail thought a moment. "What if it was a Bailey but not Ethan? The *Lilianna* arrived just hours before the engine warped out. What if they're the ones that started the fight?"

Turk nodded. "They go looking for Ethan to tell him that they've arrived, they end up on the engine while he's not there, and discover who is funding the project."

Mikhail made a note that he would have to show Captain Bailey a picture of the dead Red to see if she could identify him. "Afterward, Mary's Landing has leverage on Ethan to force him to go with them. Eraphie said that he had a minotaur and obnaoian with him, so some of his technical team survived."

"So we go to Mary's Landing and use our orders from the United Colonies to force them to turn Ethan Bailey and his team over to us?" Kutuzov said.

His crew was ready to fight someone, anyone. He could see the eagerness on their face to grapple with something other than the laws of physics, bare elements, language differences, and inscrutable but peaceful aliens.

"Mary's Landing is pre–United Colonies." Mikhail hurried to put a damper on that. "As such, it has no reason to cooperate. At the moment, it's a virtual unknown. Both Ethan and Hardin are operating covertly. Ya-ya and Fenrir authorities and most of the civilians were totally unaware of Hardin's activities. We have no justification for treating the entire landing as hostile—yet. We need to gather information and perhaps do a reconnaissance before attempting anything."

They nodded, obedient but a little disappointed.

"Hardin said he was coming to Ya-ya after he left Fenrir's Rock. We need to find out where he is. It's possible that he went to Mary's Landing instead and retrieved Ethan Bailey." Mikhail wanted to talk to Hardin before they escalated to armed confrontation. "Tseytlin, see if you can recreate that translation machine. Worst case scenario, we ask the seraphim ourselves what they want. Moldavsky, translate out those coordinates. Amurova, run every test you can think of on the minotaur children. We'll be leaving them here when we leave, so I want to gather as much information as I can before we go. Turk, see if you can figure out some type of weapon that might work on our unwanted guests."

"The seraphim?" Turk said.

The thunder of hooves overhead reminded Mikhail that they had more than one type of aliens onboard. "Yes."

Tseytlin held up a finger. "I have a few ideas on that line."

Mikhail indicated that Tseytlin should pair up with Turk. "Kutuzov, you have command of the ship, I'm going to talk with Captain Bailey. Keep on top of the repairs. I want us in fighting shape and ready to leave as quickly as possible."

Paige's fight with Turk had her family all spooked. True to his word, though, Mikhail had sent Rabbit to her, complete with his gear, which he didn't have to do. The combat suit alone was worth hundreds of yen. Whatever Turk might feel or not feel, Mikhail was obviously interested in maintaining a relationship with the *Rosetta*.

Rabbit was truly a dear thing. Once she managed to convince him that she wasn't angry with him for shooting at her, he relaxed and focused on fitting in. He was very good at it, better than Turk, and didn't even trigger Mitch into displays of dominance. The only thing was that with two sets of teenage lovers onboard there was no way she could ignore that she was all alone. That stupid idiot.

The very worst of it was knowing Turk had taken all the abuse that the cat fancier had dished out to him but had lashed out at her and her family. For whatever reason he could withstand abuse but he couldn't extend common courtesy to the people that rescued him, protected him, loved him . . .

Paige blinked at burning in her eyes, determined not to cry over the lout.

The *Rosetta* had a new engine. They were nearly done with all their repairs. And they had money left over for supplies. The

Svoboda was also nearly completely repaired and knew where to find other translators. Paige was tempted to bolt from Ya-ya and save herself the pain of having to deal with Turk again.

As if summoned by her thoughts of him, Mikhail hailed her from the dock.

"Permission to come aboard?" Mikhail didn't even have a guard with him. Then again, the *Svoboda* was close enough to spit on.

"Come on up, Misha." She used his nickname to show that she wasn't mad at him.

He came up onto the deck and watched as they passed materials down through the halls for finishing up the crew quarters. "This is the last of your repairs?"

Paige nodded, not sure what to talk to him about. She would not ask how Turk was.

"I was hoping that Ethan might have given you a location for the ship he wanted you to salvage," Mikhail said.

"No. He said he'd talk details when we got to Fenrir's Rock. Radios are not the most private way to talk. Discussing a find means that anyone listening in could decide to beat you to the claim. A hundred thousand miles is a long way to go to find out someone stole the salvage out from under your nose."

Mikhail nodded, his disappointment showing on his face.

"Why do you ask?" she asked.

"The seraphim are the bodhisattvas of the nefrim. Eraphie said Ethan told the *Lilianna* that it was a seraphim ship they were going to salvage."

Paige studied him hard. He was telling her the truth. He wasn't sure if he should trust her completely, but he needed her. And what's more, he wanted to trust her. She nodded. "I talked to Ethan a couple times before my radio died. We went over general details like how deep down the ship was, what equipment we would need—those kind of things. He wanted to know if I'd ever dealt with a bull of a certain holt. I hadn't. I figured that the holt was close to the salvage but I didn't want to ask on the open air. I asked if we were going to be trading with him, and Ethan said that we were and I should do homework on him."

"If the *Svoboda* went to see why the seraphim wanted this nefrim ship salvaged, will we need to interact with the minotaur?"

Paige groaned and covered her eyes with her hands. She should have bolted.

"We will," Mikhail guessed from her reaction. "You don't really want to come with us."

She sighed and ran her hands through her hair. "Misha, Misha, Misha. You're going to need my whole fucking ship. You don't have the equipment and know how to salvage a spaceship out of several hundred feet of water. Hell, do any of your people even know how to swim?"

He shrugged. "I—really don't know. I can. Turk can." But he didn't offer up anyone else.

She so didn't want to say yes, but it was hard, knowing that Mikhail was doing this for no other reason than to fight the nefrims. "Let me think about it."

"We also need to find Hardin's ship, the *Red Gold*," Mikhail said. "He might be here in Ya-ya, or he might have gone to Mary's Landing to get Ethan."

It was fairly easy to cross-check the harbor authority logs with the local gossip to find out that the *Red Gold* hadn't been in Ya-ya for weeks. She radioed Mary's Landing Harbor Authority, and asked them to connect her with Ethan or Eraphie. It was fairly standard practice and shouldn't have raised a commotion. The cagey answers she got, along with crude attempts to pry information out of her, suggested that Mary's Landing was lying.

It would take time to find someone in Ya-ya who might be able to connect her with an reliable source at Mary's Landing. Until then, it was a rare clear day in Ya-ya, so she took Mikhail, a young female ensign, and a guard—a Red by the name of Coffee—to the top of *Yamaguchi*.

"There is something intrinsically wrong about climbing around on the outside of a spaceship without a space suit on," the ensign complained as they scaled up the outside of the *Yamaguchi* via ladders.

"If it makes you feel better, we can go back and get you a space suit." Mikhail's eyes showed that he was teasing. Paige covered her mouth to keep from laughing as the ensign already seemed annoyed.

The top ridge of the *Yamaguchi* was the highest point for a hundred thousand miles. As Paige hoped, the view was clear all the way to Mary's Landing, thousands of miles down the axis, and a few hundred in the direction of the spin. There was a large storm front sweeping in from the Counterspin. It extended down the negative for hundreds of miles, but most likely it would miss

Mary's Landing. The ensign had a day to study Mary's Landing until the top of *Yamaguchi* became unsafe.

As usual, the sight of *Queen Mary IV* mesmerized the newcomers. The cruise liner was built to impress and it was sad to know that, three generations after it vanished, it was still the largest, most stunning ship ever created by man. Especially since it was inhabited by people with a very civ outlook at life.

If Mary's Landing was Hardin's backer, then Ethan had done more than just destroyed Fenrir's Rock when he sent back the engine. He'd started a cascade of events. Mikhail's arrival was just one of many reactions. Hardin and Mary's Landing now knew it was possible to travel back to normal space. The United Colonies knew there was a place of mystery. And they had the engine. Even if Mikhail never returned, and Ethan refused to cooperate further with Mary's Landing, the pressures of the Nefrim War would still cause the United Colonies to send more ships, only next time they might have modifications made to the engines.

The door was open. There was no shutting it.

The question now was, what would be the best future for her family, and everyone that had adapted blood? If Mary's Landing gained control of that door, and managed to keep control of policies set, then adapted and their offspring would stay things to be owned. New Washington was only slightly better, as they might see offspring as freeborn people. Under Viktor, the Novaya Rus Empire had already banned the production of Blues as immoral. Turk was proof that Reds could be considered free. And Mikhail, as the next Tsar, had offered protection.

Clearly, it was in her family's best interest that Mikhail be the one to control the door.

The hak had said that she couldn't stand still in the ocean. That she would be carried either by the current or pick her own course. If she wanted the best for her family out of this, then she had to help Mikhail.

"The *Queen Mary* wasn't that heavily armed originally." Mikhail finally broke his awed silence.

"When you have a habit of kidnapping your neighbors, you need big guns to discourage people coming and taking them back," Paige said.

"I suppose," Mikhail murmured. "Moldavsky, feed what you can into the rendering program."

"I probably can find people that can tell you details of the harbor," Paige said. "People here in Ya-ya tend to be pure human. And Ya-ya is too big of a bite for Mary's Landing to chew. Ceri might be able to tell you a little about the layout of the ship, but it's hard to say. She was very young when she left, and from what I understand, Blues really don't have run of the ship."

"I happen to have all the deck plans of the ship," Mikhail admitted.

"You do?" Paige said.

"Because of Viktor." Mikhail blushed slightly. "I had a slightly morbid curiosity about how my first self died."

"He didn't die in the crash. He—" She caught herself before finishing.

"Killed himself. Yes. Eraphie told me." Mikhail pulled a photo out of his pocket. "I hate to ask you this, but do you know this person?"

Paige glanced at the photo and instantly tears burned in her eyes. It was her cousin, Jack. "Oh God."

"He's one of your cousins?"

Paige held out the photo blindly. She didn't want to look at it again, see him so battered and dead. He'd been so strong and healthy last time she'd seen him. "It's Jack. He's Eraphie's older brother."

Mikhail took back the photo. "I'm sorry for your loss."

Paige nodded mutely. She didn't want to break down in front of Mikhail's crew. She blinked furiously, trying to clear her vision. "When you told us about the *Lilianna*, I assumed he was dead . . . but . . . but you keep hoping for a miracle."

"Yes, I know." Mikhail glanced toward the *Svoboda*, sitting like an odd gosling among the fishing boats. "I meant to say this earlier, but thank you for saving my brother. And please, don't be angry with him. Turk should have had the world on a silver platter, but that's not how it's been. He's had a hard life."

"He shouldn't have called my baby sister a slut."

"No, he shouldn't have." Mikhail considered for moment, obviously looking for something safe to say. All he came up with was, "He really shouldn't have."

Paige caught of sight of a large ship slowly moving toward Ya-ya's harbor entrance, attracting attention to a flock of pilot boats.

"What is it?" Mikhail asked.

She realized that she'd gasped. "It's a minotaur ship. It's prob-ably the parents of our lost calves. We need to get back."

Paige tried to focus on the upcoming meeting with the mino-taurs. Unfortunately, they had left Moldavsky and Coffee on the *Yamaguchi*, which meant that Turk met them at the *Rosetta* with a security detail. Nor was there time to stand and argue; the harbor authorities wouldn't want the minotaurs to come in under their own power and the minotaurs were probably not going to be patient about being reunited with their children.

As the *Rosetta* cast off, Turk followed her like her own personal thunderstorm.

"If you're going to be like that, go away," she finally snapped at him. She didn't have time to dwell on his hurt feelings.

"I'm doing my job." Turk lowered his voice when he was angry, and it rumbled like distant thunder.

"No, you're not." She brushed past him to grab her boots out of her locker. She wished she had thought to impose some kind of ban to keep the Russians off of the *Rosetta*. The boat was just too tight of quarters to ignore him. "You're following me around like a hurt little boy, like I've done something wrong when you're the one with a problem."

"You lied to me."

"No I didn't." She pulled on her boots with the steel cleats fastened to the sole. The loud stomping she could achieve with the boots was satisfying in the mood she was in.

"You told me there were no other Reds onboard."

"And there weren't. My family wasn't born out of jars and we weren't raised in a crèche."

"Eraphie can fur over. Can you?"

"What kind of question is that?"

"Can you?"

He wanted her to confess that she was some kind of monster.

"I will not dignify that with an answer." She stomped to her cabin to find her cap.

He followed close enough for her to almost feel his body heat. "Why can't you just tell me?"

"Because it's all a DNA crapshoot which of us can and can't. Where is the line of humanity? How many generations do we need to be away from the crèche before you get over your bigotry?"

"You didn't even give me a chance to—understand."

It didn't help that her cabin smelled like him. With his scent, it seemed to hold dangerous memories of being in his arms and happy. She snatched up her cap and turned to leave, but he filled the doorway, blocking her escape.

"I brought you onboard my ship with my baby sisters and my little brother and my younger cousins. I was putting all their lives on the line. I didn't know shit about you except you were wearing Red combat armor." She slapped said armor hard enough that her hand stung. It made her angrier, and she was tempted to hit him harder, but it would probably only hurt her.

"And you couldn't tell by the time we got to Ya-ya that I wasn't raised in a crèche?"

"I could tell you're a bigoted shit." She gave him a shove, wondering if he was going to force her to fight with him. "You hate being adapted." He didn't back up enough for her to squeeze past, so she shoved him again. "You don't respect people that you think are adapted." She dropped her voice to mimic his deep growl, shoving him yet again. "*Why didn't you tell me Ceri wasn't human?* What the fuck difference would it make if she was a Blue or Red or Purple, for God's sake, except in your maggoty little brain?"

"Maggoty?" he rumbled dangerously, but he'd backed up enough that she could escape him.

"You're pissing me off." She stomped away from him. "Go away before I find nastier names to call you."

The idiot followed her. "Were you ever going to tell me?"

"You left me!" She was losing it. Her volume was raising as his timbre dropped lower. "Before telling you could become an issue, you left! Why are we even having this discussion? As soon as you and your brother can track down Hardin, you're going away and never coming back."

"Did you think if I didn't know, I might stay?" He was reaching subsonic level.

"You've made it fairly clear that you were only staying with me because you were afraid to deal with Ya-ya on your own." The urge to add more hurtful things hit her and she locked her jaw against it. "Go away!"

"Can you fur over?" He pressed.

"Go away!" she shouted.

"You didn't tell me when you knew it was important to me. You knew. You knew and kept silent. If you had told me, I wouldn't have called Hillary a slut. I would have realized that Hillary would see Rabbit as a potential mate. I would have known what putting him with her would have ended up with. You totally blindsided me and then acted like I'm—*zlody*—the evil one."

"No I can't fur over," She snapped. "My mother couldn't either; she was just half-Blue, so she died of hypothermia when my parents' boat went down. Orin and Charlene and Hillary can and they survived. But we had a baby brother that couldn't—just like me—and he died—just like I would have died if I'd been with them."

She turned away because if he'd looked relieved that she couldn't fur over, she would have hurt him, with both words and fists.

Orin came clambering down from the bridge. "It's Hoto's ship! Someone must have gotten a message through to him about his kids." He glanced toward Turk, and his eyes narrowed as he guessed what was going on. "We're almost to the peace docks." They were wood floating platforms that served as neutral ground outside of the city. "The pilot boats have corralled the minotaurs to the docks, but they're afraid that the minotaurs will plow their way in if a translator doesn't show up soon."

"I'm coming!" Paige bellowed.

Turk growled with annoyance as Paige turned away from him yet again. He said one thing out of surprise—she'd lied for days and days. She was painting him as a villain without even trying to understand what he'd gone through all his life at the hands of cat fanciers. Bringing in her parents' death was totally underhanded; it had nothing to do with lying to him and causing this mess.

Orin stepped in front of Turk, blocking his view of Paige. "Don't be such a hypocritical bastard. Just leave my sister alone."

"I asked if I was the only Red onboard and she lied to me. You all lied to me."

"Well, if I'd known that you wouldn't dirty your hands with the likes of us, I would have told you. Saved my sister from a cat fancier."

Turk snarled and swung at Orin. The man ducked and danced backward.

"A cat fancier," Turk growled, "is a pervert that sleeps with Reds because he sees them as animals."

"Glad you know what you are," Orin taunted.

Turk leapt at the man. Maddeningly, the man sidestepped him and then dodged every swing that Turk threw at him. They circled in place.

"I'm not a cat fancier." Turk feigned a punch with his right and followed with a swing from his left.

Orin ignored the feint and sidestepped away from the true blow. "You slept with the disgusting animal didn't you? That makes you a cat fancier."

Turk roared and attacked without reserve. He wanted to silence the filth coming out of the man's mouth. Maddeningly, Orin ducked and weaved, avoiding every blow.

He's only half Red, I should be able to hit him. Turk fell back, panting. How was Orin dodging his attacks? "Paige didn't tell me she was a Red."

Orin laughed. "We didn't want trouble. Crèche-raised Reds won't fight with humans."

"I'm not crèche-raised . . ."

"You're acting like it. My grandfather worked in a crèche. I know what went into engineering Red gene banks. They didn't add anything that wasn't human. There's no cat or lizard or fish in our genes. It's all human. Tweaked. But it's all human. That cat shit is nothing more than screwed up behavior training."

"I wasn't raised in a crèche," Turk growled. "I didn't go through behavior training."

"You got it somewhere. You're not as deeply etched as Rabbit. But when you were young and impressionable, someone rubbed your nose in that shit, telling you lies, until you believed them. And you know what's truly sad? By refusing to see the truth, you're letting those bastards keep your nose in shit. Bad cat! Bad cat! Shame on you for thinking you're human."

Turk lashed out and this time caught Orin fast by the throat. Turk felt a flash of triumph until he realized that there was no fear in Orin's eyes. The man looked at him the same way Mihkail would; trusting Turk not to hurt him. Their eyes were even the same shade of blue.

Had the man let him win? Orin had started the fight. And now he let Turk win. What was Orin trying to do?

"Why are you doing this?" Turk growled.

"Because my sister loves you, even though you're being a complete asshole. I figured this would go one of two ways. Either you get your head out of your butt or you'd kill me. And I trusted you not to kill me."

Turk let go of Orin. It hurt to think of Paige in love with him. Of what could have been—but only if they were two different people.

Orin shook his head, sighing at whatever showed on Turk's face. "Humans are all alone in that place you're from. All they seem to do is examine each other under a microscope to find differences. Why do they feel the need to say 'you're not like me'? We don't do that here, because we have the minotaurs and the civ and obnao. If anything, we cling to each other and say, 'Thank God, you're human too.'"

Hoto was the bull from Midway. He stood a full nine feet tall and clocked in around eight hundred pounds. His coat was rust red and his horns and hooves gleaming jet-black. He wore a loincloth of cobalt blue, earrings at the tips of his jutting leaf-shaped ears, and steel shoes. The makeshift dock quaked as he stomped up it.

"Who is the mouth here? Who? Who?"

"I am mouth!" she shouted at him and gave an assertive stomp. "What's your rush? You so thirsty for beer?"

She was trying for ridiculous. Minotaurs liked broad humor, or perhaps, humans didn't understand them enough to get the finer points of their wit.

Hoto threw back his head in surprise, and then cocked it to one side to get a better look at her. "What? This little thing is mouth?" He towered over Paige as he peered down at her. "I surprised it can think!"

At a distance, you could mistake a minotaur for an animal. Close up, once you got over their sheer size, you could see the intelligence in their face. Hoto's mouth pulled to one side in annoyance, but humor flicked through his eyes. The humor was working.

"You not tall yourself!" Page shouted and stomped her foot. "You just calf! Where your bull, calf?"

Hoto roared out what passed as laughter among the minotaur, a loud braying noise that was deafening close up.

Unfortunately, any exchange of insult was always followed by ritual exchange of blows. She really hated this part. He casually cuffed her on the shoulder. She rolled back to soften the blow to something that wouldn't break her shoulder, but it still hurt like hell.

There was movement behind her and a snarl of frustrated anger. She glanced behind her to see Mikhail and Orin haul Turk back by his scruff.

"No!" Orin growled. "Stop him. Only the mouth can talk!"

"Stay," Mikhail snapped.

Apparently Turk didn't hate her totally. Somehow it only acted like diesel fuel thrown on the hot ember of hurt that had been smoldering inside of her, pain at what couldn't be flared through her. Blinking away tears, she made a fist, and hauling back, put all that hurt into punching Hoto as hard as she could, as high as she could, which landed mid-belly.

The minotaur brayed out laughter. "You hit like a calf, little mouth!"

"I'm a young bull. I will grow bigger."

"Oh yes, you will come to here." He tapped his chest and then tapped a point level with her head on his stomach. "Instead of here."

She laughed as if it was a joke. "Be careful. I might bite your ankle if you make me angry."

That made him laugh. "Ah, but I know your secret. You are smart. The little young bulls that cut out their own herds are the very clever ones. I will be on my guard around you."

Paige considered the minotaur. If she could read ages right, Hoto was fairly young himself. "Then I will have to be careful too—you are not old yourself."

Hoto brayed another laugh and then sobered. "Where are my calves, clever little mouth? Why do humans have our little ones?"

"We found them washed ashore, their boat ruined, and one of them very hurt. We brought them here so we could care for them."

"Which one?"

"The female Zo."

Hoto nodded. She couldn't tell if he was relieved by the news. It was possible that the little bull, Toeno was more valued as the only male. Or he might be more expendable, since one day he'd be Hoto's rival. Paige wasn't sure how minotaurs viewed their children as they were always kept out of sight and silent.

"Let us go then and collect my calves."

∞   ∞   ∞

The Baileys had warned Turk that the minotaurs were large and brutish. Somehow he'd forgotten. Part of it was because he could look down at the children. He'd expected the adults to be only slightly larger. The male that stomped down to meet Paige was huge. It was easily twice her size. One of its beefy arms was nearly equal to her whole mass. Its angry bellows were deafening. Paige's shouts—which had seemed annoyingly loud moments before—were like a mouse squeaking.

The two bellowing at each other was comical until the minotaur hit her.

He nearly shot it. Without thinking, he started to raise his rifle.

"No!" Orin knocked the rifle out of his hands. "Stop him."

And then Mikhail had a hold of him too, and the two of them were hauling him backward when he wasn't even aware he'd lunged forward.

"Only the mouth can talk!" Orin blocked his view of Paige.

"Stay." Mikhail got between him and the minotaur too.

"It hit her," Turk growled lowly.

"She's fine." Orin didn't even look to be sure. "This is how it works. They talk to one another. Hit each other. Drink some beer. Do business."

Turk realized his Reds were standing alert, looking to him for guidance. He forced himself to relax and watch the negotiations, flinching each time the bull hit her. Paige bellowed. She roared. The cleats on her boots gave an extra noise to her stomping. The bill of the cap that she wore sideways stuck out to one side, and she waved it like a horn, tossing her head. She thumped on the minotaur's chest to make a point, and somehow took the beating back. Each time she was hit, a jolt of fear would go through him. Fear that she wouldn't get back up.

Then finally, he realized that the blows weren't really connecting. Just like Orin when they'd fought, Paige was somehow judging when and where the hits would come and shifting a moment before they fell. As his fear lifted, he began to see the artistry in what she was doing. She wove all the minotaur nuances into a complete cloth and vanished behind it. She became a minotaur.

Just like she had all the human nuances down pat.

Eventually, the bull, Paige, and a harbor pilot headed up to the gangplank for the minotaur catamaran to be guided into the harbor so the minotaurs could be reunited with their children.

"Now what?" Turk growled, wanting to follow.

"We have a small flotilla of boats back to the harbor. Paige will stay with them, drinking beer and keeping the peace," Orin said.

The females with Hoto brought out the massive glass steins of beer. Hoto laughed as Paige struggled to lift the stein with both hands.

"We are going to Mary's Holt soon," Hoto said. "I have been trying to tell if we are sailing into trouble."

"Trouble?" Paige was glad that the bull was giving her an excuse to sip instead of chugging. It was good manners to chug the beer.

"We have seen Fenrir's Holt. We know that it was an accident that caused the ruin, but if it was our holt, we would not take such destruction lightly."

"You know that Mary's Holt caused the accident at Fenrir?"

"Mary's Holt were the ones attempting to make the engine work."

Paige suppressed the urge to throw up her hands. Was she the last one to know what her brother had been doing? "How do you know it was an accident?"

"When our people come of age, they move from their father's holt and roam, looking for a place to settle. It lowers the chance of inbreeding."

She supposed with much of one generation in a small town all being half siblings, she could see the sense of that.

"One of our young bulls, Caan, came to human waters. He is very brilliant and wanted to learn human science. He has a theory that we are not all coming from the same . . ." Hoto paused and searched for a word. "Outside place. That all that come here are coming from places vastly different and this is the only place we would meet."

Paige made the noise of understanding even though she wasn't sure what he meant. If he meant that they were coming from different galaxies or even universes that would explain the age-old human question of why they'd never known of the various aliens prior to encountering them in the Sargasso.

"Caan went to Mary's Holt?" Paige asked.

"He came first to here." Hoto motioned to take in Ya-ya's harbor. "He met many civilized and uncivilized beings. By pooling their knowledge, they'd determined . . ." Hoto paused longer this time, searching for a way to making himself clear. ". . . the common point."

"The common point of what?" Paige asked.

"Of here."

She had explained to Turk that jump drives were jumping from point A to point B with the Sargasso being point C. Human had been trying to determine the nature of point C for a long time. When navigating the open sea, the more points of references you had, the more exact you could be with your location. Ethan had combined information from three races. Or perhaps more, if he'd been able to communicate with the seraphim and the hak. And there was the civ.

"Having discovered the common point," Hoto said, "they went to Fenrir to move the engine out into open waters and attempt to send it back to human space. The humans of Mary were to make the arrangements, but something went wrong."

"How do you know?"

"Caan arranged for us to trade engine parts to the humans he was working with. We were to meet them at Fenrir. He communicated with us that they'd moved to Mary and that we were to meet him there."

What happened at Fenrir's Rock was, then, just an accident. Paige drank while she considered the implications. Minotaur beer was actually good beer. It just came in excessive quantities.

"Will we be sailing into trouble when we go to Mary?" Hoto asked again.

"I do not know." Paige did the exaggerated head shake, close to the human gesture but meant that the speaker was more at a loss of an answer than the human's simple "no" conveyed. "They are another herd. We do not get along with them but we rarely fight."

Hoto didn't like the answer and it showed on his face. "I see. Well . . . good neighbors are distant neighbors."

"What did you ask for in exchange of the engine parts?"

"Submersible pumps." Minotaurs used hexadecimal and had a method of counting on their fingers. Hoto held up his fingers to indicate they were to get sixteen pumps off of Mary's Landing. "I'm expanding my holt's fields. It will mean we can have half a dozen more calves."

"You don't care that humans have discovered how to return home?"

"Humans have discovered to blow themselves up," Hoto said. "And home? Home is the place you make."

By the time they reunited the minotaurs with their children in the hangar of the *Svoboda*, Paige was stomping in a wandering path.

"Idiot," Turk growled to himself. "She has no stomach for beer."

"Orin! I've got to pee!" Paige bellowed as she stomped up to them, still set at minotaur volume. "Come and take over."

"I thought only the mouth talks." Turk reached out and steadied Paige as she threatened to tip over.

"Minotaurs can't tell us apart." Orin snatched the cap from Paige's head and put it on. "As long as only one of us is talking at a time, everything is hunky-dory."

"Where the hell do they hide the pisspot in this goddamn ship?" Paige bellowed.

"Get her to a bathroom." Orin stomped off toward the minotaurs.

"I need to pee!" Paige shouted.

"You can stop yelling," Turk told her. "I hear fine, and I'd like to keep it that way."

She laughed, teetering on her feet. "Help me find the bathroom before I explode."

His cabin was closer than the communal latrines, so he took her there. She banged, and cursed and muttered in his toilet closet as he waited. When she came back out, her pants were still untied. They hung low on her hips, exposing her belly button and the top of her white underwear. God, why did he find her modest clothes exciting?

"You . . . you didn't fasten your pants."

"Hmmm?" She tried looking down and walking at the same time and nearly fell over.

He caught her elbow, intending only to stabilize her, but she slid into his arms. As always, their bodies fit together perfectly. Her face pressed to the nape of his neck, her warm breath tantalizingly intimate. He held her gently to him, despite the fact it filled him with sorrow, because it was going to hurt more to let her go.

"I miss you." She whispered against his bare skin, her lips brushing him like butterfly kisses.

He would have thought that would make him feel better, to know that she was suffering along with him. But it merely made him feel worse. It made him painfully aware that he was the one deciding if they were together or not. And he had chosen to be apart.

She ran her left hand down his spine. She pulled him closer to her with her right, playing with the hair at the back of his neck. When she lifted her mouth to his, he couldn't resist kissing her, tasting her again.

"You're drunk," he protested as she undid his uniform and slid her hand across his bare skin.

"I'll burn it off quickly," Paige said.

Because she was a Red.

She sensed his thought and looked up at him, her eyes filled with pain. He hated the fact that he was the one that was hurting her. She couldn't change what she was any more than he could. He kissed her, trying to smooth away the hurt.

Ensign Moldavsky's report was stunningly bleak. Mikhail was glad he decided to review the information alone. He didn't need his staff to hear this without their captain being optimistic.

"Beyond the shielding and their generators, Mary's Landing has four rail guns at the cardinal points," Moldavsky was saying. She highlighted them, making it clear that Mary's Landing had no weak backside. "They seem to be salvaged off of British and Russian ships. As far as I can tell, they all operate. Between them, there are sixteen main batteries, creating an overlapping—"

Mikhail waved her off. "You don't need to continue." He could see for himself how impossible attacking the heavily fortified city would be. If they had all their Reds, they could drop them from overhead and back off until the Reds disabled key gun batteries, which would let the *Svoboda* dart into the city. With only eight Reds and Turk . . .

Jumping to the Sargasso had been full of risk and uncertainty. Despite its label of "suicide mission" Mikhail had extrapolated from the fishing boat's existence that the Sargasso would be in some way safe. Invading Mary's Landing, though, would be a true suicide mission.

"Did you find the *Red Gold*?" Mikhail said.

"No visual, sir, but I set up *Fenrir*'s IFF system so I could use it remotely and I found the *Red Gold* here." She indicated an enclosed harbor area at Mary's Landing that seemed to have camouflage netting stretched across it. "I say he's trying to hide from us."

Trying—or appearing to try? If Hardin was indeed completely hostile to the *Svoboda* and knew they'd be looking for him eventually, Mary's Landing could be an impressively large trap. Sitting out in plain sight would make the fact that the *Red Gold* was bait too obvious.

Winning any strategy game was thinking several moves ahead. Hardin wouldn't have graduated with honors from the Academy without a good grasp on that. At Fenrir's Rock, damaged as the *Svoboda* was, Mikhail still had the advantage. He was expecting a fight. The *Svoboda* outgunned the *Red Gold*, and the *Svoboda* didn't have to worry about sinking. Hardin had been caught off guard, realized he was outmatched, and lied to give himself enough space to gain the advantage. He had to know that Mikhail would eventually discover Hardin's connection to the *Fenrir*'s engine; otherwise he wouldn't have needed to lie. Certainly, once Mikhail found the trail of evidence, there had been no attempt to cover it up. Jack Bailey had apparently thrown all of Hardin's plans askew when he started the fight that ended with the engine warping out prematurely.

Hardin had fled to the largest trap he could find and laid in wait for the chase to begin. If Mikhail was Hardin, he'd leave the IFF operating so his enemy could track him into the trap and then disable it.

"Ensign, lock onto the *Red Gold*'s IFF and monitor it for fluctuations."

"Sir?" Moldavsky looked mystified.

"We're going to contact the *Red Gold*. They're either going to turn off their IFF or move it to an onshore location."

"Shouldn't we . . . just wait for them to move?"

Mikhail shook his head. "The IFF might not really be on board the *Red Gold* anymore. We tapped it from Fenrir's Rock once already. Hardin might have gone to Mary's Landing and set up his IFF there and left already."

"Oh, I see."

"If it shifts, that means that Hardin is at Mary's Landing now and that he is using it as a trap."

Moldavsky nodded. "Yes, sir."

"Once you have a lock, hail the *Red Gold* and tell them that I want to talk to Hardin."

"Yes, sir."

Mikhail waited, hoping that he was misreading the situation and that Hardin had simply panicked in the face of the destruction at Fenrir's Rock. Leveling a human town and killing off countless civilians by accident might have made the man nervous, wary of accountability and repercussions. Operating under United Colonies orders, Mikhail could have represented the face of the law. Perhaps.

"This is the *Red Gold*," Hardin's ship answered Moldavsky's query.

"Captain Volkov of the *N.R. Svoboda* wishes to speak with Captain Hardin."

"Stand by."

Ensign Moldavsky killed her microphone and then spoke quietly even though there was no chance that the *Red Gold* could hear her. "Sir, the signal just jumped. They've moved the IFF, and are now putting me through to Hardin."

Mikhail nodded grimly. The chase was on.

"*Svoboda*, please establish a secure channel," *Red Gold* requested.

Hardin didn't want the Sargasso to learn what Mikhail was about to lay bare. Mikhail considered denying a secure channel. The conversation was sure to be tantamount to stalemate. Denying the secure channel would be tipping his hand that he knew that Hardin counted on Mikhail using the IFF to find the *Red Gold*.

"Secure the line," Mikhail ordered.

"Volkov, you want to speak with me?" Hardin came on the line after the secure channel was established.

Mikhail flicked on his microphone. "Yes, I did Hardin. My orders are from Minister Heward of United Colonies Defense. Unless you've reneged all claims to citizenship to the New Washington Colonies, you are required to assist me in fulfilling my orders."

"And those orders being?" Hardin said.

"To find *UCS Fenrir*, investigate how its engine ended up at Plymouth Station without the *Fenrir*, and return with a report."

"That last part is a little tricky, isn't it?"

"I've ascertained that you were the force behind the engine modification. You paid for all the parts from Ya-ya's salvage yards. I have part numbers on the engine at Plymouth Station and your name on receipts here. It's a very clear trail, Hardin. At this time, it would be pointless to deny your involvement."

"You have no idea what pointless is. Mikhail Ivanovich Volkov. Son of Tsar Ivan. Clone to Victor the Great. A copy—no a parody of Peter the Great; the man was dark-haired for God's sake. He died over six hundred years ago and people are still so much in awe of him that they recreated him. Every person in that root-bound family tree of yours has achieved immortality. The moment you were born, you became a footnote in history. You'll be remembered even if you fail at everything you do. Pointless is to live a life that's totally unrecorded. To be born, exist, and die to vanish away as if you never breathed air."

Mikhail hadn't expected the conversation to take this direction. "But you live it. You exist. Isn't that the real point of life?"

"To claw and claw and claw until you finally die?" Hardin asked. "My family was so obscure that I can't even find records of them living. My grandfather died poor and went into a mass grave without so much as a marker. My father's life goal was to be buried in a proper plot—and he failed. They tore down the housing project I grew up in and put new projects up. If I die here, no one will know I ever lived."

"You go back, you're a hero?" Mikhail guessed.

"I'll be Christopher Columbus. I'll be Captain Cook. I'll be Magellan. Now there's fame—don't even need the first name."

"You've done all the technical groundwork. You know the world. You'll be credited—"

Hardin laughed. "You stupid fuck. I know what will happen—what has happened over and over again. I become a nonentity around you. I was the star of the Academy. The smartest. The brightest. The one everyone expected huge things from. And then you came. It was like a black hole set down on campus. You were the only thing anyone could think about. Every appearance. Every disappearance. Every success. Every failure. I thought I escaped you when I was posted to the *Dakota*, and then it came through the grapevine—you'd picked *my* ship. And I could see starting all over again. You were all they wanted to talk about. I had to keep you off the *Dakota* or I'd never make it beyond lieutenant as long as you were onboard."

"Keep me off?"

"I heard rumors that you were in the Academy only to repair

your reputation of being slightly reckless. I dug into your past and I found all your dirty little secrets. Not enough to keep you out of the service, but there was an instability that everyone was overlooking. So I hacked the placement system and made it look as if High Command had serious concerns over your sanity. It triggered more extensive psych evaluation than normally is given a cadet. But failing it . . . that was all you."

Mikhail clenched his jaw against any retort. Hardin was trying to work him into a rage. It confirmed his suspicions that Mary's Landing was a trap.

"Sir, they've cut the connection," Ensign Moldavsky said. "Should I try to get them back?"

"No."

Hardin could now wait or move without Mikhail being able to tell where his opponent really was. Moldavsky could return to the *Yamaguchi* and try to keep visual, but Hardin probably would wait until a storm front to move between them.

The *Red Gold* might be bait but it wasn't the target. Mikhail had to keep focus on that. The technical crew that did the modifications to the engine was the true target. Even thinking of them as such made him uneasy; this all might end with the technical crew dead. He and Hardin were squaring off in a battle to see which of them would return to normal space. To "win" Mikhail would need to invade a human settlement in order to take civilians by force.

Was his action justified? He'd promised Captain Bailey to claim Georgetown as a N.R. colony and put it under the empire's protection. If Hardin had been right—that the Sargasso was a safe haven from the nefrim—then the needs of Geogetown were outweighed by those of humanity. But the seraphim were nefrims and there was something going on that Mikhail didn't understand. How could he decide what was the most appropriate path without knowing all the elements?

In the end, it all weighed on what the seraphim were attempting to do.

The hak had told Captain Bailey that the seraphim were the "enlightened" members of their race, which they knew now were the nefrim. Something had happened to the nefrim and they were regressing. If Mikhail understood the religion correctly, an enlightened being was peaceful and saintly; "angel" was not far from the truth. The regressed nefrim were the ones attempting to wipe out the human race. Were the seraphim attempting to stop the regression? Were they trying to return their race to something more civilized? If they were successful, could that mean the end of the senseless war?

But the hak had warned that if the humans didn't listen to the seraphim closely, they could make things worse. Worse for who? For the seraphim? For the nefrim? Or for the humans?

Most importantly, how closely had Hardin listened? Had he made the connection between the seraphim and the nefrim? Was he even acting as an agent for the "angels" or was that something that only Ethan Bailey cared about? Mikhail felt that the latter was probably the truth. Oust had reported that Hardin was mistreating his daughter Evangeline because she was a Blue; it was doubtful that Hardin would see Ethan Bailey as any more significant.

Ethan Bailey had started the whole chain of events. He had been listening closely to the seraphim. Whatever he heard, made him start into the engine modifications, so it stood to reason that the seraphim wanted to return to normal space.

Mikhail wondered how they had communicated this to Ethan. He couldn't imagine a language developed from anything they forced him through, unless it was a message full of grief and loss.

Mikhail paused. Grief and loss. Every single memory the seraphim had put Mikhail through had revolved around having lost something precious to him. The hak had indicated that a single event had divided the nefrim and started the process of regression. Could the event have been simply losing something in the Sargasso?

Mikhail couldn't imagine one item that could have such a profound affect on a race. But then, before coming to the Sargasso, he wouldn't have been able to guess that he'd meet aliens like the hak and the seraphim. He reminded himself to keep an open mind.

Ethan planned to have the *Rosetta* and the *Lilianna* salvage a nefrim ship off of minotaur waters. Was the seraphim's lost item, the salvation of their race, still there? Was that why the seraphim were hounding Mikhail?

He had too many questions and not enough answers. Before he waded into battle with Hardin, he would need to be sure that he was doing the right thing.

∞   ∞   ∞

Mikhail explained the problem to Captain Bailey. She had knowledge of the world that he lacked. "Taking the *Svoboda* to Mary's Landing would be true suicide and perhaps totally pointless. Hardin might have taken your brother and everything involving the engines and left."

They were sitting on a shaded part of the *Rosetta*'s deck. Or to be more specific, he was sitting, while Captain Bailey was lying on her back, eyes closed, concentrating on what he was saying. Between them, a pitcher of lemonade sweated in the heat, almost forgotten. The rest of her crew were apparently out enjoying their last day in Ya-ya.

"Hmmm," Bailey said after a long silence. "The minotaurs have a load of engine parts they're delivering to Mary's Landing. It's possible that Mary's Landing has taken over the project. Hardin might not be able to pry it out of their hands."

"Can you guess?"

"I get a strong feeling that Ethan went to Mary's Landing from Fenrir's Rock as an attempt to escape Hardin."

"I see." Mikhail hadn't considered that. It made sense though if Ethan was rebelling against Hardin's control even in Ya-ya.

"Ethan is as good as I am at weighing options. Mary's Landing is fairly unknown to me, but through his dealings with Hardin, he could have learned a great deal more. So it's possible that his assumptions are correct. Mary's Landing can protect him from Hardin. But the deciding factor might be Eraphie."

"Eraphie?"

"You said that Hardin worked hard to lure her to him. I think he planned to use her as leverage for Ethan, knowing that he couldn't pry Ethan out of Mary's Landing without Ethan cooperating."

That too made a great deal of sense. "Would it work? Would Ethan go back to Hardin to keep Eraphie safe?"

The ice shifted in the pitcher, reminding Bailey of its presence. She sat up and poured them both a glass.

"I would like to think he would," Bailey said after sipping her lemonade. "The brother I think I know is a self-centered prick, but he wouldn't allow anyone to hurt his younger cousin any more than he'd let someone hurt Hillary. It depends on how deep of waters he sunk himself as to whether he can swim clear of Mary's Landing. And Hardin wouldn't have taken Eraphie unless he knew that he couldn't bully Mary's Landing into just handing over Ethan."

They hadn't been able to maintain visuals on the distant settlement, so there was no way of telling if the three-way power struggle had disintegrated into gunfire. Perhaps Hardin was trying to lure Mikhail to Mary's Landing to distract them from Ethan. As it stood, though, it was impossible to tell who was victorious.

He'd already guessed that their only option would be to send a spy into Mary's Landing. He'd hoped that she would prove him wrong; Turk was the person best suited to act as a spy. He didn't want to lose Turk again.

"Are there passenger ships that can take Turk to Mary's Landing in a timely fashion?" Mikhail asked.

"Turk?" She gave him a hurt look. When he nodded, she swallowed down the hurt and considered his question. "I don't think that will work. We don't have ships just for passengers—like the *Queen Mary IV* had been. We might be able to find some Ya-ya cargo ships with cabins for passengers; but most have crews that don't speak any Standard. If anything went wrong, he wouldn't be able to communicate with the crew, and he couldn't arrange for passage back to Ya-ya. Besides, Mary's Landing requires adapted to be registered when a ship sails into their harbor. That includes proof of ownership, which is insane since most people are born free."

"What about a ship from one of the New Washingtonian landings?"

Captain Bailey shook her head. "Anything here in Ya-ya will be heading home when they leave. Only Mary's Landing and Ya-ya ships will be going back and forth between the two—and you don't want him on a Mary's Landing ship. You don't."

Mikhail looked past Captain Bailey at the minotaur ship. "Hoto is heading to Mary's Landing?"

"You can't send Turk alone on the minotaur ship."

"Not alone. Any human ship we use, we run the risk of being betrayed by the crew. The minotaurs owe us."

"That's a dangerously human way of thinking."

"All right. That's true. But they have no reason to betray us either."

Captain Bailey considered for several minutes and then nodded slowly. "You're asking a lot of us, Grandpa."

Mikhail had thought he couldn't feel worse. He was wrong. "I know. I'm sorry."

∞   ∞   ∞

Mikhail hated the plan. Loathed it to his core, but there wasn't a better one, short of turning their backs on all of humanity and settling down to learn how to fish.

The *Rosetta* was the first to leave, taking advantage of clear weather. Orin was acting Captain, as Paige was going to Mary's Landing with Turk. The *Rosetta* was heading for minotaur waters to do the salvage on the seraphim ship. Mikhail equipped them with tracking devices and extra radios so they couldn't fall out of contact.

The minotaurs were delayed by the wounded little female, Zo. They lingered in port for a week, waiting for her leg to heal enough to take the ocean seas. Finally they announced that they were heading out. The time had come to say good-bye.

Turk surprised Mikhail by suddenly hugging him. "Don't you implode while my back is turned."

Mikhail laughed into Turk's shoulder. "I'll be fine."

"Promise me."

Mikhail realized then that Turk really meant "if I don't come back" and sobered. "I'll be fine."

"Promise." Turk tightened his hold on him to nearly painful, as if he was afraid Mikhail would self-destruct right there. "You could make a good life here, Mikhail, if you had to. Marry a Blue, settle down, have a passel of kids. Viktor made it work."

Obviously Turk hadn't heard the end of Viktor's story.

"Oh, no, I don't want you thinking you can go getting yourself killed." Mikhail hugged him hard and then pushed him away. "Just come back and everything will be fine."

22 Mary's Landing

PAIGE HAD INSISTED THAT THE WEATHER WAS MILD AS THEY
sailed to Mary's Landing. If the gray heaving waves and dark
overcast skies were "mild" Turk decided he truly loathed the
ocean. They were apparently sailing through a trailing edge of a
storm. In the direction of the spin, they could still see the black
skies and flickers of lightning from the front. Clouds and waves,
though, obscured Mary's Landing.

They were nearly at the settlement before Turk laid eyes on the
infamous wrecked cruise ship. Surprisingly, they sailed out of the
storm and into crystalline waters. From the bow of the minotaur
ship, Turk studied the landing in awe. He'd seen pictures of the
Queen Mary IV taken when it was in space. It took seeing the
cruise liner in the ocean and sailing toward it like a water bug
to grasp the full size of it.

The massive female figurehead towered above the water, seeming
undamaged by the crash. Even her great feathered wings were intact.
A blend of the British queen and Nike, the goddess of victory, the
figurehead serenely gazed out over the water as if confident that
humans could conquer this place under her guidance. She stood
in the shallow water, waves covering her feet. The kilometer-long,
thirty-story-high hull of the *Queen Mary* flowed out behind her as
the train of her dress. The ceramic alloy gleamed pale white with
the surf rippling bright reflections over the wings and dress.

Turk wondered what the aliens of the Sargasso made of this giant human goddess stranded in water?

She was a heavily armed goddess too. Her people had created a wide harbor and then a ring of man-made islands with gun batteries, a reef-filled moat, and then a series of breakwaters to defend their ship from storms and attackers.

Hoto stomped up, bellowing, and gave Paige a rough shove toward the hatch down into the living area. Paige rolled off the shove and blushed furiously at whatever Hoto was saying.

"What is it?" Turk slid between Hoto and Paige. He knew exchanging blows was the only way that bulls socialized. They only hit each other after they built up some sort of rapport. And having watched Hoto muscle around heavy equipment, it was obvious that the male was not truly hitting Paige as hard as he could. But Turk hated the way the bull so casually smacked Paige around; when Turk could do it without interfering, he made it a point to block Hoto.

"He says the pilot boats are coming." Paige's blush went deeper, but she smiled and she quickened her step. "It's time for us to hide."

Hoto was chasing the calves down below too.

"And what else?" Turk asked.

She was grinning fully now. "That I should take my protective bride downstairs and service her until she's a good, docile female. He says based on what he's seen, I'm obviously letting you on top too much."

Behind them Hoto was braying out a minotaur laugh.

Turk discovered he could blush as deep a red as Paige.

The minotaur had only one living area. It was dominated by one large sleeping platform with a great multitude of large pillows—which the minotaurs had expected Paige and Turk to share with them. Apparently it was a show of trust for Hoto to allow another "bull" to share his space. During the long trip to Mary's, without any barriers to hide behind, Turk had to adapt to the lack of privacy. He now knew more about minotaur sexual habits than he ever wanted to. Likewise, he'd learned to ignore the minotaur's presence while being intimate with Paige. They had been careful, though, to stay under sheets to maintain the fiction that Paige was the male.

"I'm staying on top." Turk growled pulling her close. "I'm not about to become docile now."

Turk had spent the entire trip dreading what came next. All they could do now was hide and wait. He wasn't sure why he dreaded it so much; it was like the sitting in the Red pit before a jump, waiting to be dropped into a combat zone. He supposed it was because dying was easy compared to losing everything that you had.

He shouldn't have let Paige get involved. He shouldn't have let her get dragged into his life of killing and death. He should have kept her safe on that stupid ugly boat of hers. She shouldn't be here, where people would kill her or enslave her without qualm, and the only thing keeping her safe was the promise of aliens that they'd not betray them.

And he didn't want to take her off the relative safety of Hoto's ship. But she'd probably hit him if he'd told her to stay.

"Yes, I will," she whispered.

"Will what?"

"Hit you if you tell me stay here, silly man."

"You're scary when you do that."

"Yes, I know."

The plan was simple enough. He and Paige would stay hidden until the minotaurs were inside the harbor. They needed to then ascertain if the *Red Gold* was in harbor and if Ethan Bailey was still at Mary's Landing. If Hardin had already gone, taking Ethan with him, they would simply leave with the minotaurs to be picked up by the *Tigertail* once they were out of Mary's Landing range of fire. They had contingency plans, but the first step was getting into the harbor.

Outside an engine drew close and shouting started. Even muffled by the deck overhead, Hoto's bellows were clear enough. A human voice answered back and Paige hissed a curse.

"What is it?"

"The mouth is a woman. It's not Ethan. We're going to have to go looking for him."

Paige tried not to be disappointed as the Mary's Landing female "mouth" and her armed escort of four men came onboard. Since the engines were for Ethan's work, she'd hoped that he would be the one that accepted their delivery. His absence might mean that Hardin had recovered Ethan from the Mary's Landing people and already left. Mary's Landing, though, had a nearly unlimited supply of second generation Blues, most of who had some ability at translating. Some. Apparently not a lot.

They'd left a remote camera on deck. She, Turk, and the minotaur children crowded around the monitor, watching in mystification. The poor woman seemed totally out of her element. She had the verbal language down pat. She was missing, however, all the body language. She didn't try to expand herself to match the minotaur's size. She didn't stomp, shout, or make large gestures. She didn't have anything to stand in for horns, nor had she tried to disguise the fact she had long hair.

"I think this is the first time she's tried this," Paige whispered. "She's doing horrible. She's too quiet, too small . . ."

"Too docile," Turk murmured.

She gasped. "Oh gods, you're right, she's being female!"

Didn't the woman know anything about minotaur culture? Visiting bulls would speak only to other bulls; anything else was disrespectful of the host bull. Rude bulls became dead bulls.

Paige suddenly realized that as a Blue, the woman knew only one way to relate to males. And Hoto was nine feet of obvious maleness. The Blue was flirting with Hoto but it was only confusing him. The bull wasn't grasping that this mouth was female.

"Oh, this is not going to go well," Paige whispered.

Paige gasped in horror as the Blue moved unnerving close to the bull, reached out, and deftly slid her hand into his sarong. Hoto went wide-eyed and still with surprise as the woman grasped his penis, pulled it out, and attempted to pleasure him.

The calves gasped and made sounds of disgust.

"What is that bull doing to Hoto?" Toeno asked.

"Um," Paige started to make up an answer but nothing came to mind.

"Oh please tell me that she isn't going to . . ." Turk murmured.

The Blue was. She bent slightly, opening her mouth, and tried to use her tongue and lips on the bull.

Hoto yelped in surprise and dismay and smacked the Blue away. He hit her hard, catching her in the head with his blow. The woman went flying across the deck and hit the railing in a crumpled heap.

"Shit, shit, shit." Paige leapt to her feet and pointed at Turk. "Stay!"

She stumbled up the stairs built for minotaurs to get to the deck, praying that Turk would obey her. She couldn't sit back and let the events unfold any farther. There was a chance that Hoto would kill the woman. If he did, God knows what the Mary's Landing people would do.

At least one of the armed guards tried something. Hoto was busily disarming a man, carefully, as the bull thought the man was a female mate of the "bull" he'd just knocked unconscious. The minotaur's sexist culture was working in the human's favor.

A second guard was lifting up his weapon.

"No! Don't shoot!" Paige shouted. Oh please, please, please let Turk have stayed below. She didn't need to add him into the mess.

The guard turned at her voice and took aim at her.

She held up her hands to show she wasn't armed. "What the hell are you trying to do? Start a war with the minotaurs?"

"Who the hell are you?"

"Paige . . . Jones." Bailey was a dangerous name to use. Georgetown was a dangerous landing to come from. "Me name is Paige Jones. I'm out of Fenrir's Rock." Fenrir people had more of a drawl than Georgies, she laid it on thick. "You be?"

"Barry Lewis. What the hell are you doing here?"

Good question. The only positive note was that Mary's mouth was in no shape to contradict anything Paige said.

"Me boat sank off Midway. I've been cooped up with them for a couple months. They all were giving me a ride back to human waters."

"You can talk to them?" Lewis asked.

"A smidge," she lied.

"Why weren't you up here earlier?" Lewis asked.

"I was asleep!" she cried.

"Little mouth," Hoto rumbled. "I don't know what is wrong with that other bull. He tried to bite me!"

Oh gods what did she tell him? She couldn't tell him that the mouth was female or it put her own sexuality into question. "It's a calf," Paige finally said. Calves were considered even more harmless than females. "It's a very badly behaved calf. And very young. Too young to be talking to adults. I'm telling them how stupid they are."

She turned back to Lewis, stomped her foot and did a head toss of disgust. "Stupid! Don't you people know anything about minotaurs? The translator has to act like a male at all times! He thought she was a bull trying to bite his dick off!"

"He can't tell she's female?" one of the other guards cried. He was crouched beside the Blue, examining her carefully.

"With those little hooters? They think I'm a boy," Paige stuck out her chest. Her breasts were only slightly larger than the unconscious woman's but compared to minotaur females, they were both tiny. "Now put down the guns and relax or I'll talk them into taking this cargo to Ya-ya."

Mikhail was glad that they'd equipped the *Rosetta* with tracking devices. It was amazing how difficult it was to find a small boat on the open ocean. Mikhail landed the *Svoboda* on a small nearby island and took his newly purchased launch out to the *Rosetta*. The sea was rough, and the boats tossed on the waves like an amusement park ride.

"We're over the debris field," Orin cried in greeting as Mikhail jumped from the launch to the *Rosetta*. "It's right where your Ensign Moldavsky said it would be."

"Have you dealt with the locals?" Mikhail said. Paige had told him that they would need to negotiate with the nearest bull. More of a formality, she had said, than anything else. Apparently, minotaurs didn't like warships parked on their back door.

"Yes, we told them that you were coming. The bull is actually somehow allied with Hoto's group, so everything is hunky-dory there."

Mikhail nodded, hoping that "hunky-dory" meant *good*.

"It's a rich find. We're going to be out here for a while. But there's something odd about the debris field. Come here, look." Orin led the way to the *Rosetta*'s bridge. On one screen there was a scattering of dark smudges. "When ships hit the water, the debris doesn't really scatter randomly. There's a certain pattern to it. It should—it should . . ." Orin grappled for words. "It shouldn't look like this."

"I see." Mikhail was starting to understand Eraphie's "Blues have something going on up here." The Baileys made the same logic leaps that he did, only more so. Was it just the Blue crossed with Red, or was it because they were Volkov? If Orin said the debris field was off, then it was off.

Orin looked at him in surprise. "Really?"

"It indicates that the manner that the nefrim ship crashed is different from how other ships you've salvaged crashed."

Orin considered him and then studied the screen. "It—it was in pieces before it hit the water. This isn't one debris field, but three. See."

Mikhail considered the various ship pieces. "It's surprising how little coral is on it."

"Nefrim ships never seem to have much on them. It's like the coral doesn't like nibbling on their wrecks."

"This is the bridge." Mikhail was pleased to see it seemed undamaged and perhaps even airtight. They may actually find the navigation system intact and operable. But what had Ethan planned to salvage? What did the seraphim want?

"In ghost stories, spirits are always clinging to things that no longer exist," Mikhail said.

"Ethan might be many things, but he's a good translator."

Mikhail stared off across the featureless water. The only thing in sight was one of the floating islands, so distant it was pebble-sized. A blot of black moving over the water.

It felt wrong to list in the water like this, ungrounded from everything. What was he doing? How did he know this was the right thing? His mission was to find the *Fenrir*, and he had. He'd told his crew that they were coming for the navigation device but deep inside of him, he knew he had come for whatever the seraphim wanted. Why should he be chasing after phantoms? Because of his fear of his own past? Because it was easier than facing his own weakness? What if he was betraying his species? What if this was some kind of weapon that could be used against humans?

He supposed that until they found it, there was nothing to go on but memories.

Clouds had piled out around the floating island and darkened into a storm.

"You said that we would have to watch for a floating island." Mikhail said. "What did you call them? Vimana?"

Orin turned and followed his gaze. "Not that one. It's too far down the axis." He turned into the wind and brought binoculars up to his eyes. After a moment, he grunted. "Yeah, you can barely make Loki out. We have days until we have to worry. I can look up on the charts to see exactly how much time we have. We'll have to move out of its path."

"Can I?" Mikhail held out his hand.

"Sure." Orin gave him the binoculars. "Straight into the spin. Use Fenrir's Rock as a landmark, it passes just down the axis by a mile."

Mikhail eyed the oncoming vimana. Orin called it down the axis from Fenrir's Rock, but it seemed as if would pass directly over the sunken spaceship. "If you have charts, then the orbits of these vimanas are stable?"

"At least for as long as we humans have been mapping them."

"Is it possible that the nefrim clipped Loki?"

"Like you did with Icarus?"

Mikhail nodded.

Orin considered the question. "The vimanas seem to float and not collide with each other because they seem to be made of some material that repels metal and possibly heavier material. The size of the vimana doesn't seem to effect how high it travels. It's as if there is some constant keeping it in place that has nothing to do with mass—because vimanas collect water and vegetation. Lower vimanas travel faster than higher vimanas."

"That would follow basic centrifugal force," Mikhail said. "The items closer to the center moves slowly while that at the rim moves quickly."

"Paige saw you clip Icarus. Because of your acceleration, you actually spun the vimana as you and it repelled each other. It dumped a shitload of stuff off it."

"Anything that looked like Fenrir's Rock?"

Orin frowned and took back the binoculars and stared through them. He got the dreamy look that Paige would get from time to time. "Yes," he finally said. "Fenrir's Rock was part of Loki."

The nefrim ship had hit Loki hard, dropping part of the vimana, and finally falling to the ocean floor. Not so unlike himself. Mikhail had left part of his bridge on Icarus. Had the nefrims left part of their ship on Loki?

"How do we get up there to see?" he asked Orin.

Orin laughed. "We don't. The only thing that can land on the vimanas are kites."

"Can you speak their language?"

Orin laughed again. "They supposedly speak Standard. Their language is one of money and thrills. They'll do it for the kick of it; but you have to pay them to."

∞   ∞   ∞

It took every ounce of Turk's self-control to stay below deck as Paige bolted out to save the situation from spiraling out of control. Especially when Lewis turned and leveled a weapon at Paige. Turk trusted that Paige could talk her way out of trouble as long as she didn't have to explain too much. And she did, smoothly.

Things, however, continued in an alarming direction. True, a pilot came onboard and helped to steer the large minotaur ship into the harbor, just like they did at Ya-ya. There were, however, a large number of armed troops at the dock that they guided the minotaurs to. Said troops showed signs of wanting to board the ship.

"Don't leave the ship," Turk whispered, pressing his fingers to the monitor, wanting to reach out and keep Paige from moving off the ship.

Paige stood on the gangplank and argued with both sides. She got Hoto to allow on the medical crew to care for the still unconscious Blue. Once the Blue was carried off, she and Hoto followed the humans down the gangplank.

"Oh, no, no, no." Turk could barely see her now. She was the shortest person on the dock.

The medic from the medical team turned back. Turk couldn't hear what he said to Paige but saw her stiffen and shake her head. The men standing on the dock, though, slowly gathered in around her.

Turk could barely breathe. Paige hunched down into herself, not liking what she heard, but apparently unable or unwilling to flee. She shook her head a couple more times, and then, reluctantly, held up her arm to the medic.

Oh God, they were going to take her DNA. They'll know she was a Blue. Once they realize it, they might try to seize her.

Can I just kill them all?

The Mary's Landing people weren't that heavily armed, didn't have serious armor, and weren't expecting an attack from him. He might be able to kill them all. If he did kill that many people, though, they would have a limited time window to get safely out of the harbor—with no guarantee that the minotaurs would flee. Actually, minotaurs probably wouldn't flee until they got their pumps, important for their future survival. Killing all of the Mary's Landing people wasn't an option.

Can I kill everyone in this town?
Doubtful.

The medic stepped forward, took Paige's arm, and pressed a medical device to it.

Turk thought about simply going out and joining Paige on the dock. That way they'd be together and he could protect her, but the first thing the Mary's Landing people would probably do was strip him of his weapons and armor. He would have to kill them all to keep the armor and he'd already decided that wasn't a good plan.

No, he would be more effective staying hidden and following. She wasn't in immediate danger; the Mary's Landing people considered her far too valuable to hurt. He had to keep track of her though. He had a tracer that he could use, but he needed to get it on her. How did he get it on her though? One of the calves could take it down. He could hide the tracer in something and have a calf take it to her. Turk hunted quickly around the room for something to put the tracer in.

He settled on a piece of soft-fleshed fruit. The small tracer could be pushed into its side, totally hidden, Paige could tuck it into her pocket, and there would be no reason for the Mary's Landing people to take it from her.

"Toeno!" Turk called to the little bull who was the only calf that would talk directly to Paige. It got all of the calves' attention. Turk showed them the tracer. Pushed it into the fruit. Held it out to the bull. "Paige." Turk tapped the monitor where she stood and then shook the fruit at Toeno. "*Toeno.* Paige."

"*Annnno . . .*" The tallest of the females calves murmured. "*Hano nana ra sa ne.*"

"*Bowae!*" Toeno cried.

Turk had no idea what they said. He wasn't even sure if they were asking questions or not. He couldn't tell if there was any understanding in their eyes. Were they looking at him in confusion or were they perfectly aware what he was asking, only refusing because it broke one of their father's rules?

Turk caught Toeno's hand, pushed the fruit into the bull's hand, and then pointed at Paige on the monitor. He then tried to push the bull toward the door.

The females calves all reacted with outcries. Toeno dug in his heels. All of them started to talk at once, but Turk couldn't even tell if they were trying to address him. Were they angry? Dismayed? Confused? He couldn't read any of their emotion. In Ya-ya, he had interacted with humans that didn't speak Standard. He'd been able to buy food and clothes at the small Ya-ya shops. He'd ask how much something cost with a lift of his eyebrows, understood that the shopkeeper's upraised fingers indicated amount, negotiate the price with shakes of the head, agree to cost with a nod of the head, and close the deal by holding out coins. It had been almost effortless. Because they were both human.

It was starting to dawn on him what Orin meant. What a stupid time for realizations.

"How hard can this be?" he asked the calves. "Take the damn fruit to Paige! Just hand it to her!"

The calves all talked, but he got the impression that none of it was meant for him.

Fine. That didn't work. He'd throw the stupid fruit at her. The ship was high enough that if he stood in the stairwell, no one on the dock could see him. Fruit falling from the sky might confuse the Mary's Landing people, but Paige would *probably* realize that he'd be desperate to get a tracer on her.

Turk glanced toward the monitor to check Paige's position on the dock and groaned. He was already too late. There must have been a sedative piggybacked on the DNA sampler; Paige was being lowered carefully to the stone while a newly arrived woman stomped and shouted in minotaur. The new Blue had also brought more armed guards, these in combat armor; apparently they were expecting trouble of some sort.

Turk swore and flung the fruit across the room. Now what?

He had to get off the ship unseen. He had to be able to follow wherever they took Paige.

The Mary's Landing people must have decided long before they hit the harbor to take Paige. It was the only way to explain how quickly they had acted. It had only taken Turk three minutes to get over the far side of the minotaur boat, into the water, and swim around the stern to the dock. By then, however, they'd already whisked Paige away. There was no sign of her.

Killing them all was starting to sound like a good plan.

Turk swam a little farther down the dock to where a stack of crates shielded his climbing up on to the stones. There, he tucked himself into shadows and scanned the crowd in front of the minotaur ship. There would be grunts with no clue where Paige was taken, but higher-ranked humans would know. He only needed to get one of them alone and beat the information out of them.

Luckily one of the officers volunteered, breaking away to head down the dock alone.

As the man passed him, Turk reached out and jerked him into the shadows where Turk hid. "Call for help," Turk growled as he pressed his knife against the man's throat, "and it's the last thing you'll do."

"Who are you?" The man whispered hoarsely. "What do you want?"

"Where is she?" Turk growled.

"Who?"

"Paige." The name didn't mean anything to the man. "The woman that came with the minotaurs."

"The Blue castaway?"

"Yes."

"Her blood test came up positive for hCG, though God knows how. She was taken to Blue Care to determine if we want her to go to term."

What was he talking about? Was Paige really sick? "What's hCG?"

"Human chorionic gonadotropin." The man read the confusion on his face. "She's pregnant. She's at least two weeks or more for it to be picked up by the tests. Scans need to be run to see if we want the child she's carrying. We didn't think humans could crossbreed with minotaurs, but she's half Red, so anything is possible. If it's not a minotaur-mix, we'll probably abort the pregnancy. We like to control our stock."

"She doesn't belong to you!" Turk growled.

"She wouldn't have been able to pay the fine for wearing a restraint, not as a castaway. We have leash laws for a reason."

My God, a leash law here? For someone born as a human? Just like on Paradise, the law was nothing more than a reason to take what you wanted.

And then, it sunk in.

Oh my God, I'm the one that made her pregnant!

He couldn't keep the shock off his face. Where the minotaurs had been inscrutable, Turk saw the man read Turk's dismay, and Turk recognized the disappointment that filled the man's eyes.

"Oh, it's yours, not the minotaur's." The letdown colored the man's voice too. "That explains it. I know a Blue will fuck anything, but I had doubts she could have accommodated that bull."

Turk snapped the man's wrist. The man screamed shrilly, like a rabbit only maimed by a dog. "Where is Blue Care?"

"On the ship! In the Blue quarter! Gala Deck!"

Turk knocked him unconscious and then snapped his neck. He couldn't risk the man coming to before Turk found Paige and he didn't have time to tie him up securely. There was a pile of steel rods beside them. Turk slotted two through the man's belt and rolled him off the dock.

He had to get to Paige before these monsters that always acted as if he was the animal killed their child.

Using Moldavsky's renderings of the harbor and Mikhail's blueprints of *Queen Mary*, Turk was able to plot a route that would keep him out of sight as he scaled up the side of the ship to a service access hatch tucked in among the "folds" of the figurehead's dress. It had the second advantage that it gave him a good view of the harbor. The *Red Gold* was nowhere in sight. Hardin had set his trap and left.

Since the *Queen Mary* was a spaceship that was never meant to land or even dock with a space station, the hatch's lock was overly simple. The lock could be easily operated by someone in a space suit but still was idiotproof. If the security system was active, the lock would report the hatching opening and closing. Turk dismantled the lock and bypassed the security system. He half expected to find the hatch rusted shut, but it swung open to an area that had been an air lock. The second set of doors, though, had been salvaged. He ducked into the ship and closed the hatch behind him.

The only light was from red emergency LEDs at floor level. A series of similar lights stretched out in a line of red dots to his right. Turk crouched in the dark, checking his map, as he let his eyes adapt to the dimness.

The ship was designed so the crew could move throughout the entire ship, maintaining it, without the passengers' awareness. The air lock had opened to one of the many maintenance elevator shafts. As a ship that never landed, gravity was maintained by acceleration, and the now horizontal shaft had once been vertical. This close to the figurehead meant he was on a top floor. Blue Care was one of the lower floors, in other words, in the direction of the *Queen Mary*'s massive engine. From the stale air and the dust on the floor, the people of Mary's Landing no longer used this service elevator. In theory, then, Turk should be able to get to Blue Care without being seen.

The problem with theory was that it was often proved wrong.

There were two types of hatches opening to the maintenance elevator shaft. One type was like the one he'd just come through, leading to the outer hull. They weren't blocked. The other opening, due to the reorientation of gravity, should have been straight up and down. For some inexplicable reason, the Mary's Landing people had filled the now vertical service corridors with gravel.

At the first corridor opening, Turk knelt down, scooped up handful of pebbles and let them filter through his fingers. Why in the world? He examined the other side of the corridor that now led upward through the ceiling. It had been a bulkhead that would function as an emergency air lock at one time, but now a plain sheet of steel was welded over the corridor.

The second and third shaft were also filled with gravel. He checked his map again, grinding his teeth in frustration. There had to be some way into the ship, this area had some current function, otherwise the outer hatch wouldn't have been in such good working order.

Two more levels down there was the massive conservatory with the hydroponics gardens. He headed for it, growling in anger at the Mary's Landing people. No wonder they used *Fenrir* instead of their own ship to experiment on, it had far too much mass to jump intact.

Turk opened the door to Blue Care to hear Paige's howl of anger and frustration. His heart leapt to his throat. Was he in time?

They had her pinned to a table with wrist and feet restraints. Her knees spread wide, giving them access. The five people around her were formless bodies in white that he struck down. All he could see clearly was her, naked and helpless, screaming.

Was he in time?

Once the people who did this to her were dead on the floor, he tore off her restraints. Paige bolted upright and nearly pitched head first off the table.

He caught hold of her. "Easy, easy."

"Get me out of here." Paige sobbed and clung to him. "I don't think I can walk."

He scooped her up into his arms. "Did they . . . hurt you?"

"No," she whimpered.

He carried her out into the dark hall. He needed to get her back to Hoto's ship, out of the city, and out of this world. He didn't want their child growing up here. Then he nearly stumbled with the sudden realization that the most horrible part of this world was a mirror to his own universe. Mary's Landing was all the other United Colonies. Paradise had had a Blue quarter and Blue Care just as well as Red pits. That there might have been just as many Blue trapped on Paradise waiting for the return of the nefrim, only more helpless than their Red counterparts.

The Novaya Rus Empire only differed in that there were no Blues. And until the Nefrim War was ended, neither Ivan nor Mikhail could institute the kind of changes for Reds that Viktor had done with the Blues.

"The *Red Gold* isn't in the harbor," Paige said.

"I know."

"Ethan is here."

"Screw the mission," Turk growled.

Paige let go of her hold on his neck to punch him in the shoulder. "I need to find Ethan. That's why we came here, to get him, damn it, and we're going to do it."

"You're naked and drugged."

"The drugs will wear off. Ethan will have clothes. I'm going to find my brother if I have to walk there myself."

"All right, all right. We'll search for him."

"We don't have to search. I know where he is."

Paige clung hard to her rage. There was a vast ocean of fear just below her anger that would swallow her up if she let go. They'd taken her so easily. She hadn't realized the DNA test was more than just a test. She hadn't even realized she was drugged until the world slanted sidewise. While she couldn't talk, the newly arrived Blue explained to the minotaurs that she was sick, and she laid helpless on the ground, terrified that Hoto would helpfully explain she had a mate onboard. But the minotaur only nodded and asked about his pumps.

But what was truly horrifying was the way they treated her in the medical facilities. They handled her like she was a dead fish, slicing off her clothes, and pinning her to the table for butchering. How they so casually discussed how she was pregnant and if "it" was worthwhile to "let" it go to term. As if they had a right to murder her child! And they nearly did. And would try again if they caught her.

Fear washed up against her anger, threatening to flood her with its cold, dark dread. She fought the urge to run blindly back to Hoto's boat. Once she turned up missing, that would be the first place Mary's people would look for her. And they would search—Turk had arrived covered in blood. She didn't even want to guess at the death count. She didn't want to be happy that the bastards were dead.

So she focused instead on the fact that Ethan could have gone to Ya-ya instead of coming here. That royally pissed her off.

Ethan's workshop was set up in the cavernous shuttle bay of the *Queen Mary*. Like the workshop at Ya-ya, a vast array of salvaged human and alien parts sat scattered in the space. Paige quietly slipped through the machinery, searching for Ethan, with Turk trailing behind her, a thunderstorm dripping with blood.

She found Ethan at a drafting table. "You!" she snapped and caught him by the collar. "Give me your shirt."

"Paige!" Ethan only stared at her in surprise. "What are you doing here? Why are you naked? Who's the Red?"

"Give me your shirt," Paige growled. Damn if she was going to explain it to him.

"We've come to rescue you," Turk said as if he was the voice of reason between the two of them. Yes, whirlwind of death was the sane one.

Ethan turned to face Turk with all the signs of male dominance kicking in. "Well, you've made a mistake. They're not holding me here against my will. You didn't need to come."

"You're coming with me," Paige growled lowly.

Ethan blinked at her tone. "You can't just show up and expect me to leave with you."

Paige grabbed Ethan by the collar and slammed him against

the wall, surprising even herself with the violence of her reaction. "You killed all those people. Hundreds and hundreds of people at Fenrir's Rock. The *Lilianna* is gone! You killed them all! Our family. You killed our family!"

"No I didn't," Ethan said. "We were going to move the engine and there wouldn't have been any danger . . ."

"They're dead!" Paige cried. "Who the fuck cares what you planned to do? Dead, Ethan, dead!"

Ethan stared at her and then took off his shirt and handed it to her. "Paige, please. If someone torched the *Rosetta*, would it be your fault for putting it where the idiots could get their hands onto it? What if it was Orin that did it? Would it still be your fault?"

"Talking hypothical situations is not going to change things." She brusquely pulled on his shirt. She considered demanding his pants too, but decided not to, as he was smaller in the hips than she was.

"What if Orin burned the *Rosetta*?" Ethan continued with his idiotic argument. "Would it be your fault?"

"Orin wouldn't do that!" Paige snapped.

"But what if he would?" Ethan cried.

"He wouldn't!" both Paige and Turk said.

Ethan ignored Turk to focus on Paige. "If you thought he would, yes, you might be responsible for not stopping him, but you're so, so, sure that nothing would move him to that. But you're wrong. Our family can do horrible things."

"What?" Paige cried. Damn the man, he was being a Blue on her now, twisting words to make himself seem innocent.

"I had it all planned," Ethan said. "Everything carefully planned. But then, Jack found out what I was doing. We fought. He refused to see the necessity. He kept focusing on the trivial."

"Trivial?" Paige cried. "That you're working with Mary's Landing? That if they control access to the Sargasso every single person with adapted blood, no matter how removed, will be property?"

Ethan had the gall to look hurt. "Why can you trust Orin but not me? Why would you think that I would ever let that happen?"

"Orin has always thought of family first," Paige said. "You've always thought of only yourself."

Ethan gave a short scoffing laugh. "You're—you're equating childhood squabbles over candy with the willingness to destroy my family. I have a plan. It's a solid plan."

She'd had enough of him. They had to leave before Mary's people realized she'd escaped, leaving a trail of dead behind her. "Well, it just got changed. I didn't come all this way for nothing. You're coming with me."

He edged away from her, hands up. "And when the shit hits the fan, it's going to be all my fault even though you waltz in here and didn't even bother to find out what I'm doing."

She hated arguing with Blues. With Blues you never knew what was the truth and what was a clever stall. But Ethan was right. If things went wrong because she triggered something like Jack had . . .

"What's your plan?" she gave up and asked.

Ethan was at least smart enough not to look pleased at winning. "Mary's Landing is set on returning to normal space. Short of killing every single one of them, the only way to keep control of the situation is to succeed before they do. Paige, just think about it. They have all the pieces. They always did. Multiple human warp engines. Parts to modify them. Aliens with the knowledge of how their systems work. Blues that can translate."

"So you're just going to work with them? After they killed your family and leveled Fenrir? Grow a spine, Ethan."

"If you'd been on time," Ethan growled, "the *Lilianna* wouldn't have been there when Mary's Landing arrived. I wouldn't have had to explain why I was working with them. Jack wouldn't have gone all Red on me and tried to smash our work. None of that would have happened if you—had—been—on—time."

"Don't you even try to blame this on me!' Paige snapped.

"You're doing the same thing by blaming me!" Ethan said. "I wasn't the one that pulled the switch that activated the engine. I wasn't the one that started the fight. Jack had thrown me overboard; I was adrift in my own little sea. I am no more to blame than you are."

"Only in your own mind," Paige said.

Ethan glared at her for several minutes, as if by force of will he could change her thoughts. Finally he looked away. "The reason why Mary's Landing is so bent on returning is that they have something to return to. They were the richest of the human race. They have empires of wealth waiting for them."

"All the original passengers are dead," Paige said. "How can they think that after all these years, that wealth is going to be just handed to them?"

"Back then, there were laws put into place to protect travelers," Ethan said. "DNA samples were taken and estates were established, holding things in trust if and when survivors or children of survivors could come forward."

"The Nefrim War has claimed more than one fortune," Turk said.

"I didn't say it was a reasonable expectation," Ethan snapped. "Also the *Mary*'s systems are failing. Better back to normal space than to Ya-ya, where they don't have a power base."

"And this relates how?" Paige said as Turk murmured, "We don't have time for this."

Ethan ignored Turk. "What Mary's Landing doesn't realize is I'm the grandson of Tsar Viktor Volkov. I have my own power base to return to. Hardin tells me that the Novaya Rus still grovel to statues of Grandpa."

"Ethan, you idiot!" Paige cried. "No, you don't have anything to go back to! They cloned Victor! Hardin knows that."

Ethan started to shake his head. "I'd be able to tell if he lied . . ."

"Ethan, *Fenrir*'s engine went back to normal space and they sent a ship here. A Novaya Rus ship. A ship that is captained by one of Victor's clones. That's why I'm here. If anyone goes back to normal space, I want it to be someone like Grandpa, not these idiots you're helping."

"Ivan Viktorovich Volkov is Tsar of the Novaya Rus Empire," Turk said in his thick Russian accent.

Ethan stared at Turk as if seeing him for the first time. "They cloned Viktor?"

"Yes!" Paige cried and Turk nodded.

"The angels told me to go back," Ethan said with dismay. "They told me to go back to save mankind."

"Save mankind?" Turk asked.

"Yes." Ethan nodded. "They want me to recover the *Shabd* and take it back to normal space to end the Nefrim War."

Paige laughed. "You can't be serious?"

"What is the *Shabd*?" Turk asked.

Paige threw up her hands. "It's the sound vibrating in all creation, the music of the world that can only be heard by the inner ears. It's basically the essence of God. The belief is that if you can meditate on the *Shabd*, you can merge with it until your own divinity is ultimately realized."

Turk glared suspiciously at Ethan. "That doesn't make sense. How can you recover music?"

For once, Ethan didn't look confident in his plan. "I get the impression it's not music per se but a device that allows you to hear the music with your outer ear . . . or something. I'm a little fuzzy on the details. I do know that the seraphim want me to find it and return it to normal space. The war with the nefrim is because the word of God is missing from normal space. If it's returned to where it belongs, peace will ensue."

"Are you stupid or just naïve?" Turk asked. "This device could be anything. It's probably a weapon."

"No!" Ethan cried. "The war started when the *Shabd* was lost. I did my research. The date that this ship crashed into minotaur water was shortly before the start of the Nefrim War. It was being moved because some disaster was about to happen in the star system it was located in—a supernova or something like that. They were nervous as hell about moving it, but it couldn't be helped. The ship misjumped to the Sargasso, and the *Shabd* was irrevocably lost. The seraphim know where it is and they want me to return it and end the war."

"It never struck you as strange that they need you?" Turk asked.

"I'm merely fulfilling my destiny." Ethan pressed his hands to his heart. "I'm chosen. The seraphim can hear God's word in my voice. It's why they came to me."

Paige closed her eyes, trying to shut out all the questions that Ethan's claim raised and her white space threatened to try and answer. "Just shut up!"

"You can feel it, can't you?" Ethan said. "God's voice inside of us. That place inside where answers come from."

Paige held up her hand. "Do not go all existential on me."

"We have to leave," Turk suddenly said. "I'm picking up their radio chatter. They've found the bodies in the conservatory."

Bodies? As in plural dead? In the conservatory? How many people did Turk kill? Paige didn't want to know.

She focused on the problem at hand. "You said yourself, the only way to gain control of Sargasso is to jump out before Hardin and Mary's Landing does. We need to modify Volkov's engine and have him jump before anyone else returns to normal space."

Ethan nodded, as if agreeing to the plan. He started to grab things off the drafting table and shove them into his pockets. "I'd heard about the spaceship coming in response to Fenrir's engine.

All of Mary's Landing is abuzz. An intact spaceship. Hardin said it was a Russian militia ship sent by the U.C. but didn't say anything about Volkov. Mary's board of directors wanted to take the Russian ship by force, but Hardin said it would make us look like pirates. Returning with a ship sent to our rescue without its crew would look bad."

"Why not just cooperate with us?" Turk asked. "This would have been much easier if they'd worked with us."

Ethan shrugged. "Hardin opposed that."

"Why?" Paige asked.

Ethan shook his head. "He said that once the Russian ship had seen the destruction at Fenrir's Rock, that there would be avoidable repercussions. He said it would be better to destroy the ship. He claimed that Mary had to maintain a stranglehold on the information coming from the Sargasso. Otherwise laws could be changed before they returned, eliminating their claims on their estates, in retaliation for the attack on a United Colonies settlement."

"Hardin is using Mary's greed to manipulate them. No one would blame Mary's Landing for what happened to Fenrir. They can prove that they planned to move the engine and it was an accident. Not very damning considering . . ." She gasped as she realized what Hardin was truly hiding. "That snarky bastard, he's protecting only himself. If High Command found out what he did when the *Dakota* sank, nothing would save him from being court martialed."

Ethan nodded slowly. "And *Fenrir* was a United Colonies ship. That means a certain responsibility to the survivors by a U.C. officer."

"He's blocking cooperation with Mikhail so *he* can keep a stranglehold on information about himself."

"We need to go." Turk caught her by the elbow and gave her a tug toward the door they'd come through.

She resisted. "Ethan, we need to get Volkov's ship back to normal space first. Do you have what he needs or did Hardin take it?"

Ethan sighed. "Hardin has Eraphie. He'd said he'd hurt her if I didn't smuggle out the one set of modification parts that I had done. I'm trying to get another set down quickly, before Mary's Landing realizes what I did."

"So there's nothing here for Volkov?" Paige asked.

"There's these." Ethan rolled up the papers he'd been working on. "These are plans to build more. It's all we really need."

Turk only relaxed slightly when they reached the safety of Hoto's ship. Ethan had known secret ways all through the *Queen Mary IV*, so they managed to slip out without trouble. Mary's Landing, however, would probably suspect Paige would return to the minotaur ship and the pumps hadn't been brought to the docks yet.

Paige was still half naked, though, and he needed to let Mikhail know what they found, just in case the worst happened.

Mikhail sounded stable, which was a good sign. Turk wasn't sure if it had been wise for him to leave his brother so soon after returning to the *Svoboda*, but the minotaurs wouldn't wait.

"The good news is that we have Ethan Bailey and the plans for creating the modification parts for the *Svoboda*'s engine. The bad news is that Hardin has a working set. Ethan says it's fairly simple to hook up and Hardin has the engine crew from the *Dakota* on the *Red Gold*. All he needs is a warp engine. Paige says there are half a dozen landings that have their engines intact."

"If Hardin doesn't move the engine away from whatever landing he picks, it will be Fenrir's Rock over again," Mikhail said.

"I get the impression," Ethan said, "that Hardin is feeling pressure to act quickly. He might not take the time to move the engine."

"So he'll pick an landing close to Mary's Landing that still has an intact engine?" Mikhail asked.

"Not necessarily," Paige said. "There were engines closer than *Fenrir*. Hardin probably selected Fenrir's Rock because *Fenrir* had been a New Washington origin, United Colonies, military ship." Ethan nodded to confirm her guess. "There's this 'we're in this together' way of thinking with the NWUC. Challenger Landing. Omaha. Nimitz." And then, lastly, reluctantly, she added her own hometown. "Georgetown. Once they verified the registry of your ship with another New Washington landing, the *Fenrir* people treated you like you were one of them."

"Damn the man," Mikhail snapped. "So we don't know which one and they're most likely thousands of kilometers apart?"

"That's it in a nutshell," Ethan said.

"Do you know if Hardin still has Eraphie Bailey with him?" Mikhail asked.

"Yes." Ethan at least looked guilty. "He's holding her hostage to keep me in line."

"I bugged the reader I gave her," Mikhail said. "If she's with him, we should be able to pick up the *Red Gold.*"

"Good," Paige said. "We need to get her away from him before he can hurt her."

"I'll try. I might have to sink the *Red Gold* to keep Georgetown safe."

Paige look stricken but nodded. "Eraphie would want Georgetown protected over . . . over being safe."

They explained to him the item that the seraphim told Ethan to find.

"We haven't found anything unusual in the wreckage." Mikhail went on to explain his theory that the nefrim ship struck Loki and might have left the item that the seraphim were searching for on the floating island. "Orin says we'll need kites . . ."

"And quickly!" Ethan cried. "Once Loki is beyond human waters, the kites won't take us up."

"It's all a wild goose chase, if you ask me," Paige said.

"Turk, I'll leave that up to you," Mikhail said. "You know I trust your judgment."

In other words, Turk would have to decide to go or not and then convince one of the two Baileys to change their mind.

23 The Shabd

MIKHAIL CHECKED THE FILES THAT MINISTER HEWARD HAD given him on the lost United Colonies' ships. *Challenger* had been a minelayer about the size of the *Svoboda*. *Nimitz* had been a small destroyer. Both the *Omaha* and *Georgetown* had been carriers like the *Fenrir*. If Hardin used the same set of criteria, then along with choosing a post–United Colonies New Washington ship, he'd also be looking for a carrier.

Mikhail had scanned all the charts that the *Rosetta* had into the *Svoboda*'s computer. He plotted courses to both Georgetown Landing and Omaha Landing. They were eighty thousand kilometers apart. A small distance in comparison to the overall size of the Sargasso, but still if he chose the wrong landing, Hardin would have even more time to destroy the landing.

Mikhail tapped his comline. "Tseytlin, I need to find that reader that Eraphie Bailey was carrying."

"Yes, sir."

He searched out Orin. "The *Svoboda* needs to leave." He explained as gently as possible what he knew and suspected.

Orin looked stricken at the news. "I—I can't believe Hardin would do something like that on purpose."

"I hope not," Mikhail said.

"Hardin is a ruthless man," Kenya Jones said from her station on *Rosetta*'s forward gun. "He is capable of anything. He will kill anyone, destroy anything, to get what he wants. I don't know how he lives with himself, but if there's a God, he's going to hell when he dies."

Mikhail gazed up at the black woman that had said so little in the past. "How do you know?"

"I was on the *Dakota* when it went down. We cobbled together a raft of everything that would float with cots strapped to the sides of the ships to keep them from grinding together. It was a sprawling monster of a raft and it was tricky just to get from one end to the other. Because all the weight had to be evenly spread out—or at least that's what Hardin told us—so we were discouraged from moving around.

"The highest ranking officer wasn't Hardin, but the Red commander, a man named Jensen. He'd saved several hundred of his Reds. They were fiercely loyal to him and he loved them like they were all his children.

"Jensen and Harding butted heads from the very beginning. Hardin was popular with the crew, but Jensen had the Reds, and was higher ranked, so at first we did everything Jensen's way. But then Hardin started some of the crew fishing to catch 'fish.' Hardin convinced Jensen to hold onto the emergency rations because they wouldn't go bad. We would eat the 'cat fish' while it was fresh. Days and weeks went by before Jensen realized what Hardin was doing."

Jones swallowed hard and looked away. "Hardin was butchering the Reds and feeding them to us."

"Bozhe moi!" Mikhail slipped into Russian in his shock.

"Hardin was shifting the Reds around, and lying on head counts, so they'd disappear quietly, one by one, to one end of the raft. He had a butcher shop set up. He'd kill them while they were locked in restraints, hang them up to bleed out, and then cut them down to cook them."

"Jensen caught Hardin and the idiot decided to court-martial Hardin instead of executing him on the spot. Both Jensen and the emergency food were 'washed overboard' before the trial. A few of the remaining Reds tried to take Hardin down, and Hardin had them destroyed for 'mutiny.' After that, Hardin didn't bother to hide what he was doing. By then, we'd been living on . . . them . . . for weeks without realizing it. By the time most of us found out, Hardin had made sure we had to continue eating . . . it . . . or starve. I lost thirty pounds trying not to eat, but God forgive me, I got too hungry at the end."

Mikhail could only stare at her in horror. When Eraphie had told him that Hardin had "lost" his Reds, he assumed that Hardin had neglected to keep them from drowning, or let them starve. This wasn't about eating to survive, not at first. It was a coldly calculated move to eliminate Jensen's power base and take over as commander of the survivors.

Orin had gone white. "Good gods, that monster is heading to my home. Manny!" he shouted for his cousin. "Take me with you, Mikhail. Manny!"

Manny popped up from below deck. "What? Where's the fire?"

"I'm going with Mikhail," Orin said. "You're captain until Paige or I get back."

"Okay," Manny was more puzzled than alarmed. "Where are you going?"

"Orin, I don't know if Hardin's going to Georgetown yet." Mikhail said.

"But it's a fifty-fifty chance," Orin said. "And you're going to need to know all about either landing, regardless, right?"

"Yes." Mikhail had to admit that it would be useful to have Orin along, but he'd asked so much of the Baileys, he hated to put the young man into more danger.

"Half my family is in Georgetown, Mikhail. My baby brother. All my baby cousins. We thought the little ones would be safest there, so all Bailey children under the age of eight are at Georgetown. I can't sit here, knowing—something—anything—that might help you save them."

Mikhail nodded. "Okay, come with me."

He personally made sure that Orin was safely settled in. He didn't want a repeat of what had happened with Eraphie. He had just reached the bridge when Tseytlin contacted him.

"I've got a lock on the reader." Tseytlin transferred his information to Mikhail's station. Hardin was already at Georgetown Landing. Mikhail swore. Beating Hardin to his goal was no longer an option. They would have to assume that Hardin was entrenched and in control of all local resources as well as anything he had on his ship. Any resistance Georgetown Landing was offering would be crushed before the *Svoboda* arrived.

"Sir, I wasn't sure exactly what you had been hoping for with this reader, so I did extensively modify it. We can access its memory; see which novels she's read, how long she's taken to read a page, how many times she's read a page . . ."

"I fail to see the point." Mikhail trusted that there would be one, just as Tseytlin would circle it indefinitely if not nudged.

"The reader has a note-taking function. Lets you annotate as you read."

"Eraphie has been taking notes on something she's read," Mikhail guessed. She read, then.

"Yes," Tseytlin said. "But she's leaving them in English. I—I can only read a few words in English. But the novel she's annotating? It's *The Sea Wolf.*" "Volkov" translated to *wolf* in English. "And each annotation starts with your name."

Eraphie was hiding messages for him on the reader? Tseytlin had to be mistaken.

The download from the reader appeared on Mikhail's station. He opened *The Sea Wolf* and checked for annotations.

Mikhail, I hope you're as clever as I think you are. An angel took me off the Svoboda *and took me to the* Red Gold. *I thought it was doing what was best for me, so I didn't try to leave while the* Red Gold *was still in port. Stupid me. Hardin is controlling the angel somehow. Hardin wanted me so he'd have a leash on my cousin, Ethan. Please come get me.*

Mikhail swore. What an idiot he'd been. He'd assumed that Eraphie had been frightened of him and left of her own will. He should have gone after her. She'd been part of his crew. He'd have gone after any other crew member that had suddenly gone missing. The annotation was dated a few hours after Mikhail realized that she was missing from the *Svoboda*, days ago.

There was another annotation farther into the novel.

Mikhail, the angel took your Reds too. Hardin has plans for them.

Mikhail gripped the edge of his station hard in anger. Damn the lying son of a bitch! Damn him. How dare he just take Mikhail's Reds? What plans did he have for the Reds? And did he put Eraphie in with the replacements? If Hardin locked her in with the other Reds and let them gang rape her, Mikhail would gut the man. The spacing between the two messages seemed to indicate time had passed before she found out about the Reds. Hopefully that meant that Hardin was keeping her separate from the replacements.

He searched for more annotations.

Mikhail, I found out what he plans! Damn the man! He's head-ing for Georgetown. Stop him before he levels Georgetown too! Sink his damn ship if you have to!

The note was days old. There was nothing more. No sign that Eraphie was still alive. The usage log that recorded her reading noted that she had stopped all activity at the time of the last annotation. Mikhail hoped that Hardin had confiscated the reader or that Eraphie had hidden it, guessing that Mikhail could use it to find Hardin.

Paige was ready to kill Ethan.

"There are kites in port," Ethan said. "If we take them to Loki, we'll have at least a day to search the vimana for the artifact."

"No," Paige said.

"We cannot make a difference in what happens to Eraphie now," Ethan said. "If Volkov locates her via his bug, then he's going to move before we reach him. Even if we catch up to Volkov and install the engine modification, that won't change what Hardin knows. He believes he has a chance to jump out of system and arrive in normal space first."

"You could lie and say Mikhail jumped already," Turk offered, unknowingly helping Ethan.

"Then he'd have no reason to keep Eraphie alive," Ethan pointed out the logical end to that. "And every reason to kill her to punish me. The most efficient means of saving Eraphie lies with Mikhail."

"I hate you," Paige growled at her brother.

"Paige, please." Ethan managed to sound truly hurt by her statement. "I'm just being reasonable."

"You've put Eraphie in harm's way," Paige said. "And now ignor-ing the danger she's in to make yourself happy."

"I love Eraphie just as much as you do," Ethan said. "Maybe even more as I've always considered her hot and if she didn't think I was a complete twerp I'd ask her out."

"Your cousin?" Turk asked with disgust plain in his voice.

"Our fathers are from the same Red lot and raised as brothers," Ethan said. "It's not quite the same as true biological brothers. There's more genetic variation."

"Baileys have never been about blood relations," Paige said. "We're family because we decided to be family."

"Even in real family, cousins can marry cousins," Ethan said.
Paige glared at him to shut him up.

"I know what you did with Jack," Ethan continued.

"And you killed him," Paige growled.

"Jack killed himself," Ethan said.

"I'm going to hit you if you don't shut up," Paige growled.

"We need to find the item that the angels—" Ethan started.

"They're not angels!" Paige cried. "They're disembodied nefrims,
Ethan. That's all seraphim are! Out in norm space, they're laying
waste to the human race. We have no reason to help them."

"Listen to me, please," Ethan said. "Please Paige. Just listen."

"I have listened," Paige said. "And you've not said anything that
changed my mind."

"I always suspected that they weren't angels," Ethan admitted.
"Really. But that doesn't mean that helping them isn't the will
of God."

She hit him then, harder than she intended. She felt his nose
break under her fist and blood instantly scented the air. He stag-
gered back and dropped to his knees. "God damn you, Ethan!"
She controlled the temptation to kick him for making her lose her
temper. For making her hurt someone in her own family—even if it
was just Ethan. "Don't grasp at straws to justify your own stupidity."

"Just look at what's been going on!" Ethan cried, ignoring the
blood streaming from his nose. "Look at this world! Do you think
it's just some happy mistake that it's perfect for humans? Do you
think it's good luck that the human ships all land close enough
together that we can help each other? Do you think it's just chance
that made just Blues that can pull languages out of our butts so
humans can talk to their neighbors? For once, just look at the
universe and all its parts and see that the ordering of events,
throughout history, has been to the benefit of mankind."

Paige's hand jerked back in a fist before she could catch herself. "I . . . am . . . not . . . in . . . the mood for . . . theology . . . at
the moment."

"Everything has been lined up for us to rescue whatever is
on Loki," Ethan whispered. "From your engine problems, to you
contacting the *Svoboda*, to you coming here—where the kites
are—when Volkov learned where the artifact was . . . God has his
finger on us. Look inside. Use the gift he's given you and see the
truth. Please, Paige. Just—just think for one minute."

She didn't want to. If he was right, then Jake and the others of the *Lilianna* were meant to die in order to bring Turk and Mikhail to the Sargasso. It wasn't the kind and just God that she wanted to believe in. Unbidden, though, her mind was tumbling the events around in the white space, finding the links that chained them together. Turk surviving his fall. The civ fishing him out of the water before he drowned and then leaving him alive. The *Rosetta* drifting into the civ raft's path . . .

"God damn you," she whispered.

Ethan read her face and smiled, knowing he'd won. So she kicked him.

When Paige and Ethan were talking about kites, Turk assumed that they were talking about some kind of ultralight airplane. It turned out that kites were massive insectlike creatures. They had two sets of transparent wings, visible only due to black veining. They had a long elongated body, segmented so it could move nearly like a snake while still rigid. They perched with a sense of lightness that belied their huge bodies. Their six legs seemed like thin stilts from the distance, but closer up they were like massive chitinous poles. The legs were joined close to the union of the head to the thorax, with one pair fastened directly to what would be a neck on humans. Their heads were bulbous with huge compound eyes. There were various brilliant hues on their backs, but their bellies seemed to be all a uniform dark. At a distance, they seemed sleek, but close up they were pricked with short stiff hairs.

"You've got to be kidding," Turk growled as he followed the Baileys. "You can talk to these?"

"Oh, they're not intelligent," Paige said.

"Husssh, there me duckie, they be plenty smart!" cried a young man ducking out from under one of the massive insects. His Standard was so thick that Turk wasn't sure he understood the man. "Off be ya, no gawking. Less . . ." He ran his eyes down over Paige. ". . . you be a Blue under a red light?"

"Hush yourself," Paige answered with the same thick Standard. "I be gander to this here goose, and he's a right green one."

The man looked at Turk. "Pft, he be a big yun. Straight out of the jar, be he? I bet a pretty penny, though, I can take 'em."

"Yer ma teach you manners?" Paige asked. "Or business savvy? We're offering cold hard ones for wee bit of work."

"You ask me ma 'erself." The young man motioned toward an older woman in a bright blue shirt.

Paige headed toward "Ma" with the kite driver.

Turk was going to follow, but realized that Ethan was studying him intently. "What?"

"Do you have a last name, Turk?" Ethan asked.

"No." Turk wasn't sure what to make of this man. He looked much like a slightly older version of Orin with the Bailey blonde hair and blue eyes. If he'd raised one hand to Paige, Turk would have punched him regardless of Ethan being her brother or not. But Ethan hadn't hit her back even though she'd bloodied his nose. Turk respected the man for that much. Of course, Paige wouldn't have been in danger if the idiot had just gone to Ya-ya after *Fenrir*'s accident.

"I see," Ethan said. "Does Volkov own you?"

"No," Turk said.

"Are you going to stay and marry my sister?" Ethan said. "Or you going to leave with Volkov?"

"You will be if you marry Paige." Hillary gave him another grin and sang, "Oni-chan."

He'd thought Hillary had been naïve. He realized now that everyone in Paige's family expected him to marry her. They saw no reason why he wouldn't. Which meant Paige probably saw no reason either. She would marry him if he asked.

All he had to do was ask.

Paige came trotting back. "It's all arranged. They'll take us. Have to go now, though, to have the most time on Loki."

Because of the long distance from Mary's Landing to Loki, the drivers had limited their kites to a small payload. Thus she, Turk, and Ethan were on different kites. They roared over the water, far up enough that nothing in the water would be tempted to take a bite out of them. Loki grew from a black speck in the distance to a massive rock crowned with jungle.

Unlike other vimanas that Paige had seen, Loki was a misshapen thing. Once you considered the possibility, it was easy to see that Fenrir's Rock had once been part of Loki. Was it chance or knowledge that named the vimana after Fenrir's mythological father? Paige decided it only needed witnesses to the event for the places be linked. She had never heard of it in Georgetown, but the kite people had arrived much earlier.

"How much do you know about Loki?" Paige had to shout over the roar of the wing and the deep droning hum that came from the kite's wings.

"We've ne'r been up to Loki for a looksee," Mirtrude shouted back. "Fenrir's Rock is the only thing he passes by. Nigh on the edge of human waters. We nay want to come down in minotaur waters, if you follow me."

"Have you heard of any stories about Fenrir's Rock breaking off of Loki?"

"Aye, I have. Me gram saw it. A great monster of a ship came streaking in. Bam, she hits Loki and sends the bloody thing spinning, dropping all sorts of rock and dirt and such down into the water below. She came apart and spit pieces of 'erself for miles."

"When was this?"

"Hmmm, well, before you Georgies showed up, but not by long. Gram saw yuns come down too and she marked that as the two big sightings when she was a child."

The *Georgetown* was one of the first United Colonies ships lost to the Sargasso. And the U.C. formed when the nefrims utterly destroyed New Haven Colony in a surprise attack. Until that battle, nefrim were unknown. The nefrim ship that hit Loki could have been part of that very first attack.

Or was it the trigger?

No one ever knew why the nefrims came from out of nowhere and started to attack the human race. Could the attack have been retaliation for something the nefrims only thought that humans did? Was the war over this ship?

It seemed unreasonable except for one thing. The seraphim—the bodhisattva of the nefrim race—were focused on this one ship to the exclusion of all others.

They had gotten close enough to Loki that its steep black rocky sides blotted everything but the blue water straight below them. They climbed slowly, the tree crown coming into view. When they finally crested over the edge, the green canopy unrolled for miles in three directions.

Paige gasped at the thick jungle. There was no sign of the alien spaceship. There was no way they could search nearly so much land before the kites would leave.

"Wheresabout you want us to set down?" Mirtrude asked.

Paige let the question drop the whole way into the white zone and roll about. "Well, I think the ship probably impacted where it's notched." Paige pointed toward the ridge that was at several miles inland. "If anything sheared off and stayed up here, it's probably near there."

"Righty then, that's there is where we'll set ya down."

Turk gazed at the edge of the vimana after they'd all dismounted. The rim was a good fifty meters away, but somehow it seemed unnervingly close. Strange how on the kite he had no trouble with the height, but standing on the vimana, knowing how far it was down because he'd fallen that distance before, he was having weird jolts of fear. Not a feeling he liked. He was tempted to walk to the edge and look down, but there really wasn't time to deal with personal demons.

"How long are they staying?" Turk asked Paige quietly. "They're not going to strand us up here, are they?"

Paige shrugged and turned to call to the drivers. "Will you stay as we have a look see?"

"If you make it quick. We're going to see if the lakes here have any nymphs. We've never farmed up here before."

"So . . . Five hours? Ten?"

"Ten hours will give us wiggle room. Not much more than that."

"Righty then. Meet you here in ten hours."

"They're looking for . . . what?" Turk had tried to follow the conversation and failed.

"Dragonfly nymphs," Paige explained. "The adults lay eggs in the freshwater of the vimana lakes. The eggs hatch into larvae that live in the water for several years until they mature."

"Larvae?" Turk glanced at the multilegged, winged insects. "Like worms? Living in the water?" When she nodded, he shook his head. "This place is so weird."

She winced slightly and looked away. "We have a little while, but they can't stay long, or we'll be out of human waters."

"How did you plan to find the *Shabd*?" Turk asked Ethan.

"I didn't expect a jungle up here," Ethan admitted.

Paige gave her brother a look that could kill. "It's been, what, fifty, seventy, a hundred years?"

"At the start of the Nefrim War," Ethan said. "That's how I found it; I looked for crashes in minotaur waters in the right time frame."

"And you didn't expect a jungle?" Paige mocked him.

"I got the impression that Loki was stripped to bare rock," Ethan said. "So no, I didn't."

"Do you know at least how big the device is?" Turk asked.

This time Ethan managed to look somewhat contrite. "No, I don't."

Turk sighed. "I'll see if the scanners can pick up something, but they have a limited range, and this place is huge."

The Baileys started in opposite directions. Turk wasn't sure if it was some unspoken agreement between the siblings or if Paige was simply heading away from her brother rather than give into the urge to kill him. And Ethan, being clever, was giving her room to calm down. Knowing how the Blues seem to be able to speak without talking, probably both.

Turk followed Paige.

"We probably should split up," she said. "Cover more ground."

"There's something I want to ask you."

"Okay." She kept on walking.

He trailed after her. "I'm sorry I was so stupid in Ya-ya, and on Hoto's boat."

"I don't remember you doing anything stupid with the minotaurs."

"Not with them, with you. I let every woman I've known get in the way of seeing just you. It wasn't until the people at Mary's Landing took you away that I realized how much I love you. That I would kill anyone or anything that got in my way of getting you back."

She laughed. "That's very sweet in a scary way."

He caught her hand and turned her to face him. He opened his mouth and his heart leapt up his throat and for a moment he couldn't form the words. "Will . . . will you marry me?"

Emotions flashed over her face and then she looked away, blinking rapidly. "You don't have to marry me just because I've gotten pregnant."

He had hoped for "yes" but braced himself for a no. This seemed like it was simultaneously both and yet neither; it left him utterly confused. "What does you being pregnant have to do with it?"

She studied him, frowning slightly, as if she was trying to see through him. "It's usually what men think they have to do when their 'woman' gets pregnant."

"Why?"

She tilted her head slightly, frowning harder. "Your father, the Tsar, he's not married, is he?"

Correction, he had been slightly confused, now he was utterly confused. "No, he's not. I don't know if he's ever found a woman that he trusted with his heart. Even the women that seek out Mikhail just want power."

Her face softened, and she put a hand up to his check. "Oh, Turk, I love you." And she leaned up to kiss him. He wasn't sure if that was "yes" or "no," but he held her close and kissed her. It felt like he had everything good and wonderful concentrated down into a warm human form, and he didn't want to let her go.

But she eventually pulled away. "Getting married means we stay together."

"I know."

"Will you be happy here? In my world?" Her gaze demanded that he be honest.

He sighed. "On the boat? Fishing? No. But if that's what I need to suffer to be with you, then . . . I guess I have to suffer."

She cuffed him in the shoulder. "I don't want you suffering. I think we'd start to hate each other if you're suffering."

"I don't want to put you through what I went through. I don't want to be the one that takes it all away from you."

She leaned against him.

"We're supposed to be looking!" Ethan called from the distance. "Not making out!"

"I'm so going to push him off the edge," Paige murmured into Turk's chest.

So they searched while Paige considered how to answer Turk. He had committed. He would stay if she asked him to. Somehow it felt like a hollow victory. She'd seen how Mikhail leaned on him. Mikhail would be Tsar, but Turk would be a true "right hand" to Mikhail's power. It seemed petty to take a man whose dreams spanned a dozen planets and lock him on a boat. Viktor had died from it; he'd become bored to death by the monotony of fishing.

And if she was brutally honest with herself, the *Rosetta* was not the life she wanted for herself. She'd been much happier living on her own in Ya-ya, working as a translator. Two years ago, she'd abandoned her dreams to save her younger siblings, and there were many times since then she could have cheerfully drowned them all and gone back to Ya-ya.

Even though she didn't completely love the life she now lived, she was comfortable. She couldn't imagine living without the ocean somewhere close by. She couldn't imagine *space* and *night* and *winter* and dozens of other words that were in English that she knew the definitions of but had no context for.

She couldn't imagine. She had no idea. Turk didn't need to imagine. He'd lived in her world. He knew what he was committing to. Which was braver, facing what you knew you hated, or facing the unknown?

Distracted, she slipped and fell. Close up, it was impossible not to notice that the layer of dead foliage was very deep. Possibly several feet deep. The device was probably under all the compost, anywhere along the line of impact that could stretch for miles. They were not going to find it, especially in her state of mind.

Come on, you're smarter than this, think about it.

She sat up, brushed off the black earth, and forced herself to stop worrying about her future with Turk and concentrate on her current problem. A nefrim ship warped into the Sargasso and like the *Svoboda*, struck a vimana. She knew the point of impact—slightly before Fenrir's Rock because the boulders would have traveled in the direction of the Spin as they fell. The force of impact was enough to break pieces off of Loki. Massive chunks of nonfloating rocks fell to create Fenrir's Rock and its smaller neighbors. The ship came down in minotaur waters.

The question was: where is the *Shabd*?

The answer seemed close but elusive, like a minnow darting through her white space. It would help if she had a clue what it was exactly. How large. What shape. What was beyond "the music of the world that can only be heard by the inner ears."

Only be heard . . .

Maybe if she listened.

She let herself drop into a meditative state. Mediating for her had always been like dropping into an ocean of white. She became that place of answers. Ethan might call it the voice of God, but there was nothing musical about it to her. She considered why not, and the white replied: *because she didn't believe.*

She was a devout agnostic. She believed in God, and she embraced every religion of the Sargasso, but truly believed in none. In her mind God could not be imagined, not even by the hak. Since God could not be imagined, then every religion was a misperception and thus while she accepted that they were shadows of God, she rejected them as visions of God.

What if she was wrong about the basic concept of religion? That the rituals of all religions weren't how God interacted with intelligent beings, but how intelligent beings opened themselves up to God. God *was*, after all. He did not change. It was the creatures that changed. From man to man. From man to hak. By their very small and limited and thus individualistic nature, each personal belief system had to find its path to God.

If she wanted to hear the music, she had to believe it was truly there to be heard.

Part of her worried that she might be deceiving herself. Hearing something not there simply because she wanted to hear it. It was, perhaps, how she saw all the other people who were devout in their own religion. Self-deluded. But if she never allowed herself to believe anything, then there was no way of believing in what was true.

The logical part of her wanted to fight it. If there was music there, why would belief change whether it could be heard? But refusing to believe, perhaps, was like sticking fingers in her ears and singing, "La, la, la can't hear it."

There is music. I can hear it if I allow myself to believe in it. It is there. I merely have to listen. I only need to take my fingers out of my ears and be quiet for a moment.

She took a deep breath and forced herself to listen.

She floated in the white, silent and serene. After several minutes, she thought she might be hearing something faintly. She focused on it, accepting it, allowing no doubt to come to her mind. This was what she was searching for.

I believe.

And the music filled her white space with blinding white purity. It flooded out into the rest of her, pressing on the boundaries of her skin. Trying to expand her.

God was . . .

God was . . .

She could be . . .

"Paige!" Turk was holding her by both shoulders; her feet dangled above the ground. "Paige!"

She opened her mouth and was amazed that the music swelling inside of her didn't spill out. "I can hear it."

"Hear what?"

"The *Shabd*." She concentrated on the source and pointed to it. "That way."

Turk gazed down at her, too concerned for her to put her down.

"I'm fine. I can find it. Follow me."

At first she could all but run in a straight line, following the sound. But then, as they neared the source, it grew difficult to narrow down. Turk was using the infiltration scanners on the area she was weaving through, listening closely.

"There's debris all through this area," he said. "It could be here."

"It is! It's close!" Paige realized she was walking in a large circle. "It's somewhere right here."

"Shovels would have been good," Turk said. He moved slowly and carefully, examining each piece of buried debris that the scanner picked out. "Here, what do you think of this piece? It looks intact."

She came to stand beside him, and then got on her hands and knees and pressed her ear to the ground.

"Careful of bugs, honey," Turk said.

She laughed. "I think we found it."

She started to dig in the moist loose soil. Worms and bugs squiggled in panic, trying to escape the sudden excavation of their world. She could sense their fear in little bright motes of terror.

"I'm sorry. I'm sorry," she whispered to them as she continued to dig.

It was less than a foot down. It was an unremarkable-looking black box about a foot square.

"Is this is?" Turk eyed the box. "It doesn't look very . . . impressive."

Paige pressed her hand to the slick surface. It filled her with calm, as if the glory of God was leaking into her. "Yes." She took her hand away. It might be dangerous to maintain contact. Surely it would be like a moth trying to embrace a flame.

24 Georgetown

"DO YOU KNOW HOW MUCH THE *GEORGETOWN* HAS BEEN MODIFIED?" Mikhail asked Orin. Even at a distance, Mikhail could see that the wreck no longer matched the files that the U.C. had supplied on the spaceship. "Anything you can tell us would help."

"The crèche is set up in the main hangar bay," Orin pointed out. "It's powered off the engine. It's an effective hostage against everyone in Georgetown. Hardin has spent enough time in our landing to know what it means to us. The crèche isn't banks of frozen eggs and sperm to us. It's our baby brothers and sisters and cousins. Families put in as much genetic material as they take out. There's probably a score of babies in gestation. I have a baby brother there. We would do almost anything to protect it."

The Georgetown people were in a corner. If they attacked Hardin while he was sitting on the power source, he could simply shut down the freezer units on the crèche, destroying what was in storage or currently in the incubators. Only the fetuses very close to full term would survive any loss of power.

"I'm sorry," Mikhail said. "I'll try to protect it as much as possible."

"How is it hooked into the power?" Tseytlin asked.

"I—don't know," Orin said. "I do know that they talked about trying to move it to a different location but the power source has always been an issue. We've tried salvaging a few warp engines off smaller ships, but they'd always been too damaged. A few

323

years ago, we started gathering money to have Ya-ya build us a power unit."

"Smaller ship," Mikhail said. "We can use the *Tigertail* to power it. We fly in, land, run power to the crèche, and cut all power to the gun batteries, and then bring in the *Svoboda*."

And a measure of the trust in him, none of them called him insane. Either that, or they were considering his family's historically bloody path in the face of opposition and deeming it wiser not to say it to his face.

Combat was the only time that Mikhail wished he could clone himself. With Turk on Loki and most of his most trusted staff killed in the crash, Mikhail wanted to be on both the *Svoboda* and the *Tigertail* when they engaged Hardin. The mission's success rested on the *Tigertail* shutting down the *Georgetown's* many laser cannons; Mikhail decided to head up that team. He took with him Tseytlin, Orin Bailey, Ensign Inozemtsev, and what he had left of Reds. With the bridge, they'd lost the *Svoboda's* main pilot and backup. Lieutenant Belokurov was the only one left who could handle the *Svoboda's* unwieldy controls in combat situations. That meant Mikhail would have to pilot the *Tigertail*.

Luck rode with them. It was raining as they approached Georgetown Landing. They came in fast and low to the waves, flying in full stealth mode. At thirty kilometers, they'd be in range of the *Georgetown* guns. Every second they were undetected, the better the chance they'd actually survive.

The ocean was a blur of gray as Mikhail pushed the *Tigertail* to its limits. The *Georgetown* loomed far in the distance like a sleeping god.

"We're in range," Tseytlin murmured as they crossed into the cannon's range. A moment later he said, "We've been spotted. Energy spikes on all batteries. Incoming!"

Mikhail jerked the *Tigertail* sidewise and up. Like guided lightning, the cannon fire cut through the rain. The first strike missed, so close and brilliant that it filled the cockpit with light. A second later there was the thunder as the superheated air sent out shockwaves.

Mikhail weaved as the cannon fire continued to slash through the gray. The thunder became unending. They were hit and the *Tigertail* shuddered in his hands.

"We're losing shielding." Tseytlin's voice was tense with the knowledge that when the shielding was gone, the *Tigertail* would quickly become a slag of falling metal.

Mikhail could see the open hangars at mid-level of the ship. As Orin promised, the secondary hangar stood open, its doors salvaged. The *Georgetown* was expanding as they flashed toward it, growing to fill his range of vision. They were almost there. Almost.

The universe was washed to brilliance as they took a direct hit. The *Tigertail* bucked in his hands as their shields failed. They were almost at the hangar, but he had to slow down, or they'd punch through the hangar's back wall into the heart of the Georgetown. Mikhail slammed the VTOL engines into full braking and aimed at the hangar opening. The *Tigertail* shuddered like it was going to shake itself apart as its VTOL engines fought its forward momentum.

Brilliance hit them again. His controls went slack. All indicators went red as systems failed. The engines died. They hit the lip of the hangar and skipped and then slid grinding across the steel floor. They slammed into the hangar back wall and stopped.

"We made it!" Tseytlin cried.

"If you want to call that making it, yes." Mikhail checked to make sure all the fire suppressors were working. Foam was gushing out of the VTOL engines. Yes, they were down safe, but the *Tigertail* wouldn't be taking off again without repairs. He seemed to be specializing in one-way trips lately. At least their power unit was still operating, which meant they could carry out his plan. "*Svoboda*, we're in. Stand by for my mark."

"*Svoboda* standing by," Kutuzov answered.

Inozemtsev had the Reds in position. Mikhail drew his service pistol and nodded.

Inozemtsev popped the hatch. "Go, go, go!"

The Reds poured out and made sure the hangar was secure.

The laser batteries were connected to the power units in the engine housing via a main line and two backup lines. They had to cut all three lines. Before they could, they'd have to run power to the crèche in the main hangar bay.

Tseytlin rolled a spool of power lines across the hangar floor, playing out the cable as it rolled.

Coffee was on the door to the main hangar. "It's locked, Captain."

"Blow the door," Mikhail told Tseytlin.

"Wait!" Orin cried pushing through the Reds. "Let me see if I can open it. My family has an access code to the crèche."

Orin punched in a code and the door slid open with dozens of guns leveled at the door. Mikhail jerked Orin back out of the way.

"Hold fire!" Mikhail shouted at his people. Then to the people within the crèche, he shouted, "I'm Captain Volkov of the *Svoboda*. I'm here to stop John Hardin from leveling this settlement, and as Tsarevich, I've promised that Georgetown Landing will be a free and independent colony of the N.R. Empire and that all adapted from Georgetown will be considered freeborn and fully human."

"You won't be Tsar if you're stuck here!" a woman shouted from inside the crèche.

"The *Fenrir*'s engine made it back to Plymouth Station," Mikhail shouted. "That's what Hardin is doing here—he plans to take your engine back. I don't need your engine to return to normal space."

"How do we know you're telling the truth?" the woman said.

Orin put a hand out to keep Mikhail from answering, and called, "Auntie Anna, is that you? It's Orin. He's telling the truth."

"Orin? What are you doing mixed up with this?"

"It's a long story, Aunt Anna, but he's Viktor's clone! He's a good man."

There was a long silence, then, "Okay, we'll let you in."

Auntie Anna. Viktor's daughter, named after one of Peter the Great's daughters.

Orin went in first, arms high. Mikhail followed behind him. Anna looked like a weathered, female version of Mikhail's father, Ivan.

"Tseytlin, get the power," Mikhail said and then to the people gathered there, he said, "We're setting up an alternate power source for the crèche and then cutting the power to the gun batteries so I can bring in my frigate."

There was a cry of a baby among the machinery.

"We're decanting those that we can, just in case," Anna Volkov said. "But only ten of the forty are close enough to term to decant. If Hardin tries to jump out the engine, either this nursery goes with him, or it will be leveled."

Mikhail walked the room. When the gene banks were new and cranking out Reds and Blues for sale, there had been numbers painted on the gene banks. Each lot would start with the crèche code and then the number of the gene bank that the lot had been pulled from. The gene banks now bore the names of families. Carter. Jamison. Lawson. Bailey. Johnson/McCree. Farther back were the incubators. Each baby was already named. Caroline Carter. Shane Jamison. Heidi Lawson. Viktor Bailey.

Another baby Viktor whose life was in Mikhail's hands.

The tiny fetus was recognizable as a human, complete with fingernails on its minuscule fingers. But he was obviously far too young to survive being taken out of his artificial womb. There were pictures taped to the machines. "Daddy" was a Red smiling with joy at the camera; such a rare expression to see on a Red. "Mommy" was a Volkov blonde. And a group picture of the Bailey siblings from the *Rosetta*. A small stuffed bear sat waiting for the child that now might never be born.

Damn Hardin.

Orin came to stand beside him. "My father was one of twenty boys. He thought six kids wasn't enough. Mom loved him too much to say no, but she hated being pregnant. They have another dozen kids on hold here."

Tseytlin came back. "I've got it set up, sir, that I can switch over to the new power without disrupting anything here. We can cut all the power couplers now."

Mikhail was getting the impression that cornering an entire settlement of Reds and Blues would be nearly impossible. The Georgies in the crèche had infiltrated up through hidden access points; apparently there were breaks in the underbelly of the *Georgetown* open to the sea. The Georgies had swum in. There were other Georgies clearing a path for the newly decanted babies to be carried out. Hardin's crew was scattered wide and were being thinned.

Hardin, however, was locked in the warp drive housing with Mikhail's Reds in full combat gear. Ironically, since the terrorist attack on the *Queen Mary IV*, all warp drive housings on large ships were nearly impenetrable.

"How did he get in?" Orin asked what Mikhail was thinking. "Didn't you set guards after what happened to *Fenrir*?"

"Yes, we did. We don't know how he got in. *Red Gold* came into harbor, dropped anchor next to the engine housing, and next thing we knew, he was in the housing and his men were in control of the guns."

It sounded like how Hardin took his Reds. The "angel" that Hardin had must have moved Hardin's crew onto the *Georgetown*. If Mikhail could get onto the *Red Gold*, he might be able to use Hardin's "secret weapon" against him. But it would probably mean, too, exposing himself to the seraphim's mental torture. Was being dragged through his worst memories worth the edge?

He thought of the babies helpless in their artificial wombs. What kind of coward was he that he would let them die just to spare himself a few dark recollections?

"We need to take the *Red Gold*." Mikhail clamped down on the fear that facing the seraphim again triggered. "And then we can take Hardin, but we'll have to hurry. He has to realize he's losing control of the situation. He'd jump the moment the modifications are complete."

Note to self, Mikhail thought, *do not piss off the Georgetown people.*

In a stunningly short order of time, the Georgies took the *Red Gold* in an amazing display of abilities. They were not musclebound like the crèche-raised Reds, but they were still inhumanly fast and strong and completely ruthless in defending their home. They left nothing for Mikhail's Reds to do but follow Mikhail closely as he searched the ship for Eraphie Bailey and Hardin's "angel."

He found Eraphie locked in a tiny closet. She crouched against the closet's back wall, looking battered and wild. She hissed as he opened the door.

"It's okay, Eraphie, it's Mikhail. I've come to get you out."

"Mikhail!" She flung herself into his arms. She hugged him hard enough that he worried about ribs breaking. "I was starting to think you didn't get my messages."

"It took me a little while to find them. Where does Hardin have the angel?"

"Down in the forward hold." She released him and took off running, presumably in the direction of the hold. Mikhail followed, dreading having to do so.

The hold was one vast space stuffed with crates and odd pieces of equipment.

"Are these the engine parts?" Mikhail asked.

"No, no, Hardin's been collecting exotic machines for ages. I think they're peace offerings for the U.C." Eraphie wove through the maze. She disappeared ahead of them. "Here it is."

Mikhail felt the hairs on his arms lift as he walked forward. The quality of the light changed, shifting in invisible waves, like heat coming off hot pavement. But the air was cool, and clean, like a garden after a rain. The smell shifted from damp sea to cut grass to clean bedsheets. He turned the corner after Eraphie and stopped dead.

He'd been braced for a seraphim. This was something else. It writhed in a gaseous sphere held into place by a gleaming cobweb. The creature was as intangible as the seraphim, but seemed smaller by a half. Mikhail could not tell if it was in constant motion, or if it really had as many sets of wings as it seemed to have.

"See?" Eraphie whispered.

"That's not a seraphim," he whispered.

"No, it's a cherub," Eraphie whispered back, although he wasn't sure why they were whispering. "The seraphim are usually close by and will do what Hardin wants because he has it. There."

She pointed and the shadows moved and he realized that a seraphim was coiled in the darkness. Watching. Waiting.

This was the part he was dreading. Opening up his memories and letting the seraphim in. Living through the worst moments of his life to get what he needed.

Mikhail had been angry all that morning. Once again he'd had to get dressed up and attend some infinitely long and boring ceremony while Turk got to stay at home and play. It always seemed unfair that Turk never had to do any of the formal functions. He stomped into the palace and heard the screaming.

Even though his little brother never screamed, Mikhail knew the thin high wails echoing through the vast hallways of the palace were Turk's. The very sound of it filled Mikhail with terror and for a moment he couldn't move. Then he realized something very odd; no one was rushing to see what was wrong. The Red guards by the door stood statuelike at their posts, reacting only to his presence and not to the cries. One of the maids worked in the dining room, setting the long table for a state dinner. Florists were arranging flowers in the large vases in the huge foyer. All of the adults seemed deaf to the noise.

He started up the stairs, feeling like he was trapped in a nightmare. He'd been gone for hours. Were the adults deaf because they'd heard the screaming so long that they stopped hearing it? Had they been making Turk scream this whole time?

His tutor stopped him at the top of the stairs. "What are you doing back so soon? You were supposed to be gone another two hours."

"My stomach was upset. I think I'm going to throw up," he repeated the lies that got him out of the press of people and away from the countless unblinking cameras. He had wanted out of the stiff clothes. He had wanted to be able to move and talk without a dark look from his father and all the staff. Now all he wanted was to stop the screaming. "What's wrong with Turk?"

"Nothing." His tutor caught him by the shoulder and turned him away from the nursery. "Go to your room. Don't interfere."

Mikhail squirmed out of his tutor's hold. "Why is Turk screaming?"

"His trainer is with him. Just go to your room."

Turk had just turned five, and instead of a tutor like Mikhail, he'd gotten a "trainer." Mikhail hadn't bothered to find out what the man's job entailed. He'd only focused on the fact that it was yet another way that Turk didn't have to shoulder the same hardships that Mikhail did. He'd even taken some comfort that Turk obviously didn't like his time with his trainer.

Much as Mikhail disliked his tutors, they never made him scream for hours on end.

"Tell the trainer to stop whatever he's doing," Mikhail ordered.

The tutor made a noise of disgusted irritation. "I know it's annoying to listen to, but it will be over in another hour or so. Just go to your room and ignore it."

Mikhail stared at the man. Annoying? Turk's endless screaming was annoying? Mikhail glanced back down the stairs, at the florists and maid and guards all ignoring the screams. He knew from experience that if he started to scream, everyone reacted. It never occurred to him that there was a downside of not being Mikhail.

He started for the nursery, his tutor trailing after him.

"Misha, just go to your room. Put on some music to drown out the noise. This doesn't concern you."

"This concerns me," Mikhail snapped.

Mikhail jerked open the door and the smell of blood, urine, excrement, and burnt hair hit him. Turk's trainer was a large, burly man. The trainer was kneeling on the floor, one beefy hand keeping Turk pinned to the floor. In his other hand, the trainer had a shock stick. Turk was naked except for fur and restraints. Bleeding.

Covered with his own shit. Screaming in a voice worn ragged. As Mikhail stood stunned in the doorway, the trainer pressed the shock stick to Turk, and there was a terrible silence as his tiny body went rigid from the electrical shock.

"Leave him alone!" Mikhail cried.

The trainer looked up at Mikhail, and then past him, at Mikhail's tutor. "Take him away."

"I said leave him alone!" Mikhail locked his jaw against his own fear and marched into the room. "Stop hurting him. Take off those restraints and let him up."

The trainer glared at Mikhail from his kneeling position. "I am not taking them off. It's part of his training. You have no say in this."

"He is mine." Mikhail borrowed one of his father's more forceful tones. "I got him for my birthday. If you don't take it off, I'll have you arrested for tampering with private property."

"Don't be ridiculous," the trainer said.

"I mean it. I won't allow this," Mikhail said.

"Misha," his tutor pleaded from the doorway.

"Look, little boy . . ." the trainer started.

"I am Mikhail Ivanovich Volkov, and you will obey me." It was the first time he'd ever tried to use his position as his father's son.

"You're nothing but a clone," the trainer growled.

Mikhail lifted his wrist and pointed to the panic button on his security band. "Should I summon the guard and tell them that you threatened me?"

The trainer knew that the guards would act first, ask questions later. It was how they were trained.

The trainer scowled, produced a remote, and keyed in his security code. The restraints on Turk snapped opened. Mikhail snatched the restraints off Turk and flung them at the trainer. Turk scrambled up to wrap himself around Mikhail, burying his face into Mikhail's side, seeking protection.

"You're fired," Mikhail told the man.

"You don't have the right to fire me," the trainer said.

"I forbid you to ever touch Turk again, which means you can't do your job. If you can't do your job, my father isn't going to pay you. You're fired."

The man glared but gathered up items that looked like torture equipment and took himself away. Mikhail's tutor continued to hover at the door. Turk, who was never scared and who never cried, still clung to him, trembling, and a damp spot was growing on Mikhail's shirt as it absorbed silent tears.

"Misha, your father will only hire another trainer and their training methods are all going to be the same."

Turk whimpered at the news.

"I won't allow another trainer," *Mikhail promised, even though he wasn't sure if he could keep that promise. But he had to try. Apparently, no one else in the whole palace would try if he didn't. No one cared what happened to Turk except for Mikhail.*

Mikhail came out of the memory feeling like he was going to be sick. Seeing the abuse leveled on Turk had been worse as an adult than it had been when he was a child. At the time, Turk seemed like a rugged powerhouse. Now he seemed so, so small and Mikhail could see the lingering effects of the torture in his brother's psyche. Mikhail had made sure there were no more "training sessions" and Turk had never been abused again, but there, fresh before him, was the reminder that he had been resentful of Turk's lesser status and careless with him.

When I'm Tsar, I will protect all the Reds. I won't let that happen to other children just because they're adapted.

If the seraphim were picking memories to communicate something, perhaps they'd chosen that one in order to tell him to protect the people of Georgetown Landing. But they had done what he wanted. He was in the *Georgetown's* engine housing.

Alone.

Not exactly what he had in mind.

Two of his replacement Reds were there, looking at him in surprise. One was Tricks, which would have succeeded Butcher as top cat. The other Mikhail couldn't pull up a name on, nor was it important. The tom would do whatever Tricks told him. Both were in combat armor sans helmets.

"Tricks, I'm taking control of this ship." *Show no fear.*

"So you can kill me like you killed Butcher?" Tricks punched him without warning.

Mikhail went to his knees, his head ringing, blood pouring from his nose. He sensed Tricks's kick before the Red followed through and rolled with it.

And then Coffee was there, appearing out of thin air. The seraphim were moving them one by one!

"Tricks!" Coffee roared and leapt at Tricks and they went down snarling. The other replacement waded in, trying to help Tricks. Other replacements came around the corner, summoned by the noise. Who knew how long it would take the seraphim to carry others across, or even if they would bring another Red across? Mikhail aimed for the replacement's unprotected head and shot him. The Red went down in a spray of blood.

Then Smoke was there. He reacted instantly to the confusion, attacking the oncoming replacements. Bolt arrived, and Pancakes after him. The small corridor filled with bodies, dead and alive, and the smell of blood.

And then it was over.

Pancakes had been killed. Smoke was wounded. But they'd killed half of the replacements. Mikhail had to walk on the dead to reach the end of the short corridor, his boots covered with blood.

So much for protecting Reds, he thought bitterly. Eleven dead.

Georgetown's housing was a warren of twisting catwalks and corridors. The control station was at the very heart of the housing. They'd have to work their way cautiously in. Around the next corner was a long narrow catwalk. At the far end, a Red was tucked into an alcove.

Mikhail ducked back into the safety of the hallway.

"Kill him?" Coffee looked unhappy with the idea.

"Wait." Mikhail realized that the Red hadn't taken a shot when they'd turned the corner. "Did you see who it was?"

"It's Trigger," Coffee said.

"Trigger?" Mikhail called to the Red.

"Captain Volkov?" Trigger sounded young and unsure.

"You shouldn't be fighting us, Trigger. I'm your captain, not Hardin. He stole you from me but he doesn't rightfully own you. Stand down."

"He said you'd be angry."

"No, I'm not angry. This isn't your fault. And Hardin can't take you back with him. You're registered to me. If he goes back with you, everyone will know that he's a thief and traitor. He will have to put you down."

No answer.

"Trigger? Put your weapon down and come here."

No answer.

Coffee glanced at Mikhail and then growled, "Trigger, get over here, you idiot."

Trigger came scrambling down the catwalk and Coffee hauled him around the corner into the corridor with them.

"I'm your top cat," Coffee cuffed Trigger, reestablishing dominance. "You obey only Captain Mikhail and Ensign Inozemtsev from now on. Understand?"

Trigger nodded.

If they could talk down one Red, they might be able to talk them all down. Mikhail ran a patch line to Trigger's suit. The suit's chatter was encrypted. The only way to quickly link up with their comline was to hardwire.

"This is Captain Volkov. I'm in the engine housing with you. Coffee is here with me. Hardin is not your legal owner and he cannot take you back to Plymouth Station with him. He will put you all down. I'm furious with Hardin, but I'm not angry with any of you. This is not your fault. Come to the L32 access hatch. Disarm any traps you've set as you come."

He waited, trying not to dwell on having to kill them all if they didn't obey him. Some of the veterans had been with his crew for years. He knew them as well as Tseytlin and Kutusov.

They came to him, though, one by one, looking sheepish as they joined the growing pack. Coffee cuffed them all and repeated his reprimands. Not all of them were veterans either, some were the replacements. He'd lost twenty-nine Reds. They'd just killed ten of them. He thought he'd counted nineteen slinking back, but they were all mixed together now.

"Anyone that hasn't come?" Mikhail asked to be sure.

They looked at each other, taking account, and then shook their heads.

"We're all here," Trigger said.

Hardin would only have his own people now.

The last defense of the warp drive was the innermost chamber. Made of clear plasti-steel, it locked the jump controls away from all but the trusted few. Unfortunately, it was into that fortress that Hardin had barricaded himself.

"Hardin, give it up, and come out."

"Mikhail, leave now and I'll give you time to save your ship and your people."

"Either way you'll level this settlement just like you leveled Fenrir's Rock."

"They're all adapted, Mikhail."

"I'm not going to let you kill them all. I'll sacrifice my ship and its people to keep this settlement safe."

"I'll just jump with you onboard then."

"Hardin! Destroy this landing and I'll utterly erase you! I'll see you court-martialed, executed, and once you've been thoroughly humiliated for the brief time you're alive, I'll have the records sealed and every bit of evidence that you ever took in air erased. I'll make it so you've never even been born."

"You don't have that power."

"I'm Tsarevich Mikhail Ivanovich Volkov. If I bother to bend my will to destroy an insignificant piece of trash like you, I can."

Hardin wavered, hand in place, considering.

And then Hardin shook his head. "I'm done here. My only hope is to jump and that, for once in my life, God smiles on me."

"Hardin!" Mikhail leapt forward. "Don't . . ."

And the seraphim flooded into the chamber with them. They blasted over Mikhail and all the horrors of his life flashed over him . . .

. . . *they were still covered with blood. Mikhail had blood on his shirt . . .*

. . . *"Oh, no, no." His father cried in a tone so hurt and broken that it tore Mikhail's heart. His father took his brother from Nyanya, his body bowing as if receiving a massive weight instead of the slight body. "Oh please, God, no . . ."*

. . . *Mikhail pulled his sidearm, placed it at Butcher's head, and pulled the trigger . . .*

. . . *As Mikhail stood stunned in the doorway, the trainer pressed the shock stick to Turk, and there was a terrible silence as his tiny body went rigid from the electrical shock . . .*

It was a deluge of ugliness and pain that tore through Mikhail. All awareness of the room around him was blasted away by the flood. He existed only in his memories, his real body lost to him except a faint awareness that he was howling in pure wordless misery. Every moment of misery washed fresh through him. Every heartache and sorrow.

Oh God, let it end! Let it end!

He had a pistol in hand. It would be simple to stop it all. But then Hardin would destroy *Georgetown*. Mikhail couldn't let that monster win.

And the thought brought a less painful memory ...

"... *in this world, the only thing you can control is yourself,*" Eraphie had said to him. "*I don't want to be a mindless monster that concerns itself with only feeding its belly. Fix that firmly in your mind. To be is to be and no storm can change your course.*"

I've never been the mindless monster, Mikhail clung to the realization. *I have never allowed my moral compass to be corrupted. I have not let myself be swayed into evil. This hurts, but it did not destroy me then. I can't let it destroy me now.*

Old wounds opened and bled. Sorrows he'd long forgotten made him weep. But he found solace, again and again, that he had never swayed. Never compromised.

Finally it was over. His people were backed up into the corridor, staring at him in surprise and horror. Coffee was curled in a ball beside him, weeping. The Red must have tried to pull him away from the seraphim and gotten caught up himself.

"It's all right, Coffee." Mikhail tentatively placed a hand on the Red's shoulder, aware that if Mikhail startled him, the Red could kill him. "They're gone. They were bad times, but they're over."

Only then did Mikhail remember Hardin. He turned and found the man sprawled inside the warp chamber, dead. Hardin had shot himself; he couldn't bear looking in the mirror that the seraphim held up to him.

25 Out of the Blue

ONCE THE MODIFICATIONS HAD BEEN REMOVED FROM *GEORGETOWN*'S warp engine, its power was reestablished to the crèche. Mikhail sent the *Tigertail* off to pick up Turk, Captain Bailey, and the elusive Ethan Bailey. Tseytlin started work on modifying the *Svobada*'s engines. As his crew worked, Mikhail made plans on how they would return to normal space. With all he was recovering from the Sargasso, he didn't want to jump back to Plymouth Station at the heart of the United Colonies' power. But after the seraphim's attack in the *Georgetown*'s engine housing, he didn't want to jump to the heavily populated Volya at the heart of the Novaya Rus.

He was overseeing the reduction of mass on the *Svobada* when the *Tigertail* returned. Lieutenant Belokurov must have told Turk some version of what happened as Turk came and gave him a bear hug in greeting.

"What have you been doing?" Mikhail laughed. "You're filthy!"

"Digging with my bare hands." Turk let him go to show off fingernails caked with black dirt.

Mikhail laughed. "I think it's a prerequisite of visiting the Sargasso: you must at least once dig without shovels."

"At least you haven't had to fish." Turk gave a mock shudder.

"Did you find it?" Mikhail asked. "Whatever it is?"

"Yes, we did." Captain Bailey came up behind Turk carrying a plastic orange storage crate. Turk must have been worried about

337

Mikhail if he left her holding the crate. Captain Bailey carefully put the crate down at Mikhail's feet. "This is it."

Turk settled on the low seawall as Mikhail knelt and opened the crate. Inside was a cube. It was black and slick as things that the nefrim built tended to be. Gazing at it, however, reminded him of how he felt looking at the hak. The sense of glory.

"I've talked to Ethan about what the angel told him," Captain Bailey said. "With what the hak told us, I think I understand now what happened. I'm not sure if the nefrim are naturally telepathic, but they're all linked in some way. I think the linking device is the *Shabd*. In normal space, it was slowly moving them all toward transcending. But out there, the voice of God is muted, just echoes. So when the *Shabd* got lost here, two things happened. The first was that every nefrim that came to the Sargasso found itself connected to the pure voice of God and instantly transcended. It was like getting ripped out of your body because you were hardwired to this thing. Nefrim became seraphim with no ability to return the *Shabd* to normal space. And back in normal space, the time dilation of the Sargasso was transmuting what the nefrim were receiving. It's what has been driving them mad."

"Do you know why the nefrim attacked us?" Mikhail asked.

"The seraphim encountered humans and guessed that they could help, but their focus on us here made the nefrim focus on us out there."

"If we take it back and give it to them, will they stop attacking?" Mikhail asked.

"I think so," Captain Bailey said. "If nothing else, the seraphim will stop focusing on humans and there should be nothing to drive the nefrim mad."

Turk whispered something to Captain Bailey that made her blush.

"Shush you," she whispered back.

Turk gave her a smile that filled his eyes with laughter. He pulled her into his lap and nuzzled into her neck. Obviously the riff between them had healed since the two had left Ya-ya. Bailey put a hand up to Turk's hair and touched him with loving tenderness.

Bailey glanced up and saw Mikhail watching her. Her eyes filled with sadness and she looked away. She knew that Turk would be leaving.

"I get first dibs on your shower." She slid out of Turk's hold. "That puppy is yours to guard."

"I'll get you some clean clothes too." Turk stood up, hands still outstretched to her. They called her back to him and she kissed him again.

"Thank you." This time she slid free and went.

Mikhail studied Turk as his little brother watched her go. Turk was clearly head over heels in love. And Captain Bailey obviously loved him back. Was Turk going to give her up just to protect his suicidal older brother from himself? Did all the times that he protected Turk make Turk feel like he owed Mikhail to the point of self-sacrifice?

"Turk, you've found something good here," Mikhail said. "I don't want you to give it up because you're afraid that I'll self-destruct. This has put me through hell, but it's taught me to stop picking at wounds until they bleed. The only thing that could hurt me now is to someday realize that I've destroyed your only chance at happiness."

"You, you, you, it's all about you," Turk growled but hugged him hard.

Mikhail expected Turk to let go after a brusque show of emotion. That was his normal way. Turk continued to grip him tight, almost as if he was afraid to let go.

"I—I'm staying." Turk said finally. "If I walk away from her, it will tear a hole in me that I don't think I ever could fill. I've asked her to marry me."

Mikhail thought he had braced himself, but it still was like getting stabbed. He was going to lose Turk. After a moment, though, the pain dulled. Turk would be here if Mikhail really needed him for some time before the time dilatation became too great. There would always be the comfort knowing that his little brother was happy. That he would be surrounded by people that loved him. That his children would never know the bigotry that Turk had suffered.

"So, we're having a wedding before I leave?" Mikhail asked.

Turk winced. "We're still trying to work it out.

Damn the man, Paige thought, as Turk walked in and caught her searching his drawers. It wouldn't be embarrassing except for why she had done it last time and what she'd found. This time it was all perfectly harmless.

"This is not what it looks like," she grumbled.

"It isn't?" He smiled at her discomfort. He'd borrowed someone's shower and come to his room wearing just a low-slung towel loincloth that looked oh so yummy on him.

"No." She closed the drawer she had been rummaging through—slowly—so it didn't look like she was feeling guilty. "Your shower is heavenly but that automatic drying cycle makes a mess of my hair."

She tried to run her fingers through to show off the knots, but it was too tangled even for that. "I'm starting to see why you newcomers always have such short hair."

"Short hair is easier with space helmets."

"Ah." She opened the next drawer and glanced over the contents. "Do you not own a comb?"

He laughed and ducked into his shower to open a cabinet she hadn't noticed recessed into the wall. "Here."

He lay on the bed and watched as she combed her hair. She could see him in the mirror. He was enjoying the show, but there was something bothering him. His smile had a touch of sadness.

"What is it?" Paige said.

"Mikhail would like to be at the wedding when we get married."

Oh, yes, the whole future thing. It had seemed so huge and scary when they talked on Loki. Amazing what being plugged into the voice of God could do to your perspective. She saw with clarity how Mikhail's success affected her family and all of the Sargasso. Cause and effect would ripple out of Turk's universe and into hers.

She put away the comb and curled up beside Turk. "I can't stay here in the Sargasso, hoarding you to myself, and ignore your universe."

"You'll come back with us?"

"Returning the *Shabd* might stop the nefrim from attacking, but I'm the only one that can communicate with them. They're not going to go away and humans aren't going to leave them alone—not after fifty years of war. Someone has to build a peace, and Mikhail can't do it by himself. He'll need both of us. And we'll need him to change how humans see adapted."

He rolled on top of her. "So you will marry me?"

"Yes. And you won't have to fish."

Mikhail ordered the *Svoboda* stripped to reduce the mass that the warp engine had to jump. They took out chairs, tables, and unused beds. They dumped all the water and stripped most of the plumbing. After some frank talks, he also left his surviving Reds. The people of Georgetown were grateful and saw them as strong, healthy young men. Families stepped forward to take them in, even the replacements, though with words of warning. Surprisingly, a few of his crew also asked to stay. He gave them the *Tigertail* as stake money to start their new life.

Lastly, although not least, they had a joint wedding for Turk and Paige, Rabbit and Hillary. Considering they might be jumping into oblivion, it was surprisingly joyous, though at times mystifying. The Georgies had developed a surprising number of odd wedding traditions. He'd have to ask Paige later what the thing with the fishing float was about.

Mikhail had his remaining crew queue up into space suits and gathered in the engine housing. And he attached his recording of all the time they'd spent in the Sargasso to the engine itself.

For the first time in his life, he felt like he was shutting a door behind him, and walking into a future that he chose. For the first time, he felt nearly sick with fear, because death would be more than just a release from pain and a failure to his crew. For the first time, he prayed.

Taking one deep breath, he triggered the engine.

The field flashed over him, making the hair on his arms stand up. There was a deep ringing vibration, as if the whole universe had been a massive bell that had just been struck. It was a purer tone than the sound of a normal jump, which always had a muted hum. At least his vision filled with the same color of wine. There was the familiar jolt of heat and cold and smell and blindness and nausea all at once as his senses protested being shoved through a hole in time and space.

And then it was over.

"Was that it?" Paige whispered.

"Yes, that was it," Turk murmured. "Welcome to my world . . . hopefully."

"Stations," Mikhail ordered as he headed forward to see if the bridge had survived this time. "Damage report!"

The bridge had survived. He snapped on the exterior cameras. They had come out near a planet. The question was, which planet? He'd chosen to return to Krasnyi, which was Novaya Rus's least populated planet on the far edge of human space. He wanted to be in control, but he didn't want to endanger his people in case the alien device turned out to be dangerous. But had they reached Krasnyi?

"Kutuzov, find out where we are," Mikhail ordered. "Moldavsky, set up a secure channel to my father."

Moldavsky squeaked quietly in surprise and perhaps intimidation, but set to work.

"Sir, it's Krasnyi," Kutuzov said.

The planet was only recently habitable as it reached the last stages of terraforming. It no longer had its reddish cast that earned its name. Modified wild barley grass gave the vast plains a sandy hue and its seas were turning blue.

"Sir, incoming ship! It's nefrim!" Moldavsky cried.

It was one of the nefrim carrier ships, filled with fighters all only slightly smaller than the *Svoboda*. Luckily they weren't built to land on planets. The astrosphere would also deflect and defuse most of the carrier's energy weapons.

"Take us down to Krasnyi," Mikhail ordered. "Away from the ocean, please!"

Lieutenant Belokurov started them into the gentle glide into the planet's astrosphere.

"Two more ships," Moldavsky said. "Three. A destroyer. A dreadnaught. No, two dreadnaughts."

Nothing yet that could touch them on the planet. Mikhail was afraid of something like this happening. The hak had implied that the nefrims acted as one, and the seraphims had communicated mind to mind. The nefrims had picked up the return of the *Shabd* and obviously were now focused on getting it back. It was possible that the entire nefrim fleet would gather over the planet.

"Sir, a planetbuster just warped in." Moldavsky said.

Their only hope was that the nefrims' return to sanity was as sudden as their plunge into insanity.

"Sir, are we landing?" Lieutenant Belokurov obviously wanted to continue being a moving target.

"Yes. Put us down. We're hoping for first peaceful contact." Mikhail glanced to Paige, who nodded slightly.

They settled on the northern plains. Mikhail clipped on a headset, saying to Moldavsky, "Put my father through when you connect with him."

She nodded, her eyes wide with fear at her screens filling with incoming nefrim ships.

He, Turk, and Paige went down the gangplank together. Paige carried the *Shabd*.

"This—" Turk flung wide his arms. "—this is a steppe."

Paige laughed as if he'd made a joke. "Where is my borscht?"

They waded out through the knee-high grass that ran for miles in a shifting carpet of gold. The clear blue sky filled with the underbellies of nefrim ships.

"Sir." Kutuzov's voice came over the headset. "One of their frigates is coming down. It's heading right for us."

"Stand by but do not engage," Mikhail said.

"I think it's going to be all right," Paige whispered. "The seraphim are here."

In the clear day, the seraphim were nearly impossible to see, except for the slightest distortion in the air and the stirring of the barley. When they brushed against Mikhail, he had flashes of joyous memories. Turk was in every one. He glanced to Turk, smiling.

Apparently the seraphim were doing the same to Turk, as he grinned and said, "This is what happens when you shake the universe to see what falls out."

There was a faint rolling thunder of sonic booms that grew louder and louder as the nefrim frigate dropped down out of the heavens. It came roaring across the plain, growing from a black speck to a gleaming black slice of metal. At the last minute, it banked and slowed in a howl of VTOL engines. It landed a hundred feet off, beating down the barley around it.

Turk reached out and put his hand against Paige's back. His new wedding ring gleamed in the sunlight. "I love you."

"I know," Paige said and walked toward the frigate carrying the *Shabd*. The air was alive with seraphim pressing close to her.

The nefrim appeared outside their ships. They moved to tower over her. Paige held the *Shabd* out, which they took. Paige sat on the bent grass. One of the nefrim settled in front of her, and they started to commune.

"Mikhail?" A voice came through his headset, and caught up in the moment, it took him a second to recognize it.

"Father?"

"Oh, thank God, you're alive. Minister Heward sent me a communiqué saying he'd lost you. Is Turk all right?"

"He's fine." Mikhail was surprised that his father cared. "We need to talk. I've given out promises I need you to keep. And I think I'll be giving out more very shortly."

"This has to do with what's happening in the space around Krasnyi?"

"Yes."

"I take it you found more than the *Fenrir*."

"I found things beyond our understanding. And I found a new colony. And I think I found a way to end the war. And I found myself."